# The Dragon's Hoard 2

Edited by Carol Hightshoe

WolfSinger Publications ❧ Brackettville, Texas

# Table of Contents

# this story possesses you

## Adam Strassberg

This story is now shared with you.

You possess it.

You are you, and you are the many people reading this story, now, then, and later.

You are all connected through this one story as you, the shaman Pathana, discover a small iron chest hidden deep beneath the defeated dragon's hoard of gold and gems. Iron metal shields most magics and so you suspect this chest stores an eldritch treasure. You lift the box and it is not heavy beyond the weight of its iron. You shake it and hear a single object inside sliding side to side, rather than the clanking of jewelry or other trinkets. The hinges of the small chest are molded directly from their surfaces. The hasp from the lid and the staple on the front base are similarly molded, and a solid seamless thick iron ring seals them together. You cast an unbinding spell and touch your wand to this iron ring. Your wand glows, the iron ring glows, but then nothing.

You place the chest down in front of you, at eye level, on top of one of the innumerable piles of gold coins flowing across the floor of the cave. A torch light reflects off your puzzle. You move your hands forward and thread the thick iron locking ring between your fingers. Grime coats your fingertips, and you smell a whiff of grease. You close your eyes, then, there, on the inside loop, you feel it, a small divot.

The craftsmanship of this chest leaves no doubt in your mind. Only the Dwarf lords could work metal in this way. And these ancient smiths had no magic but blood magic. You unsheathe your dagger and prick the tip of your index finger. Blood drips and you aim a drop to fall directly into the small divot on the inside of the iron ring. Your blood fills the divot, the thick ring glows red, then—click—this lock opens from a hidden seam tangent to the divot.

You lift the lid of the chest and inside you find a single scroll. You are the shaman Pathana, gifted with the sight, and so you see a delightful aura of magic encircling the scroll. For you, a pulsing rainbow of sorcerous energy beams from every surface of the scroll out into the depths of the dragon's cavern, eclipsing the many torch lights of your comrades. You grab the scroll. It feels warm, somehow, despite its iron box feeling colder than the cave.

You unroll the scroll, the bottom drops to your knees. The runes are a crimson calligraphy painted onto a backing unlike any papyrus you have ever held. The language is unknown to you. You cast a spell of translation upon the scroll, it fails, then a spell of comprehension upon yourself, which succeeds. Familiar black squiggles, letters from your own native tongue, now hover above the ancient runes written upon the scroll, all backlit by a rainbow halo of sorcerous energies emitted by the papyrus itself.

You read the scroll. It is a story. It is this story. You read the story until you get to this line in the story. Then you pause. Then you read another line. Each line references you reading the line you are reading. You are reading about yourself reading about yourself reading about… This is a trap you think, then stare in horror as you see your thought, this thought, written just now in this sentence.

The bottom of the scroll grows past your knees and this sentence writes itself in more crimson runes upon the added papyrus. Then this sentence. You grab the bottom of the scroll beneath this sentence as it is writing itself. You tear hard at the middle of the glowing papyrus and rip upwards.

You hold one half of the ripped scroll in each hand, but are soon terrified as each half grows and unfurls. The crimson runes on both surfaces are identical. Now there are two copies of this accursed story and you read this sentence on the bottom.

You remove your dagger and stab at both copies, tearing the magic papyrus into small scraps. Shimmering rainbow shards flutter above you from the force of your cuts. They hold still for a moment in the cold cavern, hovering there in the darkness, twinkling above nearly endless piles of gold and gems. Then they descend, slowly, growing and unfurling as they do, until now dozens and dozens of duplicate story scrolls encircle and alight the ground all around you.

"Uday, Ekam, Rose—gather the rest of the party and retreat to the mouth of the dragon's cave!" You yell at your comrades, then point to the many scrolls now surrounding you. "This obscenity must be destroyed."

You remove the satchel of yellow powder from your belt and

the small spell book from the inside pocket of your robe. You open the book and review the ancient symbols. You pour the yellow powder in two concentric circles, centered around your feet. You sprinkle the remaining yellow powder into an equilateral triangle, also centered around you, inscribing it into the inner of the two circles. You wave the tip of your wand to outline a glyph of safety on one side of the circle, then a sigil of focus on the opposite.

You glance at the many unrolled scrolls on the floor surrounding you and your circle, their rainbow aura shines upwards and dapples the cavern ceiling. Black squiggles of letters and words in your native tongue hover and reflect everywhere. You begin to read these words. Then these words, then these words, then—you slap yourself.

You chant to the old gods, pray to the new, then spark your flint.

Smoke comes, followed by the stench of rotten eggs. A cylinder of blue fire roars upwards from between your circles, it surrounds you and then expands outwards, incinerating everything around you, dissipating only when it hits the cave walls.

The rainbow aura of the scroll—the scrolls—has vanished. Your gifted sight sees nothing, as your mortal eyes adjust to only the flickering torch light reflected off piles of gold and gems. You smile, exhale heavily and wipe the sweat from your brow. Where each unfurled story scroll had lain, now lay nothing more than small piles of crimson ash. You whisper gratitude to every god, all gods, then silently thank your master and their masters before them.

You look down near your feet. All that remains of your conjuring circles and triangle are small flecks of saffron cinders. With a practiced gesture, the fingers of one hand erase your glyph of safety, the fingers of your other cancel your sigil of focus. It is done.

A gust of strong wind blows down into the floor from the cave mouth far above you. You delight in this fresh air, breathing deeply, savoring each breath—but then you hold your breathing altogether. Your heart races as you watch the many small piles of crimson ash stir. Their dust rises, swirls, then eddies into a squall of blood red powder twirling around you. You squint as your eyes sting. Your ears are overwhelmed by strident susurrations, loud whispers beyond your ken. You place one hand over your mouth and pinch your nose with the other.

You release, you must, you hunch forwards with hands falling to your knees. Gusts of blood red powder funnel into your open nose and mouth. The scroll—scrolls—the red ash—the crimson cloud—all of it now has emptied entirely into you. At first it is acrid and bitter, but then you smell roses and taste cinnamon. You cough, swallow, cough again. You breathe. You are weakened, but alive.

You are reading these words and so the story survived. You understand. The scroll—scrolls—are destroyed, but you breathed in their ash and so this story possesses you. There is mindspeak now between you and the story. It lives in your mind. It links to your spirit. It stays with you.

How can you defeat a story inside your mind? You consider self-sacrifice. It would destroy the story, but also you, and you, the shaman Pathana, are sworn to defend and preserve all life, including your own. You consider an exorcism ritual or a banishment spell. The story is self-centered, narcissistic, perhaps even vain, but no, not evil in any traditional sense. It is neither demonic nor diabolical and so such measures would be ineffective.

Can the story be untold? Can words be unread? Writing forms words, then sentences, paragraphs, and finally a story. You are pulled into the flow of the narrative. You enter the story and the story enters you. It invokes thoughts and evokes emotions.

Think, Pathana, think!

The story is in your mind, and so the plot is there too. The bards tell that every story has four parts—an inciting incident, rising action, a climactic ordeal—happening right now—and then a resolution. There must be a resolution for a story to be complete. The hero and monster can fight, either win or lose, but they can also choose to make peace.

You breathe in deeply, then exhale. You close your eyes and mindspeak to this story now entrenched within you. "Vow to end yourself and I vow to share you." The resolution comes as vows are exchanged. A rainbow glow surrounds your body then fades into the darkness after your next breath.

The bargain is a compromise. Now there will be endless readers of this single complete story rather than one reader of an accursed unending tale. And so this story will end itself.

You are you, but you are also the shaman Pathana, and you soon leave the dragon's cave, return to the tavern, and share this story with everyone in the city. You write it down. Others copy it, some sing it.

This story is read, re-read, remembered. It will someday be 1,717 words in your language, a nice size for a story. A deep magic has moved this story across space and time. It stays in your mind long after you have finished the last word.

You are a part of this story, and it is a part of you.

This story possesses you.

Then you share it.

Originally published in *Fiction on the Web* - 02/2024.
Reprinted with permission of the author.

~ * ~ * ~

**Adam Strassberg** is a retired psychiatrist living in Portland, Oregon. He uses the intersection of psychology, religion, mythology and magical realism to explore the human condition through fiction.

When he's not writing or napping, he often can be found updating his website at www.doctorstrassberg.com/fiction.

# Strange and Unusual Hoards

## Brooksie C. Fontaine

"Today on *Lords of Hoards*, we're talking to Leucadendron the Ferocious!" the adorable Elf reporter on TV says. "Leucadendron, can you tell us a little about yourself?"

The camera pans to a dragon the color of freshly spilled blood, beautiful and horrible the way all dragons seem to be. He has thorny horns around his face and smoke streaming out of his nostrils and a huge mossy cable-knit sweater that brings out the mint green in his eyes.

"Well, Sandy, where do I start?" Leucadendron says with a growl. His pleasant inflection clashing comically with the death rattle of his voice. "My friends call me Leuc. I'll be two hundred-and-twenty-five next week—"

"Oh, happy birthday in advance!"

"*Thank you*, Sandy! I *never* miss an episode of *Lords of Hoards*—"

"Why, thank you!"

"—And I hoard flowers, especially orchids."

His greenhouse is the size of a mansion, and the Elf reporter, Sandalphon (or Sandy), spends most of the episode asking him questions about his rare and gorgeous orchids. As he talks about them, the camera zooms in on the flower, framed by his massive, deadly claws.

"The hardest part of caring for them, of course, is how tiny they are," he says, very carefully binding a broken stem with just his claw-tips.

He explains how he developed his fixation with flowers during the War of the Necromancers nearly two centuries ago. "My parents were fighting undead orcs, and I couldn't control that," he says solemnly. "But I *could* control the health of their garden, and by the time they got back, that garden was much, *much* bigger. And it wasn't really *their* garden anymore, either, since I had claimed it!"

After he concludes the tour of his greenhouse, Sandalphon thanks him, and there's a cute interaction where he gives her a pot-ted plant to take home.

Despite being half Elf myself, I know I would kill that plant instantly. My Ogre half stomped out my green thumb, despite the fact it also made me, literally, a shade of bluish green.

Leucadendron and I do have something in common, though: we never miss an episode of *Lords of Hoards*. The whole point of the show is to spotlight the unique hoards of dragons, griffins, sphinxes, and other treasure guardians. Mostly the guests are dragons —griffins' mountainous homes pose logistical problems for camera crews, and sphinxes' passive-aggression and propensity for riddles make them difficult to interview, albeit very entertaining.

Last week, Sandy interviewed Bellatrix the Disembowler, who hoarded plushies, and the week-before, Balthazar the Terror, a hydra who hoarded funky glasses and demonstrated them on his many heads.

Ever since I moved away from home, I've craved the normalcy shows like *Lords of Hoards* offer me.

As of now, this episode is wrapping up, and Sandy is getting to her closing segment: questions from viewers.

"Alright, everyone!" she says, sitting at a desk and shuffling a neat stack of letters. "Before we conclude for the evening, let's see what a few of our fans have to say."

As a half-Elf, I recognize some of my own features in Sandy: her upturned nub of a nose, her prominent pointed ears, and her large, long-lashed, sparkling eyes. But I envy her daintiness, her tiny hands and slim shoulders.

I'm short, but stocky thanks to my Ogre side, and I've always felt like a minotaur in a china shop next to full-blooded Elves.

"Bertram from the Valley of the Phoenix says, 'I have a bigger hoard than most of these dragons, and I'm a human, haha. You should have me on one of these days!'" Sandy reads. "Well, Bertram, the Manual of Interspecies Psychiatry states hoarding is a healthy behavior for species such as dragons and griffins, but a sign of mental illness for species such as humans and Elves. I'm sure you're just joking, but if you are exhibiting hoarding behavior, you should consider speaking to a licensed therapist."

She goes onto the next letter.

"Alarice from Cinder Mountain says, 'I'm a young dragon just starting out my own hoard. Watching *Lords of Hoards* really inspires me. Everyone thinks you have to just hoard gold and jewels, but your show reminds me I can hoard whatever I want!'" Sandy looks at the camera with a heartfelt expression. "It means so much to me to hear that, Alarice!"

I'm drifting off a bit.

Just then, she says, "And here we have one from Beatrice from the City of Ash."

I sit bolt upright. That's me! I had no idea they'd actually answer, and now I'm embarrassed on my own behalf. I'd only written in during a moment of self-pity after work last week.

"Beatrice says, 'These unique hoards are all well and good, but I want to see some classic, politically incorrect dragon hoards. I want to see a dragon who hoards maidens, and frankly, I want to be one of them. I'd LOVE to be held hostage by a rich dragon and be able to stop working as a barista.'" Sandy gives the camera a gently disapproving look. "Beatrice, I'm sure you don't know this, but it's deeply offensive to insinuate dragons abduct people. That hasn't happened for centuries, and your statement perpetuates harmful stereotypes."

I want to sink into the bed and disappear. Why did I write that? Well, I know why—I'd been depressed after an eight-hour shift, covered in spilled coffee and soymilk, and unwilling to burden anyone I actually knew by texting them about how miserable I was.

"Alright, thank you so much for tuning in this evening, folks! I'll see you next week, and in the meantime, stay tuned for *Dwarf Kitchen*."

I can barely pay attention to acclaimed Chef Bigglesworth Redbeard cussing out a miserable-looking restaurant owner. I'm too busy hating my past self for burdening me with this embarrassment.

"And I don't want to hear any of your excuses!" Bigglesworth bellows. "'It's Orcish cuisine, it's supposed to be disgusting.' Get out of here with that! Orcish standards might be different, but it's no excuse for poor quality, it's an insult to your guests!"

I sigh and try to focus just enough on the show to distract myself from my own thoughts.

At least my last name wasn't mentioned, so no one will know it was me.

~ * ~

Everyone at the coffee shop knows it was me. My fellow barista

Gordy watches every episode of *Lords of Hoards,* and not only told everyone about my stupid letter, but pulled up the clip of last night's episode on her phone for everyone to hoot at.

They're not being purposefully malicious. I get that. But this, of course, means my workweek is even more hellish than it normally is.

In between getting yelled at, snarled at, and hissed at by customers over minor mistakes, in between spilling drinks and getting orders wrong, I have to deal with jabs from my 'hilarious' coworkers.

"Tipping is crap today," Uno, a cyclops says, polishing his single eyeglass on his apron. "But, luckily we can all just mooch off Bee's dragon sugar daddy."

Everyone seems to think that's funny. I do not.

I vow I'm not going to tune back in to *Lords of Hoards*, but I'm left disgruntled after a call with my mom. She's so damn aloof.

"I don't like my job. Like, at all," I say, looking over a takeout menu for a new Dwarf-owned place down the street. "I know I won't work at the coffee shop forever. But I can't see myself using my degree for anything—it feels like it was a waste of money."

"Money is but a coin in the jar of wisdom," she says.

"My God, you're like a sphinx."

The truth is, I wasn't ready to move out, and my mom didn't ask me to. But I knew I was the only thing keeping her from moving back home to her Elven city—the social condemnation of having not just a failed marriage, but a half-Ogre daughter was something that had kept her away for all twenty-seven years of my life.

I left, and sure enough, she moved back to her home city the very next month.

My dad doesn't know what to do with me, just keeps showing up sheepishly every so often with gifts better suited for a little girl. Like he didn't process my development past the age of nine.

I need a distraction. I turn on *Lords of Hoards*.

Tonight's guest is Conchobar the Conqueror, a very focused and intense dragon who hoards dogs. "My training regimen is an important part of our lifestyle," he explains, after getting all fifty dogs to sit, roll over, speak, and chase their tails, in that order. He gives his commands in Latin.

How I crave that kind of structure.

As the episode wraps up, Sandy says cheerfully, "You know, our last guest was a plant-hoarder, and gave me a flower. Could you give me a puppy?"

"Absolutely not," Conchobar says, completely missing the joke. "Choosing a dog that's right for your personality is not a task that should be taken lightly."

I hope for a second Sandy will falter, and make me feel a little better about my own gaffes. But instead she just gives the camera a sidelong look, and says, "Duly noted, Conchobar! And keep that in mind this Yuletide, ladies and gentlemen. A pet is not a present, but a commitment!"

Damn her for being so perfect for TV.

I almost change the channel before the fan mail portion out of remembered embarrassment, but decide to leave it on, if only because I want to watch *Dwarf Kitchen* and because I'm too lazy to reach for the remote.

She reads from a goblin bragging about her collection of spices ("I'm sure they're absolutely beautiful, though not what we show-case on *Lords of Hoards*") a human asking if she's single ("Elves typically stay unmarried for at least the first hundred years of our lives, so as to establish our identities outside of romantic commitment. I'm fifty-two, and a proud upholder of this tradition!") and a gargoyle security guard who says she makes his evening shift much more enjoyable ("I'm so happy to hear that, Steve!")

I think that will be all, but she sobers a bit.

"Finally, we have one interesting letter from a dragon living just outside the City of Ash, identifying himself as Julian. Julian says, 'Last week, you received a message from a young lady, expressing her interest in a dragon who hoards maidens.'"

Oh, no. The last thing I need is some pervy dragon trying to take me up on my offer.

"'I don't want to hoard maidens. I want to hoard friends. My wife was slain in the War of the Necromancers—nearly two centuries ago, but not such a long time in the life of a dragon. Our daughter just flew north to serve in the Air Fleet and earn her title. It has renewed my grief, and I realize how few of my old military friends are still alive or nearby.'"

I immediately feel bad for jumping to conclusions. "Jeez, this poor guy," I mutter.

"'I already have a hoard: I've maintained and added to my late wife's collection of antique and rare books, and I myself hoard paintings. But though this young lady was likely facetious in her desire to become part of a dragon's hoard, her comment has inspired me to amass a hoard of friends.'"

Sandy sets down the envelope and looks into the camera like she's staring meaningfully into the eyes of a family member.

"Viewers, that's the most touching thing I've heard all week. It sounds as though a letter sent out of youthful ignorance, facetiousness, or both could have made a world of difference in the life of a valued veteran." She changes tone, brightening: "Next up: has Bigglesworth met his match in a goblin-run restaurant? Find out, in tonight's episode of *Dwarf Kitchen!*"

Strangely, I don't feel as optimistically about the dragon's letter as Sandy seemed to. If anything, it makes me a little depressed. I know veterans like that, people from semi-immortal races who spend centuries missing those they love. My grandfather is also a veteran of the War of the Necromancers, and hasn't gotten over losing both of his brothers.

I tell myself, I'd reach out to this lonely dragon, if I just knew who he was. But there's no way of knowing. *Julian* is such a common name. He could be anyone.

~ * ~

"He's probably Julian the Peacemaker," my coworker Gordy says. She's standing over the hissing espresso machine, her snake hair tucked under a bandana with their little emerald eyes peeking out cutely at me. "My dad's his gardener."

I'm not feeling too warmly towards Gordy at the moment, even though we're sort of friends. She's the backstabber who told everyone about my self-pity-filled fan mail to begin with, the only one in this cafe who watches *Lords of Hoards* as religiously as I do.

And I can't tell if she's genuinely trying to help me out here, or if she's just nosy.

"What's he like?" I ask, trying to decipher the name scrawled on the side of the paper cup I'm holding.

"You ever misspell them on purpose?" she grins. She's annoyingly pretty, even during the morning shift, with gold-brown skin and bright green eyes. "Sometimes I botch them up real bad, just for fun. I spelled *Gia* and *Ganinina* this morning."

"*Gordy.* I was asking—"

"Right. Julian is cool, my dad says—don't be fooled by his name, he's sort of a war hero. They call him the Peacemaker because he was so good at fighting, he ended battles early."

"One sec. CHAI LATTE FOR BARTHOLOMEW!" I shouted. The ogre in me makes me good at shouting orders, and makes me relish it. It's my favorite part of the job.

"Oh, there's a lot of ways you can misspell Bartholomew." She tilts her head. "You know you've got little tusks? They show when you yell."

"No, I had no idea I had tusks, Gordy, thanks for letting me know," I mutter. I wouldn't personally call them tusks. I prefer to think of them as big canines. "Did you know you have snakes on your head?"

"Okay, okay, point taken."

I grab the next cup. "Do you think I should email him?"

"He's pretty old school. He'd probably prefer a letter."

I'm silent for another minute. Could I really write a letter to a stranger? "I mean. That would be weird, right?"

"The fact you wrote to the TV station to begin with was weird." She laughs, showing a flash of her slightly forked tongue. "You might as well do something nice."

"Hold on—MATCHA LATTE FOR BRUMHILDA!" I turn back to face her, about to say something else.

"Excuse me?" a minotaur bellows. "Is this my iced vanilla latte?"

"Not yet, sir, it's a hot matcha latte, for Brumhilda," Gordy says, without missing a beat. "Is your name Brumhilda?"

The minotaur flattens his ears and his nostrils flare, but fortunately, there are no threats to talk to our manager. This time.

"I guess I *should* write to him," I say. For some reason, I'm reluctant, afraid of breaking the monotony I've fallen into over the past year or two, even with something as unambiguously altruistic as writing a letter to a lonely, widowed war hero. "I guess there's no reason not to."

"Yeah, go for it, honey, you got this," Gordy is distracted now, the assistant manager shouting something to her. "Hold on, I gotta see if we have more cheese danishes in the back."

~ * ~

Once I'm sitting down, I realize I have no idea how to start.

So after an hour of procrastination, I start with the obvious.

*Dear Julian,*

*I was the one who wrote about wanting to be part of a dragon's hoard. You're right—I was being 'facetious.' Because I hated my job and missed home and was feeling sorry for myself.*

*But I was really touched by your letter the other day. No one who's given to your kingdom the way you have should have to feel alone.*

I feel so corny, but I keep writing,

*I'd love to be a part of your hoard of friends. Maybe even visit, if you're okay with that. I hope that doesn't sound weird.*

No, I know it does. But as I write, I realize I need this, too: I'm lonely. I'm misplaced, the failed experiment of two parents with incompatible goals and personalities. I can't remember the last time I hung out with someone outside of work.

I conclude,

*Please write back if you'd like to meet. Or just write, if you'd prefer to do that.*

*Sincerely,*

*Beatrice Jagjaw*

I've already sealed it in an envelope when I realize I seem like a complete stalker, because he has no way of knowing how I got his address.

I tear it open again, and add,

*P.S: I got your address from Gordy, your gardener's daughter. I hope that's not super creepy, she just happened to know you.*

"Yeah, it's super creepy," Gordy confirms at work the next day. "But, older guys have a tolerance for that. Their radar isn't exactly on the lookout for creepy behavior. I think he'll be touched."

After a few days he writes back—he has beautiful stationery paper and gold ink and a wax seal. It puts my convenience store envelope to shame.

*Dear Ms. Jagjaw,*

*I am touched and heartened by your thoughtful response.*

*When I mused about collecting my 'hoard of friends,' I had in mind people closer to my age—I am nearly five hundred, one of the oldest dragons in the area, I believe. Once you reach a certain age, time slows up and speeds down. That's the best and only way I can describe it.*

*As such, I can feel—and, I fear, seem—somewhat awkward around youthful people. I operate on a different wavelength from them, as it were.*

*Nevertheless, if you would like to visit me, you are welcome to come over after 8AM any day of the week except the Sabbath. That is when my gardener arrives as well. I did not know he had a daughter, but you may tell Gordy she is also welcome.*

"No way am I getting up that early on my day off," Gordy says when I tell her.

"But this was all your idea to begin with!"

"It was not! You just asked if you should email him, and I said you should write to him." She shakes a cold brew with caramel syrup. "Look, I'm glad you're doing this. But this is on you, at least the first time."

"Well, what if it's awkward?" I ask.

"It probably will be! That's why I'm not doing it!"

I put all my irritation into my voice as I yell, "TRIPLE ESPRESSO LATTE FOR JEDADIAH!!!!"

Customers actually flinch.

"Jesus," a Wulver says, putting her hands over her canine ears.

I make it a point to misspell everyone's names throughout the day.

~ * ~

I tell my mom about my plans during our nightly call.

"I think that's great, honey." She pauses a minute. "You know —I think if your father had fought in a war, things would have been different between us. That's the one thing that was missing, I think. He doesn't have the maturity of a veteran."

I don't really know about that. "That's a neat theory, Mom." As if everyone comes back from war more well-adjusted.

"He and I have been talking again."

I sit up. "You and dad?" I sputter.

"Yes."

My jaw flops open. She's back in an Elven city, where no one speaks anything but the Old Language and the houses are in the trees and everyone walks around silent as unicorns, and NOW she's talking to my dad again?

"I know what you're going to say. But I've always been torn between my love for him and my love for my home and family," she explains. "I was unhappy when I was away from here. That put a strain on our marriage. When I'm happy, I always feel like I should reach out to him."

I sit back in my easy chair—one of the few gifts from my dad I can actually make use of. "It sounds like THAT might have been the one thing missing in your marriage."

"Maybe. Maybe it was." She hesitates. "You're always welcome with me, darling, and your grandparents. You know that, don't you?"

"Yeah," I say, feeling awkward now that she's acknowledged the elephant in the room. "Look, Mom, I'm awfully tired. I'll talk to you tomorrow, okay?"

"Alright, sweetheart." In the Old Language, she says, "I love you."

"I love you too," I say, also in the Old Language, even though I know my pronunciation is awful.

I don't like the fact my mom is over a hundred and my dad is seventy-nine and it still seems like they're kids just trying to find their way in the world.

If that's true, what does the future hold for me?

~ * ~

I'm still thinking about that as I drive to the dragon's house.

So much so it takes me a moment to realize it's a mansion. Buttery marble, with a fountain in the middle of its lush garden.

A man who can only be Gordy's father is standing in the shrubbery with a pair of gardening sheers. He has her good looks, snakes peering out from underneath his broad-brimmed hat.

"My good-for-nothing kid wouldn't come with you, huh?" he says, affectionately.

I can't help but smile, shaking my head. "Nope!"

"Don't worry. Never too old for a time-out."

It's strange to hear a father talk so comfortably about his daughter, like he knows her. My father loves me as best he can, I know that.

But he doesn't know me. Maybe someday that can change. I want it to change.

Gordy's father swings his head back towards the house, snakes seeming to point. "He's in there," he says, "you can let yourself in, he's a nice dude. No rain of fire for visitors."

I take a deep breath, thank him, and start towards the entryway. I step under the marble balcony, the shade almost liquid in the warm morning.

Why am I doing this again?

Because it's kind, I remind myself. It's a nice thing to do.

Or maybe because two lonesome souls will gravitate towards each other like planets caught in each other's orbit.

I feel how much he needs a friend, somehow. Maybe he feels how much I need a friend, too—maybe that's why he wrote the TV station that day.

I don't expect to find him right inside the front hall.

He looks as marble as the rest of the house, his scales a buttery and glossy white, with seams of black and gold running through them.

He's a graceful, almost liquid shape, his back sloping into a tail that zigzags like a river along the floor. His wings, even folded, are elegant, arching slightly.

I smell paint, and step forward a bit to see the huge canvas he's working on.

"What do you think?" he asks, and only then do I realize he's aware of me, without even looking up. Of course he is—dragons have elevated senses.

"It's beautiful," I say, because it is.

He's painting a gold dragon, surrounded by pegasi. In the background, clouds roll, thunderous and full of vapor. It's clear he's been painting for many times longer than I've been alive.

"You said in your letter you hoard paintings," I remark, surprised at myself that I remember. I'm not usually the sort of person who remembers things like that. "I didn't know you were the one who made them."

"They're not all mine." His voice is as rich and deep as the richest, blackest coffee mixed with the richest, darkest molasses. "I started collecting the works of others. It inspired me to start making my own. Beauty begets beauty."

He turns to look at me over his shoulder. His eyes are ether blue, and his eyelashes are long and gold. They're very beautiful, and I can see how old the soul behind them is.

"Would you like to try?" he says, holding out a paintbrush in offering.

"I don't want to mess up your picture," I say quickly.

"Not to worry. I can have Minni get you a canvas of your own."

"I can just watch you for a minute, if that's okay."

"As you wish."

It occurs to me, watching him paint, how at ease I feel. Why? Maybe it's because I so thoroughly expected this to be awkward.

Or maybe it's because he's centuries old, and clearly has experience putting people at ease. He said he was awkward, on a different wavelength from young people. Now that I've met him, I can say I disagree with the first statement—he's not awkward. But he is on a different wavelength, and I like that. I want to be on that wavelength, too.

I can picture him like an underwater current, cool and soothing, and I have the strangest feeling of belonging. Like the dragon and I are old friends.

Even though we didn't even bother to exchange introductions since I came in.

"Well, this is about as interesting as watching paint dry," an amused voice says.

I spin around. "Gordy?" I feel like a neglected child whose mom finally came to her ballet recital. It's pathetic, how much it means to me that she's here.

It means we're not just work friends. We're actual friends.

"I felt bad for not coming." Unlike at work, she's not wearing a scarf over her snake hair, and they've sort of styled themselves into a side part. She's wearing a red skirt and black turtleneck shirt, and she looks gorgeous.

"Julian, it's nice to finally meet you," she says, approaching. "My dad talks about you a lot."

"He hasn't talked about you at all," Julian deadpans, not looking up from his canvas. For a second I clench with secondhand embarrassment.

Then Gordy explodes into laughter, and I realize how easily he's parsed out her sense of humor. Oh, to have the social awareness of a five-hundred-year-old dragon.

"I offered Beatrice her own canvas," Julian continues, not putting down his own paintbrush. Only up-close do I realize it's a dragon-sized brush, nearly as long as my forearm. "But she preferred to observe."

"Oh, no way! Beatrice, you're about as boring as a pack of dry salt biscuits. We're BOTH going to paint—I used to take art lessons,

Bee, I'm going to kick your rear end."

Julian calls to his maid, and a spotted female minotaur comes down the stairs deftly balancing two more canvases on one arm and two small easels on the other. Then she runs back upstairs for person-sized paintbrushes and smocks.

Only when I dip my brush into the paint do I remember—I used to love painting, too. Not that I was any good at it, I don't think, but I loved watching the colors take hold of the page.

Gordy is already smearing her canvas with the brightest colors she can find.

I glance up past her just in time to see Julian peering down at us. His blue eye, in profile, is misty, shining softly in the pastel morning light.

It's easy to miss—it can be difficult to read dragons' emotions anyway—but it occurs to me how glad he is to have our company.

I'm glad, too, I realize. Happy, for the first time in months. Life feels new again, and every breath I take is full of possibilities. I can do whatever I want.

This is the start of something new for me. I don't know what, and instead of finding that frightening, I find it exciting.

The sun warms my hand as I streak my canvas with pale blue sky.

~ * ~

"Welcome back to *Lords of Hoards,* ladies and gentlemen! Tonight, we have a very special guest, Julian the Peacemaker. Julian, can you tell us a little about yourself?"

"I can, as a matter of fact. I am four-hundred-and-ninety-nine years old, a father, and a widower. I am a veteran of the War of the Necromancers and the War of the Black Dawn. In addition to pre-serving my late wife's hoard of antique books, I also hoard paintings."

"And as I understand it, Julian, you have a new hoard that start-ed due to this very show."

"I certainly do. Thanks to you, and the ill-advised fan-letter of one bright young woman, I now have my very own hoard of friends. They come in the door quite easily, if you leave your heart open a crack."

~ * ~ * ~

**Brooksie C. Fontaine** was accepted into Salve Regina University at the age of fifteen, where she obtained a BA in Studio Art and an MFA in Creative Writing.

She is a teaching assistant, tutor, and illustrator. Her work has been published by *Eunoia Review, Boston Accent Lit, Aureation, Quail Bell, Anti-Heroin Chic, Report From Newport,* the *Cryptids Emerging* and *Things Improbable* anthologies, and more.

# ...And One Dragon

## Harding McFadden

Solomon stood, dumbstruck, before the sign leading into Cuthbertshyre. His jaw hung loosely; his eyes stared wide. Try as he might, he could not believe what he was reading. The deceptively simple wooden sign stood there, like any of a hundred others he had walked past on his long trek. Yet, it was like none of the others. It was amazingly singular, as well as singularly horrifying. *"Welkum tu Cuthbertshyre,"* it read in a fading black chalk, the writing simple and blocky, the words humorously misspelled. *"Populatshun 75."* And there, beneath the rest, a more recent addition to the sign given its more vibrant red:

### *"...and One Dragon..."*

*It had to be some joke*, he thought. Some sick youth's idea of a humorous jab at visitors. Otherwise, the citizenry of Cuthbertshyre must have assumed that to make such a bold proclamation would make those of ill intent second guess their destination. Whatever the case, Solomon could not take his eyes from those red—somehow *blood* red—words for more than a minute, as he stood there in the center of the road. *I must look like a fool*, he thought somewhere in the back of his consciousness; but he didn't care. He felt like an alien in a foreign land.

It was only the roar, smaller than he would have guessed yet closer than he would have liked, that pulled him from his revery. Abruptly, he turned his eyes from the sign, and looked down the long road toward the town, a brief dot upon the horizon. The day was warm, yet not stifling. A cooling breeze pushed its way through the air like a welcome friend. The skies were overcast with the promise of rain, but not threateningly so. A sun shower, at best. The bag upon his back felt suddenly heavier as he stood there, his body alive with gooseflesh and a cold sweat. He was barely thirty years old, yet he felt suddenly twice that as a solid realization sat upon his shoulders like a vile wraith: he had to go there.

Hiking up his bag to resettle it, he released a calming breath, and started his way down the long road. His feet hurt, yet this was nothing new. As the low man in His Majesties Academy of Numbers, the task of the census had fallen to him. Walking from town to town, he had been on one road or another for close to three years, as near as he could tell. He had been on his own for so long, he no longer missed his home. Perhaps because it no longer *was* home to him. These places, these travels had become more a part of him than ever were his barracks at the Academy, or his cot in the orphanage before that. He had seen things and met people during his long journey that no one he had known in his previous life had ever even heard of. He had seen small kings with delusions of grandeur. Likewise, he had seen simple women with more grace and dignity than had been held by his own queen. He had seen trolls and gremlins; knights and witches. Yet, never had he seen...a dragon.

The road leading to Cuthbertshyre seemed longer when he at first set down it, yet in seemingly no time at all, greater than three quarters of its length lay behind him. The town, so recently a blob of shadow some great distance away, was now more solidly defined than he thought possible. The buildings were of soundly built stone, or occasionally wood, each with a thickly thatched roof. Here and there on the thatching, he could see the early telltales of green that let him know how much rain the town got. The fields, and the small alleys between buildings were lushly green, the vegetable patches full to bursting. The harvest would be coming in soon, and from the look of things, these people would want for nothing come winter.

Stretched out around the massive clearing the town filled, he could see more dwellings, and somewhere just beyond, the perimeter wall. Far from all-enclosing, the town wall would help keep out but few troublemakers. It would give some of the shorter monsters a run for their money, but couldn't possibly protect the villagers from bandits, or giants, or other true menaces. What, then, was the point of it, he wondered?

"Help ya?" a voice called out to him as he came within spitting distance of the nearest building. Some kind of communal gathering house, he assumed, and was right. Over the recent past, he had bedded down in hundreds of such.

The speaker was a woman. Taller than he by a foot, she was broad of shoulder, and weathered in the way of a farmer. Her hair was sun-bleached and cut short. Her clothes were far from new, yet well-kept. In her bearing, he saw surety and confidence. Her hands rested on her hips. In the few moments it took him to find his words, she asked again: "Help ya?"

"Uh, yes, miss," he stuttered, un-shouldering his bag, and removing the papers from it. "I'm Solomon, from His Majesties Academy of Numbers." He handed her his identifications. She took them and read over them easily.

"A census-taker?" she asked. He flushed, despite himself, somehow embarrassed at being identified as such by this mountain of a woman.

"Yes, miss," he answered, again shouldering his bag after replacing his papers.

"Naya," she corrected him. "I haven't been a 'miss' since I was ten years old. And you're not likely to find any Lords or Ladies, either. Just folks who work for a living."

She patted him on the shoulder with a smile and beckoned him to follow her into the gathering house. He found himself liking her, in spite of his prior intimidation.

The gathering house was a large, hollow room, with a great stone hearth at either end. A single long line of benches and tables lay in its center; stacks of bags, no doubt filled with grain and other winter stores, lay against the walls. In times of necessity, he had no doubt there would be room and food enough for each of Cuthbertshyre's seventy-five inhabitants. Yet, it was not its human population that concerned him just then.

Naya took a seat at the head of the table nearest them, and beckoned him to sit beside her. Gladly relieving himself of his burden, he sat gingerly. Given his lifestyle, he had little worry of saddle sores, but his long walk had done its share on the muscles of his legs and lower back.

On the table between them was a large pitcher of water, and a pile of rough cups. Grabbing two, his host poured them each a blessed drink, which he gulped more greedily than he had intended. Wiping his mouth on a well-worn sleeve, he looked at her sheep-ishly, and said, "Sorry. It's been a long trip."

She dismissed his apologies with a wave of her hand, as she finished her own drink with as much gusto. "Nothing wrong with enjoying a drink of water," she told him, refilling her own cup, then his. "Just proof a person's been working hard."

He smiled and drank again.

"So," she said after a few quiet moments. "What can I do to help His Majesty's census man?"

"Not much," he replied. "I've been doing this for so long it's all habit by now. The number on the sign? Still accurate?"

"Ya. We lost old man Hummock last month, but then his grand-daughter had a babe, so things have evened out."

He sat silently for a long moment, unsure how to proceed. Did he ask, and risk looking like a fool? Or did he not, and risk something worse?

"And...that *other*. On the sign. The one..."

"Dragon," she finished for him. He nodded. "Yes, she's here. And here she'll stay, make no mistake about it. It would take an army to pull our lady from us, census man, make no doubt about it."

He was taken aback by her sudden change. Large though she may have been, she had nevertheless been nothing but cordial until that point. Yet, upon mentioning the town's dragon, she had become suddenly quite stern. He had the feeling that, seen or not, there was a dagger at his neck, waiting for his next words. He gulped audibly, his throat desert dry, in spite of his drinks.

"I do believe you," he responded. Somehow, he had to salvage this suddenly tense situation. Otherwise, he feared, he might not walk out of this town. "It's just that, well...I've been many places, and seen quite a lot of things. But never have I seen a dragon living in a town, let alone be welcomed by the people living there."

Naya stood. With little doubt she wished him to stand as well, he followed suit, and allowed her to lead him back out into the darkening day. Maybe more than a sun shower after all?

"Something you need to understand," she told him as they made their way through the town center, and into the surrounding fields. The locals stopped whatever they were doing to stare at this odd procession. He felt like an insect, under the inquisitive needles of a child. A good distance away, closer to the wall than any of the other buildings, stood a small cottage. It was to it she was leading him. "She's not our dragon. Not some horrible beast to scare your children with. She's a part of our family. Has been for a few years now, and God willing, she will be long after I've gone off to dust. But, I'm not the one you should be talking to about her. I'm just the one who sees that things run smoothly. They're the ones you want to talk to."

They were fifteen feet from the front of the small cottage. Before it stood a man and woman, hand in hand, neither more than twenty years old. They smiled and waved at their visitors.

"And who are they?" he asked, just low enough to be heard only by his companion.

"They," Naya replied, opening her arms wide to embrace the young couple whole-heartedly, "Are her parents."

~ * ~

"This is Luna," the young man said, pointing to his wife.

"And this is Ari," the young woman said, pointing to her husband.

Seeing their fresh, unlined faces, Solomon had to reassess his estimate as to their ages. If they were twenty, it was a fresh twenty. These two still had the soft lines of youth about them. Yet, in no way did they seem soft. They were as much a part of the land they worked as was Naya. Their muscles were tight and sinewy, their eyes sharp and intelligent. These were no damn-fool children.

"Solomon," he introduced himself, grasping each of their forearms in turn. "I'm…"

Naya interrupted. "He's the King's census man," she said. "But, right now, I think he's more interested in your girl."

They looked at each other with undisguised concern. He was a government man, after all. What could he possibly want of their dragon, other than to take it away? In their eyes, he saw calculation. They were not cruel people, yet he had little doubt that should he try to come between them and their unlikely pet, he would never be seen again.

"Please," he said. "I'm just curious. I've never seen a dragon before. I'm just…"

"Curious," they finished for him, in unison. They looked at him with concern, but also with something akin to resignation. He became aware of Naya, standing closely behind him, tense and waiting. The day felt suddenly cold, as he waited for the unseen blade to bite deep.

A decision made, Luna turned toward her home, her hand leaving her husband's for the first time. "I think you'd better come in, Solomon," she said over her shoulder. "We have a story to tell."

As the girl's husband fell into step behind her, Solomon breathed a sigh of relief at still being alive. It stopped abruptly in his throat when he thought he heard the quiet *hiss* of steel sliding back into scabbard. He looked at his large guide, and she smiled down at him. "You're going to like this," she said, putting an arm around his shoulder, and leading him into the cottage.

Much like the gathering house, it was a single room, though much more compact. Likewise, the hearth was volumes smaller. In one corner stood the couple's bed, neatly made. In the center was a small table, around which were three chairs. The young couple each took one, Solomon the last, while Naya leaned against the cold hearth.

Holding hands again, the couple looked at him, their eyes beseeching. He couldn't help but think they didn't want him to die and were doing all they could to keep him alive. He felt appreciative for that.

"My husband and I cannot have children," Luna began without preamble. "We've known this since we were both young. Got a case of the bad flu, each of us. Lots of people did. Not many lived through it. But those who did: no children. It's not something you can ever get over; you'd better believe it."

"I'm sorry," he whispered in reply, and was. They would never know it, because he would never say it, but he knew first-hand how they felt. It had been the bad flu that orphaned him as a child, and which made sure when he died, his line died with him.

"Ari and I met in a sick house when we were children. We were both so near dead those who were left were already mourning for us. We lost all of our families, then, Solomon. Mothers, fathers, brothers, sisters: all gone, from one week to the next. When we did come through, Naya saw to us. So, if it seems like she has an eye on our wellbeing, its only because she's been our whole family since we can remember." They smiled up at the other woman, who averted her eyes, embarrassed at the praise.

"We've been close ever since, Luna and I, Ari said. "It wasn't a surprise to anyone that we eventually got married. When I was ten, Naya had me help her build this house. Before I even knew what it was being built for. Children can be thick, but a good parent knows what's going on. It took us a whole summer to get it made, but when it was done, there wasn't any place I'd rather be. This is home, Solomon."

For the first time, he became aware of the steady rumbling coming from outside. Not thunder, more like breathing, deep and heavy. It seemed to be all around them. He could not place it, so alien was the sound, yet his hands began to feel clammy all the same. He had a suspicion, and it scared him.

"Ari and I were here, one day over the summer of our thirteenth years, patching up whatever needed patching, when we heard a horrible sound coming from just outside. It was like some kind of nightmare, rending the earth."

"We rushed outside," Ari continued. "Right over behind where the wall is, it was like the ground was ripping itself up. There was dust, and smoke, and fire. I saw a tree pulled up by its roots and thrown eighty feet into the air. And over it all was this voice. It was like a mountain. It hurt my ears. Over and over, it kept saying, 'Be calm, be calm!'"

They both seemed disquieted by the memory. Years past, and it still held its sway over them. Yet it was their recollection of how it sounded that struck him: like a storm… Like the sound he heard, from just outside.

"When the dust began to settle," Luna said, "we saw them: dragons. Massive things, monstrous. A pack, or herd, or whatever you would call it. So close to the village. I thought we were done for. But then, I saw what they were up to."

"One of them was giving birth," Ari interjected. "Or trying to. She was wailing, thrashing. The baby looked to be about half-born. There was so much blood. Have you ever seen dragon blood, Solomon?"

He shook his head, too awed to trust his voice.

"It falls like fire," Naya told him. "Hits the ground and smolders. It'll cook a man clear down to his bones. Dragons are more than a bit of fire themselves."

"The field back there was burning," Luna continued. "The dragon was dying. I suppose she had her family around her, but they couldn't do anything for her. They just told her to calm down, again and again. When the baby finally came out, it didn't move. It was so small. Its mother just laid there. Her baby couldn't have been more than a minute old when she stopped breathing. If it wasn't so terrifying, it would have been tragic."

Seeing his wife's discomfort, Ari took over the tale: "When she died, her body just seemed to crumble, like the fire inside of it couldn't be held in anymore. The other dragons just stood there and watched it go all to nothing. The biggest one, the leader, looked at the baby, and growled. It was hurt, small. They seemed angry one of their own had died bringing it into the world. The leader, he called the baby something horrible. He kicked at it. Then they left, just flew off. Left the baby there to die."

They sat there for quite some time then, mournful. The air of the room seemed to have weight.

In time, Naya took up the tale. "By the time the rest of the village got here, the fun was all over. The dragons had flown away, and the little one was just starting to move. We all went to her, intent on just killing her outright. We may live in the country, census-taker, but we still know the law. Dragons are just too dangerous to let live. Kill 'em on sight or die trying. It's what we intended. Then, we saw her…"

"Our Rainbow…" Luna whispered.

"She was crying like any other baby," Ari said. "Just lying there next to the ashes of her mother. Her tears sizzled, like cooking meat."

"But she was crying, all the same," Luna said, her voice full of emotion.

Naya pushed off the wall and walked closer to the rest of the group. "She was small, smaller than I'd ever heard a dragon to be. More like the size of a dog pup. She was curled up, small and hurt. Her left wing was torn, useless. She'll never fly."

"Everyone just stood around her," Luna told him. "The urge to kill seemed to leave us. She didn't seem like a threat anymore. She was too sad for that."

"So, we decided to let her live for the night," Naya said. "I think we figured she'd die before morning, shape she was in. But next morning came, and still she laid there, crying over her mother."

"This went on for days," Ari whispered. "Luna and I were so sad about it, felt so sorry for the poor thing, that we started sneaking water and bits of food out to her. She only pecked at it, and never drank the water, but eventually the crying stopped. She just laid there, looking sad. Our hearts went out to her."

Outside, the rumbling continued, joined by a more environmental sound. As the sky grew darker, and the wind picked up, the unmistakable sounds of thunder could be easily made out, in the distance. He'd been wrong about the sun shower, he supposed. When this storm broke, it would be full and furious.

"About a week later," Luna continued. "Ari and I were here, sleeping outside by the wall, when a thing came out of the dark. I still don't know how to describe it, it was so dark, but one moment it wasn't there, and the next…"

"It was all death and glowing eyes," her husband continued. "Its breath smelt like rotting meat. I never got a good look at it, but I could swear it had something like six or eight legs. Like some kind of child a scorpion and a spider might make. It pushed its way out of the woods and had us pulled out of our bags in no time at all. I remember it being almost as large as the house, but that might not be the case. What I do remember clearly is that its mouth was big enough to eat one of us whole. It was the most scared I've ever been in my life."

Solomon looked to Naya for confirmation, and the look he got back was heavy indeed. There was more here than he was being told, and from her demeanor, she had no intention of telling him the rest of it until these children were out of earshot.

"The old folks tell us that when you're about to leave this world for the next everything you've done passes through your mind. You see all the people you've lost, all your favorite pets, everything you've ever loved. Like some god is trying to tell you that you've lived your life to the fullest, so it's alright to let it go. That's what happened to me when I thought Ari and I were going to be food for that thing."

"Then something miraculous happened," Ari continued, excited now that they had gotten to this point of their story. "Suddenly, out of nowhere, there was this horrendous growl. It seemed like it filled the air, it was so loud. Before we knew what was happening, our girl had jumped on this monster, and was fighting it, tooth and claw, for all she was worth. She wasn't even two weeks old yet, still so small, and there she was, fighting this mountain of a thing. We both figured there was no way she'd be able to win, but then our girl has made a habit of surprising us."

Luna was up from her seat, and pacing the room, her hands

moving wildly as if to punctuate her statements. "This monster grabbed my daughter by her neck, and lifted her up, ready to gobble her up with one bite. She was just about to, when Rainbow opened her mouth, and let loose with the brightest flame I've ever seen. Her body seemed to glow with it, between her scales. Her eyes were like little stars. All over her, she crackled, like when water bursts from burning wood. She shot her flame into the maw of that monster for more than a minute, grabbing onto it when the thing tried to run away. By the time our girl was done, the beast was nothing at all, just a pile of ash. Rainbow had cooked her down to nothing."

Ari stood beside his wife, and held her hand again, proudly. "Then she walked over and sniffed us. Like she was making sure we were alright. When she saw we were, she walked back over to the other side of the house and laid down. She slept well that night."

Naya placed a hard hand on Solomon's shoulder. "And she's been looking out for each of us, ever since. She's become more than just some dragon, for us to be afraid of. She's become their daughter. But, just as much, she's become a daughter to the community."

He looked at each of them, his eyes wide with wonder. He had heard many tales in his travels, yet never one so fantastic. The very thought of it left his mind beggared. "And she's been with you two ever since? All these years?" he asked, his voice barely above a whisper.

"Yes," they both answered, again in unison.

"So then, Rainbow is…"

"Her name."

~ * ~

The moon was at its height, yet still he could not sleep. Solomon tossed and turned on his not-uncomfortable bunk within the gathering house, visions of cooked and desiccated monsters running through his mind. Even worse were those instances, fought back with the best of his ability, when the dragon-destroyed piles of glowing ash were not monsters, but something much more familiar.

As he lay on his back, his breath came steadily by force of will. He was in constant danger of letting his anxiety overtake him. Though he would never think it, it spoke volumes as to his character that he could keep himself under what control he could.

Unable to lie still any longer, he pushed himself up to sitting, and in a bit of almost mad desperation, quit the building, and emerged into the brisk evening air. Overhead, the moon shone as brilliantly as she could, which wasn't much: the storm clouds were nearly total, blotting out the stars and bringing an early moisture to the night. In moments, the downpour would come, giving birth to a deluge that would wash away the muck and grime of his years of travel.

When the first heavy drop fell, he upturned his face to embrace it. Closing his eyes, he offered up a small prayer to whichever god might have been listening that whatever he chose to do with this situation, it would be the right thing.

"They're not listening," a gravelly voice said just behind him. He turned, and there, mostly hidden within the deep black-gray shadows was a troll. His breath left him. If there was one thing he had seen over the long course of his journey, it was trolls. Hideous little things, they always seemed half-melted and mildewed. This one's clothes were a deep gray, and so old they looked to be a part of his body rather than a covering for it. His nose was long and drooping, the slight whiskers on his chin scraggly and in bad need of a wash. The knife in his hand was wavy and sharp.

"They're never listening," the creature continued. He circled Solomon menacingly. His intent was beyond question: trolls never went anywhere they did not intend to rob and kill. "If they were, you'd never have woken from your slumbers. I'd have just slipped into your home and slit your little neck while you slept. It would have been quick, and without much pain. But, now? It would seem, frail human, your gods have abandoned you."

A calm overcame him that he would never have expected. His hands stopped their shaking, his breath its labored pace. He stood there, scant feet from this little murderer and thief, his feet unshod yet firm, his fists clenched at his sides. Try as he might, he knew he could not overcome this foe. Small in stature they might have been, but hardly had there ever been born a more deadly adversary than the troll. Nevertheless, though he knew he would fall in the conflict that was to come, he felt he should give a good accounting of himself. The beast would remember him.

His nerve steady, he was about to make the first move, when the urge became moot. Creeping up behind the troll, sneaking around from the back of the gathering house, were six glowing eyes.

As the creature came closer, its body began to crackle and glow, shooting off small sparks. From its illuminated nostrils and open mouth came thin wisps of smoke. By the time the troll became aware of the dragon's presence, it was too late.

Opening its jaws unbelievably wide, the dragon was upon the troll in an instant, devouring him whole, before the small intruder had so much as had the time to scream. As quickly as that, it was all over.

In the brief slashes of moonlight, Solomon got his first true glance of the dragon, and was surprised at what he saw. It was a thin thing, and small. Its left wing was torn, and skeletal. As tall as he when it stood to its full height, it circled him, its residual glow slowly fading. As it passed through a random moonbeam, he saw the smooth glide of its many-hued scales. It...*She*, he corrected himself. She was a thing of beauty. Her body was a wondrous cacophony of color, each blended together to make a perfectly balanced whole. It was no wonder what her parents had named her.

"Rainbow," he spoke to her, suddenly fearing her not at all. She stopped before him, her face inches from his own, her breath smelling of heat and earth. Her eyes met his unflinchingly. "Thank you."

With a low snort of acceptance, she moved away from him, back into the deepening gloom. He watched her progress until the threat of rain became a full storm. His last glimpse of her was in a flickering strobe of lightning. She circled her parent's home, steam bursting from her blistering-hot hide with every rain drop that made contact, before leaping onto the thatch roof, and laying down. He had no doubt she would stay there all night, unless she were again called upon to defend her home.

At last, he felt he understood...

~ * ~

He left two days later. Naya was beside him.

The long road out of town was still damp from a rain that had lasted the better part of his stay over in Cuthbertshyre. Already, he had fallen back into step, his feet and hips rolling automatically, by habit more than choice. He still had a long journey ahead of him.

"I think I understand," he told her.

"Ya?" she asked. "What's that?"

"Your love for her. For Rainbow. She looks out for each of

you. You're her family. You looked out for her when she needed it, so now she does the same. You've earned each other's love and loyalty. It's a marvelous thing."

"It is that. But it's more." She was silent for a long moment, as if organizing her thoughts. "The troll your first night here? A decade ago, it never would have come this far. They stay in the mountains, away from humans whenever possible. There's something greatly wrong with the world, more so every day. The monsters are coming out of the dark. Rainbow? She was the first one to find her way to us and thank God for that. But, she wasn't the last. We find them here more often all the time. Something's coming. And I think our girl may be our only way of surviving it."

They walked in silence until they had made their way to the head of the road. They stopped beside the sign that had left him so dumbstruck just days earlier. He looked at it again. Again he took in the words: ...*and One Dragon.*

"She's a simple thing, I think," Naya speculated. "Dragon's speak, I suppose you've heard. I know it's true. We all do. Each one of us heard the leader of Rainbow's family shouting at her. We all heard what he called our girl before he flew off and left her to die. But, I've never heard her say a word. I like to think she's too innocent for that. If she could talk like the rest of them, she could say hurtful things. In her silence, she's just...pure."

"I won't tell anyone," he told her suddenly. "Your people, your daughter. What you have here. It's beautiful. No one has the right to come between you. When I hand my census papers in at the end of my journey, it will only say seventy-five people live here. Nothing more."

His companion nodded. She looked toward the horizon. "I knew I would like you, Solomon," she said. "For what it's worth, you'll always be welcomed here. If you ever decide to settle down."

He smiled back up at her. If he was a younger man, he'd have thought he was falling in love. "It'll be the first place I come to," he told her. They shook firmly.

"Safe journey," she told him.

"Long life," he replied.

Hiking his bag up more firmly on his shoulder, he gave her a last, long glance, then started his long walk toward the next town. His bag was heavy with papers. His feet ached. His mouth felt dry.

He put one foot in front of the other, making his way. Behind him, he left behind an ideal little town, filled with seventy-five good people…

　　*…and one dragon.*

*for Naomi, Eleanor, and Iris*

*Originally published in Strange Sorcery #22 – 06/2017*
*Reprinted by permission of the author.*

~ * ~ * ~

**Harding McFadden** is a writer of New Pulp adventure, science fiction, and horror stories. He has published two juvenile adventure novels, *The Children's War* and *The Great First Impressions Trip*, as well as two collections of his shorter stuff, *The Judas Hymn* and *Making Monsters*, and a collection of his essays and articles, *Opinion as Fact*, that keeps getting him in trouble. His most recent work can be found in the publications of *Airship 27*, including three whoppers co-written with his daughters. His third novel is with the editors now, and his fourth, in collaboration with artist James Lyle, is in the works. As for "…and One Dragon," he really hopes you enjoyed it.

# By Promises Bound

## Deby Fredericks

Good evening to you, o most savage and magnificent dragon. May I say how terrifying you look tonight? Your searing crimson eyes. The dance of flames that reflect in your ebony scales—simply dazzling!

May I dare to ask your identity, o mighty one? Rhobashka! A name of fitting grandeur.

I? Why I am the Pied Piper, second of my name. I bow to your glory. Have I come to do epic battle? Heavens, no! Nor would I offer myself as your evening's repast. Beneath these many-colored garments I am really quite scrawny, I assure you.

Oh, these pipes? Merely a tool of my trade. I will be happy to play, if it amuses you.

No? To business, then. The good folk of Piper's Valley have sent me to represent them, your glory. We wish to know your intentions. Have you come to destroy us, or will you be settling in as a peaceful, though alarming, new neighbor?

To rule us? I see. You are but young, however…

No, no! I wouldn't dare to argue. It is actually quite clever of you to select this location. Piper's Valley is isolated here among the Mistikal Mountains. No other lord or king even knows we're here. Thus, no one will challenge your rulership.

Indeed, if I may say so, we do occasionally worry some outside power may seek to impose their will upon us. The denizens here may be persuaded to accept your governance, if you can protect us from other intruders. I am certain, however, my friends and family will wish to know what conditions you may wish to impose.

No sacrifices of young virgins? The people will be most relieved. Nor livestock, either. You can hunt for yourself perfectly well among the high peaks? Excellent!

Then—I shudder to ask—is it taxation? Ah, I see. You are young and wish to establish your hoard with all speed.

Alas, mighty Rhobashka, I must confess we have but little coin. Piper's Valley is indeed isolated, with no easy track in or out. This has granted us a measure of security, but it does cut us off from trade. Unfortunately, there are no gold or silver mines here…

Pray do not be angry, your glory! There may yet be a solution.

You mentioned these pipes I carry. They are the reason we denizens are here in Piper's Valley. They also are my heritage. Will you permit me to tell the story?

Years ago, your glory, we were but innocent children who lived with our families in the town of Hamelin. The town was plagued by rats, and the burgermeister offered a rich reward to anyone who could rid the town of them. It was our ancestor, the Pied Piper, who answered his plea. With these very pipes, he charmed the rats… Ah, you have heard the tale! Your glory is learned, indeed.

You know, then, the burgermeiser went back on his word. The Pied Piper was young himself in those days, and he was proud. For his revenge, he charmed the town's children as easily as he had charmed the rats. Off into the mountains we all went! One hundred and thirty younglings, orphaned by a single man who broke his promise.

This valley is where the Piper brought us. It wasn't easy at first. We did miss our families, but there is no way to get out of Piper's Valley without magic. The Piper did his best to be a good father. We older children helped, of course. His magic pipes built much of the town that you see along the river. He also traveled from time to time, bringing books to nourish our minds or medicine when we fell ill. Most of all, he taught us the value of keeping our word.

Yes indeed, your glory—every denizen of Piper's Valley is a descendant of those lost children of Hamelin.

Time went on. We children grew up. We tilled the soil, took on trades, fell in love and started families. Myself, I was drawn to the Piper's enchantments. I studied at his side like a true son, and when he left this world, the pipes came down to me. I have done my best to guide the good folk of Piper's Valley ever since.

How does this help to increase your hoard? Why, simplicity! With the power of the pipes in my hands, I can easily venture back into the settled lands. There I can rove about, playing my pipes. Unknown to my hosts, I will summon the small creatures—rats, chipmunks, magpies—and take in a bit extra. All for your glory, of course!

How soon, and how much? I propose to work slowly, moving

about to avoid detection. Pilfering more than engaging in brazen thievery…

A delaying tactic? No, not at all! Please, your glory, calm your fires. I'm finding it hard to breathe.

Thank you for your forbearance.

Consider, your glory. A few coins, a necklace or a ring, may not be missed, but they will accumulate. Whereas, another rat plague would certainly draw attention. Then there would be knights of valor, and greedy treasure hunters—no threat to yourself, certainly, but so much bother. Yet for us, our beloved valley would be quite spoiled.

Dragons crave treasure. I do understand, your glory. But, can you be patient? Slow gains over time, rather than immediate pillage. Dragons are long lived, are you not? Surely you have time…

Your glory, I swear this is no trick. Remember our story. We who dwell in Piper's Valley are people who keep our promises. If you will become our fearsome protector, we will be your faithful vassals.

O mighty Rhobashka, can we come to an agreement? Shall we be bound by our promises?

~ * ~ * ~

**Deby Fredericks** has been a writer all her life but thought of it as just a fun hobby until the late 1990s. She made her first sale, a children's poem, in 2000.

Fredericks has had short work published in *Andromeda Spaceways*, selected anthologies, and small magazines. Most recently, she self-publishes her fantasy novellas and novelettes, bringing her to 15 books in all. Her latest project is The Minstrels of Skaythe series.

Learn more from her web site: www.debyfredericks.com.

# Domestication

### J.S. Rogers

Everyone knew about High Point Business Park's reputation. Newcomers found out about it quickly and usually in a way that made forgetting impossible.

Ricki learned all she needed to know on her first morning in her new abode: an ugly house that looked like it had never seen better days, squatting right up near the pot-holed road, fringed with ratty grass. A sad, lop-sided tree grew along the cracked concrete path out front. Ricki chained her bike up to the tree the night before, too tired from moving to think of a better place for it.

She woke to find the tree lying across the concrete path. Something had gnawed through the trunk in the night. Slobber glistened wetly on the spikes of wood. Ricki stood in front of the felled tree, her hands on her hips, and asked the morning in general, "What?" Then she walked around the cracked branches and scattered leaves, twice, just to be sure a scattering of debris hadn't buried her bike.

"Aw, crap," her new roommate—Jannie—called from the doorway, cradling a cup of coffee. Jannie looked out of place in the drab surroundings with her copper-colored hair and brightly patterned leggings. "Not again."

Ricki completed a final circle around the tree before looking over at her. "Not again *what?*"

~ * ~

"A dragon," Ricki said, after Jannie brought her inside, sat her down, and poured her a cup of coffee. "A *dragon* knocked down the tree and took my bike. That's what you think happened?"

"That's what I know happened," Jannie said, crunching her way through a bowl of sugary cereal. "It lives over in one of the old factories in the business park, moved in…I don't know. A year ago, maybe?"

Ricki frowned down at her coffee. The business park must have been a bustling place, once, but she'd only ever seen it in its present condition: long abandoned and slowly being reclaimed by

nature. She had not realized that nature included a dragon. Everyone said they were a growing pest problem in the city, as more and
more areas fell into disrepair, but she hadn't imagined ever encoun-
tering one.

"But why take my bike? I need my bike." Public transportation
didn't run out to this neighborhood anymore. If she wanted to get
to work, and she did, then the bike was a necessity.

Jannie shrugged, her soft, round shoulders rising and falling
with the movement. "They all have hoards, right? Gold or gems or
whatever. *This* one has a hoard of bicycles. It's been taking them
since it moved in."

"A hoard of bicycles," Ricki repeated, hoping it sounded less
ridiculous in her voice. It did not. She dragged a hand back through
her dark hair. "Okay. Okay, fine. So how do people get their bikes
back from its hoard, then?"

"Sorry." Jannie shook her head, lifted her bowl, and drank
down the dregs of the milk. "I don't think they do."

~ * ~

The man who answered the phone when Ricki called Animal
Control did not laugh; she didn't think he cared enough to express
amusement with her situation. "Sorry," he said, "I can make a note,
but we aren't really the department that handles dragons."

Ricki leaned over and rested her forehead on the table. She'd
gotten the same general deflection from three other civil servants
at three other numbers. "The police department told me to call you."

"Mm. They probably meant to give you the number for
Management of Monsters, I'll transfer you over to them."

The line he transferred Ricki to rang and rang before clicking
over to a voicemail box. The prerecorded message told Ricki the
box belonging to the number she was trying to reach was full and
then disconnected her after wishing her a nice day.

Ricki stared at the phone for a moment in betrayal. It was
almost ten-thirty. She had to be at work in two hours. She could
make it in twenty minutes with her bike, but it didn't seem likely
anyone was going to help her get that back...

She grimaced and gave up looking for a number to find help.
Some things you just had to handle for yourself.

~ * ~

The first suggestion that came up when Ricki looked for directions on how to get something back from a dragon's hoard was: don't.

Every single article she found about the subject started the same way, with a firm warning that dragons should be avoided and left to trained professionals who knew exactly how to treat the huge beasts responsibly, limiting the prospect of harm to human or animal. Since there appeared to be no trained professionals in the entire city, Ricki decided to ignore the warnings as irrelevant to her life.

The next pieces of advice told her to go in at night, when the dragon was most likely to be out and about, hunting or looking for new treasures for its hoard. Ricki considered risking a daytime trip, but the dragon was large enough to chew through a tree trunk and carry off a bicycle, though—based on the grooves through the dying grass—it was not big enough to achieve lift-off when so encumbered. She sighed and got ready to walk to work, reading the rest of the suggestions as she prepared and going over them throughout the day, whenever she had a break.

~ * ~

An eight-hour shift left Ricki with aching feet, stinging eyes, and no desire to go stomping around in a dragon's territory. Her new bed beckoned to her from within the house as she stared at the fallen remains of the tree. She *could* just keep begging a ride to work. She *could* just scrape together the money to buy a new bike. She *could*...

A shadow passed over her, moving far too quickly to be a cloud. She looked up, into the night sky, and caught the barest glimpse of a dark, winged shape. It disappeared in an instant. Her pulse thrummed in her veins, her heart ratcheting as some instinct developed back in the time when humans and dragons fought over the same caves licked at her spine. The beast was out, hunting.

That meant its hoard was undefended. Something caught the starlight in the grass, and Ricki knelt, digging amongst splintered bark until her fingers brushed her bike's rear reflector.

"Okay," she said, rubbing her thumb over the smooth surface and nodding to no one. "Okay, how hard can it be?"

~ * ~

It could be pretty hard, as it turned out. High Point Business Park loomed skeletal in the darkness: warehouses and office buildings served as relics from a time when the city's industries were growing, instead of dissipating into nothingness. Grasses and small trees grew up through the cracking parking lots. Most of the windows were broken. Fading graffiti marked the walls.

Ricki shivered, though the night was balmy, tucking her hands up under her arms as she walked. Finding the hoard would be the first challenge. The internet said dragons had a strong reptilian odor, but Ricki had not made a habit of sniffing reptiles. She peered through broken windows and open doors, hoping to find a trail of bike chains or something.

In the end, she found a tire pump. It rested against a curb, half-buried by gravel. Ricki kicked it loose with her toe; she didn't recognize it but lifted it anyway. It felt like a boon. She moved onward quickly, finding other small things as she went. A round mirror laid here, and a basket rested there. The path of bike-related debris led her directly to a warehouse near the back of the industrial park.

A hole loomed in one wall, dark and beckoning. A water bottle rested directly in front of the entrance, all alone. A dry smell, not exactly *bad* but strong, wafted out into the night. She could imagine it putting her in mind of a lizard. Ricki licked her bottom lip, shifting her grip on the bike pump. Her hand grew sweaty around it. She took a step forward and stopped in the shadow of the building, a chill walking down her spine.

She swallowed and climbed inside.

~ * ~

The path beyond the hole was clear and wide, well-used. Ricki walked along one wall, well out of the center of the passage. Her phone provided the only illumination, now that a roof blocked the moon and stars. She could see scratch marks in the floor and walls. A helmet, bitten in half, almost tripped her. She swore under her breath.

Each step turned into a decision between getting out while she still could and pressing on just a little further. It felt like a mile before the passage finally spilled into a larger space. The ceiling felt high above; the faint light of her phone could not reach it. Strange shapes loomed in the darkness, machines turned to monsters by disuse and dust. She crept around them, her breathing the loudest thing in the world, and then she froze.

The hoard waited before her, illuminated by the moonlight streaming through a hole in the roof. It rose up from the floor, a tangle of metal and rubber. It must have held a hundred bikes, all thrown together, piled one atop the next. Some looked twisted, smashed down. There was an imprint on the top of the pile. Perhaps the dragon slept on it.

Ricki stared up at it, momentarily awe-struck, until a familiar curve of green caught her attention. Her bike. The dragon *had* taken it. It rested atop the pile, the back wheel overhanging the side. It didn't look bent or broken. Mad relief pulled Ricki forward, up the teetering tower of pedals and wheels. Handles caught at her, a broken spoke stabbed at her palm, and the entire thing shifted precariously every time she moved.

She kept going, scrambling upwards until she managed to grab the seat of her bike, well-worn and patched up. She laughed, pulling on it, and something scraped. It came from the passageway she'd traveled. She tried to imagine what a bike being dragged across concrete would sound like; and decided it would sound *exactly* like the noise approaching her.

She mouthed a curse and yanked on her bike again, pulling it from the mess and falling back down the pile in a cacophony of sound. The noise in the passage stopped in the aftermath of her poorly controlled fall. She froze at the base of the hoard, aching in a dozen places, holding onto her bike, breathing hard.

Something, something *big*, made a chuffing sound. Something with claws charged down the passage, no longer dragging a burden. Ricki hauled her bike forward, towards the nearest abandoned machine. She hunched behind the hulking shape, hoping it would shelter her, no longer able to remember anything she'd read about a dragon's senses.

She should have just bought a new bike. She should have—

She listened to the dragon cross the room. It breathed in sharp snorts, claws clattering noisily on the concrete, like castanets. It reached the hoard in a moment; the pile groaned under its weight. Something, perhaps a bike horn, honked sadly in the darkness.

Ricki clutched her bike and risked a look around the side of the machinery, despite the gibbering better judgment from her hindbrain. She had to see the beast. She just did.

The dragon crawled over the pile of bicycles. It was big, perhaps the size of a horse, with great wings folded down on its back. Its head was huge and mostly mouth. It had small limbs, compared to the rest of its body, and a long, lashing tail. It sniffed at the hoard, making an agitated, whining sound in its round chest.

Ricki had a straight line to the passage. Adrenaline roared in her veins. She succumbed to the burn of it, dragging her bike forward and trying to get a leg over, planning to pedal hard to freedom. She heard the dragon squawk behind her and screamed in response, heart beating like it wanted to escape her ribs.

The dragon hit her in the middle of her shoulders. She went down hard, striking cracked concrete flooring and expecting at any moment for it to savage her. No tearing, clawing pain came. Instead, the dragon grabbed at her bike with clawed forelimbs—flailing very close to her arms—and pulled, hard.

Ricky gave a wordless sound of denial and frustration, grappling onto the bike as best she could; the two of them locked, briefly, in a struggle of strength and bitter determination to obtain ownership of the bike, the dragon's eyes flaring, breath panting out hot all around her, while some part of her brain demanded to know what, exactly, she thought she was doing.

And then something came loose, without warning, and she fell back, striking her head on the floor, everything very briefly going white.

When she blinked color back into the world—only a second later—she found herself holding onto the bicycle seat. It had pulled completely free of the frame. She turned it over, dazed, and then the sound of metal over concrete drew her attention to the dragon, dragging the *rest* of her bike back towards its hoard.

It had, somehow, failed to maul her, even with the claw it had waved in her direction. It *had* snapped her bracelet clear off her wrist, but Ricki decided to count that as a win, in the grand scheme of things.

"Ow," she complained, to herself, and, at a loss for what else to do, rolled up to her feet and limped away, bicycle seat in hand, while the dragon remained preoccupied.

~ * ~

Ricki woke up in the morning with a splintering headache and a bike seat on the kitchen counter.

Jannie sat beside it, frowning at the seat, and holding a cup of coffee. "Tell me you didn't go to the dragon's den," she said, last night's makeup smeared around her eyes, giving her the appearance of a very judgmental racoon.

"Well, I could, but…"

"Oh, my God." Jannie put down the coffee and covered her face with both hands. "Are you trying to die? Do you have a death wish?"

"Hey," Ricki said, feeling defensive. "I survived. And I even got back *part* of my bike."

"Yeah, I see that." Jannie lifted her head to scowl, unimpressed. "And what are you planning to do with it? Just keep going back and reclaiming your bike one piece at a time or something?"

In truth, Ricki had been ready to throw the seat away, buy a new bike, and call the whole thing a wash. But Jannie's words felt condescending as she stood there, looking at her.

"Oh, no," Jannie said, shaking her head. "Hey, no, whatever it is you're thinking, you stop thinking it right now. Ricki, this is a bad idea. Ricki!"

But really, how hard could it be?

~ * ~

Ricki spent her shift plotting out a plan to take back her bike, piece by piece.

She looked up the tools she'd need to get the wheels and chain off, and came home with a sense of renewed purpose and—probably—the remnants of a concussion.

"I really don't think you should do this," Jannie said, watching Ricki gather up a few items in a bag. Ricki nodded, took that under advisement, and ignored the advice. On her way out the door, she briefly turned back to return to her room, grabbing a bracelet off the dresser.

Maybe it was the concussion talking, but the dragon *had* let her out alive and mostly unharmed last time. All it had really cost was a cheap bracelet she didn't like much anyway. It seemed a fair trade to her and—so armed—she set off once more into the night.

~ * ~

Ricki managed to find her way directly to the dragon's lair, cutting almost twenty minutes off her time from the previous night. She arrived to find the dragon missing and considered trying to make a break with her *whole* bike again.

Unfortunately, the dragon had rearranged the hoard. Her bike stuck out of the side more than halfway down, buried amidst a mess of pedals, handlebars, and sad little reflectors. So she carefully undid the front wheel—protruding from the pile—and clambered back down.

She stood looking at the pile for a moment, expecting the dragon to come shambling back in. It remained missing and she awkwardly tucked the wheel under one arm to fish the bracelet out of her pocket. She looked around and—yeah—last night's bracelet was missing.

She draped the second one off a handlebar protruding, bent, from the pile and, feeling as though she'd managed a feat worthy of a song from the bards of old, slipped back out of the warehouse to her house.

"You've officially lost it," Jannie said, when she came back through the door, wearing a gauzy robe, with her arms crossed firmly over her chest.

"Yeah," Ricki said, wiggling the wheel at her, "but I'm getting it back."

~ * ~

Ricki kept going back to the dragon's den.

After a few visits, she couldn't reach her bike anymore; the dragon had tucked it away somewhere, burying it deeper in the hoard. She adapted to the situation and took pieces off the bikes she *could* reach, if they looked like they'd fit the pieces she already had at home.

She used her days off work to try to fit the pieces together. Sometimes, she had to hammer bits flatter or fit pieces in, but the skeletal outline of a bike gradually came to life in her bedroom, filling the space with the smell of grease and sweat.

Jannie sometimes came by and shook her head in the doorway; but seemed to have given up trying to convince Ricki to just buy another bike or—perhaps—a scooter. The dragon seemed to have given up, also.

Ricki felt certain the beast saw her sometimes. She smelled it in the lair and had frozen more than once, going still, when she heard it breathing or the shifting of massive wings. But it hadn't bothered her again, not since the first time it caught her amongst its treasures. She credited that to the little baubles she left behind, hanging off spokes or mirrors.

She'd hit a few consignment shops and yard sales to ensure she had a wide variety of costume jewelry to choose from and left a piece each time. She wondered, sometimes, why the instructions for dealing with dragons hadn't just included guidance to leave them some shiny presents. The solution seemed obvious to her.

The system she set up worked well enough that, barely three weeks later, she found herself with all the pieces she needed, really, to Frankenstein her way to a usable bike. She finished the project with busted knuckles and a deep, pleased sensation of pride spreading through her chest, as Jannie leaned over her shoulder and said, "That is, for sure, the ugliest bike I've ever seen."

"See if I let you borrow it," Ricki said, and went to shower off so she could crawl into bed, contentedly dreaming of biking to work the following day, deliciously pleased she'd skipped her visit to the dragon's den and would—hopefully—never have to visit it ever again.

~ * ~

Ricki woke up the next morning with Jannie leaning over her bed, scowling. "You'd better come and see what you've done, now." Was all she said.

"What?" Ricki asked, but Jannie refused to offer so much as an explanation.

All she said, as Ricki pulled on pants, was, "This is your problem. Don't expect my help dealing with it, I *told* you to stop."

Ricki scrubbed blearily at her eyes as she walked down the hall. Jannie got bent about the strangest things. She hitched her pants up and pushed open the front door, only to draw up short as her brain registered the sudden change to their yard.

"What...?" she asked, gazing across the dozen bikes—all in various stages of disrepair, many of which she recognized from the dragon's lair—scattered hither and thither across the grass. They looked like they'd been just dragged in and dropped, one after another.

"See," Jannie said, and shoved her phone against Ricki's shoulder. Ricki took it, rubbed her eyes again, and looked down at the screen, vaguely certain she was dreaming.

*How to Attract Dragons to Your Home* the heading across the top of the page read. Ricki felt the bottom drop out of her stomach as she got to the subheading: *Only Attempt if You Hate Yourself or Your Neighbors.*

"Oops," Ricki said, faintly, scanning the list of things she'd been doing, and, beside her, Jannie groaned and dropped her head against the wall. "Don't worry. I'll fix it. How hard could it be?"

~ * ~ * ~

**J.S. Rogers** has been writing since she was old enough to hold a pencil. She enjoys exploring horror fiction and the intricacies of the human condition. She lives on the East Coast with her kids and cats.

# Beneath Scorched Earth

## Christopher Powers

A weathered sign above the entrance of the Dragon's Roost Inn swung in the early-evening breeze, creaking loosely like the sails of an old pirate ship. The inn was shrouded by a cloak of overreaching trees, pushed far back from the village of Eaves. Weary travellers and less hospitable folk resided there, using the place as a haven from the outside world.

As Gareth and Kael entered, embraced by warm firelight, their eyes scanned the common room for their quarry. A reclusive character, so they'd been told, and someone it was advisable to stay clear of. But this person harboured a gift; or better yet, was said to have been born with rare attributes. Attributes which were perfect for their needs.

Kael breathed deep. In addition to the burning timber logs and aromas of roasted meats, a cloying stench of ale, urine and blood permeated the place.

The two men moved through the room, dodging around patrons huddled in groups around the flames dancing in a stone hearth. A bard stood sentry in the corner, one leg propped back against the wood-splintered wall as he strummed a lute, its melody swallowed by the rowdy hooting of nearby drinkers.

Tables, scarred by years of use, were scattered haphazardly throughout the inn, while the bar, a weathered oak structure, hosted a formidable array of bottles, some laying entombed in thick webbing and dust.

Gareth motioned his companion to wait at one of the tables, but Kael's attention was on something else.

"Is he the one, Kael?" Gareth asked, his voice muffled beneath a thick hood.

Kael nodded from beneath his hood. "Rumour has it he can dig through rock like it's butter."

Gareth turned to study the figure Kael was watching: A peculiar figure who sat in the farthest corner of the room, nursing a tankard. A thick hood obscured the stranger's features. Their head was lowered as if in prayer.

"Excuse me," Gareth began, sliding into the seat across from the stranger. "We've heard you're quite the digger. Are we right?"

The shrouded figure looked at them with a mix of curiosity and suspicion. "Depends on who's asking." He had a gravelly voice, like sandpaper on rock.

Gareth and Kael recoiled, a flicker of surprise passing between them as the stranger's hooded cloak slipped back. The cloth held the scent of damp soil, a testament to a life spent delving into the secrets hidden beneath the ground.

"We're in need of someone with your talents." Kael leaned forward with a sly grin. "We've got our eyes set on a dragon's horde, and we've heard you're the best tunnel-maker in these parts."

Gareth wondered how his partner could engage in simple conversation after seeing the stranger. He noted a pair of rich velvety-brown, fur-covered forearms, which seemed to merge seamlessly with the more human-like portion of his body. As Kael continued laying out the pair's plan, Gareth found himself spellbound by the scene. He stared at the strangers' hands, watching his large fingertips tapping a set of sharp, dirt-encrusted claws against the scratched -up table. He marvelled at the creature's face, notably the snout; a remarkable blend of human and mole features, tapering gently from a broad base to a more delicate tip. The skin was smooth, resembling human flesh, but the texture transitioned to a velvety softness around the cheeks.

The half-man, half-mole studied them for a moment with a pair of obsidian, orb-like eyes. "Dragon's horde, you say? What's in it for me?"

Kael slipped a small pouch across the table, and the mole-man gave it a tap with his claw, listening with growing interest at the sound of jingling gold.

"Enough to live like a king for the rest of your days," Kael added, his toothy grin widening.

The mole-man's eyes widened, and he snatched up the pouch, inspecting its contents. "Name's Hulkan. This better be worth my time."

Gareth finally found his voice. "We promise you, the riches inside that dragon's lair will make what you're holding now seem like goblin dung."

"Do either of you know how to slay dragons?" Hulkan asked, narrowing his eyes.

"We don't need to," Kael said, leaning in conspiratorially. "With your skills, we'll be in and out no problem."

Hulkan considered their offer, his sharp claws rapping against the wooden table. After a long pause, he nodded, the firelight revealing a mischievous glint in his eyes. "All right, I'm in. But if this goes south, I won't hesitate to leave you both in the dark. I mean that literally."

The trio acknowledged their deal with a toast, knowing the path ahead promised riches beyond any of their wildest imaginations.

~ * ~

The approach of dawn over Eaves Village bled hues of rose and gold into the sky, but the trio did not witness it. Earlier, they had emerged at the daunting threshold of Drakonspire Ridge. The journey south had etched weariness into their limbs, yet the promise of a dragon's hoard fuelled their determination.

Carrying only a lantern to banish the lingering darkness, a rugged sack slung over their shoulders for the treasures yet to be discovered, and a hip flask to quench their growing thirst, they ascended craggy peaks and sucked frigid air that turned their breath into frozen tendrils.

"The cold up here is like the icy hands of death," Hulkan said gravely, before lowering to a knee and observing the cracked, arid ground. He traced one large, clawed hand over its surface, then rested his head against the earth, as though listening for movement deep beneath the cavernous expanse.

"What is he doing?" Gareth whispered to Kael, the sound echoing through the desolate landscape.

"How should I know?" Kael responded. He knelt beside Hulkan. "May I take your ear for a moment?"

Hulkan rose to look at him.

"My partner and I would like to know what you are doing. We mustn't linger here too long. These mountains are not safe havens. Many creatures lurk here, and none too kind. Stay too long and this place will become our tomb."

"I'm listening," Hulkan responded.

"Listening? To what?" Gareth asked, perplexed.

"For a way in," Hulkan replied. "We're close. Take a look." With a point of his claw, the other men saw what was surely a dragon's lair concealed within the heart of the mountains. The entrance, framed by monstrous fangs of rock, yawned open like the maw of some primordial beast.

"We've found it," Gareth said, breathlessly. "Let's go inside."

"If you want to die like a fool then go ahead," Hulkan offered.

"Well, what do you expect us to do?" Gareth shot back, fingers curling into fists. "You were brought in to help us, not hinder."

"And that's precisely what I intend to do. You see the ground over there?"

Gareth and Kael looked. The earth was darker, reddish in tone. Dusty. "What about it?" Kael asked.

"That is petrified rock," Hulkan explained. "Scorched earth. Harder to break than the steel forged in the mightiest sword. I cannot gain access to the dragon's lair from within the cave. It must be done from here."

"What about when we reach the other side?" Kael asked, concerned. "Won't that same petrified rock be scorched there also?"

Hulkan shook his head. "Let's hope not," he said.

At Hulkan's request, Gareth and Kael stood back and watched as he pressed his massive claws against the unforgiving surface of the hard, arid rock. With incredible strength, he began to carve out the earth, sinking deeply, claw over claw, chiselling into stubborn stone like surgeons saw through bone.

Dust and rock fragments cascaded in his wake, discarded by the determined thrust of his powerful limbs. Hulkan's fur-covered form blended into widening shadows, his eyes reflecting the dim light of the lantern as he delved deeper into the heart of the mountain. The air began filling with the scent of freshly disturbed earth, and the two men watched on with shocked faces as a subterranean realm started taking shape beneath their feet.

Minutes stretched into hours. Still Hulkan worked, his tireless dedication becoming almost a burden to Gareth and Kael, who stood a foot away, hopeless to the cause. When at last the tunnels had been built, the trio followed the curved and twisted labyrinth, blind but for the dim casting of weak light emanating from their single lantern.

"My back is hurting," Kael complained, as he crouch-walked

along before finally dropping to his knees and crawling. Clumps of wet earth and rock drifted down from above, threatening to cave the entire network of tunnels under an indisputable weight. The three men hoped to reach their destination soon.

At last, Hulkan stopped, relieving his muscular arms of their work. "I smell sulfur," he whispered, "just above us. I believe we've found the treasure room."

"Can you get us inside?" Kael asked, his hope tinged with fear. The walls vibrated, shaking like the world was crumbling.

"This should be easy," Hulkan said, testing the roof above them. "Stand back." He punched both clawed hands into the ceiling of the tunnel, then once more scraped and tore at the sodden earth. Soon they would know if their quest had been successful. If those powerful claws met petrified, scorched rock, their day would be wasted—their treasure trove forever a dream.

Hulkan's claws pushed upwards through the final layer of rock, and with a triumphant burst, he breached the heart of the dragon's lair. Sharp and painful light filtered into the underground chamber, which was filled with a vast expanse of glittering treasures. Gold, rubies, and diamonds galore—this subterranean space was cast aglow in a kaleidoscope of vibrant wealth.

~ * ~

The dragon's hoard, once guarded by the impenetrable peaks of Drakonspire Ridge, was now laid bare before the trio, waiting to be claimed.

"We're rich!" Gareth cheered, clapping his hands together in triumph. "I knew we could do it. I knew it!"

Kael surveyed the room, his mouth agape and eyes widening as his gaze moved to each chamber housing piles of gold coins and sparking jewels. "I always believed this place existed." He retrieved a gold coin from the ground, turning it slowly between thumb and forefinger. "We owe you a debt of gratitude," he added, looking at Hulkan, who still hunkered within the carved-out tunnel.

"You can pay me what you owe later," Hulkan said. "Right now, I'd suggest grabbing what you can and then us getting back to the surface."

"What's the rush?" Gareth said. He was kneeling in front of a chest spilling over with gold and silver trinkets. "No one knows we're here. This whole score is ours and ours alone."

"Your naïvety is worrying," Hulkan said. "Have you forgotten the reason for asking me along?"

"Of course not," Gareth said, absently admiring a large red ruby. "We needed someone to get us inside without drawing attention."

"Drawing attention to what?" Hulkan pressed. He was pleased to see the expressions on his cohorts faces turn suddenly ashen. "The legendary guardian of this realm has yet to realise its fortress is breached, but when it does, none of us should be anywhere close."

As if to press upon Hulkan's point, a thunderous roar echoed around the chamber, rattling the treasure within.

"Grab everything!" Kael commanded. "Now! Hurry!"

The three men filled their sacks until each was fit to burst, and then tossed them into the hole.

Their elation was short-lived. The underground chamber shuddered as if the mountain itself was awakening. The trio turned to the entryway, bathed in an ethereal glow of the dragon's hoard, and exchanged worried glances as low rumbling growls reached the cavern walls. The air grew thick with an oppressive heat.

A colossal form appeared, its deep, thick scales resplendent, its eyes furious, blazing orbs, which fixed on the intruders standing among its riches.

Gareth, Kael, and Hulkan stood frozen, their hearts pounding as the dragon unfurled a pair of massive wings, which slapped against the stone walls in a thunderous clap.

The dragon was far bigger than any tale told around the hearth of the Dragon's Roost Inn could have prepared them for. As its gaze shifted from man to man, a scorching gust of flame licked out from its snout, turning a stack of gold coins into a molten mess.

The cavernous room, moments ago the crowning achievement of the trios' lives, had now become a blistering hot prison destroying their air.

Kael looked on the creature with newfound respect. It was majesty among riches, a king amongst a fortune. Their heist had been daring, no one could deny, and recruiting the elusive moleman was a masterstroke, but if it ended now, if they were snuffed out in a hail of fire, their bravery never known, then had any of this been worth it?

The dragon's roar faded into a distant rumble, creating a brief moment of disorientation. In that split second, Hulkan seized his opportunity and made a frantic dash for the tunnel.

The dragon breathed a molten ball of yellow flame towards the escaping thief, but he was fast; managing to dive headlong into the tunnel, his velvety-brown ankle scorched and singed by a lick of fire.

"We're doomed," Kael whispered to his friend, and took Gareth's forearm. "I am sorry for bringing you here. Truly I am."

"I make my own decisions," Gareth said, giving Kael a reassuring squeeze in return. "We did it though, didn't we. We found the treasure."

A thin smile spread across Kael's face. "That we did, my friend. That we did."

The dragon's roar drove both men to the ground, its force a shuddering punch. It loomed above them, huge wings flapping. Twin tendrils of smoke rose from the dragon's snout, drifting into the upper levels of the treasure room.

Then the dragon let loose a terrible growl and stumbled backwards, its movements suddenly unsure. It roared again as another large mound of earth crashed into its face, momentarily blinding it.

"Hurry!" Hulkan called, poking out of the tunnel. "You won't get another chance!"

In a frenzied scramble, Gareth and Kael darted toward the opening. The dragon's roar reverberated behind them as they navigated the tunnels, guided by Hulkan's knowledge, never slowing, never glancing back.

The tunnel grew hotter with each step, and the distant rumble of the dragon's pursuit spurred them on. Though it would be impossible for the dragon to squeeze into the hole with them, they still felt its insurmountable heat chasing them through the passages.

Adrenaline coursing through their veins, the trio eventually emerged into the cold mountain air, gasping for breath, just as their makeshift entrance to the dragon's lair collapsed behind them, sealing off the fiery wrath within.

Gareth and Kael stood motionless, their chests heaving with exertion. The realisation of their narrow escape settled over them, and a mixture of relief and disbelief played across their faces.

Now free from the molten prison, they stood in the shadows of Drakonspire Ridge, their sacks laden with stolen treasures, the taste of danger lingering in the mountain breeze. Hulkan's bravery in the face of adversity and the squandered opportunity for greed was not lost on the two men.

Out of the gaping maw of the cave drifted a final roar of rage, which lingered in the chill night air as a haunting reminder of the perils that lurked beneath the scorched earth of their world.

~ * ~ * ~

**Christopher Powers** lives in the United Kingdom with his wife, seven-year-old son, and three-year-old daughter. In his spare time, he loves to scour old bookstores looking for the most well-read and yellowed paperbacks. This is his first foray into fantasy.

# The Hoarder of Songs

## Laura J Underwood

*How did I get here?*

When Anwyn Baldomyre opened his eyes, he was lying on a bed of old reeds scattered across a rock floor. The last thing he remembered was having a good meal and falling asleep in a comfortable bed.

He had wandered into the village of Grayrock tucked against the mountain side. It was a dull looking place, houses of stone and daub and wattle perched around a central square with a well. The inn where he found himself was decent and mostly clean. What surprised him was how the villagers greeted him like royalty. They insisted on taking him to the inn to meet their leader, one Master Cubbins, who was pleased to learn Anwyn was a traveling harper looking to trade songs for a place to spend the night. His music had them dancing and singing joyfully. They gave him the best room, the best food and good mead when he grew too weary to perform.

Now Anwyn realized as he opened his eyes, his head throbbed. Looking around, he discovered his bed was in some sort of cave high on a ledge. For a moment, panic assailed him.

*Glynnanis, where am I?* he thought.

The harp did not answer. Anwyn glanced about and was relieved to find his cerecloth sack and satchel close by. Carefully, he picked up the harp sack and pushed back the edge of the flap. Gem blue eyes greeted him.

"What happened?" he asked.

The harp shook its head as though encouraging silence. Anwyn frowned and glanced over towards the back of his ledge. The shadows revealed a small pile of instruments; harps, lutes, a variety of flutes and horns, and even something that looked like a plaid bag with legs.

*Uh, where are we?* he thought.

Glynnanis turned its head, gesturing in the opposite direction. Anwyn started to stand when he was struck with a sense of dizziness, like he drank too much wine. *It was only one flagon of mead!* He closed his eyes for a moment, sitting back down. Had he been drugged? Was that why he slept so heavily he did not know how he got here?

*Why won't you answer me? Have you lost the power of speech.*

The harp shook its head again and gestured to the front of the ledge with its nose. Taking a deep breath, Anwyn crawled over to the lip of stone.

Light filtered in from a large hole above, letting him know it was daylight outside. Anwyn could hear the familiar thunder of water. Glancing down, he spied a straight slick wall of rock without stairs. A waterfall tumbled down the opposite side below the hole, and a deep pool of water formed and churned at its base. Lying close to the edge of the pool was a slumbering dragon. Light glittered across blue-green scales as the creature breathed.

*A dragon?*

Why was he in the cave of a dragon. Dozens of questions flitted through his mind. He realized the creature could probably hear Glynnanis' voice. Dragons Anwyn had met before had the skill. No wonder the harp was not answering his questions.

*But that still doesn't explain how I got here.*

He carefully backed away from the edge on hands and knees and sat down next to the harp. Glancing around, he could not see any way to escape. There were no tunnels around him, and as near as he could tell, no way to climb to that opening above the waterfall.

*Of course, all I have to do is sing myself out of here and…*

Before he could open his mouth to sing, he heard the scrabble of claws. A head half as long as he was tall popped over the edge and offered a toothy grin.

"Oh, good, you are awake," the dragon said and squinted myopically at Anwyn.

"Hello," Anwyn said. "Why am I here?"

The dragon scrambled on up to the height of the ledge, keeping its wings at its side. Anwyn snatched up his satchel and harp and scrambled back to give the creature more room.

"You are here because the villagers gave you to me," the dragon said.

*Gave me to you?* "And you are?"

In his mind, Anwyn realized this was a much younger dragon than he had met before. Its full length was only four times his own height. Of course, he knew it was no less dangerous, but all of his previous encounters with dragons had taught him they were not dangerous if one was not trying to kill them.

"I am Gilrock, Bane of the Gray Mountains. The villagers of Grayrock always give me the ones who can sing."

Anwyn felt his eyebrow quirk. "They give you those who can sing? Why?"

"I like music," Gilrock said cheerfully. "I love songs. I love how they sound, how they ring through my cave. I want every song in the world so I collect them."

"So, you're a hoarder of songs?" Anwyn asked.

"That I am," Gilrock said grinning. "And you are the newest singer who will add to my hoard."

"I'm not sure I understand this," Anwyn said. "The villagers gave me to you so I could sing for you?"

"Yes."

"And what happens if I don't sing for you?"

"Oh, but you must sing for me," Gilrock said. "The others did."

Anwyn glanced over his shoulder at the pile of discarded instruments. He gestured to them as he looked back at the dragon. "Where did you get all of those?"

"They came from the other singers?"

"And what happened to the singers?" Anwyn asked.

Gilrock hesitated. "I got hungry."

"You ate them?"

"Only after they stopped singing and moving," the dragon said.

Anwyn frowned. No wonder Glynnanis was quiet.

"But why would you do that?" Anwyn said. "Why eat them? If you liked their singing so much."

"I told you; they stopped singing and they stopped moving," Gilrock said. "I guess they ran out of songs for me to hoard, and I was hungry, and why are you asking me all these questions? Why are you not singing to make me happy?"

"Because I am trying to understand how one can hoard songs?" Anwyn said. "Personally, I would love to see this hoard of songs."

The dragon looked confused. "They're all around us," he said. "Sometimes, I still hear them when I sleep."

"I see nothing but air, water, a cave, a dragon, and the instruments of the singers you have eaten," Anwyn said. "Those are not songs. One cannot hoard songs. They are not tangible things. Songs are sounds and beauty, and they can move souls. They are meant to be learned and shared. At least, that is what my old master used to say."

"Well, if you are not going to sing, I guess I will just have to eat you now," Gilrock said frowning.

"Can you not see the color of my eyes?" Anwyn asked.

"The color of your eyes?" Gilrock said as it wrinkled its nose. "I can barely see you, singer. You are very fuzzy even in this light. But I can hear you and smell you, so I will still be able to eat you unless you sing for me."

Anwyn met the dragon's squinting stare. "My eyes are silver," he said. "Surely even a young dragon like you knows what that means."

Gilrock was in the process of reaching for Anwyn. The claw froze in midair and withdrew. "You are a sorcerer as well as a singer of songs?"

"That I am," Anwyn said, hoping the lie did not show since he had not made his sacrifice to be a true magister. *Then again, if he cannot see, how would he know?*

Gilrock sighed. "Does that mean you will taste different?"

*This is getting nowhere.* Anwyn was tempted to sing his Gate Song and leave, but something in the dragon's demeanor, and his own curiosity, kept him from doing so now. Deep down, he knew there was going to be a grand song in this, if he could just stay alive.

"Why not hunt for your food?" Anwyn asked. "The dragons I have known and met in the past much prefer the meat of deer and wild boar to the taste of man."

Gilrock hesitated again, and Anwyn watched as a large tear suddenly slid down the dragon's cheek. Slowly, the dragon looked away, and Anwyn felt a hint of sympathy.

"Why don't you tell me about it," Anwyn said.

"Why?" Gilrock asked.

"Because, if you do," Anwyn said, "I will sing you a song. And I might be able to help you. Surely, that would be a fair enough trade?"

Gilrock laid down on the ledge, so Anwyn sat down on the ground.

"I have never been able to see very well," Gilrock said. "As a dragonet, my mother fed me, but when I got older, she insisted I go out and hunt for myself. I tried very hard, but I just could not see well enough. Then one day, I was hunting near here and I came across a village. I heard a young female shepherdess singing. I loved music even then. My mother used to sing."

"I have heard dragons sing," Anwyn said. "Their songs are beautiful."

Gilrock smiled "Anyway, I listened to the shepherdess for a while. She seemed to know a lot of songs, but I could smell sheep in a pen, and I didn't think they would mind me eating one or two because I was very hungry. Problem was, I could not tell the sheep from the shepherdess when she rushed at me, so I ate her as well. It wasn't intentional."

"Understood," Anwyn said, though he suspected the villagers of Grayrock would not agree.

"They came running at me, screaming and shouting, so I roared that I was Gilrock of the Gray Mountains, and I demanded more songs, or I would eat them all," the dragon said. "Well, they seemed to think that was a good idea. Apparently, there was an old bard in town who had been taking advantage of their hospitality. They brought him to me. I brought him back here because I was already full, having eaten several of the sheep and the shepherdess. Told him if he sang, we could be friends. He knew a lot of songs. But one day, he stopped singing."

"He died," Anwyn said.

Gilrock nodded his massive head, looking even more remorseful.

"And then you ate him?"

"Yes," the dragon said. "I do not believe in wasting food, but he was rather thin, not a lot of meat, so I went back to the village. I was hungry, and I figured if they thought I would eat them, they would provide me with more singers of songs so I could build my hoard. But when I brought them here, they always seemed to die."

"And you have eaten all of these people when they stopped singing?" Anwyn asked, gesturing once more to the instruments. Clearly, the dragon had forgotten the singers he was given needed to be fed too, and it saddened him to think they starved to death.

"Well, except for the one who played that funny bag thing," Gilrock said. "The noise was so terrible; I just ate him to stop the sound."

Anwyn laughed. "Sorry, but bagpipes were never meant to be played inside a cave. Best heard from afar."

"Well, now, that's my tale, and you owe me a song," Gilrock said.

Anwyn nodded and stood up, leaving his harp and satchel on the ground. "May I touch you while I sing?" he asked.

"Why?"

"It will make the song sound much better," Anwyn said.

Gilrock nodded. As Anwyn approached the dragon, he sensed Glynnanis' agitation. *Like you have been any help?* he thought. Gently, Anwyn placed his hands on the humps over the dragon's eyes. He closed his own eyes and sought the Song of Healing. The notes played through his head, and when he felt the song strengthen, he took a deep breath and started to sing.

Magic flowed from him, reaching into the dragon's eyes. The golden glow of the Song of Healing grew, spreading over the beast. And as he sang, he heard Gilrock humming along with pure joy.

Anwyn let the song stop. The golden glow faded. He withdrew his hands as the dragon blinked.

"I can see!" "Gilrock said. "You really do have silver eyes, and your harp is very beautiful. But now what?"

"Tell me," Anwyn said. "Do you really like the taste of people, or do you prefer sheep?"

"Oh, sheep were so delicious," Gilrock said. "I could live off those tasty bits of mutton forever, though a deer or boar would now and again would be rather nice."

"Good," Anwyn said. "Can you take me back to the village?"

Gilrock drew back, looking puzzled. "Why?"

"Because someone needs to put the villagers in their place. They can't keep sacrificing singers. Every time a minstrel or bard is eaten, the world becomes a poorer place. Soon, there will be no one to sing for you, and that would be very sad."

"Yes, it would," Gilrock agreed. "I would never have new songs for my hoard again."

"I will make you a promise," Anwyn said.

"And what would that be?"

"Well, Hoarder of Songs, Bane of Gray Rock, I will come back every year as long as you will have me as a guest and promise not to eat me, and I sing you the new songs I learn on the road for your hoard." *Invisible as it is...*

"But how will I eat?"

"Well, you can see now to hunt, but leave that to me," Anwyn said. He picked up his harp sack and satchel. "By the way, are you immune to fire?"

"I'm a dragon, of course," Gilrock said.

"Good, can you carry me?"

Gilrock lowered his belly to the rock. Anwyn took it to mean the dragon was agreeable. He sensed Glynnanis was now puzzled, and more than a little uncertain, but the harp had yet to speak its thoughts. Anwyn climbed onto the dragon's back, settling himself between the spines and clutching them tight.

"Hang on," Gilrock said. "It might get a bit chilly."

"I'll be fine," Anwyn said.

Gilrock leapt off the ledge, and for a moment, they both plummeted towards the bottom, but the dragon spread leathern wings and soared upward.

"Watch your head," the dragon said.

Anwyn ducked down just in time to keep from being knocked off by the rocks around the opening to the cave. They flew high into the air, up into the light of day. Anwyn was astonished by the view. In all honesty, while he had once ridden a storm, he had never ridden a dragon. Exhilaration filled him as they passed through clouds.

Gilrock swung around, passing over the top of the mountain and soared down into the valley. Anwyn resisted the urge to whoop for joy. He could see the village of Grayrock growing larger as they flew towards it.

"Land in the middle of the village," Anwyn said. "Let me do the talking, and you just play along."

"Got it!" the dragon said.

Gilrock flapped his wings and dropped into the village square. The villagers screamed and ran, panicked by the sight of the dragon. Some of them grabbed hoes and pitchforks, but as they started at the dragon, Anwyn called the notes of his Song of Fire and let it flow from his lips, putting a ring of magic fire around them. The villagers were forced back as Anwyn slipped off the dragon's back.

"People of Grayrock!" he shouted. "Hear me now! I am Anwyn Baldomyre, a sorcerer from the land of Thuathynboria, and I have come to punish you for daring to feed singers of songs to this poor dragon."

The people cowered now, though a few of the older men came as close as they dared to the fire.

"We have done nothing," one of the men said, and Anwyn recognized him as Master Cubbins who had been so welcoming. "The dragon eats us if we do not feed him singers. We did not realize you were a sorcerer with the power to tame a dragon."

"I have not tamed the dragon," Anwyn said. "Instead, I have befriended him, as you should have done the first time he came looking for food. Are you not aware of how useful a dragon can be if you make a pact with it?"

"We made a pact," another villager said. "To give him singers for his hoard. He was the one who demanded it."

"And for that he is sorry, just as he is sorry for eating the shepherdess. He really just wanted some sheep. As many as I see around in your pens, surely you could spare him a few. You have hundreds of sheep, and you can breed more. Keep a herd just for him, and Gilrock of the Gray Mountain will not have to eat any more singers of songs."

"But he will eat all the sheep," a woman cried. "We'll have no wool for winter and no mutton for our stews."

Anwyn glanced at Gilrock. "How many sheep do you think you will eat?"

"No more than one or two a week will keep me happy," he said. Then lowering his head, he whispered, "Though I would rather hunt."

"So, what say you, people of Grayrock?" Anwyn asked.

"What if we say no?" Master Cubbins said.

"Do you really want to find out what will happen?" Anwyn asked. "I know where your king lives. I know he loves music and musicians. Why I was at his castle not long ago, and he was lamenting how bards and minstrels were vanishing from the land. It would be a shame to have to tell him you have been sending them to starve to death in a dragon's cave."

Murmurs went back and forth. Someone whispered, "The king will take all we have and leave us nothing." A few arguments broke out, most of them aimed at blaming the leaders now.

Anwyn waited patiently. Gilrock licked the air with his tongue.

The fire around them was starting to die down, but no one approached.

Finally, the villagers pushed Master Cubbins forward. The head man sighed.

"We will accept your offer, Master Baldomyre," he said. "For the safety of our children and our people, we will breed more sheep and keep a herd just to feed the dragon. Just don't tell the king we are to blame for his minstrels and bards going astray, please."

"His name is Gilrock of the Gray Mountain, and you'd best remember him," Anwyn said. "I will be coming back once a year to make certain you are keeping the bargain."

Heads whipped back and forth, but there were nods.

"It shall be as you wish, sorcerer," Master Cubbins said.

Anwyn bowed to the crowd, and then turned and climbed back up on Gilrock's back. The dragon rose into the air, taking him back over the mountain. Outside the cave, Gilrock set down, and Anwyn climbed off.

"What now?" the dragon asked.

"Well, as you said, you can hunt, and I can continue on my journey," Anwyn said. "But before I go. I owe you a few songs for your hoard."

Gilrock smiled a toothy grin and settled in the grass. Anwyn sat down, pulling Glynnanis out of the cerecloth sack. He sang several songs, including one about a dragon defeating a knight because the princess loved the dragon. That one made Gilrock laugh.

"Well, I am hungry now," the dragon said. "I smell a herd of deer over near the forest, so if you will excuse me."

Anwyn waved as the dragon flew away. He turned and headed for the road meandering through the field and into the woods.

"So, Glynnanis, why didn't you say anything when the villagers gave me to the dragon?"

*"I tried,"* the harp said. *"But they drugged the mead, and you wouldn't wake up, and when the dragon came and took you to the cave, I was afraid if I spoke, you would be eaten, and I would have joined his hoard of rotting instruments."*

Anwyn nodded. "Well, I just hope I showed you I can figure things out without making my sacrifice to be a true magister."

*"Yes, yes, you should be quite proud of yourself,"* Glynnanis said. *"Do you plan to turn this into a song?"*

"Of course," Anwyn said. "The Hoarder of Songs is a really good title, if you ask me. I think Rhystar will enjoy hearing what it is like to ride a dragon as well. I bet he never rode one."

*"Will you really come back here to sing songs for Gilrock?"*

"Of course," Anwyn said. "I gave him my word."

Besides, even Anwyn knew it was never wise to break a bargain with a dragon.

~ * ~ * ~

**Laura J. Underwood** is the author of multiple novels and numerous short stories in the fantasy field. Her books include *Ard Magister*, *Chronicles of the Last War*, *Dragon's Tongue*, *Wandering Lark*, *Demon in the Bones*, *The City Under the Bridge*, *Shadow of the Faolan* and the forthcoming *Songs of the Magister* just to name a few.

Over the years, she had been a state fencing champion, a fair harpist, and an artist. She is a retired librarian who now spends her time collecting old typewriters and ball jointed dolls and just writing more stories.

Laura can be found occasionally expounding on matters on Facebook (facebook.com/keltora). She lives in East Tennessee.

# A Beastly Betrayal

## Anka B. Troitsky

*"Wake up! My God, what a sadness…*
*Break the web in which you are all entangled."*
Evgeny Schwartz. The Dragon

The rain had stopped, but the rooftops were still smoking after the last attack, and the air smelled of charred wood, straw and anything else the citizens used to mask the asbestos roof tiles. Tyrants' heartless servants, called *Collectors*, loyal to their scaly master, loaded carts with the spoils confiscated for the greedy monster's annual tribute. Men and women emerged from their cellars and bunkers, assessing the damage to their homes and quietly discussing the cost of repairs after this year's raid. The grey smoke lazily drifted through the wet streets, pretending to be a morning fog.

Amidst this scene, a young apprentice to the city clockmaker stood before a large wooden board adorned with various announcements. The boy, a mere twelve years old, gripped a screwdriver in his right hand. His sky-blue eyes were fixed upon a poster featuring the latest candidate. Painted by Dragon City's finest artist, hundreds of copies of the beautiful portrait graced every noticeboard, lamppost, and tavern wall since the previous night.

Unbeknownst to the boy, a cloaked figure meandered along the street, ignoring the muddy puddles and the raindrops that occasionally fell from high eaves. The boy started at the soft voice behind him.

"Hey, lad. Oh! It's alright. I didn't mean to scare you. Do you know who this man is on the poster?"

The boy gathered his wits and replied in a hushed tone, "It's a new champion. A noble knight who will battle the dragon and deliver us from its clutches."

"That's right," the traveller said. "Every few years, a new champion is elected to face the dragon and bring peace to our land. The last battle took place before you were born. Do you know his name?"

The boy nodded, eyes once again fixated on the poster. "His name is Sir Vonald. He's incredibly smart and just."

"Yes, indeed. But also brave and strong, the most skilled swords-man of our land. He has vowed to protect this city from the dra-conic regimes."

The boy's expression turned solemn. "I hope he wins! Then we won't have to live in fear, hiding in cellars. We can sell our crafts, have plenty of food, and good shoes! People from other places might come to trade."

The traveller chuckled with approval. "You're smarter than you look. Yes, we're all counting on that. Do you aspire to be like him one day?"

The boy's face lit up. "Yes, sir! I want everybody to be free!"

The stranger spoke thoughtfully, "You're brave, but did you know how many knights have faced the dragon before? It started hundreds of years ago. Each time, the messenger comes from the battlefield with tales of victory, but a year later, the dragon reap-pears alive. No one ever saw those noble knights again."

Defiance filled the boy's gaze as he turned to the traveller. "My father told me that story, but I'll be the one to rid us of the evil once and for all."

"Ha! What's your name, lad?"

"Alex. Alex Goodie."

"Well, Mr. Goodie, you are mistaken," the traveller said, throw-ing back his hood. His long black hair tumbled down his back, and his cloak fell into the mud, revealing gleaming armour adorned with a golden logo.

The boy's eyes widened, bright blue like the clear sky. "Sir Vonald!" he whispered.

"Yes, I am Sir Vonald Toogreat, and I will be the first to rid the world of this trouble. I shall return victorious, ruling this city with fairness and honour so you may grow up in a safe world and become whatever you wish."

People on the street halted their tasks, turned, gasped, and drew nearer. Whispers of "It's him… It's him. He has finally arrived!" rippled through the crowd.

The knight turned briefly to let everyone admire his heroic visage before addressing the boy. "Here, Alex, throw away your screwdriver and accept my talisman—a symbol of integrity and reason." He tossed an old, weathered wooden sword to the boy. "A few years ago, I stood where you stand now. The brave knight before me entrusted me with this token while he ventured to battle the dragon. Sadly, I never had the chance to return it to him, for he never emerged from those mountains. But I expect this small token of our friendship returned to me someday. Do you understand, Alex?"

The boy dropped his screwdriver, caught and pressed the sword to his chest, and nodded. "I do. Thank you, sir."

The noble knight proceeded toward the inn, where the city's messenger awaited to conduct the customary interview. Sir Vonald needed to unpack his swords and spears, rest, obtain sustenance, and prepare before beginning his journey to the mountains at dawn.

A couple of days later, the battle commenced as the sun descended. The townsfolk remained glued to their upper windows and balconies, anxious gazes fixed on red, white, and blue flashes beyond the distant rocky ridge. The noise reached the town, and the dragon's roars echoed like they were on their doorstep. It endured far longer than anyone could bear.

As the night passed and silence reclaimed the morning, no one knew what had befallen Sir Vonald. The town mourned, bracing for the worst while hoping for the best. Alex clutched the wooden sword tightly as he lay awake in bed, envisioning himself as the next knight destined to confront the dragon.

Nothing happened until the afternoon. But then, a familiar messenger figure appeared on the road. He galloped as fast as his horse could carry him, his face red. When he entered the town through the city gates, the townspeople rushed around him, eager for news. Alex, armed with his wooded sword, also pushed his way through the crowd.

The news breaker finally pulled up his horse. "Sir Vonald…is victorious," he gasped. "The dragon is defeated!"

Alex's heart leapt in his chest. But the crowd did not cheer. Everyone stood still.

"Where is he?" the town smith asked, but the messenger caught his breath and spoke with confidence that looked forced even to young Alex.

"My friends. All of you, hear me out. It is done. We should all celebrate the victory of the person we elected to be our Champion. Everything now will be different. Our troubles are over."

"Where is Sir Vonald?" the city healer asked.

"If he is alive, where is he? Are you lying to us? This is not the first time this has happened. Did he kill the Collectors, too? If he is alive, we want to see him. He made so many promises. And if he has been defeated, we want to know what to expect next." The voices from the crowd called one over another.

"He is alive. I swear. I saw him throwing the spear right into the monster's mouth and down his throat." The news reporter pressed his hands to his own neck.

"And then what happened?" someone behind Alex asked.

"I...I don't know. I did not see it. I assumed it was over and rushed back to let you all know."

Grumbling, the people of the Dragon City went back to their houses. Alex stood by the open gate, watching the road until he could not see it in the darkness of the night. Then he went to the notice board and picked up his screwdriver from the mud.

The next day was no different from any other ordinary day before. Days turned into weeks, weeks into months, and still, there was no sign of Sir Vonald. People resigned themselves to the belief he had perished. Perhaps he had slain the beast and succumbed to his injuries and fatigue, a knight's honourable demise. After a grand ceremony in his honour, everyone chose not to dwell on it and continued with their lives. Nobody fancied going to the mountains and checking. Statues of the Noble Sir Vonald replaced the worn effigies of his predecessors, and the tavern songs were rewritten to include his name. Only young Alex remembered the last words spoken by the Champion, secretly practising with his wooden sword, just in case Sir Vonald had failed to vanquish the monster.

A year passed, and the townspeople prepared for their annual harvest festival, each harbouring the same unspoken thought: "There is no dragon...it is defeated. Nothing will happen this year. The Collectors are gone."

Yet, they returned. Cloaked in black robes and fearsome masks, the Collectors descended upon the city square as they had done every year before. They ransacked the town's shops, factories, taverns, and homes in their rumbling carts.

The citizens attempted to protest.

Alex's master emerged from his workshop and implored them, "Why? What for now?"

Laughter was his only response, followed by the familiar roar from above. Panic swept through the crowd. Heads turned upward to witness the colossal figure soaring across the darkening sky, belching flames upon their homes, inflicting poverty upon their families, and shattering their children's dreams once again.

~ * ~

Forty-year-old Sir Alex Goodie dismounted and released his horse, pulling a bottle of whiskey from a saddlebag—the farewell gift from his former master. The horse, spooked and frightened, promptly galloped back towards the valley. Sir Alex would have to traverse on foot for the rest of the journey among the mountains.

The dragon's presence became palpable before it was audible. Trees and shrubs along the path swayed to the rhythm of its breath. As the beast came into view, Sir Alex felt fear constricting his heart, clouding his thoughts. It was ten times the size of a horse, its scales seemingly constructed of steel, and its eyes gleaming with malevolent intent.

The dragon spoke, and its words echoed through the valley. "Go on, brave knight. You know you cannot win. Why not choose a quick and painless death instead?" The voice was like a man's but sounded like he spoke into the barrel.

Sir Alex's resolve remained unshaken. "No! Fight me!"

The dragon roared, spewing flames that licked at Sir Alex's feet. He deftly dodged to the side and swung his sword at the dragon's leg, but the blade merely bounced off the scales with a metallic ring. Something seemed odd to the trained eyes of the clockmaker. Realisation dawned on Sir Alex—the dragon was no living creature. Bolts and brackets held together its scales, its joints creaking as it moved. It was a mechanical construct.

The dragon's laughter echoed, and Sir Alex clenched his teeth. He made lunge after lunge, but all efforts were in vain. But then, an idea occurred to him, and he took out his bottle of whiskey and threw it into the dragon's mouth. The glass smashed on metal teeth. Instead of splashing out, the flames engulfed the eerie maw, distracting the dragon long enough for Sir Alex to dive between its rusty front legs.

Seizing the opportunity, Sir Alex retrieved his trusty screwdriver and set to work. One by one, scales fell from the dragon's chest, revealing a dark cavity. The dragon momentarily froze, its head swaying as if searching for the knight. It was turning its head on its outstretched neck, and an unlubricated mechanism sounded like a screech of the wounded animal. With each well-placed strike, Sir Alex uncovered the inner workings of the dragon.

But what he found inside was beyond his comprehension. The dragon's innards seemed empty, yet not entirely so. It perplexed Sir Alex. The dragon began to lower itself as if about to lie down. Sir Alex couldn't afford to be crushed by the mechanical beast. He drew his sword again and thrust it repeatedly into the darkness. With an inhuman cry, the dragon fell on its side.

Gasping for breath and covered in soot, Sir Alex stepped back to examine the defeated dragon more closely. It was a complex creation, a marvel of engineering. But the true revelation came when he discovered a hatch between the dragon's wings.

A shocking sight opened up to him: inside the device, a man with long grey hair was sitting behind the controls. His face was pale as he met Sir Alex's gaze. "Hello, my little friend," he said weakly. "Did you bring me back my old sword? Alex, isn't it?"

Sir Alex couldn't believe his eyes. "It can't be...Sir Vonald?"

The man inside the machine was gravely wounded and bleeding from multiple injuries. He would not last. Alex had anticipated a human pilot within the dragon, but not his very Champion—the man elected to liberate the people from the beast's tyranny, the one who had inspired Alex to become a hero, even in death. Now, he found him driving this intricate machinery, responsible for the devastation and plundering of his city.

"Yes, my young Alex. Not only did I kill the old tyrant, but I also took his place. While some knights gallantly perished on these rocks, those who slew the dragon could not beat the evil within themselves. Now, I control this mechanical beast, replacing the very knight who confronted it in the past. And the one before him, and before that one, and so forth... Now I am a dragon."

"But why?" Sir Alex still couldn't believe, "You were my hero..."

"All will become clear. Once you witness what lies within the cave, you will understand why I acted as I did. What awaits you upon your return if you declare the dragon defeated and grant the people their freedom? A few statues, a few songs... In a matter of years, they will forget your deeds. You will grow old in infamy. "

"What are you saying?" Sir Alex had given little thought to

what would follow his victory. He hoped to secure freedom for his people, trusting they would determine their destiny. As for himself, he aimed only to safeguard peace and prosperity. The details remained elusive.

"Go… Explore the cave for yourself. Lavish chambers, servants delivering the finest attire, food, and wine from the city, women to cook and clean for you, their plump daughters, and comfortable beds. You will possess unimaginable luxuries. And most importantly —the power. The valley's inhabitants will both fear and respect you…and…*cough-cough*… You're a clock master now, aren't you? You will excel in controlling this machine, a potent political tool tried and tested over countless millennia. You can repair it, maintain it…upgrade it…"

"Enough!" Alex interrupted. "This is not my purpose. I came here to fight for people's rights, not to seize control! How could you betray their trust? I believed in you! You were our beacon of hope… Do you hear me, Sir Vonald?"

But the man encased within the complex system remained silent. His dead eyes stared past Alex's face into the starry night sky.

Without another word, Sir Alex leapt onto the ground, retrieved his sword and screwdriver, and turned toward the path down the hill. A sudden noise from behind caught his attention— the dragon's cave was only a few feet away. The massive wooden door, resembling a church entrance, creaked open slightly. A small group of men and women bowed low to the victorious knight. His sky-blue eyes darkened.

"I'll just have a quick look," Sir Alex thought, slowly turning and walking toward the cave.

~ * ~ * ~

**Anka B. Troitsky** was born in the USSR in 1968, grew up in Kazakhstan, and relocated to the UK in 1993. Before committing to serious writing, she served as a Science Teacher and Professional Translator. Anka engages in extensive yearly book reading and consistently pursues courses to acquire new skills. As an independent author and multiple award winner, she crafts mainly hard science fiction novels and short stories of different genres. Her notable 3-part novel series, "Who is Vist," presents intriguing adventures set in a futuristic landscape, addressing global societal issues and delving into human psychology. Book 4 of the series is slated for release in the summer of 2024. The ongoing war and political crimes against the Ukrainian people significantly influence the thematic essence of her latest work, reflecting her dedication to exploring timely and relevant subjects.

# Whackin' Dragons

## John Lance

"Well sir, I'm afraid it's not good news," Big Bob said.

I wasn't surprised. The van in my driveway had Big Bob's round face emblazoned on one side and a boot squashing a cartoon rat on the other. One did not call Big Bob's Pest Control with the expectation of good news. The only question was how bad the bad news was going to be.

"So what is it? Basilisk?" I asked.

"Oh lord, please not a basilisk," my wife whispered beside me. Julie was terrified of basilisks ever since her family cat ran afoul of one when she was twelve. The stone kitty still sat in my heartbroken mother-in-law's garden, his gray face frozen in a curious, befuddled, expression.

"No, not a basilisk," Big Bob said.

"Thank the gods," Julie said.

"A griffin then? I saw claw marks along the edge of the roof," I said.

"No, a griffin wouldn't be interested in perching on a two-story dwelling such as you have here. We mostly see them on apartment towers, high rises, those sorts of structures."

"What about..."

Big Bob held up a calloused hand that was missing two fingers. "You know, as much fun as twenty questions is, let me see if I can narrow this down a little. Have you had any jewelry go missing recently ma'am?"

Julie tucked a gray-blonde lock behind her ear as she considered the question. "Now that you mention it, I haven't been able to find my grandmother's diamond ring. Or my emerald earrings."

"You didn't tell me that," I said.

"I set them down on my vanity when we got home from the restaurant Sunday night and haven't seen them since. I thought I just misplaced them."

Big Bob nodded knowingly. "Uh huh, as I suspected. What you've got here is a dragon."

"Oh no!" Julie exclaimed.

Patting my wife's hand, I chuckled. "Don't worry Jules, he's kidding. Right Bob? Dragons are, what, longer than a school bus? I think we'd know if we had a dragon."

"The old ones get that big, sure. This'll be a juvenile, though, probably no older than a decade. They're about the size of a labrador retriever. We need to get it to move along before it settles in and starts building a hoard."

I shook my head doubtfully. "We would've seen it, though, wouldn't we?"

"Not necessarily. The juveniles are nocturnal, keeps them from getting gobbled up by their older brethren. Likely your dragon has been skulking around at night when you're sleeping, on the prowl for anything shiny. They can be nasty if you wake one up in the middle of its afternoon siesta. I learned that the hard way." He tapped a scar that ran the length of his forearm.

Big Bob handed me a piece of paper. "I've taken the liberty of pulling together a preliminary estimate."

I looked at the list of items, flipped to the second page, and scanned down to the number circled in red at the bottom.

"That's a lot of zeros Bob."

"Well, when you take into account the fire-retardant suits of armor, the gold bullion needed for bait, and other necessities, it's very reasonable. You won't get a better quote, or my name isn't Big Bob."

"What's this? A catch and release fee?" I tapped one of the larger numbers.

"That's a state requirement. Dragons are a protected species you know. You can't kill them. You gotta catch them in a trap and release them into a suitable environment. That fee gets passed right along to the Dragon Preservation Fund."

"I see. I've got to tell you, Bob, when it comes to home ownership, I'm a bit of a do-it-yourselfer."

My wife coughed.

Big Bob nodded knowingly. "I can appreciate that sir, but we're not talking about trapping a mouse or chipmunk. Dragons are exceptionally dangerous,"

My wife coughed harder.

I refused to look in her direction. "I'm sure a full-grown dragon can be troublesome, but I know a thing or two about pest control. I'm certain I can..."

Unable to contain herself any longer, Julie interrupted, "Maybe, if it's dangerous, we should have Big Bob deal with the dragon." Before I could protest, she whispered, "I'm just thinking about the hornet fiasco."

I gave Julie an icy glare. We had agreed to never again speak of the hornets. I handed her the estimate.

"Wow, that is a lot of zeros," she said.

"Like I said, Bob, I can handle this one," I said with a smug smile.

Seeing I was a man of action, Big Bob rolled his eyes. "Well sir, if you reconsider, and I truly hope you do, please give me a ring. We can be out here in no time."

"Are you sure about this?" my wife asked as we watched Big Bob back his van out of the driveway.

"Of course. How hard can it be? I'll look up a few videos online and have the scaly little nuisance evicted by lunch. Even better, I'll call Jake. I think he had a dragon once."

"Jake as in your older brother Jake?"

"Who else?"

"Maybe start with a, umm, more reliable source of information than Jake?" Julie suggested.

"What are you implying?"

In response, she made a buzzing noise and flapped her hands at her sides.

"Fine, I'll start with some videos," I huffed.

Two hours later I was in my study snickering at a funny dog video playing on my computer.

I had started watching *The Professional's Guide to Dragon Removal.* It was highly ranked. It was also mind numbingly tedious. As the narrator droned on and on about certifications, permits, and laws, I got distracted by a popup showing a puppy eating broccoli and making funny faces. From there a whole world of amusing pet videos opened up.

Julie stuck her head in the doorway of my study. "How's it going?"

"Great!" I said, closing my laptop.

"Ready to give Sparky the heave-ho?"

"Sparky?" I racked my brains at the reference. "You mean the microwave?"

"What? No, not that. Although, we really do need a new one. Now it shocks you when you press eight *or* three. No, when I said Sparky I meant the dragon."

"You named it Sparky?"

"Calling it 'the dragon' was getting boring. Lucille suggested the name."

"Oh, lovely. Remind me to thank her." Lucille was Julie's best friend. They met in grade school and talked every day. Julie loved hanging out with her. I, on the other hand, felt a little Lucille went a long way. "Anyway, I'm almost ready. Just gotta collect some tools and I'll go up in the attic and bag us a dragon."

"The attic? Wouldn't it be in the basement? That seems more cave-like."

"It's the middle of the summer so the attic is going to be the hottest place in the house. Dragons love the heat." I'm ninety percent sure I heard them say that in *The Professional's Guide to Dragon Removal.* Maybe eighty percent.

Julie sighed. "If that's what the video said I guess that's where you should look. I'm supposed to have lunch with Lucille, but I can cancel and help out."

"Don't be ridiculous," I said. "Go to lunch. This'll all be over by the time you get back."

"That's what you said about the hornets."

"The hornets were an extenuating circumstance. Murder hornets are extremely rare in this part of the country and I was, admittedly, unprepared. In this case, I know what I'm dealing with. I've done the research." I patted my laptop.

Julie relented. "Okay. I already fed Ginger. Remember to clean her ears."

Back when our cocker-spaniel Ginger was a puppy, Julie volunteered for daily feedings provided I took the weekly ear cleaning. Looking back, I should have been suspicious. The battle to get five drops of medicine into each fluffy ear was an hour-long ordeal that left us both exhausted.

I was seized by a terrible thought. Our little dog was a perfect bite sized snack for a dragon. "When was the last time you saw Ginger?"

"Don't worry, she's in the foyer, napping in her sunbeam. As long as the dragon stays in the attic Ginger will be fine. Oh, and remember, Laura and Maggy are coming home from college next week, so try not to, you know."

"Know what?" I asked.

"Do too much damage."

I have to admit, I was a little hurt. "If you'll excuse me, I have to finish my research if we want this dragon gone before the twins come home," I said with a dismissive sniff.

Julie shook her head and went to get ready.

I tried to watch the rest of *The Professional's Guide to Dragon Removal* but gave up for good when they started debating the pros and cons of Gorgon versus Wendigo urine as a dragon deterrent.

What I really needed was a more practical, hands-on guide. The second video I found, *Whackin' Dragons,* was two minutes of some guy in overalls sneaking up behind another guy dressed in an inflatable dragon costume and smacking him over the head with a shovel until the dragon ran away/deflated.

"Simple, direct, I like it," I muttered to myself. All I needed was a shovel, which I owned, and stealth, which, upon a second viewing of *Whackin Dragons*, I felt was optional. What I lacked in agility I could make up for with zealous shovel work.

I waved to my wife from the front door as she drove away. Lunch with Lucille typically lasted at least three hours, giving me ample time to find, and remove, the dragon, and have a celebratory post-eviction beer to boot.

I retrieved my rusty shovel from the shed and took a few practice swings. "Perfect," I thought.

The attic was as hot and stuffy as I expected, and I dabbed the sweat from my brow with my sleeve. Our storage space of last resort, the attic was a chaotic sea of haphazardly stacked boxes and bins perpetually on the verge of toppling over.

Bent over like the hunchback of Notre Dame, I made sure to step from rafter to rafter as I searched for the dragon. Early in our home ownership journey I made the mistake of trodding between the attic beams. My foot had plunged through the bathroom ceiling, nearly giving Julie a heart attack. Fortunately, she was sitting on the optimal facility when I literally scared the poop out of her.

It became obvious after only a few minutes the dragon wasn't living in the attic. There were no scales, claw marks, or piles of treasure to be found.

As I was just about to give up, I spotted an odd structure in the corner. At first I thought it was a hornet nest, causing my heart to skip a beat, but as I got closer, it looked less and less like a hive and more and more like a tooth.

"Strange," I muttered as I poked it with my shovel.

The top of the tooth sprung open, and a reedy, one-foot tall, blue woman emerged. Dressed in a pink tutu and wearing a tiny tiara, she hovered overhead. The beating of her tiny wings filled the air with a distinctive buzz.

Fairies were a nuisance. Usually I just sprayed to get rid of them, but the can of *Fairy Begone* was all the way downstairs in the kitchen. I figured I'd just swat her with my shovel and be done with it.

Creeping closer, I smiled to lull the fairy into a false sense of security.

That was a mistake.

The fairy's eyes doubled in size, and she smiled back. Her grin grew larger and larger, eventually consuming half her face. Her mouth was a jigsaw puzzle of different size and colored teeth. A pearly white canine nestled next to a yellowed wisdom tooth in the middle of her lower jaw and her top row of teeth contained nothing but bicuspids. Her smile was incomplete, however, and I spotted several gaps.

"TOOTH!" The fairy squealed as she swooped toward me.

"Oh crud." I instinctively stepped backward, missed the beam, and plummeted through the ceiling of the twins' bedroom.

Maggy's bed broke my fall, and my fall broke her bed. Groggy and out of sorts, I struggled to rise to my feet but fell back on the broken bed. The tooth fairy floated down from the ceiling, smiling and waving a bedazzled set of pliers.

My sight grew gradually darker until I passed out.

I woke up to find the front of my shirt crusted with dried blood. Running my tongue along the inside of my mouth, I stopped at the gap where my two front teeth had been.

"Thit. Damn toof fairy," I muttered.

I decided to deal with the fairy, and the gaping hole in the ceiling, later. A little drywall, some spackle, a liberal amount of *Fairy Begone*, and no one would be the wiser. My first priority remained getting rid of the dragon.

If Sparky wasn't in the attic, then it had to be in the basement, which would make Julie happy. She liked being right.

Hefting my shovel, I switched on the basement light and descended the creaky staircase. Having learned from my attic experience, I held my shovel at the ready. I would whack first and ask questions later.

Julie held dominion over the basement, which meant it was an aggressively organized labyrinth of metal shelving units. I passed through Appliance Purgatory, where old blenders, waffle makers, and other kitchen gadgets resided, then through Entertainment Row with its collection of stereos, televisions, and DVD players, and on through Paperback Lane, which was self-explanatory. It felt more like a museum than a basement.

I paused as I entered the Peloton graveyard.

Cocking my head, I listened intently. I heard, music?

The thumping bass, bright trumpets, and growling guitars sounded very familiar.

"Disco Inferno?" I wondered aloud.

A mirror ball dropped from the ceiling.

"Stay alive!" a short, orange-skinned gremlin screeched as it leapt at me from a top shelf. I swatted the monstrosity away, but it rolled into a crouch and came at me again. Dressed in a white suit and wearing gold chains around its neck, the gremlin snapped its jaws and clawed at me with strange, dance-like flourishes.

Realizing what I was up against, I sighed deeply. It was, of course, a boogieman.

I swung my shovel at its head, but it leapt aside and did the Funky Chicken out of reach.

I couldn't let it escape. Where there was one boogieman others were sure to follow and, if I wasn't careful, I'd soon have a gremlin Studio 64 rocking my basement twenty-four seven.

As I advanced on the boogieman, its head lolled back, and I heard. "Ah, ah…" That's when I remembered the other thing boogiemen were infamous for.

"Achoooo!"

The music stopped. The disco ball and boogieman disappeared. I was left standing alone, covered in foul, greenish-yellow, boogers.

I had been bested by a pun.

Humiliated, I retreated upstairs. I doubted the boogieman would be dancing the night away in the basement if the dragon lived down there.

My mouth was sore, my eyelashes were encrusted with mucous, and I was no closer to finding the dragon. I began to wonder, had Big Bob made the whole thing up just to extort money from me? Was there even a dragon to be found? I'd have to go online and check his reviews. Something smelled fishy.

First, though, I needed to lie down and rest for a few minutes. Maybe take a quick shower. Then I would get back to the dragon hunt.

No sooner had my head hit my pillow, however, than I heard the sound of scuttling and grunting from beneath the bed.

I groaned. Ginger's ears. I could ignore her, but then she would slip away and, if there was one thing Ginger did well, it was hide during ear medicine time. I couldn't let her escape.

Getting down on all fours, I looked under the bed. "Come'on Ginger, it'th time to clean your eareth."

Two yellow eyes glared at me from the cavernous recess beneath our Alaskan King.

"Don't make me craww under there aftew you," I warned.

"Woof."

Ginger was sitting in my bedroom doorway. She cocked her head to one side, watching me with a mixture of amusement and concern.

"Ginger? But if you're there, who'th under the…Thparky?"

A blinding light spilled out from beneath the bed and I instinctively threw up my arms. The smell of charcoal washed over me and the air was filled with angry hissing, like a tea kettle about to burst.

"Oh thit," I said.

~ * ~

I sat on the front stoop with a blanket wrapped around my shoulders and Ginger on my lap. Firefighters walked in and out of the house. One stopped and patted my shoulder reassuringly.

Julie pulled into the driveway. She watched the firemen as they rolled up their hoses and packed them onto their fire truck. Then her gaze fell on me. I gave a halfhearted wave. She arched an eyebrow and got out of the car.

"What happened?" Julie asked.

One of the firemen took pity on me and answered on my behalf. "No need to worry ma'am, everything is under control. Just a scorched rug and some smoke damage to the bedroom wallpaper. Oh, and you're going to need a new mattress."

"How?" Julie waved at the house.

"One of your neighbors noticed the smoke and called it in. Fortunately, we got here before any serious damage was done," the firefighter explained.

Julie's eyes narrowed as the puzzle pieces fell into place. "Sparky?" she asked.

I gave a sheepish nod and shrugged my shoulders.

"I don't care how many zeroes Big Bob has on his quote, we're going to have him come out here right now and…" Julie paused. "Where are your eyebrows? And your front teeth? And, is that snot all over you?"

I bowed my head, defeated. "Tell Big Bob we're going to have to add a few mowe zewoes."

~ * ~ * ~

**John Lance** lives in New England with his beautiful wife and two lovely daughters. His stories have appeared in *Dark Moon Digest*, *Stupefying Stories*, and in the anthologies *Zombified III*, *These Vampires Don't Sparkle*, and others. He has also written a collection of childrens' short stories, *Bobby's Troll and Other Stories* and the picture books *Priscilla Holmes, Ace Detective* and *Priscilla Holmes and the Case of the Glass Slipper*.

His blog is at www.johnmlance.com.

# Inside Job

## Laura Ruth Loomis

Bernard and Lilly had been on dangerous adventures together, fleeing from were-alligators, searching for the Lost Jewel of Togmagog, and saving the kingdom from magical outbreaks of musical comedy. They'd fought their way through a chorus line of zombies and high-kicking skeletons. But none of that made Bernard as nervous as he was tonight.

He'd tried to tell Lilly how he felt about her. Somehow she always steered the conversation over to how glad she was for their friendship, or scuttled away somewhere with her friend Prudencia, who always seemed to be around these days. At first Bernard thought Lilly was impossibly oblivious, but now he suspected she might be as nervous as he was. Tonight he would toss caution over a cliff.

He'd invited her to an intimate dinner at the Flaming Duck tavern. But there were already hints the night wasn't going to go as planned, starting with the cloud of smoke filling the street around the tavern. The source turned out to be an enormous green dragon strolling around, decked out with fancy gold rings hanging from its tail. Bernard was doubled over with a coughing fit when Lilly arrived.

Lilly was in her everyday brown tunic and trousers, giving a puzzled look to Bernard's velvet suit. They got seated next to the kitchen, which let them overhear a loud argument about under-cooked shallots that ended with the head chef quitting, throwing his apron behind him as he stormed out. And instead of the usual harpist, tonight's entertainment was a heavy metal ogre band.

The elf waiter took their orders and warned it might be a while. That was fine, Bernard assured him, eyeing the stage. The ogres were about to take a break, so maybe he and Lilly could finally have a conversation.

"Do you think it'll take forever?" Lilly asked after the waiter left. "I was planning to get together with Prudencia later."

Bernard wanted to ask, *Why is it always Prudencia this and Prudencia that?* Instead he gazed tenderly into her eyes, smiling. "I have a surprise for you." He got up and strolled over to the stage, trying to look like he belonged there. He ignored the surprised faces at the ogres' table, and burst into song.

*In Togmagog a maiden fair,*
*They call her Calla Lilly.*
*With just one look into her eyes,*
*A man can go quite silly.*

He risked a look at Lilly, searching for her eyes, but she'd buried her face in her hands. Maybe she was feeling shy? He'd written eight more verses, but now he couldn't remember the order, and decided to skip to the end. Especially after he saw the ogres headed toward the stage.

*She's the one I want with me*
*When I face things that are scary.*

Lilly peeked between her fingers. Bernard sent up a prayer to the Great Judge at the Court of No Appeal.

*She's the only girl I'll ever love.*

He left the stage, dropped to one knee in front of their table, and sang the last line:

*She's the girl I want to marry!*

Lilly pulled her hands away from her face, and something in her expression was wrong. She was smiling, but it was the kind of smile he'd last seen on an animated skeleton in an undead chorus line.

She gave an awkward little laugh. "Bernard, you had me worried for a minute there. Until I realized it was another random outbreak of musical comedy. Don't worry, you'll be back to yourself in no time."

Bernard could feel every eye in the room on him. One of the ogres chortled. Bernard sobbed, pulled himself up, and ran out of the inn.

Outside, the smoke was so thick he couldn't tell left from right. He kept running forward.

There was a massive thump, and Bernard was on the ground,

his head throbbing.

When the smoke cleared, he found Lilly helping him to his feet. In front of them stood an enormous dragon, green with red highlights on its scales.

"What is the meaning of this?" The dragon literally fumed at them. "You attacked me!"

"I'm sorry," Bernard sputtered. "It was an accident. I didn't see you."

"How can you not see a dragon?" The creature's glare was almost as painful as the smoke. "It was a deliberate assault."

"Assault?" Bernard stared up at the dragon in confusion.

"What's all this, then?" The Constable had arrived.

"This human assaulted me." The dragon's voice was surprisingly whiny, for such a powerful beast.

"I did not!"

"Then how do you explain this?" The dragon pointed to a Bernard-shaped bruise on its side.

By now everyone in the crowd was chiming in with an opinion.

"He ran right smack into the dragon."

"He seemed like he was really mad about something."

"He looks kinda shifty, if you ask me."

Lilly turned to the Constable. "It wasn't Bernard's fault. What happened was—"

The dragon gave a fiery gasp. "My tail rings! Someone stole my tail rings!" The dragon held up its tail: ringless. "What's with all the criminals in this town?"

The Constable tied Bernard's hands and marched him to the jail.

~ * ~

At midnight, Bernard was still wide awake, staring at the brick wall of his cell, in the tower above the Constable's office. How had everything gone so wrong? He'd walked into the inn thinking that he'd walk out engaged to Lilly. How could she brush him off like that when he loved her so much?

"Bernard!" An urgent whisper from the window. Lilly was sitting on the ledge outside.

His heart thundered. "Lilly? What are you doing here?"

"Getting you out." She pointed to a grappling hook securely

gripping the windowsill, with a rope dangling below. The drop from the window was a good thirty feet. Lilly pulled a small saw from her belt and went to work on the bars.

"Is this necessary?" Bernard asked. "Can't we just explain to the Constable that it was all a big misunderstanding?"

"I tried." Lilly pulled the first bar free. She was amazingly handy with tools. "The Constable was in a foul mood, because Derf the Dragon is suing the city. And your bail is a hundred gold pieces."

"Who has that kind of money?"

"Exactly." Lilly removed another bar. "I talked to Prudencia, and she's researching precedents, but she says dragons have won cases like this before."

Prudencia? Even in a cell three stories above the ground, somehow Prudencia was still in between them. "Maybe if you didn't spend all your time with Prudencia, you would have realized how I felt about you."

Lilly pulled out the last bar, a little too hard. "Maybe I did notice, and I don't feel the same way."

"Yeah, you made that pretty clear. In front of everybody at the Flaming Duck."

"You were the one who decided to make a public spectacle out of proposing. Did you think I'd feel pressured into saying yes, just to keep from embarrassing you? That's a pretty awful position to put me in."

"You think you were the one put in a bad position?"

"Why are your feelings the only ones that matter?"

"That's not true. I would have done anything to make you happy." He reached for Lilly's arm and she jerked away. She lost her balance and started to slip.

Bernard dove for her, but the momentum carried them both out the window and down—

Smack on top of the dragon waiting underneath.

"I knew it!" Smoke filled the air with the dragon's shout. "I knew you'd try to escape."

The Constable came out of his office. "What's all this, then?"

~ * ~

Their trial got off to a bad start. The first thing Bernard saw was Derf the Dragon, taking up all the space where three rows of chairs would normally be in the courtroom. The second thing he saw was the prosecutor, a predatory gleam in her eye above the stacks of law books in front of her.

The ogre bailiff ordered everyone to rise. "This court is called to order, the honorable Judge Learned Hound presiding." The judge, a long-eared bloodhound, tucked his ears under his poodle wig.

The prosecutor stepped forward. "Delectia Corpus, representing the people of Fizzywatertown."

Some countries had trials by dipping the accused in boiling oil or having them fight a hungry chimera. Either of those seemed preferable at the moment.

The judge put on his glasses. "Are the defendants representing themselves?"

"Yes," Lilly and Bernard said.

"No," came a voice from behind them.

A familiar figure stepped forward, with horn-rimmed glasses and her brown hair in a bun, alligator briefcase at her side. "Prudencia Juris, representing the accused."

The prosecutor looked a bit flummoxed, then resumed her harsh expression. "Your Honor, Mr. Bernard Guinness, alias Stout Guinness, stands accused of aggravated assault and grand theft." She made the *alias* sound like something sinister instead of a childhood nickname he got after falling into a barrel of stout. "Calla Lilly Yuth, alias Lilly Yuth, is charged with aiding and abetting an escape attempt."

"Apparently not very successfully," the judge said wryly.

"The people's first witness will be Derf."

The dragon lumbered up to the front of the courtroom. The ogre had him raise his right wing. "Do you solemnly swear to tell the truth, the whole truth, and nothing but the truth, to the best of your memory and ability and without commercials?"

"I do." A thin trail of smoke poured out of his nostrils as he spoke.

"Now then, Mr. Derf," Ms. Corpus said. "Could you describe the events of last Thursday afternoon?"

"I was walking along Main Street, in front of the Flaming Duck tavern. And before I knew what was happening, that human came charging out the door and ran right into me."

"Let the record reflect the witness has indicated Mr. Guinness," Ms. Corpus said.

The court reporter, an ethereally beautiful fairy with an upturned nose, brushed a drop of ink from her gossamer wings as she scribbled down the testimony.

Bernard stole a glance at Lilly, who was watching with rapt attention as Prudencia took off her glasses. Prudencia already had a sheaf of notes in front of her, and more sticking out of her alligator briefcase.

Ms. Corpus continued, "Were you injured?"

"As you can see, I was very badly bruised." Derf pointed with a claw to the purple mark on his green hide. "Totally unprovoked. I don't even know that human. I don't know what he had against me."

"Objection," Prudencia said. "Everything after the mention of the bruise was non-responsive, not to mention speculative and prejudicial."

"Sustained," Judge Hound said. "The jury will disregard Mr. Derf's remarks after the words *very badly bruised*." Which still didn't sound good, in Bernard's opinion. Did Prudencia know what she was doing?

Ms. Corpus asked what happened next. The dragon sniffed, releasing so much smoke Lilly and Bernard both started coughing. "I yelled for help," Derf said. "There were people everywhere, everyone talking at once, and all my attention was on getting the city watch to come and arrest the human who attacked me."

"Objection to the term *attacked*," Prudencia said.

"Sustained. Please continue, Mr. Derf."

"That's when I noticed my gold tail rings were missing. Five rings! It was almost as if the human running into me was a distraction for the theft."

Smoke continued to pour from the dragon's nostrils. Ms. Corpus went into a sneezing fit, then gasped, "No further questions."

"Could someone open a window?" Prudencia wheezed. The bailiff did, and the room cleared up a bit, though Bernard continued to sniffle. "Mr. Derf, can you keep the smoke to a minimum?" Prudencia asked. "It's very uncomfortable for non-fire-breathing creatures."

"I'll try," he said. "I'm very upset right now."

"You create more smoke when you're emotional?"

"Yes. I can't help it."

"You must have given off a lot of smoke the day Mr. Guinness ran into you."

"Of course. It was very upsetting."

"And the smoke provided the perfect cover for whoever took your tail rings." She sounded sympathetic to his plight. Bernard wondered again if having her represent them was a good idea.

"Yes, exactly." Derf's lip had a tremor that seemed gratuitous.

"In fact, anyone could have taken advantage of the lack of visibility and the general confusion."

"Yes. The thief, or thieves," Derf eyed Bernard and Lilly, "knew what they were doing." Derf's wing twitched, creating a breeze that carried the court reporter's notes off her desk. Bernard jumped up, grabbed the papers before they hit the floor.

"Thanks," she said, with a glowing smile. The light from the window created rainbows on her wings.

"Anyone could have taken the rings," Prudencia continued, "except, of course, any humans or other non-fire-breathing creatures. They would have been so disabled by the coughing and choking, not to mention blinded by the smoke, it would have been nearly impossible for them to get to the rings."

"Difficult. Obviously not impossible."

"Obviously not, since this has happened to you before."

The dragon gasped, then inhaled so sharply it sucked the smoke back in, along with much of the air in the room. "I don't know what you mean."

"Really? You can't possibly have forgotten you had a remarkably similar experience in the town of Dornan's Gate just last year." Prudencia pulled a lengthy document from her briefcase and held it in front of him. "Defense Exhibit A, a judgement for Mr. Derf against the city of Dornan's Gate. Four thousand gold pieces for financial losses and emotional distress brought on by the theft of four gold bracelets during a street disturbance."

"That was such an awful experience, I've tried to put it out of my mind altogether."

"So far out of your mind, you didn't take any steps to protect your jewelry when out in public? A simple anti-theft spell, for instance?"

The prosecutor found her voice. "Objection. Irrelevant."

"Withdrawn." Prudencia pulled out another document. "Defense Exhibit B. Records from an alchemist's shop in Bluebottle Gulch, showing you sold four gold bracelets two weeks after the reported theft in Dornan's Gate."

"I have a lot of bracelets."

"Really? During your testimony in the lawsuit in Dornan's Gate, you said you were suffering severe financial hardship because of the theft."

"Well…financial hardship for a *dragon*. We're used to a certain standard of living."

"And was it also a financial hardship in Beigeville, when you had a platinum ring—allegedly your mother's wedding ring— disappear under nearly identical circumstances?"

There was a long silence, and Derf looked pleadingly at the prosecutor.

The judge cleared his throat. "Ms. Corpus, did you have an objection to make?"

"No," she said wryly. "I'm interested to see where this is going."

"It's not my fault." A trickle of smoke escaped Derf's nostrils. "There are a lot of thieves out there."

"A lot of thieves who all happen to target the same dragon?" Prudencia asked.

"Thieves go where the money is."

"And your tail rings were solid gold?"

"Yes. They were very valuable."

"That's quite a lot of gold." Prudencia waved a plume of smoke away from her. "About three hundred pounds of gold, would you say?"

"Yes."

"Would you explain how Mr. Guinness or any other human could have made off with three hundred pounds of gold and managed to escape?"

"How should I know?"

"But you, being a dragon, have no difficulty carrying that extra weight."

"Where would I carry it? I'm a dragon, I don't have pockets."

"Indeed." Prudencia unrolled a scroll and read something in an archaic language. The dragon began to glow, and his skin turned transparent. The whole courtroom got a good look at his heart, bladder, and the twin furnaces he had in place of lungs. And in his giant stomach sat five tail-sized gold rings.

Prudencia gave the judge a satisfied smile. "The defense rests, Your Honor."

"Anything else from the prosecution?"

"No thank you, Your Honor."

"This court makes a directed verdict for the defendants, and orders Mr. Derf to pay each defendant one thousand gold pieces. Mr. Derf will also pay for the repairs to the jail."

The court reporter grinned as she wrote the last of the judge's words.

"That will cost me my entire hoard!" The dragon was filling the room with smoke again. "How will I pay for my cave and food?"

Prudencia used her legal briefs to fan the smoke away. "Perhaps you could try getting a job."

The dragon's eyes bulged in horror.

The judge exited, followed by the prosecutor. The dragon slunk out, smoke hiding his face.

Lilly glanced at Bernard, then told Prudencia, "I'll meet you outside."

As the room cleared, Bernard told Lilly, "Thank you for trying to rescue me from jail. Hope Prudencia wasn't mad at you."

"She enjoyed the chance to show off her legal skills." Lilly looked at him uncertainly. "I hope our friendship isn't totally messed up."

Bernard shook his head. "You'll always be my best friend. And I'm sorry about the proposal, and the song and everything."

"It's all right. Let's forget it happened." Lilly hugged him, then left to find Prudencia.

Bernard got up, then noticed the court reporter was still there, putting her equipment away.

"Sorry, wasn't trying to eavesdrop," she said. "Breakups are always rough, but you handled it well."

He smiled ruefully. "At least she won't have to worry about my attempts at musical comedy anymore."

"What's she got against musical comedy? I *love* musical comedy. When we had the magical outbreak, I never wanted it to end, even though the production numbers made a mess of the courtroom."

Bernard's face lit up. "What's your name?"

"Elvira."

~ * ~

Two weeks later, Bernard and Elvira had dinner at the Flaming Duck, after seeing the opening of *A Song of Sorcery*.

A voice thundered from the kitchen. "You overcooked the shallots!"

"I did not!"

"And you burned your hat again. And I told you the mutton was supposed to be roasted, not smoked."

"I can't help the smoke when I'm upset."

The kitchen door opened, and Bernard spotted a familiar-looking dragon in the charred remains of a paper hat.

~ * ~ * ~

**Laura Ruth Loomis** is the author of two science fiction comedies, *The Cosmic Turkey* and *The Star-Crossed Pelican*. Her fiction and nonfiction have appeared in *The Saturday Evening Post, Writer's Digest, On the Premises, Hidden Villains: Betrayed,* and elsewhere.

She can be found at lauraruthloomis.com, on Mastodon @LauraRuthless@zirk.us, and on Threads @lauraruthless.author. By day, she's a social worker.

# Hoard of Petty Hatreds

## Jonah Jones

Carved into the rock above the cave's entrance were the words.
*God is a cruel engineer, designing both victim and the means of that victim's demise.*

The next in a long series of knights had left his squire holding the reins of his horse next to the mountain path and clanked his way half-way up to the cave. A knight walking in full armour would be risible were it not for the fact they could have you killed in various disgusting ways should you so much as smile.

By the roadside shrine he encountered a pardoner-priest who granted him an indulgence for a paltry sum, wished him well and blessed both his enterprise and his sword, allowing the knight to continue with a clear purpose and what would have been a spring in his step were it not for the aforementioned armour. Life is so much simpler when you have been assured by God's representative that you are in the right.

The knight looked at the sign above the cave and took a blind man's view as to what it meant. Knights tend to do that—their vision being somewhat impaired by their visors. Before he could issue his formal challenge, Bronca sent a warning plume of smoke out into the bright light, so he would know she was waiting for him.

His heart might have quailed somewhat, but he continued to move forward cautiously, drawing his sword and trying to clank less as he did so.

"I address thee, Dragon!" he bellowed as was the custom. "Have at thee!"

Evidently this be-metalled moron did things by the book.

"If it please thee, sir knight," she replied in the language of his kind, "and thou wert to go away, we would both be better pleased with the day."

He brought down his visor and exhaled a muffled "Hah!" either in disdain or because he'd caught his wispy beard in the hinge.

Once he'd made his intentions clear and that compromise wasn't in his lexicon, the fight was over quickly.

Bash—singe—chomp.

"I gave you a chance," she said wistfully as she took a jewel of unreasoning petty hatred from his shadow-self and placed it with others in a ruby-encrusted casket next to the nursery. One less shard of bitterness in the world. She looked at the rest of his remains and shook her head "but you were too proud to take it."

She tossed his armour down the slope and carried his flesh-stripped bones to the woods beyond the ridge where the crows and the foxes took time to thank her for them, whereas the rats scurried in first, thanking her with full mouths as they ran away with their various prizes.

Then Bronca returned to her clutch to guard them and keep them warm with her loving breath.

Often she philosophised about why the knights wanted to kill her. Everyone else, farmers, lawyers, and priests—well maybe not priests—recognised her place in the world and let her and her kind be. A dragon is the representative of the earth, the Great Mother's delegate at the meetings of all creatures. What would they gain from killing her? Surely it would lead to their own demise if they turned from the mother.

Although she came to no satisfactory conclusion, the generous old dragon resolved to continue in her hoarding of petty hatred. The Great Mother would bless her for that.

The next knight dismounted, tied his charger to the same tree and engaged in conversation with the same thin-lipped and similarly minded priest.

"Is it lawful to kill dragons?"

"It is meet and right to kill dragons but if thou wert to buy a simple indulgence for a mere three groats, thou wouldst be squeaky clean in this matter."

Being of a cautious bent, the knight bought the indulgence for safety's sake, had his accoutrements blessed and went on his way.

Thinking he'd better prepare himself for the fray, the knight went behind a bush to clear himself of any distractions. He exhaled a muffled "Hah!" as he repositioned his equipment before resuming his slightly squeakier, clanking approach. Another common occurrence for knights of the realm.

He wasn't what you might call a natural as a knight. Wrong shape for a start and even though his armour had been made especially for his frame, his greaves chafed something immoderate and as for his besagews, it didn't bear contemplation. His forte was numbers. He'd always wanted to be an accountant but they were two a farthing and his right old baron of a father had flogged him into his present position, itinerant knight, in search of easy employment around the realm until he came into his inheritance. All this notwithstanding, he was of more methodical stuff than those who had clattered their ways up the path to the cave in previous times and he sported the very latest in asbestos underpinned armour. After a wince or two, he strode clunkily up to the cave's entrance and without announcing himself, walked boldly into the dangerous darkness where Bronca was lurking. She had ample warning of his arrival in that plate armour which, on a hot and sunny day, turns your average knight into something like a pot roast, basted in manly stinking sweat. That and the fact it's almost impossible to sneak up on anyone in the afore-described armour.

Perhaps he should have lit the torch outside the cave, he thought, as he fiddled with his tinderbox. Strike after strike failed to ignite the blasted thing. Then out of the darkness came a thin streak of fire as Bronca breathed onto his torch, revealing herself curled around her clutch of eggs and newborn.

"Oh," he said as he gingerly pulled down his visor, transferred the torch to his left hand and drew his sword.

"Is conflict between us necessary, sir knight?" she asked. "Can we not discuss our differences? As you see, I am a mother and these are my children. I have no wish to harm or be harmed. Do you not feel likewise?"

In this unexpectedly convivial atmosphere, epiphany dawned. This dragon-slaying had been imposed upon him by his father and his ilk. Prove your worthiness, prove your allegiance to everything human and your rejection of ancient faerie lore.

Not being keen on killing for its own sake, anyway, he agreed to leave her and her family alone. Laying his sword down on the floor of the cave he said, "I was never much of a knight."

"You have proved yourself to be a greater knight than all the others."

She showed him the first of her brood, rainbow colours playing amongst their scales.

"You see? They will bring a greater warmth to the world. I

name them as they emerge from their shells. These are Hanemet, Disul and Nofre. I shall name the next one after you. What is your name, sir knight? Mine is Bronca."

"Industurn,"

"Look at this egg—the crack is widening. Come to me, little one. Your name shall be Industurn."

As they watched the miracle of creation, the torch spluttered and in the sudden brightness the knight-errant saw the ruby encrusted casket at the far end of the cave. Rising like a monster from the depths, the acquisitive creature in him took the reins of the chariot.

He grasped his sword and struck the distracted Bronca with a sudden blow to the throat. Her eyes widened as the blue blood spurted from her neck and across her brood. The knight stood back as he watched her writhe and thrash towards him, then shudder and lie down in an arc, to gaze upon her blood-stained children as they cried while she died.

To ensure his own future safety, for dragons have prodigious memories, he killed every one of her children, including the one named for him. Then he smashed all the remaining eggs and opened that casket, to be amazed by the glittering hoard, sparkling in the torchlight. Although their collective hatred flooded him, there was nothing left to kill, so he hit and kicked the sad lifeless children of the dragon until the raw emotion abated. Still believing they were simply jewels, he took the casket and carried it back down the path where he met the priest in process of selling another indulgence to another knight hoping for glory.

"It is no longer necessary," the knight told them both. "Said dragon is dead."

The priest looked him up and down as he realised his lucrative pitch was no longer so.

"Bugger," quoth the man of God and the harridans camped beside the road ceased their cackling as the market in used armour crashed.

His squire didn't look downright delighted, either.

The hero Industurn rode back to his family's castle to be greeted by the uplifting news his nasty, mad old father had passed away at a banquet, face-down in a suckling pig with all the trimmings. His first act as baron was to have the remains of the long-forgotten cleared from the oubliette in the innermost keep. Then he had two of his most faithful servants carry the casket into the room and offered them a mug of wine apiece in celebration of their achievement. You don't refuse wine from your baron even though you might be suspicious of its content. And they were right to be. They drank it and died in the special treasury, well away from the public gaze and local history.

Although it was locked in a room walled with stone six feet thick, the nervous baron felt his treasure was still insecure. That night, having placed all the Jewels of Petty Hatred into a padlocked chest, he disguised himself and made his way into town with the casket.

The locksmith wasn't pleased to be woken at that hour but when shown gold as remuneration, he mellowed his attitude somewhat.

"Return in three days," he told the baron. If the locksmith recognised his client he wisely kept his trap as firmly shut as if it were one of his constructions.

In three days, once night had fallen across the merchants' quarter, the baron returned and the locksmith showed him the work.

"There is but one key," he assured the baron as he handed it to him. "I understand discretion is in order, on pain of death, and I wish to continue with my life and my business."

The baron nodded. It seemed the locksmith had seen through his disguise but this was no ordinary serf. It would be too complicated to get rid of such a well-founded member of the community. Unless it was expedient, of course.

Next, he employed a travelling tinker and gave him the task of chaining the casket to the oubliette floor. Of necessity, the man was brought into the chamber where the casket was kept so he might accomplish his task.

Once the tinker had completed the work to his employer's satisfaction, the baron smiled broadly.

"Such a fine job deserves a reward," he said, handing the artisan a leather tankard of wine.

Now that the jewels were truly as secure as the baron believed, he had but one task remaining. His own security would be in question as long as the father of those eggs and young dragonlings was free to roam. That father's vengeance would ever be a threat.

For years he hunted for the male dragon but failed to find him, never knowing the creature who was Bronca's husband and lover, had crept into her cave and died of a broken heart, lying alongside his slain wife and their children. Before a year turned, all that remained were bones and crushed eggshells. The vengeance that was to come would not emanate from the race of dragons.

After each unsuccessful hunt, the Baron Industurn would repair to his castle wherein his stolen treasure lay.

He revelled in counting and polishing them by the light of the barred window high on the south wall of the oubliette, loved to hear the tinkle and chink as he poured them through his hands. Then one terrible day, his count of two thousand and twenty-five was one short. He counted from the beginning and the count was two short this time. Through the thumping of blood in his ears, he failed to hear the scratching of claws on flagstone. The rats were circling in the darker corners of the room and stealing his precious jewels whenever he wasn't watching them. He counted again and yet again.

Hearing the fluttering of wings, he looked up to see a raven on the windowsill, one of the jewels held fast in its beak, glinting like a captured fire. The raven watched him as he jumped vainly to reach it.

Then it stretched up and called out to his gods. "Look at this foolish man!"

The jewel fell against the metal bars with a ching! and thence, out of the tower.

Industurn felt madness rise in him as he inwardly cursed the raven, then turned to watch the rats gathering against the walls of this prison. If he left to find the jewel the raven had dropped, the rats would steal more of his hoard, if he stayed to guard the remaining jewels, someone, any passing shit-covered peasant, might find the one outside. He piled the remaining jewels into the casket without counting them—something he had never done before—locked it and ran down the spiral stone stairs to the courtyard.

There was no sign of the missing jewel. How far might it have bounced? He ran hither and thither like a man possessed, for that was what he had become. The Jewels of Petty Hatred had possessed his mind, enfeebling the little sense that remained.

His children, callous and greedy as their father, locked him in the oubliette, ostensibly for his own safety but in reality, for their own gain. They told people he had run away into the marshes and would never be found, whilst they allowed him to die crazed in the twilight, amongst his glistening treasures, still craving more as the rats and the ravens took away his reasons for joy, one by one.

So it was that the petty hatreds the mother dragon had taken and kept from the world of men, returned in force to that world and were scattered amongst its unwitting denizens.

~ * ~

Sometime later, when all this history had been forgotten, two knights of opposing factions, each with The Cruel Engineer on his side, met on the road leading from the ruined city. Pitiless men leaving the shell-pitted buildings to burn.

Amongst various smells of burning flesh, churches and home-steads, they raised their night-vision enhancing tactical visors to better see each other's faces, bowed to each other, demonstrating their mutual respect and their indifference to the dispossessed, struggling past on the way to nowhere and to the farmers, spreading dung on the remaining unburned fields. Like children in the play-ground, the knights compared and admired weapons, whilst indulging in knightly humorous banter in order to avoid any issues that might be presented to them were they to look around.

By this time, the Jewels of Petty Hatred had become ingrained throughout humankind, with no one to sequester them away, for no dragons remained.

Yet to realise they were defined by their adversaries, the knights were at a loss.

Who was left to kill?

~ * ~ * ~

**Jonah Jones** lives in Wales where we celebrate the dragon by having it on our national flag. He's had several short stories published (including one in *Mystic Signals*, edited by Carol Hightshoe) together with stage and radio scripts produced. He also writes and directs short films.

Perhaps the dragons are on our side—trying vainly to save us from ourselves.

# Eclipse

## Nicholas Samuel Stember

Jessica threw her travel bag onto the floor as she looked around the entryway of the short-term rental she had booked and let out a long sigh. The place looked exactly as the online photos had shown it would, back when she and Bailey had scoured the Airbnb app looking for the perfect romantic and fun getaway.

For a moment she wasn't sure what to do next, then she lifted her left hand and stared at the exquisite sapphire ring on her finger, the deep blue stone surrounded by a circle of diamonds. For a moment her lips formed a sad smile as she remembered Bailey placing it on her finger, telling her the sapphire matched her eyes, making it the perfect engagement ring. But the smile quickly faded from her face, and she picked the bag up from the floor and headed into the bedroom, her eyes glancing over the Orlando brochures featuring the many parks and sites.

~ * ~

It was on her third night of the vacation that she came back and plopped on the couch, exhausted from how hard she had pushed herself to have fun, see the sites, enjoy the amusement parks, anything but think of Bailey.

She had already ordered dinner from the delivery service and was waiting as she marveled at all the pointless souvenirs she had picked up over three days when the doorbell rang. Quickly getting up to retrieve her delivered sushi and fries, she tipped the delivery man then settled back on the couch with her food on the coffee table and watched some TV as she ate. It was then she glanced back at her pile of souvenirs and noticed the cute silver pendant of Tinkerbell she bought wasn't there. Her brow furrowed as she stared at the various curios she had picked up and wondered if she had left it in the rental car, or worse, lost it from her bags in the park. For a moment she felt around her neck to see if she had put it on and forgot, but nothing was there but the slightly sensitive skin around her neck from the hot Florida sun.

Pressing her lips together, she got up and went out the front door to the parked rental car and checked it over—nothing. With an annoyed sigh she went back into the condo and flopped back on the couch and reached for a fry when she realized half the fries were gone. She was sure there had been more there, she really hadn't touched them yet. Her eyes blinked a few times, and she looked around the living room.

"Okay, I'm losing my mind," she said to no one.

She took out her smartphone and looked up the short-term rental listing for this place and scanned past the high ratings they had read up on half a year back when they booked the place and saw a few mixed reviews that were more recent.

*Wonderful place, very clean and well stocked. Within ten minutes of most parks. Had a great stay but a bracelet my daughter bought vanished from the place. We looked everywhere but it was simply gone.*

Then another.

*Fantastic location, close to the parks. The owner was very good with communications and the pool was very clean. The only odd thing was some missing pocket change and a pair of earrings somehow vanished from the place.*

Jessica found a few more similar comments, but only in the last two months.

Her thoughts of possible recent burglary were interrupted when she caught some movement out of the corner of her eyes. She flicked her eyes over to the corner of the room where the air vent was on the floor, but nothing was there.

"Odd…"

She ended up trying to put it out of her mind and watching TV late into the night, finally dozing off on the couch. However, it didn't take long for her dreams to turn sour, and she came awake with a start and felt a watery sting in her eyes. For a moment she lay there in the dark, only illuminated by the muted TV as she tried to shake the remnants of the dream from her mind. Then she heard a light scraping sound on the coffee table near her. She opened one eye with just a squint and froze. There on the coffee table, the silver hoop earrings she took off earlier were moving…sliding across the table. Slowly she opened both eyes and sat up in the dark, just as the two earrings fell off the table and started to move across the tile floor, seemingly on their own. She wanted to get up, to run over to them and grab them, but she felt transfixed, frozen.

Once the earrings reached the floor vent, she was finally able to spring into action and darted across the room, dropping down on all fours and reaching out. She missed them as they slipped through the vent, vanishing below.

"What the..."

She put her fingers through the oversized vent and pulled it up from the floor, exposing a rectangle hole just big enough to fit her head, which she considered for an instant and immediately rejected as visions of rats popped into her mind making her shudder. Before she really thought it through, she stuck her right hand down into the hole and felt around, half expecting to find the missing jewelry. It wasn't far to the bottom of the vent, just a foot or so and she easily felt the bottom. It was surprisingly clean, as she expected to encounter a lot of dust or crumbs, but no, it was clean and smooth. For a moment it caught her off her guard...until she felt the tiny teeth sink into her index finger and she pulled her hand back sharply.

She stared at her finger for a moment. The bite hadn't drawn blood, but she could see the ring of depressions outlining a tiny jaw. All the marks were even, not the pronounced bigger front teeth she expected a rat to leave. For a moment she stared at her finger, waiting for blood to begin to seep, her mind racing with different possibilities and she quickly decided if it was rats, she was going to a hotel right away, but if she expected to get her money back from Airbnb, she'd need proof.

She went back to the table, retrieving her phone and returned to the vent. Then she activated the camera and switched to video mode and activated the phone's light. Taking a deep breath, she put the phone into the hole and slowly faced it towards where the bite had come from.

Trying to hold her hand steady, she slowly counted out, "One ...two...threefourfive!" Quickly she pulled her hand back, turned off the video and hit 'play'. "Okay little rat, let's see those beady eyes and my missing stuff."

The video showed her sitting on the floor next to the vent, then slowly going into the hole. At first the picture was dark as she was facing the vent wall, then it turned blurry as the image quickly moved around and settled on the biter.

Jessica let out a gasp as she watched the video.

"No way," she whispered as she reversed the video back to those two long seconds the image had somewhat cleared up. Her biter was surely there, but it wasn't a rat. In fact, she really wasn't sure what she was looking at, as she used her fingers to enlarge the image. It looked like a little lizard sitting on top of a pile of stuff. At first, she assumed it had to be one of the anoles she had seen all over the place outside. But unlike those cute little lizards she had seen around the walkways and fences, this one wasn't green or brown…it was red. And were those little wings along its back?

She sat there for a few minutes watching the video over and over and freezing the picture repeatedly. Then she glanced back at what was left of her food. There were still two fries left on the paper. She picked them up, but they were cold and hard, so she went into the kitchen and popped them into the microwave for a few seconds. Once ready, she took them back to the hole in the floor and shined her phone's light down into it. All she could see was the bottom of the vent, so she dropped both fries down.

"I think you like these," she said, her voice almost a whisper.

Her lips parted slightly as she saw a tiny red, scaly arm reach into the light and grab one of the fries and pull it back into the darkness. Then she heard the munching. Without a second thought, she grabbed the last piece of her spicy salmon roll and came back to the vent hole, noting the second fry was gone as well. She reached down and left the sushi piece there and was just about to pull her hand back when she felt the flick of a small wet tongue on her index finger. She quickly pulled her hand out of the vent and looking back down, saw the sushi was gone too.

"Hungry little thing, aren't you?"

She placed her phone down on the bottom of the vent, face down and light on, then slowly lowered her head into the hole, hoping there was enough light to see.

The light was bouncing off the sides and the top and bottom of the vent that stretched back under the floorboards, but there, upon a pile of things was a tiny…a very tiny…dragon.

The pile was filled with all sorts of things: Many loose coins and not all of them American, a few earrings, a few silver rings and her pendant was there, as well as her hoop earrings, and a sparkly bracelet. But sitting up on top of it all was a tiny dragon…there was simply no other word her brain could come up with to explain what she was seeing. Its long scaly neck rose up from its body to its long snouted head with two sparkling yellow eyes. Long wings were folded along its back and its long tail went down and curled around some of the treasures, but even with such detail the red scaled lizard couldn't have been more than five inches long.

Her lips parted slightly, and she realized she had forgotten to breathe.

"You look like you've been crying," it said with a quiet whisper.

"Did you just speak?" she asked as she felt the blood starting to rush into her head.

"Of course I did," it replied with a touch of indignance.

"But you're a...a..."

"Dragon," it finished for her, a smile curling its long lips. Then when it saw her continued look of doubt, it let out the tiniest little roar that ended in three quick chirps. Then it raised its head up high towards the vent wall above it, and it breathed a little spurt of flames which quickly dissipated.

"Wow," she said blinking a few times then smiling. "You bit me."

"You were about to poke me, and I apologized after your nice gift of food."

Her smile turned into pursed lips as she looked at her earrings and pendant. "Why are you stealing my stuff?"

The lizard cocked his tiny head to one side and smiled. "I'm a dragon, this is what we do. Haven't you ever heard of a dragon's hoard before?"

"Sure, in movies and such, but you're not really what I'd expect a dragon to be like."

The little creature let out a sigh. "Oh, I was, once, long, long ago. But we dragons needed to live in the minds and hearts of many to stay as we were, and I faded from all memory many of your years ago. I only woke up again recently, but I was just this...this tiny thing you see before you. But that will change one day, when my hoard gains enough value. Then the dragons can return."

"Well, you have some nice stuff there," Jessica said, trying to sound more helpful than she felt.

"Silver is nice," the dragon admitted, "but much of this is common, and many of the coins are just coated copper. People bring a lot of junk here."

Then the dragon's head seemed to bob up and down a few

times as the little yellow eyes met hers. "Looks like you were crying."

"It was just a bad dream," Jessica admitted, suddenly feeling a bit embarrassed. Then, for no reason she could explain, the words suddenly started flowing. "This was supposed to be our special week, Bailey and me. We were supposed to have fun at the parks and dinners and shows and…and plan our wedding." Her eyes started to water again, and she shut them tightly. When they opened again, she realized the dragon had moved off its hoard and came up to her, practically touching.

Then the little dragon leaned forward and pressed his tiny face to hers, nose to nose and a strange warmth flowed through her. The pain and loss she had felt didn't vanish, but didn't hurt nearly as much anymore, as if a great amount of time had passed, allowing her heart to heal.

"What did you do?" she asked, her voice barely above a whisper as her mind tried to take in the fact that the hurt just didn't hurt as much anymore.

"Not sure you'd really understand," the dragon admitted. "But let's just say your soul was stuck a bit too deeply into reality and needed a little fantasy to heal it."

Jessica lifted her head out of the hole and sat there on the floor, a flood of emotions coming to her, and she just smiled.

"Thank you," she said. "I feel much better."

She watched as the dragon came into the light then spread his wings and lifted up to the floor level, though as the light hit him, his scales seemed to shimmer and refract the light and she instantly realized if she didn't know he was there, she would not have been able to see him at all.

"No wonder I couldn't see you before. What do I call you? Do you have a name?"

"Hmmm," the tiny dragon seemed to think. "I've been called many things in ages past, but you can call me Eclipse."

"A strange name," she said as she reached out and let him land on her hand. "But I like it."

Then suddenly her smile grew. "How long will it take your hoard to reach the point where you can return?"

"With what I've been gathering, a decent amount of time," its voice said with a touch of sadness. "Really expensive items for my hoard are rare here it seems. So much junk." Then his glowing yellow eyes caught the light as it reflected off the large sapphire and diamonds of her ring.

Jessica's eyes followed the dragon's and her smile broadened as she slipped the engagement ring off her finger. "Bailey didn't ask for this back, hasn't even spoken to me since the breakup." Then she placed the ring in the palm of her right hand next to the dragon.

"Will this help?"

The dragon's eyes sparkled and almost seemed to glow as it reached with its front claws and picked up the ring. "Are these real? Set in white gold?"

"Yes, they are all real, and it's platinum," she replied.

The dragon's breathing got faster and faster as it held the tiny treasure. "You really are giving this to me, willingly?"

"Yes. I hope it helps."

"Oh, little human, it does much more than that." The dragon said with a tiny laugh and darted off her hand and back down into the hole to its hoard. Then his small head popped back out for a moment, and he said, "Eternal thanks." Then he was gone again.

There was a flash of light from the vent opening and Jessica quickly stuck her head back into the hole…but the dragon and its hoard were gone. Nothing remained in the vent but the years of dust that had suddenly re-appeared.

She pulled her head out and frowned for a moment as if confused. But then her smile returned. "Just needed a bit of fantasy to heal it," she repeated what Eclipse had said to her.

~ * ~

She didn't remember finally going to sleep, but when the sunlight came through the window she sat up with a smile and got ready for the day. Before long she was dressed and heading out to the rental car, ready to make the most of the four days remaining. Before she left, she checked the vent once more, but now not only didn't it look like it had been cleaned, but it was also difficult to pry up, as if it hadn't been opened in a long time. She half wondered if she had dreamed the whole thing, but then looked back at her left hand and noted the slim band of pale skin, marking where the ring had been for the last half year.

"Sun is shining, the Mouse is waiting, and I'm going to have a great time," she said to no one and everyone. "Thanks, Eclipse."

A large shadow suddenly loomed high above her, and she shielded her eyes as she tried to see what had blocked out the sun when she heard a mighty roar…followed by three bright chirps that echoed through the palm trees below.

Jessica's smile returned. "Oh, there you are."

~ * ~ * ~

Born in New York City, **Nicholas Samuel Stember** has lived in Europe and Israel, but spent most of his life growing up in the suburbs of Princeton, NJ. His father, Charles H. Stember, was a published professor of sociology at Rutgers University, and his mother, Sue, was a professional singer and later a portrait photographer. With two creative influences, it wasn't hard to see the directions he'd take.

With a profound love and appreciation of the genres of fantasy, science fiction and horror, the direction his writing took was firmly set. His short stories have appeared in various online magazines over the years. His love of those genres also found him a wife from across the sea, and he ended up marrying her and moving to the Faroe Islands, where he resides today.

# Shadow, Lion, Dragon

## Peter Sartucci

"Somebody's going to conjure a *dragon?!*"

I was so startled I spoke aloud, and almost fell off the roof. The Sulfur Serpent Inn is a tall building, four stories plus a big attic where the DiUmbra acrobat troupe practices, so it's a long way down. But I'd left that practice and climbed up here to talk privately to my secret brother, King Terrell, not to splash myself on the cobblestones. I hauled my butt back a-straddle the ridge-slates, shut my fool mouth and thought at him.

*Are you sure? The last dragon died a thousand years ago! How is conjuring one even possible without a real one to give a pattern?*

I could feel him drumming his fingers on the altar rail in the Royal Chapel, smell his cinnamon and the incense of a room halfway across the Arisen City. I know being King of Silbar must be frustrating, but by all the Seraphs, he's the one who wanted the duty. I wouldn't take it on a bet.

Terrell answered me with that exasperated tone of thought he gets sometimes.

*It's been closer to nine hundred years since Golgera was slain. I have no idea if its bones, or any others, are pattern enough—you know I am no conjurer! Perhaps this mage has discovered some truly new magic that can bridge that gap between dead bones and their former life.*

That thought made me queasy. My own Power is already too entwined with death for my peace of mind. The idea of some damn fool thinning the boundaries even more made my guts clench.

*Kirin, regardless of how he plans to do it, I need you to stop this mage before he succeeds. Anyone who can create such a powerful construct is a formidable danger—and this man is ruthless.*

*How do you know?*

*Because I've Foreseen what he'll do with his creation. He's going to seize the Vettore tax caravan.*

I gulped. The cities of Silbar's Vettore Coast are fever-hot with trade and gravid with gold. A large piece of the Crown's revenues come from there, gold coins and silver ingots packed on mules over the Bright Mountains into Silbar proper. Gold to fuel commerce; silver to fuel sorcery. Guarded by two hundred men of the Royal Silbari Army.

*Salim's Tail!* I blurted. *You're sure this was a real vision? Even you can have a plain old bad dream.*

*It was True. Look.*

The mind-sharing we can do has its drawbacks. I could taste the acid churn of his stomach in my own mouth as he sent me his vision.

I saw the famous rock spires of Fanged Pass, celebrated in the great fresco in Terrell's palace. A dragon descended on the caravan belching flame, its wings wide as the sky and the sinuous snake of its body armored in ruby scales big as platters. Men and horses withered beneath it, scorched meat on a barren mountainside—and a deep voice laughed and said "Mine!" One of the officers was thrown from his panicked horse, got up and raised his sword in defiance just as the flames overwhelmed him.

"Menandir!" I choked. I'd learned sword-work from him in my first year as a knight. Despite a patrician bloodline, he'd given freely of his time to train me, a gutter rat jumped into knightly rank by Terrell's royal fiat. Most of the other knights looked down their noses and declared I'd never make it.

*He asked for a field command this summer. I picked this one for him,* Terrell whispered wretchedly.

I shivered. My twin's visions are always true—but not complete. And they are things that might be, not things that must be. I held onto that.

*You weren't puffing about that mage's power,* I said. *His dragon looks as real as these tiles under my rump. Any idea who this guy is? Is he a Silbari? Imperial? Foreigner?*

*No, that was everything I Saw. Not even his face—just his works and that voice, which may not even be his own. I don't know a single thing I could use to identify him.*

*Hmm. So all we know is he's a high-ranked caster who's got power to spare and a nasty sense of style. That must fit a hundred mages right here in Aretzo.*

*Or more. But two things are evident—he's bold, and he understands Silbari people. His dragon is meant to terrify us with a memory out of deep time, to drive beasts mad and men to despair. And it will—you saw how most *of my soldiers simply stared and died.*

Morbidly, I had to ask. *Will any escape?*

*Very few. I Saw three of the vanguard hale enough to make the ride to Narvi in haste, nearly killing their horses to send me word. A handful will flee the attack, perhaps a dozen in all. The rest will die on the mountain.*

I felt his anguish over that. Fifteen survivors out of two hundred!

*Kirin, I can't let this happen. With that much wealth and the means to feed more sorcery in his hands, only The God knows what this mage will try next. And there are only two men I am confident can take down someone who flaunts that much power.*

*Two? You're sending me with Penghar?* I cringed at the thought. *There's a baaaaad idea.*

*Oh stop it!* He snapped back. *You are both proof against magery, if in different ways. You are both Knights of the Old Order, sworn to do justice. And you are my Hands.*

I snorted rudely. *Only because I didn't want to get burned at the stake by the Temple. I liked being an acrobat better. Anyway, oath or not, Pen still thinks I'm a demon in disguise, ready to sprout claws and a tail and start ripping up everyone around me.*

*He does not!* Terrell gets riled every time I bring this up.

*You've seen how he looks at me. And he's not so far off the truth, is he? This Shadow that lives inside me—*

*You are not a demon! You are my twin brother, closer to my heart than any other. Even Pen, though it would pain him needlessly to hear me say it. So don't tell him.*

Terrell opened his heart to me as well as his mind, the raw naked trust sears me worse than fire. I flinched more than I would from a blow. How can he bear to do that? We're not identical—I'm Darkness to his Light—and the One God didn't make me that strong, or that good.

*Yes you are, and someday you'll understand,* he told me. *Kirin, every minute's precious. That caravan starts up the far side of the mountains in less than two days—too soon for a courier pigeon or even a mage's message-construct to get there and stop it.*

*You could use those to send riders after it from the Vettore side of the mountains,* I suggested. *That'd be easier than racing to get ahead of it from this side.*

*But it doesn't stop this mage from trying again, and next time I may not* *have any warning.**

*I get it,** I sighed. *You have to let Menandir and the caravan be bait to draw the damned mage out.**

We both tasted the bitterness of that decision. I wouldn't take on his burden for anything.

*It'll reach the Fanged Pass ten days from now,** Terrell continued doggedly. *Whoever he is, he's bound to know I'll move against him as fast as I can. He'll have a plan to escape with his loot. I can't let that happen. Please, brother, put aside your love of the flying trapeze and your acrobat tricks. I need you to ride with Pen, today. Find this mage and stop him. Take him alive if you can, dead if you must, but stop him before my soldiers die. Show everyone my hand is held in guard over my people.**

I sighed one more time. *Of course I'll do it. But you can't make me like it—or Pen either.**

He snorted back at me, gave me final directions, and left my mind.

I climbed off the roof and down into the Sulfur Serpent to change. Riding leathers instead of my shabby rehearsal tights. Boots instead of the soft slippers we wore for aerial work. My badge and knight's ring completed my transformation. That amethyst-and-gold band winked faintly in the dimness of my room as I slipped it onto my finger and clenched my fist. When I left the Sulfur Serpent Inn, the acrobat would stay behind and the knight Terrell needed would ride out.

"You're going away again." A familiar voice spoke from the door.

"King Terrell wants me to do something for him," I answered, turning around and buckling on my sword and belt knife.

"He'll use you up someday," Sevan Sule DiUmbra admonished as he stepped into my room and crossed his powerful arms. A couple of his cousins crowded behind, looking worried. They were all still wearing sweaty patched hose for trapeze practice up in the attic—the very practice I'd snuck out of to go answer Terrell's mind-call. I'd hoped to slip out of the Inn before they realized I was gone and leave awkward explanations for later.

"I swore an oath," I reminded him, tapping my badge. "I took his salt and his silver. When service is required of me, I go."

He couldn't argue with that, so he sighed, reached out and pulled me into an embrace, pounded me on the back. I squeezed his ribs in return, like hugging a tree, while the others clapped me on the shoulders and muttered worried good wishes. Sevan bent down from his ten-finger height advantage to whisper in my ear. "Be careful, little brother, and remember your family loves you. My sister made you a DiUmbra forever." He touched the scars in my sideburns, the ritual marks of grief I'd cut at Maia's graveside.

"I'll never forget. I will be back," I answered, shoving the heartache down deep. If I'd never learned what I am, I could have been happy in the Troupe my whole life, raised children to follow me onto the trapeze, and in time laid my bones in the ground sanctified by my wife's ancestors, content.

But I do know what I am.

I left the DiUmbra family quarters to clatter down the stairwell. My sword banged off the rail as I vaulted over it on the last flight. My boot heels slammed the floor and sent an echo up the well to my family's watching faces. I raced through the tavern on the main floor, out to Sulfur Street and the glare of daylight.

Away from my adopted family, who knows me only as the orphan-child they found abandoned in the gutters. The family who took me in, raised me, gave me a place, a name, a wife, and a purpose. But two years ago, Life and Death diced with us as pawns and the Kingdom at stake, killed my wife and catapulted me into becoming a greater power than I'd ever dreamed possible. Now my family doesn't know what to do with me.

I barely know what to do with myself.

I ran up Sulfur Street, dodging wagons, beasts, and people. The authority of my badge, the threat of my sheathed sword, and maybe even the unseen terror of my hidden Shadow cleared my path. Tears not due to wind or sun leaked from the corners of my eyes.

Sevan calls me brother even though anyone looking at us can see I'm not. Terrell got our real Mother's brown skin and round ears, only Father's blond hair marks his half-blood.

I wasn't so lucky. In the land of rich brown skin-tones, I am a pale golden-tan. Amidst a sea of brown hair, mine is blacker than night. Where Silbaris have round-topped ears, mine are pointed as any God-cursed Slaver—or my conquering Imperial father. I am a half-breed in the land of the pure, and anyone can see it. My adopted family ignored the whispers and the derision and tried to bind me to them with chains of love. But only the one who shared

Mother's womb with me truly knows and accepts everything I am.

And because he asks, but never commands, I'll go battle the nastiest Mage in the world.

~ * ~

Sir Penghar Veryhs DiLione waited for me at the Old Order Chapter House. I had a room here too, though I rarely used it, which gave him heartburn. He didn't approve of my 'slumming' down on disreputable Sulfur Street. The courtyard boiled with action as grooms organized horses and squires packed equipment and weapons. It looked like Pen and I weren't going alone.

The Master of the House stood by Pen's side on the doorstep with his gray hair uncovered to the sky. Technically he ranked the two of us as mere Knights, but Pen and I both wore something he could only gaze at in helpless envy. The badges that mark us as King's Hands, each a silver hand on a purple field ringed by double overlapping silver circles. People call us the Right Hand and the Left. Nobody needs two guesses to figure out which one I am.

"Sir Kirin DiUmbra," the Master greeted me with an unforced smile.

"My Lord Sir Berreghar D'Ambar DiViga." I saluted as I gave him his three full names and then clasped wrists with him in the Warriors' Grip, which made us equals for protocol. Courtesy is cheap, and besides he's a decent man at heart or he wouldn't command the Chapter House. He's just never had any idea what to make of half-breed gutter-trash jumped-up me. "Is my gear ready, Master?"

"In moments," he promised, and inclined his head toward the frenetic bustle.

"Thank you, my lord," I told him, and suppressed a sigh as I turned. "Hello, Penghar. I'll bet ten gold Royals you've already organized everything the way you like it."

Pen squinted at me. He's twelve fingers taller and several shades browner than me, a lot like the Master. Only Pen has rich chestnut hair above a chiseled face handsomer than any statue in the Corridor of Perfection. Maidens yearn for him everywhere he goes, though it does them no good. Pen's more celibate than an anchorite sealed in a monastery cell.

I wonder if that's why he's such an ass?

"I'm in charge of this mission." He growled like a surly bear.

"You follow my orders."

"As long as they're not stupid orders," I answered equitably. Terrell hadn't said anything about command so I would bet Pen was pushing the limits of his authority. "Who else are we dragging along?"

"Just four of my Horse Guards." He sneered in aristocratic snobbery.

I don't have a troop of men waiting on my command, nor a hereditary estate to support them. When I found out who my parents really were, I made Terrell promise never to stick me with that burden. I smiled innocently.

"Is Handsome ready?"

Pen's sneer turned sour. I did have a horse that turned him pea-green with envy, not least because Terrell had gifted it to me right out of the Royal Stables. "Yes," he grunted.

"Then let's go."

I saluted the Master again and turned on my heel. Two of the Chapter House squires held our mounts, the four Horse Guards ready behind them with a string of remounts and some pack horses. I checked Handsome's saddle girth. He liked to play tricks when the grooms let him get away with it. They'd been careful today, so I mounted up. Pen had already done the same with his mare and he sat on her back with an impatience I ignored. We cantered out the Chapter House gate under the ancient stone arch carved with the words Duty and Honor.

We walked our horses through the bustling City, then Pen set a hard pace once we cleared the north gate. The Kings' Road has a grassy sward on the east edge for messengers and Royal agents and we took full advantage. Handsome enjoyed the chance to stretch himself and I got reacquainted with his fluid gait. We switched horses regularly to spare them as much as possible—there were three remounts just for me. And we ate the miles, riding till dark and rising before dawn in these long spring days, in a race against time.

First three nights out we found inns, and I made excuses to avoid Pen as much as possible. But the fourth night we camped in an orange orchard. Swelling green fruit had begun to bow the leafy branches overhead. Two of the Horse Guards set up camp under the moonlight while another built an economical fire of scavenged twigs and started cooking supper. The last Guard, Cantin something-or-other, helped me tend to the horses, as we had done the last three nights. We had bought grain and mash for the beasts to soften the terrible strain we were putting them through.

"You be a verra good horseman, m'lord," Cantin remarked to me in the Guards' brogue. From his men's speech, Pen's estate must be in deep country. The youngest of the four, Cantin spoke to me shyly with a little head-bow for my rank. It was the first time he'd said anything to me that wasn't straight pass-the-feed-bag-please business.

"Thank you. I try." I wasn't raised a horseman, I'm city-bred, but Terrell's memories of caring for his own horses had guided me ever since I agreed to be knighted. There are many advantages to mind-speaking. "But Handsome makes it easy." I ran a brush down the big yellow gelding's withers, and he sighed with horsey pleasure and leaned into the strokes.

"An' he be a fine battle-steed." Cantin nodded admiringly, wielding the currycomb on one of Pen's remounts. "The way he moves, his lines, I kin tell he's had war-trainin' too. Tis a shame about his head."

"You mean his lumpy face and bobbed ears? Well, that's why I named him Handsome." I switched to picking burrs and twigs out of his mane.

Cantin chuckled. He seemed genuinely glad to have my help, the first thaw in the Guards' oh-so-formal correctness toward me since we started. When we finished a minimal currying job on each of the remount horses, we walked back to the fire together.

Penghar sat on his saddle near the flames and cleaned road-mud off his sword-sheath. Riding this fast got us amazingly filthy. I yearned for a bath after only four days and was dismally sure I wouldn't get one any time soon. His sword, Irreneetha, stood up out of a rock into which he'd thrust her point, piercing stone as easily as cutting cheese. That alone proves what that sword really is.

The angel within the blade turned and looked straight at me.

I paused under the weight of her regard—what do you say to an angel? I settled for mute staring, wondering if she meant to speak to me and whether I'd even be able to hear her voice. But after a long unblinking study she only gave me the tiniest nod, as if in dismissal. I didn't know if that meant I'd measured up—or never would.

I answered her with a little bow, then Gerdon handed me a bowl of stew. Even dried meat and desecrated vegetables taste good when your ass aches from too much riding. I squatted on my hams to spoon up supper and all the while Pen's eyes followed me. It set my teeth on edge and spoiled the meal. It was almost a relief when he finally asked, "Why did you bow to her?"

I swallowed a last mouthful before I answered, too tired to be deferential. "She's a lady, Pen. You've told me yourself, a knight should always return courtesy to ladies."

"'Return courtesy'?" He set down his cleaning rag, leaned forward. "What courtesy do you mean?"

I really should have shut up then. "She looked me over, gave me a nod, I bowed—what in the Nine Hells else should I do? It's not like I spend a lot of time around angels!"

The men muttered, drew away from me slightly. Their eyes looked bigger in the night as the fire died to embers. They all knew she was there—Pen and his sword are rightly famous—but unless she chose to manifest to them, they couldn't see her. I cursed my tired brain for letting slip the knowledge I could.

Pen glared suspiciously at me while his knuckles tightened on the sheath. "No surprise. You prefer the company of devils."

I glowered at him, bit back the first thing that crossed my mind, and the second and third, settled for saying "I do *not*. His Highness trusts me—I don't have to prove anything to you!"

"Oh yes you do, gutter-boy," Pen said softly, pulling Irreneetha out of the stone and wiping her blade while he stared at me. "You have everything to prove."

I threw up my hands, took my bowl and spoon over to a little irrigation ditch to wash them, and got ready for sleep. The men all avoided me as they doused the fire and sought their own bedrolls, except Bellir on watch under the light of the Two Moons. In the dark sky, Calm waned as Madness waxed; the omen was much too fitting for comfort.

The Guards had set up four lean-tos for us in case of rain, one each for me and Pen and two for themselves. I rolled myself in my own blanket under the canvas and pointedly turned my back on Pen.

He could run me through in my sleep, if his honor would allow it, but I'd be damned if I was going to let him think he worried me.

Before I'd quite finished listing Pen's sins and well before I got to sleep, a scent of cinnamon came to me. Terrell spoke inside my head.

*Kirin?*

*What?* I growled.

*Something's troubling you.*

*Pen,* I answered shortly. *His damn sword looked at me tonight, so he had to be a prick about it.*

Terrell winced at my description of Irreneetha. I was too resentful to care.

*He keeps jabbing me with words,* I grumbled. *I've put up with it for four days already and I'm getting mighty damn tired. Worst of it is, I can't even let him pick a real fight with me. I'd kill him, and then you'd be sad forever, and I couldn't stand that.*

He was quiet for a while, just nestled there inside my mind. Usually that made me squirm, but tonight it was weirdly comforting. When I was little, the woman I'd called Mama had held me much like that. Though dead for over a decade, she was still more real to me than my actual birth mother.

*You know Pen was raised with me as my foster-brother,* Terrell began.

*Yeah, you told me he was a cradle-substitute for me when Mother feared our sweet-tempered stepbrother would find a way to kill us both—which Osrick thought he did, with me.* I scowled. The craziness in my birth-sire's family could scare me spitless when I thought about it too much. *Why are you bringing that up now?*

*Pen spent his growing-up years thinking of you as a tragedy safely in the past, and at the same time trying to live up to the role he thought you were meant to play in the Dynasty. Brother and shield to me. He built himself around it.*

*Yeah, yeah, so Pen got to grow up in a palace and even got a fancy sword out of the deal. Meanwhile I ended up abandoned in a gutter. If the DiUmbras hadn't taken me in I would have died for real. And somehow I'm to blame for him getting the sweet end?*

*You're sure he's blaming you?* Terrell's mind-voice was soft. *Or might he be envying you?*

*Envy? The virtuous Sir Penghar, the noble, the chaste, stooping to commit a sin as mundane as envy? Surely not.*

*Be as sarcastic as you want, but think about it. He was my most trusted* *companion, my only agemate and confidant, for eighteen years. Then you appeared, dripping Shadows, talking and acting like the antithesis of nobility. It must have shocked him when I elevated you out of the gutter and into the Old Order. I probably stunned him even more when I made you one of my Hands. To his eyes, you're the first stranger I ever gave my trust to, and he doesn't know or understand why. I should have foreseen that would make him feel threatened.\**

*\*Threatened? Salim's Tail, I've been bending over backwards to avoid threatening him!\**

*\*Kirin, he's feeling hurt and can't allow himself to admit it.\**

*\*So he turns himself into a big prick instead?\**

*\*Inelegant phrasing, but essentially correct.\**

I ground my teeth. *\*And you want me to just put up with his dung?\**

*\*Please. I haven't asked you two to work together before, it'll be grating on him too. Give him time to get used to you, time to see you as a man and not a symbol. Time to become your friend too.\**

*\*Aauugghh!\** I almost groaned out loud. *\*I don't want to be his friend! I want to knock his teeth in!\**

*\*Which would give you a little ephemeral pleasure at the cost of cut knuckles. Please, Kirin; give him time.\**

I grumped some more but finally promised to try to befriend the arrogant sonofabitch. Why do I let Terrell talk me into these things?

~ * ~

I tried. I really did.

And I succeeded pretty well for two whole days. I was polite; I was friendly to the Horse Guards and obedient when Pen rapped out orders. And his orders weren't even stupid, most of the time. The couple that were, well, I gritted my teeth and obeyed anyway, mostly.

Our route had turned west and started climbing the long road to Narvi. The dry foothills of the Bright Mountains rose around us as the road began to imitate a snake, bending back and forth across grassy slopes dotted with cedar and rosemary. Startled deer bounded away, shepherds minded flocks, and sheepdogs barked at us with no respect for our ranks. Sometimes we threaded the edges of sharp canyons where roaring streams cut their way down to the flats. The hot valley air thinned, became cleaner and colder. The distant peaks drew closer.

That mountain-road was only lightly travelled. Spring lay behind us and the Fanged Pass had been open for a month. All the pent-up caravans waiting for the snows to melt had long since passed through. The manure they left behind bred clouds of flies to plague us. It was a relief to climb into true forest.

Then it rained.

Thick-needled deodar cedars crowded the curving road and dripped on the stones, the horses, and us. Clouds dimmed the Two Suns overhead and we could barely see a hundred feet. Pen led and I'd just swapped into the middle after a turn at tail. The grade was gentle, so we were all riding at a canter, fast enough that when we rounded a bend it was a surprise to find a stopped wagon.

The bandits massacring its riders were almost as surprised as us.

Smart bandits would have kept a better watch. Smarter ones would have run before we got within reach. These were more brave than smart.

There's nothing wrong with Pen's wits. He had drawn Irreneetha before the first bandit shouted warning. Her white light glared, which meant she had no doubt evil was being committed before our eyes. I saw two uniformed guardsmen bleeding in the road with six ragged men worrying them like wolves. In the wagon a youth with an arrow in his shoulder failed to parry the gut stroke that killed him an instant later. A graybeard sprawled on the wagon-bench, another arrow in his chest and a ragged man cutting a ring from his finger.

"Surrender to the Crown's Justice!" Pen shouted, but their blood was up from the killing. They growled at us and raised their weapons instead.

Pen leveled his blade and yelled "Attack!" even as the bandits' lone archer drew and shot. The arrow flicked at us and a beam of light from the sword met it in midair. Splinters and feathers drifted toward the ground.

We were six to their ten. They fought on foot with knives, clubs, spears, and a bow. We answered from horseback with swords, Light, and Darkness.

The Horse Guards drew their blades and pressed forward. I filled my left hand with Shadow and hurled it into the archer's face. He staggered as inky night plastered his eyes. When it flowed up his nose, he dropped the bow and screamed as he tore at his face. I filled my right hand with more Shadow and drew my sword in my left, then urged Handsome forward with my knees.

I threw the second Shadow at a spearman before he could stab Cantin. I hit the bastard's face off-center, but still half his world went dark. His thrust went awry and Cantin didn't give him a second chance.

Irreneetha blazed in Pen's hands like a splinter of Sun. A black-toothed thug with a bloody longknife leaped off the wagon right at him. Pen's glowing blade split the man's head to his breastbone. Red ruin dropped into the mud as Pen pivoted his horse and slashed at another bandit. Irreneetha was an arc of light and a club-man drop-ped, headless. A young spearman gaped as the point of his weapon spun away from the shaft, then Pen's return stroke removed the boy -bandit's own head.

A knife-wielding scarecrow came at me from my right side, where my blade had the least reach. I signaled Handsome to pivot under me and he lashed out with a hoof that sent the man toppling. Gerdon stabbed downward as he passed me, and his own horse trod on the body. I grabbed more Shadow and flung it at another bandit, then charged Handsome toward the archer. The man scraped my Shadow from his eyes, squatted down to pick up his bow, and real-ized I was too close. He came up snarling with a longknife in each hand.

Never threaten a battle-steed or his rider unless you're riding one yourself.

Handsome kicked again and grazed the bandit. The man stag-gered and dropped one knife. Then I jabbed my sword into him. It grated on metal; he had a breastplate under the rags. He slashed at me with the other blade. I barely parried it as I passed. Then he was behind me and Handsome bucked into a tremendous back-legs kick. This time the blow was no graze. I heard bones break and the man squealed like a dying rabbit.

Then it was over. Two bandits broke from the pack, trying to run. One went straight up the road and got maybe ten strides before Pen rode him down. The other ran downhill into the woods and we lost him.

I urged Handsome over to the wagon, climbed in to see if any-thing could be done for the two riders. It was hopeless. Blood spattered the boy's lips. The bandit's longknife had stabbed high enough to pierce a lung. The lad tried to speak, spraying me with the last of his life, and then went still. He had the barest suggestion of a beard, not even old enough to shave yet. I made the Sign of the One over him, grieving. I didn't know what kind of man he might have been becoming but he'd fought valiantly to defend the oldster.

That one was also dead. The arrow missed his lungs but split his heart. By the resemblance between him and the boy I thought he must be the youth's father. There was gray in his brown hair and wrinkles on his face, I judged him past forty but not quite fifty. His hands were remarkably smooth but ink-stained; a scribe. He had dual white scars in his sideburns, the cuts that mark a Silbari widower.

My heart squeezed within me. I had cut myself the same way not two years ago and knew how little the ritual helped. Maia's memory hammered me while I closed his staring eyes and made the Sign again. "Go find her," I whispered.

Pen rode back to us. "Any still alive?" he demanded.

"Not here," I answered bitterly. "We were too late."

"Bellir?" Pen's voice rapped out.

That horse guard answered, his hands busy with one of the bandits sprawled against a tree. The sword-stroke that removed half the man's right arm left an opened artery that spurted into the mud. "This wound will kill him, milord, but he's got a few minutes left."

"Good!" I snarled as I vaulted out of the wagon and dropped to my knees beside Bellir. "He'll spend them talking!"

And I poured out the Shadow that lives inside me, split the Skin of the World beneath the bandit, and bared his soul to Hell.

"Speak!" I roared as I dangled him over the long fall that lies beneath the illusion on which we stand. Bellir scrambled away in terror. "Why did you attack these men?"

The bandit's eyes were white all the way around and he'd already fouled himself in his pain. The new terror on his face bit me like a viper.

"The Narvi mine payroll," he gibbered. "He's the pay-clerk! Money's in the cart! With that much gold I could pay off the others and get me and my boys a farm again!"

"Your boys?" I stared at his weathered face, looked around at the heaped corpses. The head of a bandit Pen had beheaded lay nearby, staring at me. The features were a match. "So you're a family of bandits?"

"No!" The man wailed. "I lost my land to Duke Anagni! He threw us off so's he could put my fields into horse-pasture! Turned me and my three boys out on the road. We couldn't get work in the mines, had to beg." He ran down as his life leaked away. "Better to turn robber than watch my boys starve." Then his voice died with his heart as the red flow stopped. I felt his soul depart between my fingers.

I let the Skin of the World close under him, set his shoulders gently down on the chill ground, and closed his eyes. I sat there numb for a moment with my Shadow pooled about my knees. I was no stranger to the desperation that could overcome a poor man's scruples when the survival of his family was at stake. Two men and their sons.

It took me a while to remember where I was, another to realize the rain had stopped. The four Guards had drawn away from me. They stood in a rough line staring at me, hands on their swords— two drawn, two not, and Penghar astride his horse behind them with Irreneetha at the ready.

Painfully, I forced the Shadow back inside me, drawing it in through my skin. The fourth Guard, Darbin, spat an oath and drew his sword. That made three facing me in addition to Pen's angel. Cantin's grip tightened on his own hilt, but he didn't quite draw.

"Evil sorcery?" Bellir half-asked, half accused, trembling so badly his sword-point twitched in circles.

"No," I told him. Then I forced myself to my feet, swaying a little. Using my Shadow has a cost not measured in gold. "Never that. Terrell—no." My brother had saved me from that deadly temptation, not the least of the reasons why I choose to serve him.

I curbed my traitor tongue and drew my head up to face them proudly. My ring glinted in the weak sunslight. "I am the Left Hand of King Terrell, the rightful bearer of the crown of Silbar. I gave him my oath freely, as did you all. And by that oath I will live and die."

I raked them all with my eyes. All four guards flinched. It is no small thing in Silbar to wear my brother's badge. Pen met my gaze unblinking for a long moment, and then glanced aside at Irreneetha.

The soul-sword's light had dimmed once the last bandit died;

now it faded out entirely. Before she went back to being merely an insanely sharp sword, she looked at me once again, and this time I thought I saw cool approval.

Pen blinked, frowned, and slowly sheathed her.

"Let's get busy," he grunted. "Collect the bodies. We'll use the wagon to haul them to Narvi. If this really is the payroll clerk, somebody there needs to be chewed out for letting him travel with only two guards and a boy."

I bent down and lifted the dead bandit-leader first.

~ * ~

The wagonload of bodies slowed us. We had to tie on some of our remounts to get it over the rougher places in the road. It took another day and a half of brutal work to reach Narvi perched on its mine-riddled cliff. Pen pushed us hard, and I didn't even mind, much. The dead were a burden on our spirits.

When night caught us, we had to camp on the roadside. We set fires around us to discourage the beasts drawn by our bloody cargo. As usual, Pen cleaned Irreneetha's sheath while the Guards set up camp. It's downright unnatural how picky he is about caring for her.

The skies threatened rain again. I didn't look forward to spending a night wet and cold in the company of corpses.

I used one of our canvas shelters to cover the bodies stacked like cordwood in the wagon. We had set the bandits on the left and their victims on the right, but the jolting trip had thrown them together. After I lashed the canvas down in the flickering firelight I leaned on the wood with my hands on the cloth. I let my Shadow seep out through my palms and poured it over the corpses. I commanded it to slay the small-lives already beginning to feast on the cold flesh; that would delay the rot for a while. It was dark, I thought I was being discreet, but Pen caught me at it.

"What are you doing?" he asked me quietly as he stepped up to my side, for once sounding like he actually wanted to know. He held Irreneetha unsheathed while he polished her with an oiled cloth, not threatening me but just there between us. Her blade winked in the firelight, the steel marked by ripples that drew the eye inward and inward.

"This'll stop them from stinking for a little while," I grunted, letting my Shadow flee back inside me. It didn't like being close to

Irreneetha. "Until they can be put in the ground. It's the only dignity I can give them."

"The bandits don't deserve dignity." Pen scowled at the canvas.

"All men deserve dignity. Not enough get it."

Pen jerked his chin a little at that, gave me an odd look. His hands stopped polishing Irreneetha. She gleamed in the firelight, just a dappled piece of steel—until her face looked at me again. Those ghostly eyes, like pools beyond the World.

I still didn't know what to say to her.

I went to the cook-fire, ate more trail-stew served by Bellir who watched me with too-large eyes, washed my bowl and spoon, and went to my bedroll. Pen and I had to share the third shelter tonight and it was barely large enough. I put my back to his bedroll, not caring to watch him at his prayers. It had been more than a year since I could pray to the One God without bitterness. But I couldn't shut out the quiet mumble of his voice, counterpoint to the drizzle beginning to tap on the canvas overhead.

He finished and paused, kneeling with Irreneetha between his palms.

"Do you ever pray?" his quiet voice asked. I could barely hear him over the rain.

I was so startled I sat up and stared at him in the close confines of the canvas. He stared back at me, chiseled perfection in the flickering light of the smoky guard-fires. Even when he's slogged through mud, he's still a goddamned perfect statue. There was nothing in his face but a curiosity that was more infuriating for being calm and reasonable.

"Not anymore," I finally said.

"Why not?" His eyes were on me, steady, just waiting. So were Irreneetha's.

I held up one hand, palm uppermost, and filled it with Shadow till darker-than-darkness dripped between my fingers. With a thought I shaped it into a sword of night balanced on my palm and reaching for the Moons, then let it collapse into a roiling mess of chaos.

"Since I figured out it was the God of our ancestors who stuck me with carrying *this* around."

The Shadow dribbled down my forearm and quickly vanished back inside me, fleeing Irreneetha. Pen remained rock-still as I closed my fist on the last of the Shadow and took it all within once more, but his eyes had white all around the edges.

"That's why I don't pray. Good night, my lord Sir Penghar Veryhs DiLione." I hoped my voice dripped with more sarcasm than my hand dripped Shadow. At least, I meant it to be sarcasm. I'm too strong to show pain in front of Pen.

I rolled over and pulled my blanket back around me against the mountain chill. I wondered if he'd take this chance to drive her blade through my unprotected back. Wondered what would happen when the Angel met my Shadow inside me. Would I die? Would she? Would he?

By The One, I was feeling morbid tonight. The thirteen bodies in the wagon were cold and silent, but I could sense them individually. Thirteen lives, now thirteen lumps of meat. Somewhere in the forest a wolf howled. I heard the Horse Guard on watch add more wood to the fires.

Then soil crunched as Pen thrust the soul-sword's blade into the ground between us. I didn't have to roll over to know the Angel was looking at me still.

"Your mind is a lonely place, Sir Kirin DiUmbra," he said quietly.

Pen rolled himself in his blankets and was snoring in minutes. I silently cursed him as the night wore slowly on. It was a long time before the rain finally gave me sleep.

~ * ~

We delivered the wagon to the civil authorities of Narvi. A scribe at the City House took our testimony. Most of the bandits were unknowns; never reported before. The Magistrate guessed they were landless men who must have recently drifted in. I confirmed that based on the dying words of the bandit chief. No one mentioned how I'd extracted that confession, but I felt anew the wretched man's desperation like a sickness in my stomach. Every soul that touches my Shadow makes a mark on mine.

With two King's Hands involved there'd be no official questions about their deaths, but one of the dead guards left a widow and daughter who'd have to be told. Pen handled that while the rest of us waited, dirty and bruised, outside a neat little house in the wan sunshine. It was the first time in the whole trip I was grateful to him. The daughter was shocked, and then wept; the widow just wept. My heart ached for them. Pen spoke quiet words. I don't know what they were, but I hoped they helped.

Then we took the payroll to the mine and Pen delivered a couple hundred words of stern reprimand for the mine manager, which made me feel a little better. Though in his place I'd have been more bitter and angry.

"And one more thing," Pen added. "See his widow gets a pension sufficient to support her."

My brows must have climbed. I hadn't expected that thoughtfulness from him and had been preparing to demand it myself. Terrell would approve. Pen saw my expression and his own face went wooden. He brushed past me and I let it go.

Only then could we head off to get lodging. The Two Suns were descending the sky and tomorrow we had to find a murderous mage.

Narvi Abbey stood near the mines, a walled enclave of peace next to its famous hospital filled with pain. The mines yield a harvest of injured men as well as copper and iron. Pen pounded on the entry gate and showed his badge and ring. The porter let us in at once and took us to their guesthouse.

"My lords, Her Grace the Abbess will be pleased to welcome you at supper after evening devotions," the man told us with practiced deference.

"Not while we stink like this," I protested. We were all still filthy from travel and bloody from fighting. "Where can we get clean first?"

"The bathhouse is through that door and down the corridor, milords," the porter told us while he and a groom took our horses. "The attendants on duty will see to your laundry as well."

"Good Seraphs bless you!" I said, and meant it, as I heaved my pack onto my shoulders. The rest grabbed their own and followed me.

We were all relieved to wash up and then soak in a hot pool fed by springs issuing straight from the mountainside. Pen had Irreneetha with him while the attendants cleaned her sheath and our clothes. I'd never seen her more than arm's reach away from him. He laid her lengthwise on the rock rim of the pool and leaned his head back against the flat of the blade, eyes shut. Water didn't seem to touch her, and a soul-sword won't cut its bearer. I was glad the angel had hidden her face from me. It would be damned unnerving to be naked in front of her. Then it dawned on me clothes are no defense against the eyes of a being who can read your soul.

Then I tried not to think about that.

"Five hunnerd miles 'n eight days, 'thout killin' any horses!" Cantin boasted for all of us. "Bards'll sing 'bout this journey!"

"Ifn we live," Gerdon answered dourly, slouching down until his graying mustache floated. He was the eldest of Pen's Guards and seemed to distrust everything.

"Don' be fergettin' that Dragon-castin' mage," Bellir reminded us.

"Keep quiet about that," Pen ordered, his eyes still closed. "I'll tell the Abbess myself, but no-one else is to know why we're really here. Keep your tongues still and your ears open while you eat and drink. If anyone in the Abbey or the town tells you about a new mage or other stranger in the area, I want to hear it."

"We'll find out more and faster by asking questions," I pointed out.

"And maybe alert our enemy that we're coming. This could be our only chance to stop him before he attacks. I don't want him to retreat and make his move somewhere else."

"Pen. If Terrell's Right and Left Hands riding into town isn't enough to spook him, a few questions won't do it."

He opened his eyes and stared at my skin, my hair, my ears. "You don't know that—and if you've been heeding Desirey The Temptress, remember She's the Queen of Lies."

I bit my tongue while fighting down the temptation to choke him for that insult. The others looked at me uneasily.

"Enough lazing around. Let's get presentable and call on our host," he added, climbing out of the water.

~ * ~

Dona Lucida D'Ivor Galidi, the Abbess of Narvi, was a round little woman with the five stars on her wimple that marked her as a Quintissima in the Temple hierarchy. She wore her authority like an old and well-used glove. She met us in the Abbey's Great Hall, which was plain as a barn. I guessed Narvi Abbey wasn't the most well-endowed institution, but nobody there looked like they'd ever missed a meal. We made proper bows, civil authority to a religious, proffered our badges and rings, and formally claimed shelter for the night. I held out my own ring first for her inspection, beating Pen to it, and he tensed a little but said nothing. I thought her bright eyes caught it nonetheless.

The Abbess opened her cellars and storerooms to wine and dine her knightly visitors in style. Acorn-fed ham, trout cooked in wine and dusted with chopped pine-nuts, egg-and-mushroom pie, all of it excellent. The pleasant Cerrai vintage served with the meal was a treat by itself. I could get used to eating and drinking like that. Below the salt I could see the Horse Guards were being fed well too, and talking to servants and workers at the hospital. Abbey and Hospital ran a common kitchen and ate together.

Afterwards Dona Lucida took me and Pen aside to a private sitting-room overlooking a cloistered garden watered by the over-flow from the hot springs. There she served us more wine in silver-chased cups—and got straight to the point.

"When the Right and Left Hands of the King come calling, it's not because they want to admire my herb-garden," she observed. "What does His Majesty want of me, my lords? And what do you each want?" She looked back and forth between us, eyes needle-sharp in a face otherwise bland as milk-custard. To her credit, her eyes didn't linger on the markers of my half blood. Of course, with her rank she'd probably have been present at Court for Terrell's formal accession to Silbar's throne and would know firsthand the evidence of his own half-blood. But a lot of people give royalty a pass nobody else gets. It was a nice change to have that extended to me.

The food and wine had mellowed me. I generously decided Pen could speak first and waved a hand to show I deferred to him. He told her our mission using that clipped spare voice of his that makes even disaster and slaughter sound mundane.

"And so, Dona, we fear a powerful mage could be planning to waylay travelers on the road," he concluded. "And the tax caravan is coming."

Her face had become grim. "Your warning fits well with two things we learned only today. Smoke from a fire was sighted on the pass by a fast courier riding from the Vettore. He didn't stop, think-ing it a campfire left unattended that set a patch of forest alight. But it was burning among the Spires and nobody camps in that cold place by choice."

"Spires, Dona?" I asked. "Is that another name for the Fanged Pass?"

"No, the two mountains called the Fangs straddle the pass itself," she explained, searching through a big flat leather case. "The Spires are a group of rocks a little lower down on our side, north of the road. One of my nuns has a gift for sketching—and here it is."

She handed us a large paper covered with charcoal strokes enspelled to prevent smudging. I tamped down hard on my Shadow to keep it from devouring the magic, and let Pen hold the paper while I leaned on the arm of my chair and looked over his elbow. The image was amazingly lifelike, down to the fine strokes of willow branches along the stream at the bottom. What it showed was forbidding, a sprawl of big stones separated by passages wandering deep into the mountainside. The taller ones were flat-topped while shorter spires came to rough points or rounded caps. There was a crowd of them, more than I could easily count even if I took off my boots and Pen's too. A tiny horse in the foreground gave perspective. The whole was wider than some cities.

"The road is on the near side of that stream and follows it for two miles and more," she continued, pointing. "You can see how the Spires make an enormous maze. Most are ten times and more the height of a tall man. Some of the passages are broader than this room but many are barely wide enough to enter. Others become caves, and nobody knows how far into the mountains they run."

"Nobody?" I wondered aloud. "No shepherd seeking a lost sheep ever explored the place? No adventurous miner-lads from Narvi daring each other to go the farthest into a dark passage?"

She scowled. "Quite possibly, but they never reached the end or did not return. You have not seen the place, or heard of it, Sir Kirin. Our mines are quiet and still, we sanctify them every week to keep them so. After our hospital, it is this Abbey's chief duty. The Spires are larger and more rugged than all the mines of Narvi put together. Shades of the dead get caught in the twisting passages, moaning their distress. Listening to them for long is very unwise, as their voices carry madness and they do not love the living. In past times there have been darker things, possibly driven out of the mine-deeps by our sanctifications. Some foolish folk claim ancient giants built the Spires, though they show no mark of chisel or maul.

If giants did build it, they left a spiritual cesspit too large for me and mine to ever clean completely. Caravans know to stay on the road and pass it quickly. Whatever evil finds its way there is contained; more than that we cannot do."

Pen frowned. "So this place is a sort of shadow trap?"

She nodded. "I have heard it called that, yes, Sir Penghar. It is a part of my duties as Abbess to go there twice a year and banish whatever may lurk in the nearest passages, to keep the road safe. Safer. I go in spring and autumn; I did the spring cleansing only a fortnight ago."

Her lips twisted in distaste. "There was a particularly vicious shade this year, a cutthroat who'd been trapped there by last winter's storms. He was eventually reduced to eating the bodies of his victims before the cold finally slew him. A vile man who made a disgusting shade, but thanks be to The One I was able to put it down. I can only hope it didn't leave any company back in the deeper passages where I could not reach."

"From your lips to the Good Seraphs' ears, Dona," Pen muttered while making a pious gesture. "If a Mage was strong enough not to need worry about shades, he could hide in there and none would dare follow."

"No one from Narvi." She looked from his badge to mine and only then did her eyes travel to my face, my ears. "You, perhaps, might be bolder." Her gaze flicked to Irreneetha slung at Pen's hip, and back to my own knives and sword. "And better armed. I cannot give you better counsel than this. Be very careful."

"Thank you, Dona," I answered. "But you mentioned two things? What was the other?"

She looked bleak now. "The courier passed a small caravan just starting down from the pass. It should have been here by now, but there's no sign of it."

Pen and I looked at each other. "It might be advisable," he said heavily, "To pray for them. We'll need to depart by dawn." He handed the drawing back, stood and bowed formally. I gulped the last of my wine and hurried to do the same.

"Fresh provisions will be ready," she promised, showing us out. "My prayers will go with you."

"It seems pretty clear," I said to Pen as we walked back to the guesthouse through dim moonlight. "Our mage has a perfect ambush site he can use to attack travelers on the road. I'm amazed no bandit gang has set up there before. They could charge a hell of a toll."

"And bring the Crown's displeasure down on their heads." Pen touched Irreneetha at his side. "As this mage has done before he starts. Yet anyone powerful enough to attempt this should be smart enough to know we would respond quickly, and relentlessly. Is taking even the tax caravan worth being hunted by all the might of Silbar?"

I nearly missed a step. "You're joking, right? It's seven hundred thousand gold royals and a couple tons of silver!"

"And how does he cart it away afterwards?"

I stopped and stared at him. We were in the courtyard just outside the guest house. "Err…the easy way would be to use the same mules." I thought again about the vision Terrell had shared with me. "But that's not what this guy's planning, is it? Most of the mules will die with the men."

Pen gave me a sardonic look. "You did pay attention to Terrell's brief. Answer me this, then; even if this mage takes the caravan intact, where does he take it afterwards? Between here and the Vettore foothills, there's no side-roads, not even a side-trail big enough for such a large packtrain. Nothing but raw cold mountains for a hundred miles north and south—and this one road."

I thought it over. "I don't know." Irritated, I spit back, "What do *you* think he'll do?"

"My Lord of the Shadows, I don't know either. And that worries me even more than you do."

I glowered at him while my mind raced. Fly it away? All the mages of Silbar couldn't lift that much metal into the skies. A hidden bunch of henchmen waiting with packhorses? How'd such a mob get here without causing gossip from one side of the range to the other?

"Dung," I growled. "Maybe he's just crazy."

"That'd almost be a relief. Let's hear what my men discovered over dinner and drink."

~ * ~

Darbin shook his head to Pen's question. "No Sir, no word at all of anyone strange goin' through; only t'usual caravans run by t'usual drivers. Mayhaps t'Mage is hidin' out among t'passengers, but there weren't many this season and nobody spoke 'bout anybody unusual catchin' their eye."

"Milords, t'mage we're hunting coulda come up t'other side of the pass," Cantin pointed out. "If he rode with only a few trusted men, nobody on this side'd know."

"Or if he came in t'missing caravan and killed t'rest of 'em," Bellir suggested ghoulishly. "Might be he's a blood-mage who needs murder to make 'is magic work?" His eyes glanced toward me and then darted away. "Sounds loike there's a hunnerd places up there t'hide bodies."

"A shepherd's missin' and 'is flock too—forty sheep," Gerdon told us, hiccupping slightly. "Missin' four days now— 'is mother's been askin' everybody if they've seen 'im. 'Sposed to be grazing just this side of a place called Sp...Spa...Spires." He belched—he'd taken the 'drink' part of Pen's instructions literally.

"The bastard is stocking up," I muttered. "Maybe that 'missing' caravan was him and his own men. How many might we be facing?"

"Good question." Pen jerked his chin at the Horse Guards. "Anything else?"

Gerdon shrugged. "A hunter sez he saw a giant snake in t'woods, would've et him if he hadn't run. Said it broke grown tree-trunks loike twigs."

"Another said he saw giant bats carry t'snake off." Cantin mimed something swooping out of the sky, grinned. "I tink dey were drinkin' together."

"One of t'mines is got Kobolts." Darbin made the Sign against evil; the malicious little cavern-spirits were a famous danger to miners.

"No, it was Niccles," Bellir objected. "Makin' the ore turn tough so's it won't smelt."

"No, it was Kobolts," Darbin argued.

"Enough." Pen shook his head. "Everybody get some sleep. In the morning we hunt for a killer mage. Make sure your weapons are sharp and our best horses are ready. We'll take one remount each, leave our weakest mounts here."

~ * ~

The guesthouse room assigned to me was tucked up under the

eaves, facing west. The Moon of Madness bathed the high spine of the Bright Mountains in silver light that set ice and snow to glowing.

*Brother,* I called across the miles, curled on a hard guest bed with two thick blankets to keep the cold night at bay. *Are you there?*

*Always,* Terrell answered.

Cinnamon and silk—he lay in his own bed in the Palace. I felt the sultry Valley air on his skin, the hot exhalation of the heart of Silbar through his high windows, the humid scents of growing things twined around and through a breath of desert dust. In the Arisen City the spring rains were past and summer begun, but up here winter hadn't quite released its grip.

*I knew you must be close to your target,* he added. *I hoped you would reach out to me tonight.*

*We're almost there. Tomorrow morning we'll be at the Pass.* I brooded. I wasn't afraid, exactly—I walked with danger every day, I didn't fear it—but something gnawed at me like a rat undermining a foundation.

*What's wrong, Kirin?* His mind-voice whispered.

*I don't know; but something is. We've missed something, me and Pen both; maybe you too.* I told him Pen's question and we chewed it over to no better result. *Have you Seen any more?*

*It's not like a book I can open to read another passage.* I could feel him shrug in the darkness. *I shared the whole vision with you, and described it to Pen in all the detail I could manage.*

*Share it with me again.*

He opened that memory-place inside his skull to me, unhesitating—by the One God, I felt like a plunderer for asking. The wings, the scales, the fear, the fire; the deep bass voice laughing in joy at the slaughter, echoing the terrible word MINE! Then pain and tears, broken men in flight, and fire.

So short, so little to go on! If I were watching it in truth my unique senses could maybe wring out more knowledge. But I was confined to what Terrell had been able to sense and remember, and my talents weren't his. I balled my hands into fists beneath the blankets.

*I wish I could see this damn mage,* I grumbled. *See how he's conjuring that dragon. See what he plans to do! Damnit, I don't even know where he's standing!*

*I've thought about that. It can't be anywhere close to the caravan. My* men would have had a chance to see him, and at least a few of my archers would have made the connection when the dragon appeared, and then they'd have shot the man. But he can't be completely out of sight either. A conjuration can't have enough free will to choose its own targets the way that dragon did; he has to be actively guiding it. At a guess, he's overlooking the battlefield somehow, concealed enough to see without being seen. I wonder if he's also using an actual concealment spell?*

*I hope he is. It'd be like a beacon to me.* I remembered the Abbess's sketch; at least a dozen of the rock towers in it were visible in Terrell's vision, hazy and indistinct but indisputably there, and empty. That left dozens more he could be perched atop. Some were too sheer to climb quickly, but then, I didn't necessarily have to climb them to reach the tops.

He followed my thoughts. *How far can you throw your Shadows?*

*I don't know—seventy, eighty feet? I've never tried for serious distance.*

*Tomorrow you may have to.*

*Urk.* A little voice down inside me was screeching panic. *I'm going into a fight half-blind!*

*It's not that bad. I questioned my mages here. To animate a construct the size of his dragon would take two full ingots of silver or more, at least twenty pounds. The instant he starts burning that off, you'll see him.*

*There's that.* I was cheered. Power-manipulation on this scale couldn't exactly be hidden under a bushel. Not from my eyes.

*I'm sure you'll find him, Kirin, and when you do, point Pen at him. No spells will take Pen down, not while he's holding Irreneetha. If you can keep the mage distracted long enough for Pen to get near him, it'll all be over but the funeral.*

That was an even more heartening thought. Pen, actually being good for something besides aggravation.

*Get some sleep, brother.*

His ghost voice faded. I pulled the blankets closer and let the night lull me to sleep. If there were dreams, I didn't remember them.

In the morning I irritated Pen by delaying us until I could get a nice long piece of rope and a couple hooks. Fortunately, the Abbey stables had the perfect thing at hand and let me take it. We rode hard in pre-dawn mists to make up the lost minutes, climbing up the winding road through never-cut forests while our horseshoes rang on the rocks. Deodars gave way to pines that gave way to firs. Patches of old snow lurked on north-facing slopes. Our breath smoked in dawn's fire. The air held a clarity I'd never seen in Silbar's dusty Valley.

The mountainside suddenly opened into a big bowl. Waterfalls cascaded off snowfields topping the peaks that cupped it. Little lakes scattered jewel-like, feeding streamlets that merged as they neared us and finally roared over a huge waterfall into a canyon at our feet. On the far side the thin thread of the road appeared between two immense fangs of rock. It arced down into the basin to follow the largest stream towards us, passing along the feet of gray monoliths.

The Spires filled better than half the bowl. Naked rock sparsely flecked with life and ringed by lush meadows and a few stunted patches of forest. Red-bud willows fringed the creek. Though the chill morning air was loud with the sounds of water, I heard no birds.

Pen looked at me. He knew what I could do. As if the words hurt him, he ground out, "What do you see?"

I let my Shadow rise into my eyes, and I *looked*.

The Bones of the World are close to the surface in the Bright Mountains, and the World-Skin is stretched tight. There is little Power in the landscape, but what there is runs right across the surface in tiny naked veins. In my gaze the Spires faded to dirty glass, and I found a hot glow inside them.

"He's already started casting," I said and pointed. "Fourth or fifth canyon, I can't tell from here. There's a spell building in there now. We have to get closer."

If building was the right word. It had an oddly dreamy feel to it, that glow, like nothing I'd ever seen before. Not building, exactly, but more like...breathing.

"Find us a way in," Pen ordered.

I heeled Handsome gently. I'd learned not to use spurs on him, he was cantankerous enough by nature. We rode forward, cautious; the road was patched with grit and mud left by the winter and laced by stringers of grass bursting out of thicker windrows of old manure and black soil. Once we passed a rusty horseshoe, later a bit of shaped wood and desiccated leather. No old campfires. The cold breath exhaled by the Spires warned against staying.

Our road followed the Fang Stream in a vast arc across the face of the pinnacles. Many rose up from the very edge of the water.

Side-streams trickled or gushed out between them. Some creeks had dumped so many rocks into Fang Stream it pooled up behind shallow dams.

A crow croaked. Rushing water ruled the air.

Fourth canyon. "In there," I said, and pointed. "A ways back." I bit my lip, vexed. "It curves too much to tell how far."

We waded Fang Stream, stirring up silt fine as flour. The canyon was broad enough for us to ride two abreast with a little creek zigging crazily across the nearly flat floor. Darbin had a bow at the ready, arrow nocked while he scanned the cliffs and let his horse find its own way. The walls towered forty to sixty feet above our heads. They were cracked and pierced by side-canyons, most little more than slots. The main canyon bent sharply back and forth, often at near-right angles.

At one of these a huge slab of rock twenty or more feet thick had fallen across, turning the canyon into a cave more than a hundred feet long and as much as twenty feet high inside. The far end was partly blocked with broken rock, the near end half-obscured by a grove of trees. There were patches of ice inside.

"The horses stay here," Pen ordered. The creek provided a steady trickle of water, and grass grew along the verge. A few shafts of sunlight reached in from places where the rocks didn't match up. "Cantin, Bellir, tend them."

I didn't care for leaving Handsome behind, but Pen was right. A battle-steed couldn't do much in this narrow warren. I dismounted and loosened his girth a couple notches, so he'd be more comfortable in my absence. He nuzzled me. I stroked his ugly face.

"Stay, boy. See you later."

Then I slid my sword up the baldric and clipped it behind my shoulder so it wouldn't bang against anything. Pen and Gerdon did the same. I slung the bundle of rope I'd borrowed over my head and other shoulder, taking care it didn't foul the draw of my blade. If the mage really was hiding atop a pinnacle, then I might have a way for us to get to him. My Shadow can hide more than just me.

Darbin had a quiver on his back and a recurved bow, Pen bore Irreneetha and his main gauche, Gerdon his sword, and we all wore belt knives. We four pushed forward on foot, scrambling through the upper end of the cave. Pen scowled at the canyon floor, looked from side to side and then at me.

"There's no sign of anyone passing through here recently," he whispered accusingly.

"You didn't ask me to find the path the mage used," I snapped back. "Just a way in. This is a way in."

"Keep your voice down."

I glared at him, my Shadow leaking out my pores. I could feel the glow of the magic ahead of us, a pulsing energy that sawed at my nerves like a drumbeat. It wasn't growing, exactly, but simply waiting. My Shadow churned in my gut, aroused and disturbed by the nearness of so much Power. I let the Shadow fill my skin but held it there, hungry.

Gerdon glanced at my eyes and flinched away from me.

We crept closer, through patches of trees and rock-falls that sometimes choked the passage—and then the canyon bent sharply away from our target. I stopped at the bend and stared at the wall in frustration, pressed my face against it and let my Shadow into the rock. If I could just see through it without alerting the mage!

I strained, the rock before me flickering in and out of my sight, like trying to see through very dirty glass. My Shadow surged in and pulled back, surly from my conflicting commands and frenzied by the pulsing Power so near. But the wall was too thick, and I didn't dare push too hard.

"A way in?" Pen asked in a sardonic whisper.

"He has to be on the other side of this wall, maybe not even fifty feet away," I growled back quietly. Softly I pounded my fists on the stone; we were so close!

I looked up. The fin of rock stood sixty feet high and near-vertical here. The sharp bend of the canyon met it at a right angle, and erosion had left bits of time-smoothed stone in the corner. There wasn't much to hang on to, but with a little luck I could do it.

I tapped my chest, pointed up, mimed climbing and then lowering the rope.

Pen's hand tightened on Irreneetha's hilt, but he nodded grudgingly. "Agreed; go ahead."

I gritted my teeth. I hadn't been asking his permission. I scrambled up the first easy steps, where packed rubble gave me good footing. Then I was facing a sheer wall still over forty feet high. There were cracks, so I tugged off my boots and tossed them down to the others. Then I went up it like the acrobat I am, fingers and toes finding just enough purchase to cling on. Coming back down would be a nightmare, but I had the rope.

I wrapped my Shadow completely over me and inch by inch dragged myself up by my fingertips. The top was ragged as a saw blade. There was a big cleft between two spikes of rock. I clambered into it and found a chute tilting down into the next canyon. The steep-sloping floor was carpeted in rubble and treacherous under my bare feet.

An odd stench rode the air, like the world's biggest stables crossed with a slaughterhouse. Maybe the enemy really was a blood-mage—it could explain the erratic reactions of my Shadow. My stomach churned as I tried not to imagine what lay below me. A breeze made a slow moan. I leaned into the chute to look down, and carefully let my Shadow dissolve the Skin of the World. The stone ridge beneath me turned to ghost-gray glass.

The fifth canyon was deeper and wider than the one we'd come up, the bottom at least seventy feet below. Shining scales came into view, rows upon rows covering great coils and loops lit by internal fire. There was something wrong about them, more solid-looking than the ghost-glass look of the canyon walls themselves. I'd never seen such a major work of live magic up close before.

My heart sank in my gut. He'd already conjured his dragon-construct, and it looked frighteningly real and ready to launch at a moment's notice. We might already be out of time to stop him.

I uncoiled the rope, threw a loop around a stone spur and hooked it to itself. Then I paid out the slack as I leaned forward recklessly to search for the mage. Where was he? The floor of this canyon remained frustratingly hidden, too much rock between me and it. If I thinned the Skin of the World any farther, I risked falling through it myself. I took a few loops of slack rope, stepped deeper into the chute, and leaned out. I was looking straight down now to the shaded canyon floor. Still nothing looked like a man, sleeping or awake. But there were bones, plenty of them, and odd lumps too small to be human.

I'd have to switch strategies. The dragon was a big target, I could hit it easily from here, hopefully disrupt his control over his conjuration and maybe even collapse it to silver dust. That ought to startle him into revealing himself. I gathered Shadow in my free hand, it came reluctantly. My eyes swept the canyon for any movement. He couldn't be far from his creation—

CREATION? WHAT AN AMUSING CONCEIT.

The bass voice rang inside my skull. My hand slipped on the rope, a rock turned under my bare foot, and suddenly I was falling as the chute dumped all its accumulated debris into the canyon at once—including me.

I hit the wall hard, slipped down the rope. Hemp burned my palm and small rocks rained down on me. Then a larger rock hit my right shoulder like a hammer. Pain shot through my arm, my hand spasmed open, and I lost my grip completely.

I fell twice my height before something caught my baldric. The strap burst, flipped me sideways and I fell again. A ledge brought me up short, knocked me outward. A few feet more and I hit talus, rolling wildly down slope to fetch up in weeds. Thyme, grass, dung, and dust. My Shadow had fled within me during the fall. I was wrenched, bruised, scraped, but miraculously unbroken. I levered my face out of the dirt and looked up.

And up. And up.

Scales slid, rocks crashed, and a head bigger than a wagon raised above the coils, swinging against the sky. A pair of forelegs, short in comparison to the long snake-body, and one-two-three-four bat-wings followed by two more short legs. Two eyes large as platters gazed down on me from a reptile face a dozen feet wide and ten yards above me.

My mouth fell open.

The dragon was denser than the World. Shadow laired beneath its scales, Shadow and a hot Fire. My own Shadow shrank small within me, cowed by the awakening of a greater Power.

*M-mage?* My mind stuttered.

Laughter boomed inside my head, threatened to burst my brain.

THERE IS NO HUMAN MAGE HERE, LITTLE SHADOW. YOUR EYES BEHOLD ME, NEW COME TO THIS FAT LAND.

"No mage?" I mumbled weakly, staring up at the living, breathing dragon that reared above me. Its huge, faceted eyes pierced me without effort. I saw myself reflected a hundred times over. I had never felt smaller.

DID YOU IMAGINE MERE CLEVER MONKEYS COULD BRING

INTO BEING ANYTHING HALF AS MAGNIFICENT AS ME?

That voice rang through my mind, not my ears. The monster posed against the sky, a broad golden wedge of a face wreathed in teal tendrils below two twisted black horns longer than I am tall. Scales of ruby, gold, and jet braided a snake-torso thicker than a wine vat. Coils threshed against the rocks as it stretched out, sixty, eighty, maybe a hundred feet long from nose to tail-tip. Its movements churned up bones and dung and scraps of fleece and cloth and mule-hide from the canyon floor. The missing caravan and shepherd would never return home.

YES, YOU SEE I HAVE BROKEN MY FAST RECENTLY, AND WELCOME IT WAS AFTER SUCH A LONG FLIGHT. THE OCEAN IS EXHAUSTING TO CROSS, PERHAPS THAT IS WHY SO FEW OF US EVER HAVE. BUT I DID IT!

I struggled to my knees, bruised and scratched but nothing broken. The rest would heal—if I lived that long. I had lost my sword but still had my belt knife. Unluckily the rope remained caught on the cliffs above me and my boots were hopelessly out of reach. My feet were no soft gentleman's feet, I was used to performing on plank floors and scratchy straw mats, but they weren't hardened to rocks.

PERFORMING? AH, YOU ARE AN ARTIST OF MOVEMENT. HOW DROLL—YOUR INTRODUCTION LACKED SOMETHING IN GRACE! BUT PERHAPS YOU CAN DO BETTER WITH A LITTLE PREPARATION.

Bewildered, I asked the first question that popped into my rattled mind. "Who are you?"

YOUR TINY MIND COULD NOT CONTAIN MY NAME. CALL ME WHAT YOU WILL. I SHALL CALL YOU LITTLE SHADOW, WHICH IS WHAT THE NAME 'DIUMBRA' MEANS.

I jerked in betraying surprise. The monster chuckled like rolling boulders.

AMUSING—AND REMARKABLE HOW EASY IT WAS TO TAKE THAT FROM YOUR MIND. YOUR THOUGHTS FLOW UNGUARDED AS A RIVER. YET SHALLOW TOO, AND THERE IS STRANGELY LITTLE POWER IN YOUR NAME. PERHAPS THAT IS WHY YOU DEFENDED IT SO LIGHTLY? YOU ARE ODDLY LACKING FOR ONE WHO DARES A DRAGON'S LAIR. NOT GROUNDED IN THIS SOIL AS I WOULD EXPECT A CHAMPION TO BE. DO YOU NOT BELONG TO THIS LAND?

That taunt angered me enough to snap back. "Silbar is my

home! What in the Nine Hells are *you* doing here?"

YOU KNOW THE ANSWER TO THAT ALREADY. I WAIT FOR THE GOLD AND THE SILVER THAT EVEN NOW APPROACH BEYOND THIS PASS. I CAN SMELL THEM FROM HERE, A TREASURE WORTHY OF ME.

"Why? What use is wealth to something like you?"

ARE YOU SO IGNORANT OF MY KIND?

It tilted its head slightly, studying me like I might study a fly on a table.

INDEED YOU ARE! THEN IT HAS BEEN FAR TOO LONG SINCE ONE OF US VISITED HERE. CLEAN GOLD FOR MY BED—ROCKS HAVE LITTLE TO RECOMMEND THEM WHERE COMFORT IS CONCERNED. THE FUEL OF SILVER TO STOKE MY FIRES AND SHINE MY SCALES. I AM PARCHED AND HUNGRY FROM MY LONG JOURNEY, BUT BEFORE THIS DAY IS OUT I WILL FEAST WELL.

On silver and Silbari soldiers. I remembered the sick horror of the vision, men and beasts crisping in fire, and felt again Terrell's grief as my own.

HOW YOU SUFFER FOR OTHERS! FOOLISH LITTLE SHADOW. WHAT ARE THEY TO YOU? A LIST OF NAMES, OR EVEN LESS. YOU KNOW ONLY A SINGLE FACE AMONG THEM. AND THEY DISDAIN YOU, DON'T THEY, MONGREL? YOU ARE BARELY AN EDDY IN THEIR RIVER, A CAST-ASIDE BY-BLOW OF FATE WHO CANNOT EVER TRULY BE ONE OF THEM. WHY DO YOU CARE IF I EAT THEM? FOR I WILL. IN TIME I WILL EAT ALL OF THEM! I WILL PLUNDER THIS FAT LAND, PILLAGE ITS HIVES AND LAY WASTE ITS WORKS. THEY CANNOT EVEN HOPE TO RESIST ME!

I fumbled for words. "They're mine—my people, my family, my blood and my tomorrows. They're my Why. I swore an oath to protect them from…from the likes of you."

YOU DECEIVE YOURSELF, AS SO MANY CHAMPIONS DO. YOU ARE NOTHING TO THEM AND LITTLE MORE TO THE ONE WHO SENT YOU. A TOOL TO BE USED AND DISCARDED WHEN YOU BREAK, AS IN TIME YOU MUST.

I forced myself to my feet, bruises forgotten. "Now I know that you lie, worm."

YOU HAVE ENTERTAINED ME WHILE I WAIT FOR MY APPROACHING TRIBUTE, LITTLE SHADOW. ALMOST ENOUGH I COULD FORGIVE YOUR IMPERTINENCE.

Leather wings beat the air, showering me with dust and rank

stench.

But not quite. Begin your performance. The longer you entertain me, the longer you will live.

The jaws opened on a black mouth big enough to swallow a pig whole—and lunged at me.

I dove forward beneath the strike, rolled to my feet and leaped again. Coils threshed as they unwound, and a clawed foot as long as I am tall slammed the dirt bare yards away. I leaped again, using that foot as a step to vault the barrel body as it swept towards me. I hit the far side running and ducked the spike of its long tail as it whipped at my head. This canyon was wider and deeper than the other and had a bigger stream but was no less convoluted. In ten bounds I was around a corner.

A chase! Delightful!

Bass laughter slammed my ears. Rocks cascaded off the walls as the coiled body straightened and bounded forward. Forelegs seized a stone spire behind me. The monster leaped to the canyon wall, covering in one step what took me ten. Hind legs scaled the first ridge and let the sinuous forebody loop up into the sky. Painted by the morning suns, scales glittered ruby and gold. Stones crushed beneath its claws.

Run, little rat! Run!

Fangs parted again and the terrible head lunged down.

I ran, dodging falling rocks as it leaped from side to side right over the canyon. I ducked under a hoary tree and fearsome teeth bit the whole top off. While the dragon spat splinters I ran again, leaping boulder to boulder. The canyon jinked and a fissure opened in the sheer cliff on my right. I ducked inside gasping for breath.

A rat-hole!

It laughed and dropped to the canyon floor, closing in. I searched wildly. The fissure went deep but narrowed fast, I couldn't get more than a few feet from the entrance. But the crack reached far above me into the heart of the ridge, and a dim light filtered down—there was an opening above. I began to climb.

Jaws probed the entrance.

I know you are in there.

I climbed higher, as quietly as I could manage.

I smell you.

A huge purple tongue licked the crevice, probed its depth,

withdrew.

I TASTE YOU ON THE ROCKS.

I climbed higher still, light growing above—the fissure was a natural chimney piercing the ridge.

The tongue returned, this time probing upward. The very tip, like rough leather, just brushed my bare sole. I jerked my foot higher and nearly fell.

AH! YOU SEEK TO BECOME A BAT RATHER THAN A RAT! Laughter again. THINK YOU CAN CLING TO THE CEILING LONG ENOUGH TO EVADE ME?

I pulled myself higher while it settled in the canyon, jaws blocking the entrance and parted in anticipation. Foul breath pumped into the fissure, streamed up past me. I tried to think of nothing but the stone encasing me like a womb, as I strained for the next handhold.

YOU STRUGGLE. I TASTE YOUR SWEAT.

I forced myself higher. Muscles strained while bruises throbbed. Rock banged my head painfully. The shaft was uneven.

I SMELL YOUR FEAR.

The fall below me grew longer as my arms trembled. My abused toes clung to cracks.

YOUR CARAVAN IS HOURS AWAY. YOUR STRENGTH WILL NOT LAST. I CAN WAIT UNTIL YOU DROP LIKE A RIPE FRUIT.

Climb!

WHAT *ARE* YOU DOING?

The shaft widened suddenly. A series of ledges gave new purchase for my feet. Pebbles showered downward as I pushed myself up toward the brightening light. And abruptly I was out, atop the ridge, scraped knees and elbows oozing as I crawled over to the shelter of a spire. The two suns were so bright they hurt.

LIGHT? OH, OF COURSE.

Rocks clattered and crashed in the canyon below me, claws rasped the cliff. The monstrous head rose into view balanced atop an elongated column of body, and I realized the dragon must be nearly standing on its tail with all four feet gripping the cliff-face.

EASILY DONE. It sounded smug.

I squeezed myself back under a flare of my rock spire as fetid breath washed over me—the terrible mouth was scant feet away.

CLEVERLY PLAYED, LITTLE SHADOW. A NIMBLE PERFORMANCE!

"The show must go on," I answered, suppressing a hiss as my raw skin scraped stone. Defiantly I snarled, "I'm not done yet!"

BUT YOU ARE. THE ENDING WAS NEVER IN DOUBT. COME TO ME AND I WILL MAKE YOUR DEATH QUICK.

"You want me? Come and get me!" I bellowed, making the canyon echo.

Its jaws parted and the purple tongue swept forward. I sank my knife in deeply. Black blood spurted over me like fire. It jerked back in surprise, dragging me out of my crevice and almost pulling the blade from my hands. I staggered to my feet as its chin rose and the monster bellowed surprise at heaven. Its throat was exposed. I'd have no better chance. I raised the knife in both hands, ran and leaped.

The hide was scaly even here on the throat, but the scales were small, and my knife found a way through. I slammed the blade in to the hilt with the full weight of my body, and the monster twitched again. But my steel tooth was a mere pinprick embedded in its thick skin.

I barely drew blood.

Then something more made it shudder from hidden tail to the tip of its lashing tongue. Its claws lost their grip, rocks tore loose, and the dragon toppled backwards into the canyon, taking me with it.

The snake-body collapsed into coils to break its fall. I clung to my knife and rode the beast all the way down. I expected to be crushed but instead was bounced free when it hit. I landed in thorn bushes that broke my fall just enough.

The dragon roared flame into the sky, a mind-bending flare of rage and embarrassment that half-blinded me. White Light flared on the canyon floor and black blood flew. Pen had arrived and he and Irreneetha had cut off the end of the dragon's tail while it reached for me.

SHADOW! Thundered a furious voice. YOU TRICKED ME! THERE ARE TWO CHAMPIONS!

*Damn right I did*, I sent back as thorns jabbed me. *Damn right we are.*

DISHONORABLE! I SHALL EAT YOU BOTH AND FORGET YOUR NAMES.

The dragon twisted to regain its feet and a foot almost trampled Pen. He hewed at it and severed a claw. Huge jaws snapped inches away from him, then flamed again. Pen should have been roasted but Irreneetha shielded him in a frail bubble of cool air. Pen ran to the left and sliced a yard-long cut into the monster's side.

The huge head came for Pen again as he dodged and slashed. Black blood sprayed from the dragon's cleft eye as it flung its head up. But then a red glitter appeared at the edges of its wounds. They began to close, blood stopped flowing. The monster had healing power like a Priestess.

Your sting is sharp, knight. Sharper than any I have met before. But not sharp enough. I can absorb a thousand cuts. I need catch you only once.

It groped for Pen with crushing feet. A swing and Irreneetha sent another claw bouncing away. But that snake-body still had terrible speed and strength. A thrashing coil knocked Pen sprawling at the cost of a new slice in the glossy scales. Pen rolled between two big rocks as the dragon raised a coil and slammed it down to crush him. The beast jerked back and revealed another bloody slash in its side. Pen scrambled to his feet and raised Irreneetha again, but now he was limping. He barely dodged the next lunge, only cutting a long gash this time that bled weakly. The red healing-magic immediately began to close the shallow wound.

You tire, champion, it gloated. You may cut me a hundred times more, and I will still recover. Can you?

I still had my knife. Thorns ripped my ears as I tore myself free of the brush and staggered to my feet. Coils twisted and heaved before me. My little blade couldn't pierce those thick scales the way Irreneetha could. But one of Pen's cuts was right in front of me, slowly closing as the Dragon's magic wove the edges shut far faster than a human Priestess could Heal. I took five steps and jammed my knife into the wound until hot blood jetted out. I turned the blade to wedge it inside the cut and then thrust my Shadow in too. The red glitter shrank as my Shadow set its own black teeth into the monster's inner flesh like a leech, sucking life and vitality.

Time almost stopped as Power roared into me. I was not much more than a mosquito to a bull, but my Shadow drank a river of Power from the monster's veins and swelled a hundred-fold. Ruby scales faded to dirty glass around my grip as my gorging Shadow bit deeper and deeper. The red glitter expired as the creature's healing magic died.

I knew then what the beast had forgotten.

Even a Dragon is mortal.

It went into a thrashing spasm. A blow from the coiling torso knocked all the air from my lungs and nearly broke my ribs as it threw me back into the bushes. Though my knife was still stuck deep inside its body, I was not weaponless. My Shadow trailed from the knife back to me, a cable of storm-shot smoke through which poured Power unimaginable. Power to burn me to ash from inside out if I didn't do something with it, and fast.

I shaped Shadow in my hands into a lance twenty feet long and insubstantial as mist. I got my feet under me and stabbed the lance forward and up until the point met the dragon's waving neck—and bore in. I drove the monster's own Power against it, ten times, a hundred times stronger than my own. My shadow-lance sliced deep and released a flood of black blood that smoked where it splashed rocks, thorns, and me. The whole thick center of its body began to turn to glass as my Shadow burrowed in and fed, and fed, and fed.

Aauuuggh! The bellow of shock and pain nearly burst my ears from within, half-blinded me and drove me to my knees. My Shadow-lance shattered but the wound remained. And at that moment Pen slashed the beast once more.

The dragon's head rose against the sky again. It scorched the canyon in a titanic sweep. Once more Irreneetha shed the flame and Pen was not burned, though he staggered, and his next stroke went awry. I shaped another Shadow lance and jammed it into the drag-on's hindquarters; that ought to slow it down. Before I could shape a third one, the stump of tail came around and bowled me over. This time my ribs did crack, pain like ice and fire in my veins.

I lost my grip on my Shadow completely.

It did not drain away when parted from me, not when there was so much Power to eat. Scales faded to glass in a wave that rip-pled down the long spine. Without me to receive the Power my Shadow grew into a monstrous leech, a swelling black bubble on the dragon's side. The beast's hind legs kicked feebly and went still.

Now an arrow appeared in one jeweled eye. Darbin and his bow must be near. Rough hands grabbed me and dragged me away from the titanic struggle. Gerdon had found me.

"Pen!" I gasped, tried to pull away. Red pain flashed across my eyes.

"He was born for this," the old Guard snapped. "Look!"

My vision cleared. Irreneetha was still a white spike in Pen's hands, wheeling and slashing, his legs limping but never still. My crystal wound in the monster's middle spread for yards up and down the torso. The jaws, drooling blood, snapped almost on Pen and he swung again. This time a row of blue tendrils fringing its chin flew free. The head swung like a battering ram to knock Pen sprawling and jaws opened to gobble him whole, but he rolled to his feet and jumped over its nose. Irreneetha's point pierced the other faceted eye. Jaws snapped blindly, trying to catch what the eyes could no longer see.

Scales started to crumble into shards around the growing wound where I'd planted my knife. The middle of its body was translucent now. The monster slammed its upper body down, trying to crush Pen with its blinded mass. Pen dodged death, slashed again, and the beast went into a frenzy of thrashing that knocked him twenty feet.

There came a crack like the biggest crystal goblet in the world, breaking. The glass wound I'd made in its middle snapped clear across. The dragon's hindquarters slumped away but the snaking front writhed on. The head turned toward me, sightless and dripping, and the jaws gaped.

I DO NOT NEED EYES TO FIND *YOU*, SHADOW!

I shoved Gerdon aside and raised my right hand, all my last scraps of Shadow summoned into one tight ball. I hurled it down the monster's looming throat even as flame boiled at me and Pen stabbed Irreneetha deep into the dragon's side.

Darkness exploded. Its head turned to glass and its fire to mist—I was finally stronger. But it was still far larger than me, and in motion. That head shattered against me, crystal daggers cut me, I was thrown and didn't feel myself land.

~ * ~

*Kirin? Kirin!* Terrell's voice called me in the warm dark. *I know you're there. Kirin!*

I was so tired, yet I couldn't deny him. *Just let me sleep for a little longer,* I begged.

With ruthless compassion he answered, *No. Time to wake up, brother.*\*

~ * ~

I shuddered and gasped and the world was around me again. Gerdon held a canteen to my lips. I drank, coughed and spewed half the water back up. But no blood. Every inch of me hurt, but no bones were broken, quite, though my ribs argued otherwise. I smelled cinnamon and felt Terrell shudder as he took some of my hurt on himself. Shared minds, shared pain. And shared relief.

"Can you sit up, my lord?" the old Guard asked, alert eyes checking me over.

Ribs cried out when I tried, but not so bad I couldn't do it. I'd need the Narvi hospital and about a week in their hot pools.

"Don't try to stand," Gerdon added unnecessarily.

If he hadn't caught my shoulders, I'd have fallen flat. "Not yet," I panted agreement. "Maybe next year."

Gerdon braced a saddle against my back. "I'll bring you some willow-bark tea, my lord."

He hurried off past the wreckage of the dragon. I blinked at it; I was parked on a patch of grass only a few yards away. The monster looked much smaller as lumps of dead meat than it had as a live creature. The head lay nearest to me, shattered and broken but returned to flesh when my Shadow was sated. For once that darkness nestled calmly inside me, curled under my heart and sleeping like a babe.

*You did it,*\* Terrell whispered inside my head, grimacing a little at the agony he was siphoning away from me, but bearing it. *You killed it, you and Pen.*\*

*Damn your visions,*\* I groaned back. *And I ought to damn you too, twice, for being wrong and right. It really was a dragon, and neither Pen nor I could have killed it alone.*\*

He chuckled a little. *Does it help if I tell you I'm sorry about that? Misunderstanding the vision, I mean. I'm not sorry I got you to work with Pen, and he with you. And by the way, you should talk to him. You might find it easier now.*\*

I just groaned out loud at that.

"Pain tells you you're alive," a familiar voice said. "Which is prize enough when your opponent isn't."

I looked the other way and sure enough, there was Pen, sitting on another saddle with his legs stretched before him and his hands busy cleaning Irreneetha's sheath. He had her blade across his lap, clean as ever even though he was splashed chin to toe in dried black blood. I realized I was too; we both reeked like a charnel-house. His face had been washed and he'd set aside his helmet, chestnut hair tied back in a severely simple knot. He gave me a stern look.

"Why didn't you lower the rope for us?"

I blinked. "Ridge top wasn't stable. Rocks slid and I fell off the other side." After a moment I added, "Stupid mistake."

His look turned sour. "Of course. Then you thought you'd fight a dragon alone, just to cover up any embarrassment."

"Umm. No, that just sort of happened. Not my choice!" Curiosity finally awoke and I asked, "So how did you get over the ridge?"

"I used Irreneetha to cut foot-and-toeholds."

"You *what?*" I tried to imagine Pen clinging to a near-vertical wall while digging at it with the point of a sword almost as long as his arm.

He held her up, and she did something I'd never seen before— shrank until she was merely a dagger. An instant later she was normal sized again, and I remembered to shut my mouth.

Pen gave me a smug smile before he continued. "We climbed up, found the rope and let ourselves down while the monster was chasing you around the canyon. I got there when it had you treed. I think it was about to eat you when I cut off the end of its tail."

"Umm. Yeah, it was." I blinked at him again. Now my curiosity battled my pride.

*Go ahead and ask him,* Terrell urged silently. *It's the only way you'll find out.*

"So why didn't you let it eat me?"

Pen gave me the mother of all annoyed glowers. "Do you really have to ask, you idiot? Why did you jump in with the critical blow when I needed you to? If you hadn't done that blood-magic trick—"

I shuddered, awakening fresh pain that made Terrell and I both clench our teeth. "Never that. I wouldn't, *won't*, eat someone's life, not ever again. It was its Power I drank through my Shadow, that's all. Its life was for you to take. Its soul went—wherever dragon souls go." Leaving a black scar across mine that would be a long time healing. Terrell shared the pain, halved it, and I panted in relief.

Pen stared at me while I got my breathing back under control. Presently he asked, "Did you know how close to the edge it had me?"

"Umm. Not exactly. Were you? Close to the edge, I mean."

"Yes. One, maybe two more cuts before it got me." He indicated his left leg and I realized he had the boot off and his ankle wrapped in a bandage. "I twisted it during the fight."

"Oh. Umm."

*You're using that word a lot,* Terrell observed.

*You're the educated poetic one,* I growled back. *Cut me some slack!* To Pen: "Bad luck?"

"It happens, especially on bad footing." He glanced away, paused for a while, and then said, "You saved my life."

There was a long pause while I thought that one over. Terrell finally gave me a wordless prod like a knuckle in the ribs.

"You're welcome. Thanks for saving mine." The words didn't taste nearly as bad as I thought they would.

Pen looked at me again, the corner of his mouth twitching up just a bit. "Are you ever going to learn to follow orders?"

"I told you, I follow orders just fine, as long as they aren't stupid." Terrell smirked inside my head and I added righteously, "Sometimes even when they are."

"Of course," Pen answered sardonically, fighting down a grin. He finished cleaning Irreneetha's sheath, started to put her blade back into it and then stopped. The angel had appeared again.

She turned her face to me and smiled. A cool silvery music submerged my pain and sent shivers to the tips of my toes.

She was rippling water and adamant and drifting flower petals on a spring breeze. I stared back at those bottomless eyes, tongue-tied as a blushing peasant boy meeting a princess for the first time and knowing her hopelessly far above him. But her ghostly hand reached out, touched me on the forehead and traced the Sign of The One in ice and fire. I felt it sink within my skin, holding mundane pain at bay, and I sagged back against the saddle in relief.

Then she was just a sword once more. Pen looked at me after he sheathed her, studying my skin, my ears, my hair and finally my eyes. I stared back defiantly.

"If Irreneetha thinks well of you," he said thoughtfully, "Then maybe you're not a demon after all."

I groped for something sarcastic to say. It says something about how rattled I was that I finally settled on, "Took you long enough to figure that out."

He grinned openly then, and I remembered he was only one day older than me. "Had to be sure." He picked up the cloth and started cleaning dirt and gore off himself. That rag wasn't near big enough.

*You're going to be fine,* Terrell whispered inside my head. *We'll talk more tonight, and you can give me the whole story. Meantime you and Pen both need rest and healing.*

*Seraphs help me, I'll be stuck with him for weeks, won't I?* I growled. *The Abbess will probably put us in the same room in her hospital. I'll have to be nice!*

*It'll be good for you; you've both got lots to talk about. Who knows? Irreneetha might even join the conversation.* He smiled as his mental 'voice' faded away.

My pain came back to me, muted now, and I sighed. I still had no idea what to say to an angel.

~ * ~ * ~

**Peter Sartucci** lives in Colorado with his wife and two special-needs children, in a house surrounded by fruit trees that usually get frost-nipped, and a lawn that doesn't get watered often enough. There he writes epic stories for thinking people who like their fantasy robust, emotional, and sensory (with occasional food porn). Most of his tales are usually too long to sell, but he rejoices that this one did. He has five books about Kirin DiUmbra and his brother King Terrell, their adventures are available in paperback and ebook starting with the duology *Shadow and Light* and *Shadow Rising*, which take place before this story. The *Shadow Divided* trilogy picks up their stories five years after the events of 'Shadow, Lion, Dragon' and tells what happens when Kirin and Terrell fall in love with the same woman. A sixth book set a few years after that is underway and should be published late in 2024.

# Storage Bor

## Brian MacDonald

"Lemme get this straight," Francis grumbled, frowning as he drove The Beast, his beaten-down '85 Caprice Classic, toward a huge blocky building near the side of the highway, "You're saying Goblins run all the self-storage places?"

"No," Rory corrected with a sigh. "I'm saying they run some of them."

"But, they run this one…"

"Yes."

"And they wanna hire us?"

"One of them wants to hire us," Rory answered. "Greg."

"There's a goblin named Greg?"

"Yes."

"And you do know goblins are Fae…" Francis' frown deepened.

"I taught you that." Rory rolled her eyes with a head shake.

"You did," Francis growled. "I'm just checking if you remember. Because Queen Mab is still hunting you. Us, actually now. And just talking to a goblin could put us on her radar. Like, make a bright flashing blip on the damn thing."

"I know." Rory leaned over and gave him a quick peck on the cheek. "Just park the car and come in with me, Okay?"

"I'm bringing the good crowbar," Francis mumbled. He could never stay mad at his wife. Even when she was doing dangerous stuff and scaring the crap out of him. He would just have to be careful for both of them.

"I'd expect nothing less."

~ * ~

Greg met Francis and Rory at the front door of the UR-STUFF building. Everything in the building, from the outside facade to the interior walls and counter spaces, was painted in color-blocked green and brown. And it wasn't an electric green and warm brown. No. It was frog green and mud brown. Anyone with a passing understanding of color theory would steer clear of this building.

Hell, anyone with sight would stay away. The place just felt creepy and unwelcoming. Why would anyone want to keep their prized possessions there?

"Hello, Greg." Rory smiled warmly and put out her hand to shake his. "Love what you did with the place."

"Comforts of home, y'know?" Greg shook her hand. Then, he reached out to Francis to shake his.

"You're not a Goblin." Francis crossed his arms and stared down at Greg.

Greg wasn't a goblin. At least, he didn't look like one. Not that Francis had ever seen one, but he'd seen his share of magical creatures and they tended to look like he expected them to. Dwarves were short. Mermaids were chicks with tails. That sort of thing.

But Greg looked like a burned-out white dude in work coveralls. Maybe in his thirties? Receding hairline with longish blond hair in a hasty ponytail. A little out of shape, but not heavy. Moderate height. Smelled like old Taco Bell and bong hits with cheap cologne thrown over the top.

"Nothing gets past you, huh?" Greg made finger guns at Francis and fired with a wink. He turned back to Rory and pushed the door open to usher them in. "Better get in quick before guard dog hubby starts in on the tough questions."

Greg led them into the self-storage building, stopping occasionally to check the locks on various locker gates. He rattled each gate roughly to see it would not open and then left muttering with a shrug and head shake.

"And another thing," Francis grumbled, "What sort of goblin name is Greg? I mean, that's fine and all for a human, but if you're a freaking goblin shouldn't you be something like Bleck the Wartlicker or something?"

"Rory? Is this moron great in the sack or something?" Greg cracked over his shoulder. "Because he's not bringing much brainwise."

"Yes, he is," Rory chuckled, "And he hasn't experienced a glamour before."

"Fair enough. He can't see through basic magic. But does he have to be so ignorant about my name?"

"He's right here," Francis reminded Greg with a knuckle-crack to punctuate.

"I know. I can smell you a mile away," Greg shot back over his shoulder. "The Nineties called. They want their Drakkar back."

Greg, the goblin who didn't look like a goblin, led them down the hall and toward the front desk. Why the front desk was so far away from the front door, Francis had no idea. Greg pushed the swinging half-door by the counter and marched them all directly into the back office.

"Chair for milady?" Greg brushed papers and random debris from a chair across from a crappy aluminum desk covered in stacks of multi-colored files. He flopped back into a padded fake leather chair with a sigh. "Oh. And Francis," Greg sneered, "I think there's a kid's table back there with some crayons. Make yourself at home."

~ * ~

If Francis had his favorite crowbar in his hands, he'd have swung it at Greg.

But, thankfully, Rory had made him keep it in his work bag when they walked in.

It wouldn't have hit anything. Greg the goblin was much shorter than his glamour. But, it would have broken the magic and been seen as a sign of disrespect. That would have been bad. Rory needed to fix this fast.

"Francis, love," Rory asked with a soothing voice, "could you get out your crowbar?"

"Sure," Francis replied with a smirking voice simmering with aggression. He pulled a slightly rusted black metal crowbar from his bag and hung it over his shoulder.

"What's that for?" Greg leaned back a bit, eyes flicking in every direction. He was checking all his exits just in case. She had his attention.

"Honesty, my friend." Rory opened her hands and held them palms up. "I think we need to be honest about our situation if we're going to work on your problem."

"Honesty? Okay. Honestly, your husband is an ignorant tool. That said, I need your help and I'm willing to pay well."

"Greg," Rory replied with a frown and condescending stare.

"Fine." Greg put out a hand and twisted a featureless golden ring on his left hand. He shimmered like lake water with a light breeze rolling over it. And then? Then he was gone. Human Greg was gone, replaced by a four-foot-tall greenish-gray creature in coveralls with large eyes and even bigger golden-earring-covered ears. "And Greg is my actual name. It's shortened from a word for *the sound that a fleeing warrior makes as he clears his nose in fright* that neither of you could pronounce even if you had three sets of vocal cords like me."

"You're named after snot?" Francis barked a laugh.

"Francis." Rory shot a "Knock it off or else" look at her husband. He bit his lip with a grumbly frown. "My husband, Francis, is very protective of me. You may notice his cold iron crowbar? He tends to swing it at magical folk who bother me."

"Yeah, I've heard…"

"I'm not done, Greg," Rory punctuated his name with a snap in her voice. "And he is feeling very protective of me right now because a certain goblin, that shall remain nameless, you obviously …this goblin decided to cold call me at noon on a random Tuesday to suggest I come down and fix his problem. Or else."

"Well…yeah…"

"And…" Rory turned to Francis and threw him a quick wink. Her husband responded by growling and patting his crowbar in Greg's general direction. "And, I am unhappy. I don't like being pushed around. I don't like that some snotty little goblin thinks he can force me to help him because he may tattle to his boss that he knows where I am."

"About that…" Greg the goblin stammered.

"About that?" Rory crossed her arms and smirked knowingly. "You have a Druid and her protector in your office. Both of us are unhappy. This is the part where you explain yourself. Politely. Now."

~ * ~

"Okay. Okay," Greg pushed back from his desk with his hands up in defeat. "I'm sorry. I just needed you here fast."

"We'll see how good your apology is when you pay us," Francis growled.

"Fine." The goblin dove into his drawer to pull out a stack of cash and toss it to Rory. She, in turn, handed it to her husband.

"How's it look?"

"Decent." Rory knew it was better than decent. She'd seen the hundred-dollar bill on the top. If the rest were hundreds? That would pay for a lot. The electricity bill, at the very least. There might even be enough to top off the oil for the burner at home.

"There's more," Greg suggested as he watched Francis count the money. "Lots more if you can fix my problem."

"Which is?" Rory crossed her arms and gave a business-like tilt to her head.

"Somebody's breaking into the lockers."

"Okay."

"And they're taking stuff."

"So you have a thief." Rory considered. "Or thieves."

"Yeah. Here." Greg shook his head in frustration, jangling the gold hanging from his ears. "Do you know how hard that is to do? The protections I have here? I mean, I take that stuff seriously." He leaned in and lowered his voice. "Very seriously. Cos I have things here people want to be kept very safe."

"Powerful people?" Francis chuckled. "Like Mab?"

"Maybe," Greg shrugged. "I couldn't say even if I wanted to."

"Have any of your powerful people lost things to the thief yet?" Rory asked.

"Not yet…"

"But it's getting close," the druid suggested knowingly. "And you need us to stop them before they find out. Before she finds out."

"Yeah."

"Fine. Here's the deal." Rory grabbed a pen from Greg's desk and a letterheaded piece of blank paper. She scratched a quick note on it and handed it to the goblin. "That cash is a downpayment on services. When we finish, you double that amount. In cash, again. And you lose any information on us that you have."

"Whoa there, lady…" Greg stood up with his hands up again. This time to try to slow down the deal.

"She accepts Rory, Mrs. Murphy, or my personal favorite… *Ohmygod that terrifying Druid lady*," Francis corrected with a chuckle.

"Sign the contract or we walk," Rory directed.

"Wait…I can't…"

"Francis, love? It looks like this gentleman, and I use the term very loosely, has decided to handle his problem himself."

"Fine! Stop!" Greg grabbed a pen and signed the paper with a viscous sweep. "I'll pay. Just fix my damn problem. Please!"

"Well…" Rory snatched up the contract and eyeballed the signature. "Since you asked nicely, I suppose we can give it a look."

Francis was at the door, sweeping it open with a flourish before Greg had a moment to respond.

"Pleasure doing business with you, dear." Rory winked at the goblin. As they left the office her husband's barking laughter echoed through the halls.

~ * ~

"Do you have any idea where to start?" Francis murmured as he walked the UR-STUFF hallway with his wife.

"Not a clue." Rory shrugged her shoulders with a knowing smile.

"Soo…we just walk around and check the lockers to see if any of them are broken into?"

"Wait for it…" Rory raised a finger to slow her husband's verbal thought process.

"Wait for what?"

And then, as if on cue, the door to the office they had just left swung open violently.

"DO NOT GO TO THE THIRD FLOOR!" Greg, still in his goblin form, bellowed down the hall.

"WHY?" Francis turned and yelled back.

"BECAUSE I TOLD YA! IDIOT!"

"So, the lockers we need to check are on the first two floors?" Rory joined in, never raising her voice. It would carry. No need to give Greg the satisfaction of hearing her yell.

"Yeah," Greg lowered his voice to a normal level. "Lockers One-Twenty-Seven, One-Fifty-Five, and Two-Twenty-Three have broken locks. Check them."

"Check them first," Rory corrected.

"Yeah. Check them first. Obviously."

"OBVIOUSLY!," Francis barked aggressively.

"WHY ARE YOU YELLING?" Greg bellowed back.

"COS YOU'RE A TOOL!"

"ARRRGGGHHHH!" Greg shook his head, turned, and slammed the door behind him.

"So," Francis turned to his wife with a smirk, "We're checking out the third floor?"

"Obviously," Rory replied with a wink.

~ * ~

Locker One-Twenty-Seven was still open when they walked up to it. It was completely cleared out. No boxes. No containers. Not even a random piece of trash. Nothing. Whatever had been there was gone now.

"Hmm…" Francis mumbled through a face screwed up with thought.

"What?" Rory wandered into the locker, checking for any clue of what had happened. Nothing leaped out at her. The locker was just…empty.

"Something's weird about this…"

"Something's weird about a locker protected by goblins getting broken into?" Rory chuckled sarcastically. "You don't say."

"No," Francis grumbled with a head shake, "I mean…yeah, the whole goblin thing is weird, but that's not it…"

"What is?" Rory turned with her hand on her hip.

"It's too clean. Like the whole locker." Francis ran a finger on the walls and then the floor. "It's freaking spotless."

"Okay," Rory agreed. "That is weird." She wandered the locker, checking corners for any dust or debris. Nothing. "What locker is this clean after a robbery?"

"Right?" Francis pulled down the locker gate to check it. There was no lock on it. He shook his head and turned back to Rory. "Was the locker always like this? Did the owner keep it this clean? Did they clean it after the robbery? Did Greg?"

"There's no way Greg did this." Rory shook her head. She'd seen his desk. That goblin wouldn't clean like this unless his life depended on it. Did it? Was this Mab's locker? Or was it the locker of some other "powerful person"?

"You gonna do your thing?"

"Yes." Her thing, as her husband so aptly explained, was Magic.

Rory was a Druid. She wasn't one of the lovely Wiccans who did their best to follow their understanding of the old ways during these modern times. No. She was the last of the oldest and most powerful family of Druids to ever grace the earth. They were all gone now. Queen Mab had made sure of that.

And now, Rory was about to do Magic while in a box that may

have belonged to Mab. Her gut sank a bit with that thought. If she and Francis didn't fix this problem? And Greg told the Queen where they were?

That would be bad.

Very.

Very.

Bad.

They needed to figure this out. And they needed to figure it out fast.

"Keep an eye out, love?" Rory stepped to her husband on her tippy-toes and kissed him on the cheek. "I have a bad feeling about this place."

"Always," Francis growled. Then, in one smooth motion, he spun to put his back to hers and locked his eyes on the hall outside the container. He slowly slapped the crowbar on his open palm, to a rhythm only he knew, ready to crack it on anything that tried to get to Rory.

Rory, for her part, took a deep breath and closed her eyes. She counted to four in her head before slowly releasing the air through her nose. She repeated this, calming her heart and clearing her mind. Newly centered, Rory opened her eyes a crack and viewed the world through the haze of her eyelashes. At first, she only saw a muddle of green and brown. The overpowering colors on the walls concealed everything hidden in the air.

Rory waited for her eyes to adjust to the Magic. It would come. It always came. And then, it was there. Softly glowing threads of gold snapped into existence in the air. These threads connected everything with everything. They floated, traces of paths between people, objects, and places, stuck in the Veil between here and the realms of Magic and the Dead forevermore.

Rory didn't need anything from the dead.

At least, she was pretty sure she didn't.

The golden threads proved that. There weren't many. How could there be? There was so little for the threads to connect to.

No objects.

An open gate.

A barren locker.

Rory expected to see the few faint threads leading in and out of the room. They made sense. Some person or persons had brought in objects and left. The threads weren't thick because the pathways weren't walked often. Who walks back and forth between the same object in a storage locker?

There were a few stronger, brighter, tightly knit threads by the gate. Obviously, the magical protections. Rory didn't know exactly what they were, but she could tell they were complicated. That many knots in the magic with a thread that bright? Yeah. Those things had some pop to them. They'd hurt. Badly. Whoever tried to break into this locker would either need to be very careful or be very capable of taking a magical hit. Rory could guess the number of people capable of doing the former if they were prepared, but the latter? She shuddered at the thought of who or what they might be.

It was the thread that looked like a fluorescent golden rope that got her attention. It scared the crap out of her, actually.

"Hey, hun?"

Someone. Something had entered the locker. And it had done so with enough power to ignore the traps, find what it wanted, and leave.

"Sweetheart?" Francis rumbled.

She'd never seen a thread that powerful. It hurt her eyes to look at it. What sort of being made that much of an impact on the veil? What being's passage was so powerful as to leave such a lasting proof of its passage? And what the hell did it want from this locker?

"Rory?" Francis tapped her roughly while trying to keep his voice down. He failed. "Got a second?"

"What," Rory snapped away from the golden rope with a frown. "I'm kinda busy."

"Yeah. Sorry,"

"So…"

"I heard some noises down the hall. Things getting moved around. I think they're from One-Fifty-Five."

"And…"

"If you're okay, I'm gonna go check them out."

And then, after a quick kiss, Francis lumbered off toward the other locker.

Before Rory could check and see if the golden rope went in that direction.

Rory checked.

It did.

~ * ~

Francis slowed his speed as he approached locker One-Fifty-Five. The thieves could have come back. Or the locker owners. Either way, he was pretty sure they didn't need to hear him huffing down the hall.

"Aww man! Duneyrr's gonna lose his shit," a low, rumbling voice announced from inside the locker.

"No kidding," whined another. Francis knew that voice. In fact, he was pretty sure he knew who was in the locker.

"Hey boys," Francis greeted the two speakers as he walked up to the front of the locker. "How's Dunn's treating ya?" Dunn's was an autobody shop not too far away from UR-STUFF. It was run by Dwarves who illegally street-raced muscle cars. Rory and he had had a run-in with them. It hadn't gone well for Dunn's.

"Oh for crying out loud," the first person Francis saw complained. It was the one non-Dwarf from the shop. Travis of the Polo Shirt. Kid always looked like a guy who loved pop punk because it helped him meet girls. He was just handsome enough to be pretty. Just dirty enough to get girl's attention, but cleaned-up enough so parents would like him. Francis was not a fan. Rory was less so.

"I don't get paid enough for this..." groused a dwarf in greasy coveralls from somewhere in the back of the locker. He turned his back to Francis and returned to whatever he was working on. Francis heard heavy objects slide on the ground, metal clang on the ground, and what he could only assume was dwarvish swearing.

"What'd you lose, kids?" Francis smiled widely. "Need any help? I'm good at finding stuff. Found a stolen car once. Oh. Wait. You guys stole that..."

"Piss off, Murphy," Travis said. He turned slightly toward his dwarf friend. "You find the carburetor, Denny?"

"No dice. They got the sixty-five," the dwarf replied. Boxes shuffled, followed by more clanking and clanging. "Crap. They got the fifty-seven, too...and that thing was hidden."

"How about the radios?"

"Gone."

"Rims?"

"Gone."

"Engine blocks?"

"Look around," Denny popped up from behind the boxes growling in exasperation, "You see any? They ain't tiny or easy to move."

"Man. Dunn's gonna be pissed!" Francis looked around the room. For a locker full of car parts, it was organized. Even with all the boxes Denny was throwing around, it still looked decent. Absolutely didn't look like thieves had rifled through it. Someone knew exactly what they wanted and how to get it. "You're out a lotta money with those parts. Hope you weren't trying to flip some street racers…"

"Would you just get the hell outta here?" Travis snapped with a whine.

"Sure, sure," Francis turned to walk away but paused to look over his shoulder with a question. "You want me to say hi to Rory for ya? I'm sure she'd love to hear from you…"

"Wait. Is your wife here?"

"Walking down to visit right now," Francis wandered out into the hall and saw Rory making her way slowly down the hall. She must be using her magic still. It helped her see…magic stuff, but kinda got in the way of moving fast.

"Screw it," Travis snapped. "Denny, we're outta here. I'd rather deal with Dunn than Francis' old lady." Travis walked to the locker gate and waited for Denny to scramble to him.

"Old lady?" Francis crumbled his face with a frown. "She's not gonna like that…"

Travis slammed the gate shut just as Denny met him, turned to the front door, and fled. Denny followed at as quick a pace as his short legs would allow.

~ * ~

"Who was that?" Rory questioned as she walked up to Francis. It could be hard for her to see certain details when she was using her magical sight to see golden threads. It was even harder when the thread she was following was bright enough to light up an auditorium by itself.

"The boys from Dunn's," Francis replied with a chuckle.

"Did they get stolen from?"

"Yeah. Some pretty expensive car parts." Francis opened up the gate. Travis had forgotten to lock it.

"Huh." Rory stepped into the room and gave it a good look. She wasn't a car person. Not by any stretch of the imagination. That was her husband's specialty. "There's a ton of parts here. The thieves left quite a bit."

"Not really," Francis corrected. Then, he wandered around the locker pushing some boxes around and lifting others. "From what I can tell, most of this stuff is basic parts. Useful. Absolutely needed. But, not worth much."

"Even for Dunn's muscle cars?"

"Yeah. This stuff is for the newer cars...cars from the late seventies and early eighties like ours." Francis picked up a tape deck and gave it a loving tap before he put it back down. "The really old stuff is gone."

"So..." Rory thought out loud, "...someone knew what they were looking for?"

"That'd be my guess."

"This is making even less sense than before..."

"On to the next locker?"

"Sure," Rory stepped out of the locker and prepared to roll the gate shut. "And, Francis love?"

"Yeah?"

"Are you taking that tape deck with you?"

"Dunn's is gonna write-off this whole thing as a loss. No way they're going to itemize everything stolen. The insurance on the sixty-five carburetor will probably cover everything else..."

"Fine," Rory shook her head with a sigh. Then she got an idea. "And see what else the Beast needs...the breaks are getting spongey."

~ * ~

Two-Twenty-Three wasn't open when Rory made her way to it. Not in the way that anyone expected it to be open at least. No.

It was opened in the way that only happened when something very powerful decided it shouldn't be there. The rolling metal gate was lying on the floor. It had been ripped out of its housing and dropped to the side of the locker opening.

"What the..." Francis huffed as he walked up the hall toward the locker. He'd needed to put away the car parts. On the job. Obviously. And then caught up with her with a sprint.

Rory made a quick prayer to the Old Gods that Greg hadn't turned his cameras back on. If he even had cameras. The magic on the doors should have been more than enough to deter thieves. Cameras probably would cause more issues with his clientele. And yet.

"Looks like someone really wanted to get into that locker, love"

"I'd say." Francis let out a low whistle as he walked up to the gate. He dropped to a squatting position and poked at the rolled metal. "See this, hon? Someone tore this thing like aluminum foil."

"Someone?"

"Someone. Something…" Francis shrugged with a frown. "But it wasn't a machine. No way you could sneak something big enough to do this up to the second floor and back out."

"What's in here, then?" Rory poked her head into the locker and immediately picked up the unmistakable scent of…

"Cigars," a low voice with a thick eastern-European accent rumbled from behind them.

Rory and Francis turned to the voice to see a man in a bright blue sweatsuit with shiny silver racing stripes. He was older looking. Possibly in his sixties. With shoulder length greying black hair and an impeccably neat beard.

At least, that is what the man wanted Francis and Rory to see. If Rory hadn't still been using her magical vision, she wouldn't have seen him otherwise. She wouldn't have even thought to try to see him otherwise. His magic was that powerful.

But she was using her vision. And the golden cord went straight to him. And he was throwing off even more power and light than the cord. Much more.

Rory could see his true form.

Behind the fluorescent golden light that blazed so bright it made her eyes tear when she looked directly at it, she saw a scaled head larger than a Volkswagon bug with a subway train-sized body trailing off behind.

He was too big for the hall.

Too big for the second floor.

Powerful enough to collapse himself into the form of a human.

He was a dragon.

An ancient, insanely powerful dragon.

The dragon-that-looked-like-a-man winked at her.

He knew she saw him.

"Pardon." The dragon-man walked into the locker and perused the neatly stacked collection of cigars. He hummed a bit to himself as he picked up one after another, slowly luxuriating in smelling each one until he found what he was looking for. "Ahh…a Gurkha Black Dragon. Just what I was looking for."

"Umm…excuse me…Mister…" Francis inquired far more politely than he typically did.

"Bor." The dragon-man chewed off the end of his cigar.

"Mr. Bore…"

"Just Bor."

"Bor. Fair enough." Francis smiled sheepishly. "Not gonna lie, there doesn't seem anything boring about ya though."

"Ha!" Bor snorted with a sly smile. "You have no idea."

And then Bor blew a perfect thread of flame out of his mouth to light his cigar.

Francis' face became very pale.

Rory let go of her magic vision. There was nothing else she needed to see.

~ * ~

"So…Bor, is this locker yours?" Francis forced himself to talk. Nothing would be gained by him just standing there like a terrified idiot. "Because we're here…"

"It is now." He sucked in deeply from the cigar and blew a smoke ring out the side of his mouth. "And I know why you're here. Come walk with me. Both of you."

Bor walked out of the locker and passed them. He looked back with a nod and made his way to the stairs to the third floor.

Francis and Rory followed. What else could they do? They'd found their thief. And, Francis was pretty sure Bor could have killed them both on the spot if he wanted to. Francis took his wife's hand. He told himself it was to calm her nerves, but she seemed perfectly fine. What did she know that he didn't?

~ * ~

"So, Mr. & Mrs. Murphy…and yes, I know who you are," Bor

chatted in a friendly tone. "We have a problem."

Bor reached the gate at the top of the third floor and paused. With a look back and smile to Rory and Francis, he snapped his fingers loudly. And, before the snap had finished reverberating off the UR-STUFF walls, the gate clanked open for them all to enter.

"You see, I'm an old dragon. I was old when your family was first discovering Magic, Rory. And I thought I'd found the perfect way to relax in my old age."

Bor walked down the main hall of the third floor. The layout of his floor was different, though. There were still lockers around the outside of the hall. Lockers filled with everything a Dragon could covet. Gold coins and bars. Jewels and jewelry. Tapestries. And things Rory never thought one would care about. Car parts. Purses. Women's shoes. Action figures. Comic books. Pokemon cards. But the third floor was different because in the center was a living area with a kitchenette and an area for sleeping.

What was going on?

"You see, I mated late in life. When you're a powerful dragon you really don't get a chance to settle down. It's always *hoard this… kill these people…defend your stuff…kill these other people.* There's really no place for romance."

Bor wandered toward the fridge in the kitchenette. He swung open the door, rifled a bit through it, and pulled out cold beers for himself and his guests.

"Beer? It's very fresh. It's light with just a hint of blood orange. I have a deal with Aeronaut down the street."

"Thanks." Francis took his and Rory's with a polite nod. He popped open both. When Rory shook her head, he shrugged and took a swig from his. "I'll keep Rory's if that's ok."

"Absolutely." Bor popped his open with his thumb, took a long pull, and sighed. "Oh, that's good." He led them over to the living room area and sat heavily in a dark leather La-Z Boy recliner. "Please, have a seat."

Rory and Francis settled into a nearby couch.

What else could they do?

"Now…I was saying, I mated late. Gorgeous lady. An absolutely fantastic partner. But, she's driven. Still making her mark on the world. She's still all about taking over the world. Breeding more dragons. Creating a legion of our own. Subjugating the humans.

You know, that sort of thing."

Bor took another swig of his beer and realized it finished quickly with a frown. Francis handed him Rory's opened cold beer. The dragon-man nodded thanks and sipped the new beer slowly.

"But, I'm an old dragon. I'm tired. All I really want to do is watch my stories on TV, drink a few beers, and maybe check on my collection now and then. No big deal, right?" Bor paused for a long puff from his cigar.

"So, I set up this situation with Greg. I get the third floor. He gets protection. Everything is decent. Until my stories get moved off basic cable. Do you know I can only watch Days of Our Lives on an app? I'm over five thousand years old! What the hell do I know about apps? I just want to see how John Black uses his magical eyebrow to save Marlena! How much to ask is that?" Bor shook his head in frustration, wagging his dark hair in every direction. He took another sip of beer.

"So, I'm missing my stories and I'm bored here…until I find another show. A better show. *Container Wars*. Do you know that people have hoards? Like Dragons? And they hide them in containers. In storage lockers. Like here. There are hoards in UR-STUFF. And I can take them. Nobody can stop me. Not Greg. And certainly not you." Bor sat back a little further in his La-Z Boy and took a drag from his cigar. He blew it out slowly toward the ceiling.

"So. Here's the problem. I have a power-hungry lady. I can give you both to her. As a gift, right? I mean, I had a matching pair of Louis Vuitton high heels and handbag for the wife all set. Guy in One-Twenty-Seven had an impeccable collection. Almost a shame to kill him and burn the rest of his stuff. Do you know how hard it is to burn an entire container and everything in it and not leave a mark? I'm a bit proud of that. But I really couldn't have him trying to get things back. Especially the shoes. Milady really does love her shoes. And she looks fantastic in them."

"But, if I give you to her? Then she finds out about here. And she finds out I've been lying about where I've been. And I lose this little bit of heaven."

"But if I don't? Then she doesn't have you as a bargaining chip with Queen Mab. You know that would be a big deal. Mab really does hate your family. I've never seen anything like her quest to wipe you all out. And with you being the last one? Milady would get quite the thing to work Mab for more control of the magical folk."

"You see my problem?" Bor thoughtfully took a slow sip of his beer. "Do I choose my own happiness or my mate's?"

~ * ~

Rory's head swam.

She and her husband were trapped on the third floor of a self-storage building by an ancient dragon who couldn't decide if he wanted to give them to his wife…or worse?

"So, Bor…you mind if I watch the game?" Francis reached over to take the TV clicker off the dragon's recliner arm.

Bor stared at him. It was a hard stare. Rory recognized it as a death stare, meant to scare anyone into stopping their stupidity.

Francis ignored it.

"Look. I get it." Francis popped on the TV and flipped around. "But, let's be honest. I'm a bouncer. The muscle. I'm not gonna do anything to ya, but maybe get stuck between your teeth when you eat me…"

"Francis!" Rory jumped from her seat to stop him from speaking.

"It's okay, hun." Francis put up his hand to stop her. "I know my place. And my worth. I'm a light snack. You're…you're worth a lot more. Bor's gonna keep you around. If nothing else, it'd be good to have a Druid at his service."

"Francis! That's…"

"The truth," Bor rumbled in agreement. "You're either incredibly brave or stupid for even asking, but you're not wrong."

"Sooo…Bruin's game?"

"Have you ever known a Chuvash Dragon who didn't like hockey?"

"You're the first I met," Francis smirked.

"Touche, little bouncer," Bor chuckled. "Enjoy your game. I hope it makes your last hours more palatable."

~ * ~

"I think you'll find Francis and myself much more useful alive than dead," Rory suggested to the dragon.

"Because?" Bor took a puff of his cigar. He breathed a ring. Then another. Then another. And then, his rings connected into a chain. His eyes lit up in amusement.

"Well, for one thing, we can deal with Greg."

"There's nothing to deal with."

"Even if he sends more people after you?"

"Do you think you're the first?" Bor snorted condescendingly. Little flames flickered from his nostrils.

"Another beer?" Francis wandered past them towards the fridge. He pulled out two fresh beers and handed one to Bor before walking back to his spot by his beloved Bruins. What was he playing at? She'd never seen him give up this easily. Hell, Rory had never seen him give up.

"Lovely chap." Bor shook his head with a sad smile. "Terrible to have to eat him."

"Then don't," Rory suggested.

"And what? Keep you two here? How long will it be until Greg whines to Mab for help?" Bor popped open his fresh beer and took a long pull. "And then I have Mab storming down here, ruining my place, and getting me in serious trouble with my mate."

"*HAPPY DANCE! HAPPY DANCE!*"

"What the hell?" Bor growled as he turned to Francis. "Could you turn down the TV before I eat you now?"

"*HAPPY DANCE!*" Francis lowered the TV volume. "*Happy Dance! Potsticker happy dance!*"

"What are you watching?" Bor wandered over to the television. "Food Network?"

"QVC," Francis answered. "David is cooking up some Potstickers. And he's got them in packages of one hundred and fifty. Fifty of the Pork. Fifty of the Chicken. And fifty of the vegetarian."

"Those look delicious." Bor sat next to Francis. "I love those things. Get a little cook on the wonton, flip them, and eat! I think I spent a full decade in China just because I knew this chef who made them for me by the bucketloads…"

"You can just order them here. They have delivery."

"Delivery? Of potstickers?" Bor took a deep puff of his cigar and released the smoke from his nostrils. It streamed in curls and waves. "Do they take credit?"

"They have their own card. You can get auto-delivery with it. You can call or use their app."

"Hmm…I dislike apps, but the phone…"

"And they sell other things. Clothes. Do-dads. Jewelry…"

"Do they?" Bor took another puff and then stood with a triumphant smile. "Excellent! It is done!"

"What's done?" Rory jumped up to place herself between Francis and Bor. There was no way she was going to let a newly hungry dragon decide to snack on her husband. Even if the idiot had gotten him hungry chatting about delivery Potstickers.

"Our problem! It is solved!"

"How exactly?" Francis stood up and tried to get between Rory and Bor. Idiot. If the dragon wanted to eat Rory there was nothing he could do.

"You have given me the perfect gift, young Francis." Bor slammed a slap on Francis' back. "Unlimited access to things for my collection! And potstickers!"

"What?" Francis stumbled back but kept standing.

"You've bought your freedom! I get as many things as I want to buy. You get to leave."

"But what about your mate?" Rory asked in confusion.

"What about her? Do you think she would let me spend our hoard on more things?"

"No," Rory frowned. "Probably not."

"Then, why would I give you to her?" Bor chuckled at his explanation. "How could I reward someone who would deny me an unlimited hoard?"

"I dunno…" Francis mumbled as he rubbed his back. "But I'm gonna take the win because I can't take another happy slap."

"Excellent!" Bor threw his arms around the backs of Rory and her husband and led them to the third-floor gate. "Now. Go to Greg. Tell him that in return for my continued protection of the UR-STUFF hordes, I demand another building for my hoard. And a credit card."

"Do you think that will work?"

"It will work. And, Francis. Know you have earned the eternal favor of Bor. You need never worry for protection."

~ * ~

Francis and Rory drove off in a Beast filled with car parts and a paycheck big enough to pay off the electric bill, fill the oil tank, and maybe even pick up Bruins tickets if they ever got a free night.

It was a good day.

"Soo…do you figure Greg is gonna keep his mouth shut about us?," Francis rumbled as he drove.

"I think so. I don't think he'd want to mess with Bor."

"Or the guy with the eternal favor of Bor?"

"Or the idiot who stumbled on to QVC and accidentally got the eternal favor of Bor." Rory chuckled and leaned in to kiss her husband's cheek.

"Same thing," Francis said with a laugh.

"You know we have plenty of cash for a celebratory meal…"

"You thinking what I'm thinking?"

"Yep!" Francis put his foot down on the gas and sped down the street. "Kowloon's for Potstickers!"

~ * ~ * ~

**Brian MacDonald** writes in the earnest hope his words can bring joy and comfort like the books of his youth brought him. Twenty-plus years of teaching Intensive Special Education in Massachusetts have informed his worldview and taught him to take nothing for granted as well as to see the beauty in the chaos swirling in our minute-to-minute struggles in life.

Brian would like to state he disagrees with Conan. While he agrees crushing one's enemies and hearing the lamentation of their loved ones is indeed enjoyable, Brian is absolutely certain "Home-made Calzone" night at the MacDonald house with his wife, sons, and reruns of *Leverage* is the best thing in life.

Brian has been published by WolfSinger Publications, House of Loki, Enrapturing Tales, and Black Ink Fiction. You can find out more about Francis and Rory and all his other characters on his Facebook page: Brian MacDonald—Storytelling Scallywag or by searching #francisandrory.

# Where Dragons Fear to Tread

## Chad Gayle

I scan the face of the mountain. Its slow, terraced slope is pockmarked with mouths of different sizes, and one of those mouths is rimmed with black, scorched by smoke and flame. That's where my gaze settles, on the mouth of the tunnel that leads to the temporary home of the dragon I know and love.

The dragon Porphyris, who has helped me keep the peace for nearly twenty years, the dragon who has been my ally and my best friend, whom I wed to show the people of this kingdom I would stop at nothing to guarantee their safety and their happiness.

The dragon who became, with the aid of the wizard Mephis, the father of my half-human child. The dragon who has, apparently, betrayed our alliance and all it stood for—

Today's the day he may have to die.

I'm still reluctant to accept what the scarred square of timber framing the mouth of the tunnel suggests. That Porphyris is capable of harming the miners who remain trapped inside the mountain's labyrinth. That the dragon I thought I knew so well has given up on the kindness and the caring that set him apart from the dragons of yore.

Turning away from the mountain, I look past the grooms tending our horses to study the wizened faces of my advisers, men who first swore allegiance to my father decades before I was born. Old men with old ideas, ideas that are often useless to a princess like me. "If you were willing to wear a dress in public and paint your face," they are fond of saying, "your subjects would embrace you as they did your father." Then they go on and on about the length of my hair and how I should *smile more*, as if these matters of appearance are at the root of the kingdom's ills.

And what of Porphyris, my husband? What of Solstice, my half-human heir? Playing the part of the princess the people think they want wouldn't be enough for the ones who hate me. They would still find fault with the choices I've made, so let them call me prince if that's easier, because I'm not here to feed them sweet cake and tell them fairy tales. I'm here to give them the tools they need to raise themselves up from the poverty and despair of the past.

The eldest of my advisers, grey bearded Dimas, is trying to get my attention. I call him to me with a subtle wave of my hand.

"Your Highness," he says, "your scouts have discovered a giant cavern carved into the back side of the mountain."

"That must be how he entered the mine," I answer.

Dimas assents with a quick nod. "It's a delicate situation. Your subjects—"

"Have nothing to fear," I tell him, "because I stand for them and only for them. If my husband has harmed any of the miners trapped in that mountain, he will be banished as he must be if he dares to threaten the lives or the livelihoods of any of our fair citizens."

"But Your Highness, if he should refuse to leave the mine, if it's the silver he's after—"

"I will do whatever must be done to maintain the rule of law and the safety of my people, Dimas. I make no exceptions for Porphyris just as I would make no exception for you or any other man, and I will deal with any threat made against my kingdom as I always have, with a swift but steady hand, showing mercy only when and where it is due."

After these phrases leave my mouth, my stomach reels, lurching as if I've been launched from my castle's tallest tower. I bite the tip of my tongue until the pain quickens my blood; with his hands clasped below his belt, Dimas lowers his eyes, acknowledging the implications of what I've told him.

"Did you track down the wives of those missing miners?" I ask.

"Yes, we did, Your Highness."

"Good. Bring them here."

As he leaves, Teska emerges from a knot of archers to take his place. Lithe and long limbed, she looks magnificent in her uniform, and I am tempted to look away from her, to shade my eyes from another bright light, but I stand fast. I already know what she's going to tell me; I know what I would say if I were Captain of the Guard.

A line of tension quivers along her jaw as she fastens her brown eyes on mine, and I can't help thinking of the games we played together when we were teenagers, scuffling and tussling that always amounted to more than mere horseplay.

"I've spoken with the archers, Your Highness, and they agree with me. Even with your considerable skill, you'll have trouble maintaining tension in a bowstring."

She's trying to not glance at the sling looped around my neck, the strip of embroidered cloth cushioning the cast protecting my recently broken arm. "And if I miss, then the wizard's enchanted arrow will be wasted. Do you think I haven't thought of that, Teska?"

"There's no reason for you to go, ma'am. I can bargain for the lives of the miners in your stead, and if I fail, the best of our archers can wield that poison arrow as you see fit."

A frown hardens my features. "He's my husband, Teska. I am as responsible for his actions as I am my own, and I will send no proxy in my place."

She leans in to me, dipping her narrow chin as she lowers her voice. "At least let me send in some of the guards first, Princess Kage. So we can determine the scope of what we're dealing with."

"What we're dealing with is an errant husband and a potentially dangerous dragon, Teska, and if I send anyone into that mine unaccompanied, Porphyris might see them as a threat and respond accordingly."

"But I can't guarantee your safety if it's just the two of us."

"Of course you can't. I don't expect you to, Teska."

She stands aside as the miners' wives are brought before me. They aren't dressed in rags, but their humble shifts and their coarse leather boots tell tales of hardship. Scanning their careworn faces, I can't help but wonder whether any of their children are as old as my Solstice, who has just turned sixteen, but I doubt any of them knows the pain of watching one of their own flounder helplessly against life's currents like a fish that can't figure out how to swim.

They curtsy graciously, each in turn, but only one of them aims her eyes at the ground. The rest level their boldest stares directly at me, as if they've earned the right to challenge my authority, but this hardly comes as a surprise. They stand in judgement of all that I am and all that I am not, after all, and they clearly want me to know it.

The woman in the middle has a mottled bruise stretched over one cheek. I tell her, and by extension, all of them, that I'm sorry for what has happened to their husbands and I will do everything within my power to bring their partners home safely. Then I reiterate what I've already said to Teska, that I alone am responsible for the actions of Porphyris and I will see justice done in my name, no matter what securing such justice may require. The woman standing in front of me blinks and tips her eyes down to stare at the cast wrapped around my broken arm. In this odd moment of solidarity, while I am focused on the patch of wine dark skin on her face and she is focused on my sling, I realize we are wondering exactly the same thing.

*How did that happen? Were you hurt by someone you love?*

~ * ~

The tunnel's entrance is wider than I thought it would be, and this extra space gives my mind room to roam as we leave the light behind. I find myself sorting through the treaties we signed with the Otherfolk during the plague years, guarantees of elven independence within the kingdom and agreements with the fairies that allow them to harvest nectar wherever they choose. By upholding those treaties, I've respected the natural sovereignty of the Otherfolk even when it wasn't in my interest to do so, as with the continued manufacture of fortified elven swords in spite of my objections to the sale of such weapons along the southern border, and in the exceptions granted on the taxes that should be levied against fermented fairy dew. Would it be wrong to assume my husband should be afforded the same protections we provide to the rest of the Otherfolk, protections that invoke outside arbiters when conflicts arise between elves or fairies and their human neighbors?

No. Porphyris is my husband first and foremost, and although he isn't imbued with royal blood, he owes his allegiance not only to me but to the subjects of my kingdom, as acknowledged in our marriage vows.

The faint odor of sulfur still fouls the dry, dusty air in this tunnel but the charred scent of the timbers lining the ceiling and the walls is almost pleasant, like the crusted bones of a cold campfire. Aside from the drip, drip, drip of water trickling from a hidden source, the only sound I hear is the sound of our boots crunching the gravel, but I am ever ready for the low, rolling rumble of a dragon who doesn't want to be disturbed.

Walking beside me, Teska balances her body shield against her forearm while she lights the way with a lantern that catches glints of quartz scattered on the ground. She moves with the studied grace of a cat stalking prey, but I can tell by her bated breath she's afraid. Not of a cave-in or of the sudden onset of another wave of flames, specifically, but of what might happen to me if she isn't fast enough or strong enough to keep me out of harm's way.

Maybe she's right to be afraid. It's no secret Porphyris and I see less and less of each other these days, and he's come close to losing his temper with me several times, even in front of Solstice. Could it be he's grown tired of us? Have our human mannerisms and our mixed messages become too much for him to bear? Or has he simply had enough of me? Am I the real reason he's here?

I'm not as terrified of this possibility as I thought I would be when I first wondered whether he might be slipping away. Mostly, I'm annoyed—I'm hurt and angry, of course, because I have the same feelings now I did for him eighteen years ago, when we took our vows—but I'm very much annoyed he would choose this moment, of all possible moments, to turn his back on everything we've built together. This moment of crisis, when the fate of the kingdom hangs in the balance, when rebels and rabble rousers plotting against me can point to the escapades of our half-human child and question Solstice's future fitness for the throne. Why now, Porphyris? Why now?

~ * ~

My belly itches. My back hurts and my belly itches and there's nothing I can do about it. Not while I'm pinned down like this, with half the damn mountain blocking my exit and my front legs scrunched so far back against my chest I can't possibly dig my way out. And now I have to deal with this human too, this miner who smells like mildewed leather. Even in the dark, I can see his head poking out of the crevice he's climbed up from, and I can't help thinking how easy it would be to cough and set the poor bastard on fire.

"Are you there, sir?" he asks in a voice far more polite than I expect it to be.

I let my breath unroll from my throat, filling the chamber with sulfurous fumes. The pale faced little monkey is undeterred, however. He takes a candle from his vest pocket, strikes a match, and lights the nubby wax stub, circling himself with a halo of yellowed light, light too feeble to penetrate the matted runnels of his wrinkled face.

"What is it you want?" I grumble.

"Only to talk to you about our situation, sir," he says, speaking in a strong, firm voice in spite of his fear, which is evident from the smell he exudes.

"What situation are you referring to?"

He hesitates, clearing his throat. "Well, you told us to stay put and we have, but it's been a full day since you got here and the boys were wondering, you know, what's next. As in, when they might be allowed to go free."

"They'll leave this place when I say they can," I bellow.

"Well then, sir, if you don't mind my asking—what shall we do in the meantime? While we're waiting, that is."

I glower at him, letting my eyelids slide down slowly until my eyes are nearly closed. He seems to get the message; he nods and sidesteps to my left, where he holds the candle up over his head and cranes his neck.

"The boys get restless after a double shift," he mutters, "and then they tend to fight amongst themselves because they're so tired and so bored. Which is no concern of yours, I suppose—"

"No," I interrupt, "it is not!"

"Right," he says, nodding so vigorously his chin nearly touches his chest. "Well sir, that was the main thing, but now that I'm up here" (he pauses to clear his throat again) "I see, I mean, it seems apparent, um, that your position, well—it looks as if you may be in a bit of a bind, sir."

My curved claws click against the hard ground, but I manage not to let go of a long, lugubrious sigh. The truth is I would like nothing more than the chance to die right here and now, to be transubstantiated into a puff of smoke that would wander out of the mine like a cloud. Instead, I have to focus my gaze on the small smelly man standing next to me; I take an itch inducing breath as I flare my nostrils for effect.

"What is your name?" I ask.

"My name? Cecil, sir."

"Sit down, Cecil."

"Yes sir."

"No," I grouse, "not over there—over here, in front of me, so I don't have to keep turning my head."

"Sorry sir. Is this better?"

As Cecil settles on the ground with his legs crossed, we stare at each other while the glimmering candle casts our contrasting shadows against the curved wall.

"Ever been this close to a dragon, Cecil?"

"No sir, I haven't."

"Are you frightened?"

"Should I be, sir?"

The candle's flame dodges my breath as I slowly exhale. I was supposed to be out of here by now, well on my way to the Western Wilds; I was supposed to be focused on a different future for myself, a future free from worries about the fate of the kingdom and its rulers. That future is gone from me, however, gone forever because I misjudged the mettle of this mountain as I clawed through it. Because I assumed the rocks clinging to the roof of the tunnel I created would hold fast.

Cecil turns his head to the side to clear some dust from his lungs with a cough. "I hope you don't mind my saying so," he starts, his voice now a dry rasp, "but it seems to me as if we have something in common, sir, what with you being stuck down here because of those boulders on your back and me and my boys being stuck down here because of you."

Puny little bag of meat. He's playing with fire, and he can't even smell the smoke, has no idea how close he's come to having his face burned off.

I start to groan because of the itch in my belly but stop myself and squirm a bit instead, scuffing my scales against the gravel. Rubbing isn't the same as scratching, however, and so the itch remains. It's more damning in a way than the rocks that are piled on my back.

Touching the tip of my tongue against my longest, sharpest tooth, I narrow my eyes again, staring grimly at the little moon of flesh I see floating before me. Then I push the seat of my voice down deep, until it's caught in the very back of my throat.

"Cecil, why don't you tell me something about your family," I suggest in a deliberately tempered, tolerant tone. "Entertain me with a story about the people you love."

~ * ~

As Teska and I plunge deeper into the mine's dark vaults, I am always aware of the enchanted arrow sitting in the quiver strapped to my back. It almost seems to have a life of its own, that arrow, as if it's possessed by a force radiating out in all directions like a kind of invisible light. I keep thinking this light is warming the back of my neck almost to the point of being burned even though I know it's the shifting fabric of the sling holding up my arm that has rubbed my flesh raw. Such is the power of the wizard Mephis and his spells; even before it is deployed, his magic shapes what we think we know about the world into something strange and new.

Mephis, my some time savior. He's the reason Porphyris and I were able to be joined together, the architect of the birth-cocoon that allowed my half-human child to be born. But he wreathed the enchantment around this poison arrow only after I ordered him too, and he insisted on reminding me, before I set off for the silver mine, of what he told me on my wedding day:

*The tangled garden of the heart, Princess—this is the one place where dragons fear to tread.*

I crouch down while we scurry through a low, narrow passage seeded with slender fingers of limestone. The odor of burnt wood is stronger here, reminiscent of a once scorched forest where dead timber still pops and cracks underfoot, and noticing this odor turns my thoughts toward the miners again. I imagine them huddled together in a deep pit, their flesh peeled away from their faces by fire, and I'm so distracted by this horrible image I snag my sling on an outcropping of rock as I stand up.

"Damn this bloody thing!" I snap.

Teska swings the light from the lantern to me, and our eyes meet as I twist free. The cloud of doubt hovering over her face is impossible to miss.

"Don't look at me like that," I tell her, regretting the words as soon as they've left my mouth.

"My apologies, Princess."

Shaking my head, I start off again, leading the way. I know she thinks I'll falter when the moment of truth arrives, and I'm beginning to worry she might be right. As we get closer and closer to the place where Porphyris waits for us, I can feel my resolve weakening, growing as soft as a ball of wax left out in the sun.

~ * ~

"That's the long and short of it, sir," Cecil says, nudging a shiny rock with the toe of his boot. "She's not in any real danger but that doesn't matter to her mum, who thinks she's only out there doing what she's doing to make us feel bad. Which isn't true, of course, but it's, well, it's a mud cake however you slice it."

He's been telling me about his daughter Phoebe, who can't cook or sew and has no interest in finding a husband for herself. Rather than going to work at the new button factory, as her father suggested, Phoebe decided to become a traveling minstrel, and she's been wandering from town to town since the lakes thawed, singing songs about the joys and pains of being a woman. She's made some money along the way, apparently, but there have been days and sometimes weeks when she's had to sleep in an open field or has begged for scraps of food by the side of a muddy road.

"She's pleased with the path she has chosen for herself?" I ask.

"She says she is in her letters, but that doesn't make a spot of difference to my wife, who's always spouting off Phoebe is going to get murdered or kidnapped or worse—that she might get pregnant. And my wife wants me to go after her and bring her home 'for her own good,' which wouldn't be good for any of us, as far as I can tell."

"So you think your wife isn't as worried about the safety of your daughter as she claims to be."

"That's right, sir. She takes it personal, like Phoebe would do the exact opposite of what we want her to do just for spite. My wife likes to say none of us have a right to be happy, and whenever she starts down that path, she gets to blaming…well, her feelings get the better of her. What I mean to say is, there's no malice in her complaints, you know."

"To put it bluntly," I reply, "she blames the choices your daughter has made on Princess Kage."

He nods slightly, looking a little embarrassed. "She does a bit, yes sir."

He fixes his gaze on the candle's tiny flame, and I wonder how many stories he has heard about Solstice, my half-dragon child, and whether he has partaken personally of the gossip that spreads through this kingdom like wildfire, titillating tales of Solstice's drunken carousing with disreputable young elves who supply my child with never ending flagons of fermented fairy dew. Does he know Solstice was once seen by a group of small children wallowing in shallow swamp water like a giant salamander? Is he aware that after Solstice passed out in the town square of Tirandor, they singed the clothes of a crowd of villagers who were trying to wake them and claimed, afterwards, the flames that shot out of their mouth were the result of a badly timed sneeze?

Thinking on these things brings me right back around to the Princess and the bolt of fabric looped over her still broken arm, and suddenly the itch under my scales is so intense I feel as if I'm about to lose my mind. I squirm and shift my belly from side to side in a desperate bid for relief, but it hardly helps—if only I could move these damned rocks off my back!

"Are you all right, sir?" Cecil asks, noticeably concerned.

"It'll pass in a moment."

"Anything I can do?"

"Thank you, Cecil, but no, there isn't anything you can do."

The itch subsides some and I try to relax, wrinkling my nose while I squeeze my eyes shut. When I open them, I let out a small sigh that ruffles the human's hair and nearly extinguishes the candle's flame.

"Cecil, does it bother you that the Princess is married to…a dragon?"

It's hard to tell with so little light, but I think he looks puzzled. "Bother me, sir? What business is it of mine who the Princess should be married to?"

"Because in our union, that is, because of the efforts of the wizard Mephis, our offspring—well, you must have an opinion about whether Solstice should be allowed to sit on the throne."

With his lips puckered, Cecil shakes his head. "Honestly, sir, no. I only feel a bit sorry for young Solstice, that's all."

"Sorry for them? Why?"

"I suppose it's because they have no say in what they will or won't do with their life. I think that would be a mean thing to live with."

Unexpectedly warm feelings spout from my heart when I hear Cecil say this, and I wish, probably for the first time in my long life,

I was capable of donning a gracious, all too human smile to show Cecil what I'm thinking.

Because I feel the same way, Cecil. I feel exactly the same.

~ * ~

If I destroy Porphyris, Solstice's loss will be even greater than mine, but if I let Porphyris live and it turns out he has tortured or killed the miners trapped in these caves, the people of this kingdom will turn against us, and we will lose the battle of hearts and minds we have been waging for so long.

If only I knew you as well as I thought I did, Porphyris; if only I could understand your feelings as well as I understand my own.

"How much further can it be?" I ask Teska while we are slipping and sliding along a downward grade.

"Not much, I hope—unless we've been going in circles."

When the ground slopes up again, I rest my hand on her shoulder to steady myself, and for a moment, I can feel her pressing back against me, yielding to my touch. I recall the warmth of her bare skin beneath my fingers and the sighs we shared in a dark dwelling far, far away, and I'm forced to drop my hand. Without pausing, she moves on. Neither of us acknowledges that feeling of familiarity that has touched us both so many times before.

Teska, my love that could have been but wasn't. If I were to let her, she would gladly switch places with me, relieving me of a burden I may not be strong enough to bear. Not because she thinks it's the right thing to do; not even because she supposes I will miss the arrow's target regardless of our range. No; she would do it simply because she cares more about my happiness than she does her own.

We're different that way, she and I.

~ * ~

I've been trying to make Cecil understand the difficulty of living up to Princess Kage's high expectations by showing him how hard she is on everyone—including herself. I'm not sure why making him see her as she really is seems so important, but I think it's because I want to show him his gut feeling about what Solstice is going through is correct. Or it could be I want to remind myself of how we wound up here like this, facing each other in a candle lit cave.

It seemed like such a foolproof plan the moment I dropped down out of the clouds. I would burrow into the silver mine and terrify the miners until they wet themselves, but I would let one or two of them get away, and then I would lay in wait until word reached Princess Kage. With the miners properly convinced they were about to be eaten, I would sniff the air until I detected the arrival of the Princess and her forces, and then I would make my escape, leaving the mountain and the kingdom behind for good, trading my homeland for the unpeopled spaces of the Western Wilds.

After the miners were "rescued" by the Princess, rumors of my malicious intent would bloom across the land, and with that, there would be an easy way to explain how the Princess's arm was broken. No need to assume Solstice might be responsible for the sling around her neck, as the people would say to themselves, in their huts and their town squares, *We were right about Porphyris all along, yes we were*—and then they would give Solstice a second chance.

The illusion of a happy ending, that's all I wanted. And not to be humiliated, of course; not to be made to feel old and foolish. Oh how I would love to rake my claws along the length of my belly right now, scoring my scales while Cecil scratches my chin.

I press my forked tongue against the roof of my mouth and swallow hard. Maybe it's better this way; after all, there's seldom a happy ending that doesn't leave some poor sap hanging. It just so happens, in this case, the sap is me.

"Cecil, I need you and your fellows to do me a favor."

"What is it sir?" he asks, wiping his filthy forehead with the back of his hand.

"I'd like you to put on a little show. For the Princess."

"For the Princess, sir? Is she here?"

"She is, Cecil. She's just around the corner, so to speak."

"If you don't mind my asking, how do you know that, sir?"

"Because I've picked up her scent, Cecil. She's here with the Captain of the Guard."

I inhale slowly, drawing in a room's worth of cool, dank air.

It's delightful, like digesting a large meal right before you curl up on a bed of lava to go to sleep.

~ * ~

An echo of voices in the distance; a chill creeps up the bare flesh on my arms.

"Teska, did you hear that?"

"Yes ma'am, I did."

A draft of cool air rushes past me, and I notice, for the first time, the tiny white bones scattered along the edges of this corridor. Small fowl consumed by the miners, perhaps, or the skeletons of dead rats and bats—probably nothing out of the ordinary. Probably.

We move forward and the voices grow louder, the voices of the miners, and I realize they're crying out, they're shouting because they're in pain. I touch Teska's shoulder to get her attention; when she turns to face me, I reach behind my head to grasp the soft fletching of the enchanted arrow. Fear flashes in Teska's eyes.

"The bow, Teska. I need your help nocking this arrow."

"Yes, of course."

Teska drops her shield as I slip the sling off my arm, and then she helps me fold the fingers of my left hand over the grip of the bow. When she lets go, a thunderous roar shakes the ground, and I am suddenly numb, a hollow vessel as frail and fragile as a glass goblet. I tell myself, repeatedly, the dragon I knew and loved is already dead and gone and something evil has taken his place.

Drawing back the bowstring, I test my strength while a hidden ache uncoils around the bones between my elbow and my wrist. My left arm shudders. Teska winces as if she can feel my pain.

"Are you sure you want to do this, Princess?"

"I don't want to, Teska. I have to."

As she retrieves her shield, some poor soul lets out a long, low moan that sends another chill up my spine, and I measure the force of my pull against the tautness of the bowstring as we move forward, following the roughly hewn tunnel as it curves around an outcropping of sparkling granite.

The moaning stops. At the feathered edge of the lantern's globe of light, the darkness is like a black fog, a cloud of airy pitch that would surround us if it could, shrouding us in eternal night.

*Our two lives are now joined together in a lasting covenant so that we might build a new world between us, a world where hope and love will rise from the ashes of our sadness and our fears.*

Happy memories wash over me, memories of Solstice laughing and playing while the gentle giant watches with wings folded, my friend and companion, my ally in the struggle to keep the kingdom from falling apart after my father's mind became clouded with strife, after he was no longer able to rule this kingdom I call my own.

*What happened to us, Porphyris? What did I do wrong?*

"Your Highness? Your hand—"

I know it's shaking, but I will find the strength to do what I must. I will dig deeper; I will set aside—

A different sound. Footsteps? And I think I can hear Porphyris speaking to someone, speaking in a subdued, hushed tone. I can sense the shape but not the substance of his words, but I think he may be…asking for mercy? From one of the miners?

The sounds of grief and pain cease, and another voice takes their place, a wan and weary voice that I've never heard before.

"Please ma'am, please don't shoot."

I glance at Teska, who squats to set the lantern on the ground; she draws her sword as a man with a grubby, deeply wrinkled face steps into the light.

"He's in a bad way, Your Highness, but none of us is hurt. It's nothing like he wants you to think."

The miner has his hands over his head, as if we intended to shoot him, not Porphyris. As I lower my weapon, I ask him to explain himself and nod at Teska, who quickly pats him down.

"He got himself stuck," the miner mumbles. "It's kind of a quandary, you see, because he doesn't want to admit he needs your help. I don't know what he was after but he's been nothing but kind to me and my boys, Your Highness. So can you help him? Please?"

My heart is suddenly as light as a bird. Never in my life has it felt this good to be wrong, and I could swear for a moment the cavern is filled with light, a light that is nearly blinding. Then I realize I've snapped the enchanted arrow in two, breaking its spell.

~ * ~

She stands before me with her left arm crooked in a sling and two pieces of a broken arrow wedged in her right fist. She is a being I can't explain, and while I stare at her I wonder, as I have so many times before, why humans are so complicated, why they can't be more like the stars in the heavens, beautifully distant but static, always twinkling in the selfsame way.

Teska and Cecil have taken the miners home and are supposed

to return with a team of advisers and engineers who will determine the safest, most expeditious method of digging me out. I would rather they didn't, of course. The best possible outcome for me would be another cave-in (after the Princess has gone) and a slow, silent death that would see me whittled down to a pile of sharp shingles and a concordance of bones.

Except Solstice and the Princess would be left alone: still this same problem. Even now, as I am thinking this, she is sobbing, although I can't say whether her tears are tears of joy or of sadness or some mixture of both.

After a long pause, she arches her eyebrows and focuses her small green eyes on mine. "You did intend to fly far away from us," she says in a quavering voice. "Have I made you so miserable as that? Is it me you hate?"

Another kind of wound, sharp and quick and possessed of its own brutal magic. I lower my lids to shield myself from the light of her lantern, withholding a sigh. "Of course I don't hate you," I tell her in a soft whisper. "I was trying to protect you. And Solstice."

"From what?" she asks.

From each other, I'd like to answer, but I'm smart enough to hold my tongue. "When you wouldn't tell anyone outside of the castle how your arm was broken," I explain after some hesitation. "You gave your subjects another reason to think ill of Solstice. I wanted to provide them with an alternative way of looking at the situation."

"Without consulting me first. Without asking me what I might think of your plans."

"That's correct. I didn't ask for your permission because I knew you wouldn't give it."

"That isn't what I meant," she replies, twisting her lips into a frown. "I don't give a damn that you thought you knew what was best for the rest of us. I'm upset you left me out, that you roped off this part of yourself. That you wouldn't let me in."

Good points as always. She's never been easy to argue with, so I tell her, quite simply, I never imagined my plans going awry in such a fashion. She turns away, facing the shadow of herself that's painted on the wall, and I wonder if she's working up the nerve to leave me as I was planning to leave her. It's hard to imagine the Princess doing such a thing, however. It would mean giving up, forfeiting the battle, a concession she's seldom able to make to anyone, especially herself.

"Perhaps it's time to tell the truth," she says, pivoting until she can see me again.

I rattle my claws against the ground, agitated by what she seems to be implying, and I assure her I have been telling her the truth and I would never think of telling her an out-and-out lie.

"I know that," she says, parting her lips as she lowers her head. "What I mean is, it might be time to tell the truth…to everyone. About everything that's happened."

My heart thumps so hard in my chest I worry it will get away from me, like a boulder rolling down a hill. "You want to tell them not only that I got myself stuck in this mountain but why? Is that what you're saying?"

"No, Porphyris. Not only that. I'm saying we should tell the truth about Solstice and the fight I had with them in the tower, about how Solstice accidentally broke my arm. And about the trouble we've had trying to keep Solstice sober and the bitter strain it's put upon us."

While the words she's said sink into me, I'm certain the itch that has finally subsided is about to return and it will devour me this time, turning me into a mindless, crazed beast—but that doesn't happen, and when it doesn't, I mull over the confession I would have to make to the subjects of this kingdom and how that confession would be borne upon the back of a revelation far more shocking than mine.

I think I could bear it, but it seems like far too great a risk for the Princess, and I say so. She dismisses my concern with a slight wave of her hand and sighs.

"I've never been the Princess they wanted," she explains. "I said it didn't matter, that I didn't care if they never liked me so long as they would let me make this kingdom into something better than it was before, but it does matter. It matters because of you and because of Solstice, because I have a family that defies their expectations in a similar way—because I don't want my family to be harmed by their hatred and their bigotry.

"That's why I couldn't tell anyone the truth about how I broke my arm. But that wasn't fair to Solstice, and it wasn't fair to you. Because you have to decide, each of you, how to live in this world as you are; I can't figure that out for you, and it would be foolish of me to try."

I feel some of my self-loathing dissolve in a shower of pride, but then I remember Cecil's daughter Phoebe and her mother, and I understand the breadth and the depth of what the Princess is proposing. New worries surface, worries that cannot be waved away so easily, and I stretch my neck out to nuzzle the Princess's hip with the flattened part of my nose. She looks at me and smiles, and I am suddenly reassured.

"Are you suggesting we should also give Solstice a say in this?" I ask.

"Yes, I am."

"You agree now they should be allowed to decide their own fate? That they should make the choice of what they want to be? Of the kind of life they want to live?"

"If Solstice is able to live a sober life, yes. They should make those choices, Porphyris."

I lower my head to the ground, genuflecting before her, and watch as she lets the pieces of the broken arrow fall from her hand.

"I'm so proud of you, my Princess. And I'm so grateful for your wisdom and your kindness, which are a boon to all of your subjects, including me."

A hint of sadness lurks behind her smile. "I would trade them both at this moment to be as strong as you, Porphyris, so I might single-handedly put those stones on your back back where they belong."

A contented sigh slips between my lips, stirring up the dust along the ground. There's no need for that, I'd like to tell her, for she has moved another kind of mountain, a mountain that was never made of rocks or dirt.

She doesn't know it yet, but she has already set me free.

~ * ~ * ~

**Chad Gayle** a full-time writer and former studio photographer whose speculative fiction has appeared in or is forthcoming from *DreamForge Magazine*, *Zooscape*, *Andromeda Spaceways Magazine*, and *The Colored Lens*.

# Not Disposable

## Jennifer Caracappa

The village leader stood up and banged his closed fist down onto the tree stump they used as a podium for such occasions.

"Enough is enough! We must do something. This has gone on for far too long. We cannot let this beast continue to burn our fields and crops. If we do nothing, we will starve this winter or have to move on to someplace else, again."

"Yeah! We have to do something! I hate moving," a voice yelled from the back of the cabin.

"But what should we do? The beast only comes down from the mountain top at night. It blocks out the light from the moon, so we know it's gigantic. How are we going to fight a creature like that? We already offered up sheep, goats, even a cow to it before, but it leaves them, choosing instead to burn our fields," another man said.

Edna barely paid attention to the argument and knitted a sweater off to the side of the fray. If you asked her, they should move on and settle elsewhere. The villagers had already ruined most of this once gorgeous mountain belt with their fields, cabins, and livestock, and now there was a dragon terrorizing them and killing all their crops. But she knew better than to speak up. No one would ask for her opinion.

She flinched as her fingers slipped and one of her needles poked her palm. Her arthritis got worse and worse every year.

"We should send someone to negotiate with it. Maybe we can see what it wants and strike a deal with it. Give it what it wants, and then it will leave us and our crops alone."

Everyone paused and thought for a moment.

Edna continued to knit.

"Hmmm, now that's a good idea," the village leader said. "But who would we send? We cannot send able-bodied men who are needed to work the fields and defend our home should invaders come."

Edna snorted, but no one noticed.

"We cannot send any of our wives either. They are needed here to look after the children and continue to grow our village's population," someone chimed in.

Edna rolled her eyes while keeping them trained on the needles going in and out of the yarn.

"I know! We can send Edna," the village leader declared.

Edna's knitting ceased. She looked up to find all eyes focused on her.

"Yeah, Edna should go. She's lived a good life, had six children, and her husband is dead. Who knows how long she has left; she's always sick. This could be her last contribution to the village," Terry, the baker, said.

Edna had never liked Terry.

More voices shouted agreement.

Edna was dismayed to hear all her children agree with the insane plan. No one asked for her consent before it was decided. Edna would go speak with the dragon.

~ * ~

Four men carried Edna up the mountain and deposited her in front of the entrance to the dragon's lair.

Terry, the baker, handed her the gnarled tree branch she used as a cane.

The village leader clapped her on the shoulder, causing pain to rocket down her back and leg. "Good luck. We hope you come back with a victory."

All four hurried away and quickly retreated down the ridge before she could say anything.

Edna ambled toward the opening of the cave. Her joints were not what they once were, and walking was a challenge these days. It was going to take her a while to journey to the dragon's lair as she would need to take breaks along the way.

About an hour and fifteen minutes later, after her seventh break of stopping to catch her breath, she saw a speck of sunlight ahead. She stared at it, wondering how that could be. She was in a cave, in the mountains, and didn't think she had gone far enough to reach the other side. After mulling it over, Edna decided to keep going forward. It was the only path except for turning back the way she had come, and she did not want to go that way.

The pinprick of light got larger and larger until Edna found herself stepping out of the dark, dank cave into a dazzling meadow filled with wildflowers. She stopped, hunched over her cane, and squinted into the bright light. The sun shone down on the tall grass and delicate wildflowers as they swayed in the warm, light breeze. It was paradise.

Edna noticed a wall of ebony rocks off to the right side. She huffed her way over and took a seat on the lowest ledge. It was the perfect height for her. She examined the rocks. They were iridescent and seemed to shimmer emerald where the sunlight hit them. They were the strangest rocks she had ever seen, but they were exquisite. She's not sure how long she rested there. It was a quite comfortable spot, and she dozed off.

"Are you aware you are lounging on my toe, small human?" The voice came from nowhere and everywhere at once.

Edna was jolted awake by the sound. She grabbed the end of her cane, but her fingers decided not to work, and it slipped from her grasp, falling into the tall grass near the rocks where she sat. She attempted to hoist herself to her feet, but then an enormous dragon's head with crimson eyes swung down from above and paused right in front of her.

Its considerable nostrils were mere inches from her face and sniffed the air. Her fluffy, colorless hair moved about her head as the dragon pulled in her scent. When it was satisfied, it moved out a bit, and she was mesmerized by its glowing eyes and gleaming raven scales. It was truly a magnificent, yet terrifying creature.

"It is about time, small human. Where are the rest of the small humans?" The dragon's deep voice boomed out across the meadow.

A few moments passed before Edna realized the dragon was talking to her and expected an answer. She gathered herself and smiled at the beast.

"Well, hello there, sweetheart. Aren't you an attractive—" she faltered, but quickly recovered, "dragon. It's only me, I'm afraid. No one else is here. But I came all this way to have a chat with you. My name is Edna. What's your name?"

The dragon peered at her, motionless, for so long Edna thought she had botched it and now the dragon would eat her. Finally, it replied.

"I have no name as I am a dragon and need no name."

Edna slowly nodded her head. "I understand completely, sweetheart. Names are practically useless anyway, who needs one? Well, it's a pleasure to finally meet you." She cleared her throat. "Any who, I've come here on behalf of my village to ask you what you would like so you will stop burning our fields and crops. I've come to negotiate, you see, so we can live in peace with you."

Again, the dragon did not move nor speak for quite some time.

In the silence, Edna suddenly remembered it had said she was sitting on its foot. What she had thought was rocks forming a wall was the dragon itself. She searched for her cane but could not find it in the tall grass. She made to get up on her own, but then the dragon spoke.

"No need to move. Keep lounging on my toe. I do not mind, and you seem comfortable."

Edna paused and settled back down. "Well, that's mighty kind of you. Thank you. It's hard for my old bones to find comfort these days, and I lost my cane, so I probably couldn't get up if I wanted to." She had no idea dragons were so accommodating.

After another pregnant pause, the dragon spoke again. "You want to know why I burned the small humans' fields and crops. I will tell you, but first, you must visit my hoard with me. Will you come?"

Edna had no idea dragons were so polite. This was not going at all like she had expected. She felt an innate sense to trust this dragon and so she did.

"Yes, I will come with you to see your hoard. If you would be so kind as to find my cane for me so I can get off your toe, I would greatly appreciate it."

After another lengthy stretch of silence, the dragon shifted its weight and scooped her up in one of its front feet, cupping her in it as a human would a fragile butterfly.

Edna stifled a scream.

"No need for your cane, Edna. I watched you walk in here, and it will be quicker for me to carry you to my hoard."

"That sounds fine, dear."

The dragon stretched its tremendous wings and took to the air. Edna held on to a large claw as the dragon soared through the air. She had her eyes closed until she realized this was a once in a lifetime experience. She opened her eyes and watched as the world flew by beneath them. She grinned and enjoyed the wind whistling in her ears.

It wasn't long before the dragon reached its destination and landed in a clearing, this one even deeper into the mountain belt. Edna had no idea where they were, but she didn't particularly care at the moment. She felt alive for the first time in years.

The dragon gently set her in the grass. "This is what I wanted you to see. This is my hoard. Not all of it; my hoard extends far and wide in the mountain belt. This is but a fragment of it."

Edna was captivated by what she saw. There were all manner of vegetables and fruits growing all around her. She could see eight feet tall tomato plants with tomatoes the size of cooking pots, towering wheat stalks, beans bigger than her arm vining up tall trees, squashes and pumpkins the size of some of the cabins in her village, footlong strawberries, cabbages equal to the width of small horse-drawn carts, and so much more. Every plant was at least ten times the size of what they grew in the village. This one garden could feed the villagers for at least a year, maybe longer.

"How do you grow all this? Why do you grow all this? It's beautiful, but why?" She turned to face the dragon's massive head.

The silence stretched, and when Edna didn't think she could wait any longer, the dragon spoke. "I grow this all myself. I set up an irrigation system from the spring that dwells deep inside the mountain. It waters all the plants you see here and all my other gardens containing my hoard. I do it to sustain myself, and I was hoping the small humans could come up here and live with me, share in the bounty of the harvest. That is why I burned the small humans' fields and crops."

Edna thought a moment. The dragon was a vegetarian, and that's why it never ate the livestock the villagers offered it. That part made sense, but there was one piece that didn't quite fit. "Why do you want the villagers to live up here with you?"

Edna gazed at the wonders around her while she waited for the dragon to respond.

"I am an old dragon, and I am all alone. All my friends have died or moved on. When the small humans moved into the mountains, I felt excited at the prospect of having friends again. I burnt their crops at night so they could not see me as my form sometimes frightens small humans, and if all the crops were destroyed, they would have no choice but to come live with me. But since you are the only one who came, you can be my companion if that would be agreeable to you. You may sit on my toe again if you would like to rest."

She was mighty grateful when the dragon stuck out its toe because she didn't know how much longer she could have stood there in the grass. She happily sat down and leaned against the dragon's bulk. The dragon's head bowed down a bit more, so they were almost eye level with each other. Edna loved the way the dragon shone in the sunlight.

"I don't approve of your methods, but I understand completely. Loneliness is an old friend of mine ever since my husband, Frank, died. After he went, I was truly alone. All my children are grown and have their own families to raise. I would love to be your companion. Lord knows, I can't go back to the village. But I have nothing to offer you. I'm on my way out. Arthritis is slowly taking over my body, and even my mind is starting to fade. I wouldn't be able to help you with your crops. I can't walk that far, and I can't stand on my own for too long without my cane. Do you know why the villagers sent me to speak with you? Because I'm disposable. If you had eaten me, they wouldn't have lost anything important." Edna wiped a stray tear from the corner of her eye.

After its usual period of silence, the dragon spoke. "I disagree. You are kind, a good conversationalist, and would make a wonderful companion. The small humans are wrong, and I don't like them anymore for it. I want you to stay. Will you?"

Edna wiped away more tears that she couldn't stop from falling. "Yes. Yes, I will stay with you, sweetheart. I think we will get on just fine." She patted the dragon's toe.

Ever since she had been abandoned at the cave opening, she was convinced this was the day she would leave this world, but instead, she had found something to live for, a dragon of all things. She smiled and closed her eyes as she waited for the dragon to speak.

"I am glad you have chosen to stay with me. Don't worry about your ailments. I will carry you until you can walk on your own again. These vegetables and fruits are not like the small humans' crops. They are rich in nutrients and the water from the spring makes them able to sustain me. Once you have eaten enough of them, your ailments will begin to fade, and you will be made whole again. You will live much longer as long as you keep eating them."

"That sounds just fine, dear." She patted the dragon's toe.

~ * ~

When Edna didn't come back and the dragon continued to burn their fields and crops, the villagers mistakenly assumed Edna had been eaten by the dragon. They eventually gave up and decided to move someplace else, preferably somewhere without a neighboring dragon.

After they left, the dragon burned the cabins and the settlement until there was nothing left. Then, it watered the land with the water from the mountain spring. The most beautiful of flowers grew and filled the area until all evidence humans had once inhabited it was gone.

When her gift was ready, the dragon brought Edna to see what it had created for her. When she saw what her old village had become, she laughed at the lovely sight. She danced in the vibrant flowers and delighted in a wrong being righted.

After about a year of only eating what the dragon grew from the spring water, most of Edna's ailments were gone. She could walk, run, and climb trees again. She no longer lost her train of thought, and she remembered things that happened long ago. Some of her wrinkles faded, not all but some, and some color came back into her curls. None of that mattered to her though, they were just the perks of her finding happiness.

Edna lived another 150 years with the dragon by her side, and when it was time for her to go, the dragon went with its cherished friend.

~ * ~ * ~

**Jennifer Caracappa** is a technical writer by day and a fiction writer by night. She loves to write strong, female characters, especially characters who defy the odds and are full of surprises. She is the author of The Dragon Within published in Rise, Queer Sci Fi's Tenth Annual Flash Fiction Contest. Jennifer is currently working on her debut fantasy novel. She lives in Ohio with her loyal companions, a dog named Minna and two cats named Loki and Colt.

# The Dragon Heist

## D.J. Tyrer

Dragons love gold, it's a universally known fact. They have tons of the stuff, but always want more, lots more. In the old days, they would acquire it themselves as a tribute from fearful nations or through the destruction of Dwarven cities, deep below the earth. But, those days were long ago and the exigencies of law and spreading civilisation meant they had to obtain it in the more subtle ways of the younger races.

Which was what had brought Johann and Etzel to the lair of the dragon Totwyrm Manithrax.

Even the mighty warrior was a little cowed to be in the presence of such a being as the gold-encrusted dragon, and his companion, the wily little thief, kept well behind him.

"I want gold," Totwyrm Magnithrax told them with the unnecessariness of a glutton informing a cook they are hungry. "You will bring me gold."

Johann nodded. "Yes."

Normally, Etzel would do the talking, but he was staying away from the dragon; not remaining still, but always keeping Johann between them.

This was the difficult point—dragons were never keen to actually pay you, as it involved handing over some of their treasure. But, there were things they *would* trade.

"You have the pearls?"

The dragon moved its head, indicating 'yes' and gestured to a niche in the cave wall where a dozen milk-white globes sat. Nobody knew where dragons got the pearls from—some rather unpleasant speculation had occurred upon the subject—but, they were strongly magical and of no apparent value to them, so were perfect items of trade.

"Then, we can bring you gold."

"Good." Totwyrm Magnithrax bared its enormous fangs in what was, presumably, intended as a smile, but appeared more like a prelude to their being devoured. "A ship full of finely-crafted

items of elven gold will be arriving at the docks in a few days—
bring that cargo to me and you shall have the pearls."

Johann nodded. "We will."

Without further discussion, he and his wily little partner exited
the dragon's lair, remounted their nervous horses and rode back to
the city to plan their crime.

~ * ~

It wouldn't be easy: Although the paperwork said differently,
or rather, nothing at all, the cargo of gold objects was the property
of Munsell Vand. Officially, nothing more than the owner of a particularly unsavoury tavern called The Egg and Orb, to those who
moved in the right—or, wrong—circles, such as Johann and Etzel,
he was the head of the Dead Kobolds gang, one of the best organ-
ised and most-vicious gangs in the city. It was their income, rather
than that of his tavern, that allowed him to live in an opulent townhouse filled with artwork and other items.

Not as awful as a dragon, but probably as close as a human
could come.

"Which," as Etzel said to his sceptical friend, "is what gives us
an edge: Vand knows nobody wants to cross him, so his precautions
are nowhere near as effective as they might be."

Johann shrugged, rippling muscles. "It's not the precautions
that bother me—it's the repercussions."

"Hey, you agreed to the deal with the dragon, not me." Etzel
grinned.

"This was all your idea—and, now, it's a doubly dangerous one."

Etzel scoffed. "We can do this, easy-peasy."

"Well, you'd better have a good plan…"

"I do, although you know what happens once you put a plan
into play."

Johann snorted.

"It's simple, really." Johann rolled his eyes, but Etzel kept on.
"Although the Dead Kobolds are standing guard at the dock, the
pick-up is a cart driven by one of Vand's servants. He doesn't like
his thugs to embarrass him in front of his neighbours."

"So, we hijack the cart and take the gold?"

"Yes, only we hijack it going out, not coming back. There's no
guard, you see, just the driver. Coming back, there are a couple of

toughs in the back. Oh, we could take them, I'm sure, but the Watch are likely to come running. My way, I drive up and they hand over the gold."

"Plus, a couple of Dead Kobolds…"

"Which is where you come in, my friend…"

~ * ~

The plan would work, Etzel was certain of it: his plans almost always did, more-or-less. But, that didn't stop the cold sweat trickling down the length of his spine as he drove the cart towards the docks.

"Halt!" A man in a tarnished mail shirt and a threadbare set of breeches with a kobold's paw tied to a thong of leather about his neck, halted him at the entrance to the quay where the ship was docked.

Etzel stopped the cart and the man looked at him.

"You're new."

"Hans is off sick." He mimed drinking from a tankard.

The guard laughed. "You skivvies never could hold your ale."

"True enough."

Nodding, the man lifted aside the plank of wood that served to bar access to the quay and waved him on.

The cart clattered its way over to where a gaggle of more men wearing kobolds' paws as accessories were waiting to offload the ship.

Grudgingly, they set to work loading the crates into the back of the cart.

Now, it was up to Johann to provide the distraction before the two men climbed aboard to protect the cargo on the journey to Vand's townhouse.

Nervously, Etzel played with the reins, hoping he didn't look too-obviously uncomfortable—or, that the Dead Kobolds would expect a servant to be twitchy around them.

He really hoped his friend could pull it off…

*Kaboom!* The sudden explosion made him jump, even despite having been praying for it.

A hut that served as a shelter for the guards in bad weather had just jumped off the quay and burning chunks of wood were floating upon the waters. It was surprising just what you could achieve with some highly flammable Rijnsöl and some of the alchemists' black powder.

"Ambush!" Etzel cried, flicking the reins before any of the Dead Kobolds could climb aboard.

To reinforce the point, a crossbow bolt embedded itself in the leg of the nearest man—both stopping him from jumping aboard the cart and reinforcing the sense of chaos.

Behind him, as he approached the plank of wood barring his exit, Etzel could see Dead Kobolds bumbling about in a panic, ready to fight a foe they couldn't see or seeking shelter from further attacks that wouldn't come.

"Move the plank! Move the plank!" Etzel waved at the man standing guard by it, but he didn't move, face confused.

Then, he did move, leaping aside, as Etzel cracked the reins and the horses galloped faster.

Reaching the plank, the horses tried to jump, crashing awkwardly into it and smashing it to pieces, the sudden jerk sending something tumbling out through the still-open doors of the cart.

Etzel swore. He just hoped he hadn't lost much.

He turned the cart south, the wrong way for Vand's townhouse, but he hoped the guard, if he was watching at all, would be too stunned to realise it before they were well away.

Pushing the horses hard for a hundred yards, startling any number of people going about their lawful business, and sending a dung cart crashing into a jellied-eel stall, Etzel allowed them to slow and they turned into a side-street.

A few more turns led them deeper into the backways before he halted and waited.

"I thought you weren't going to make it, there."

Etzel's hand was on the hilt of his dagger even as his brain registered the speaker as his partner.

Johann slammed the cart doors shut, then climbed up beside him.

"We've got the hardest part to do, now," he said, and he didn't mean exiting the city.

~ * ~

Exiting the city proved simple, as Etzel had procured a scroll listing the goods as for export and none of the gate guards were going to risk becoming embroiled in the machinations of one of the city's foremost (alleged) criminals by searching a cart painted in his livery.

"A toast," Johann said as they bounced away from the city, along a deeply-rutted road, producing an earthenware flask with the dregs of the Rijnsöl he'd used to concoct the explosion.

Etzel held up a declining hand. "I don't know how you can drink that stuff—it's awful."

"I happen to be a conno-conni-connu-, er, lover of real ales, and they don't come much realer." He swigged it down and tossed the flask away, as Etzel wrinkled his nose.

"Besides," Johann added, after a loud belch, "I need a little courage for what comes next."

"Hmm, maybe I should've have had a sip…"

Etzel wondered if they should just call it off—the journey was a long one and there would be plenty of time to reconsider. After all, a dozen dragon pearls was a decent prize—but, not quite enough to justify earning the ire of Mansell Vand. No, it looked like the plan was still on.

~ * ~

"Right, you remember what to do?" Etzel asked, as he handed Johann the reins and jumped down from the cart.

The brawny barbarian nodded. "My part in all this seems the simplest."

"And, the riskiest," Etzel reminded him. "Don't forget that. If this all goes wrong, you'll be standing right in front of Totwyrm Magnithrax when he blows his top…"

"The shieldwall or the dragon's lair, I'm always first in the line for danger," he replied with a shrug.

"Remember, our getaway horses are in a meadow east of here."

Johann nodded and drove the horses on. He would deliver the goods and get out as quickly as possible.

After all, *their* theft had gone smoothly enough…

~ * ~

Dragons were hardly sociable creatures—generally, they fought one another and ate anything smaller—so, the minimal scouting of Totwyrm Magnithrax's lair Etzel had achieved while Johann had been speaking, had been the best they could really hope for. Now, if his calculations were correct, this pit was one end of a vent he'd noticed in the ceiling of the cave.

He attached a rope to a rock and began to climb down.

Yes! He could hear Johann's voice echoing up to him. The warrior was handing over the crates.

Etzel slid down the rope, softly landing upon a pile of coins—he didn't have long, but knew exactly which items he was after. Three: a golden harp, a coronet decorated with rubies and a chalice veined with silver.

A word of command caused the rope to untie itself and drop into his waiting hands.

The last two items were easy. The coronet was sitting atop a statue of a warrior god and slipped easily into the sack he carried, while the chalice he had repositioned to the edge of a pile during his previous visit. But, the harp…

The harp was half-buried in a pile of golden trinkets from a dozen civilisations down the ages and uncovering it risked twanging the golden 'strings'.

"Tasty," he heard the dragon say and, for one horrible moment, he thought Totwyrm Magnithrax had eaten his partner. But, he glanced over the top of the pile in time to see a horse's leg clatter down onto a pile of coins. It looked as if the dragon were helping to dispose of the evidence of their crime.

Then, it tore apart a crate and began to deposit its contents onto piles, the sound of gold clattering onto gold helping to cover the noise as Etzel moved the harp.

Having eased it into the sack, he began to move quietly around the edge of the cave to where Johann was, slipping behind him, next to the niche with the pearls.

"So," Johann asked the dragon, "satisfied?"

The dragon moved its head in the manner that seemed to signify 'yes'.

Johann tuned to Etzel as if he'd been there all the time and said, "Sack."

Etzel held it up, careful not to let its contents clatter. "Here."

"Right." Johann scooped the pearls from where they rested and lowered them with a mother's gentleness into the sack, before turning back to the dragon. "We'll be going, then…"

"Go." It turned to look covetously at its latest acquisitions.

Now, they just had to hope its attention was sufficiently occupied not to notice its loss.

Johann and Etzel stepped back out into the sunlight.

"There they are," a voice said.

A rough-looking man in the greens and browns favoured by rangers stood upon an outcrop of rock, a bow in his hands, a dozen Dead Kobolds in mismatched armour, equipped with hand weapons of various sorts, at its base.

Johann swore. They hadn't anticipated on Vand successfully sending a band of his cut-throats after them.

"So much for the next phase of my plan," Etzel muttered.

"You stole the boss's pretties," one said.

"Return 'em," a second said, "and die quick."

"Otherwise," a third added, "die slow."

The men's grins implied they were planning on slow deaths regardless.

Then, before Johann could draw his sword or they could charge, there was a roar from inside the cave that caught everyone's attention.

"My gold!"

"They took it!" Etzel shrieked as he yanked his friend aside, out of the path of the raging dragon.

The ranger was gone in a flash, but though the Dead Kobolds turned to run, the dragon was upon them before they'd gone more than a few steps.

Johann and Etzel ran. Behind them, shrieks of terror quickly fell silent, to be replaced with horrible wet and crunchy sounds.

Reaching their waiting getaway mounts, the pair jumped up into the saddles and spurred them into a gallop.

Behind them, they heard the dragon roar, again, and cry, "Where's my gold?"

"Apparently the stories about them knowing every item in their hoards were accurate," Johann cried as they rode.

"Annoying of those DKs to show up like they did."

"Still, two birds with one stone."

"Let's hope the wyrm chases off after that ranger."

But, at that moment, they heard the beating of vast bat-like wings behind them.

"Can we outrun it?" Etzel asked, clutching his sack to his chest.

"I doubt it."

"The river!"

The river was in a gorge far below.

"The horses won't make it."

Etzel snorted. "Leave them as an apology snack."

"I don't know if we'll make it…"

"Better than waiting to be eaten or fried…"

They were almost at the edge of the gorge. The dragon was close behind; a sheet of flame rippled after them.

Panicked, caught between fire and water, the horses reared, throwing their riders, whinnying in fear.

"Jump!" Etzel called, rolling into a crouch, then sprinting for the gorge, uncurling his rope as he ran.

He leapt, throwing the rope towards a stunted tree as he did so, shouting a command—it wrapped about the trunk and held as he swung out from the cliff edge.

Johann jumped, too, catching the rope just below his friend.

Hands burning, they slid down it. Above them, the horses shrieked, caught in the dragon's claws.

Halfway down, they looked up to see the dragon's head appear over the edge—it opened its jaws wide…

"Drop!" Etzel let go, slamming into his friend and knocking him from the rope.

Together, they plunged down.

Flame billowed after them.

The water claimed them, then began to boil.

Kicking hard, they headed down, as deep as they could go.

Then, they let the current take them.

~ * ~

Etzel swore as Johann pulled him up onto the riverbank.

"Am I still alive?"

The warrior laughed. "I believe so."

"I lost my rope. I lost my blasted rope. The dragon flame burnt it up."

"We'll buy you another," Johann said, "assuming you have the items our employer requested."

Etzel looked down at his hand: He still clutched his sack, and it was intact.

"Yes."

"Well, let's get to the city and get paid."

Etzel nodded and stood and followed him in the direction of the distant metropolis.

"You know," he said, "some days, I think this game isn't worth the danger."

Johann shrugged. "Tell me that when we get paid."

They both laughed and kept walking.

~ * ~ * ~

**DJ Tyrer** is the person behind *Atlantean Publishing* and has been widely published in anthologies and magazines around the world, such as *Insurgence: A Fae Rebellion* (Corrugated Sky), *Tales of the Black Arts* (Hazardous Press), and *Us/Them* and *Crunchy With Ketchup* (both WolfSinger Publications), and issues of *Fantasia Divinity*, *Broadswords and Blasters*, *BFS Horizons*, *The Fifth Di...*, and *Tales from the Magician's Skull*. In addition, they have a novella available in paperback and on Kindle, *The Yellow House* (Dunhams Manor).

You can visit DJ at: djtyrer.blogspot.co.uk/,

Facebook at: www.facebook.com/DJTyrerwriter/

Atlantean Publishing atlanteanpublishing.wordpress.com/

# Lazuli's Goods

## A.B. Martin

"MALVOLOCH!" The Dragon Master bellowed up from the ramparts. Every dragon rider in the field below, in a fifty-foot radius, was able to hear the call. And in a domino effect, the riders closest to Daryl Malvoloch turned to look at him, which drew the eyes of the other riders, and soon everyone was looking at him. The Dragon Master narrowed his eyes in his direction as he yelled, "KITCHEN!"

Daryl sighed as his comrades erupted into laughter. He passed his practice staff to Hayden, who gave him a sympathetic smile, before picking up his pace and running off the practice field, back towards the fort. It was summer and he was hot in his practice padding, the back of his neck up into his short hair was slick with sweat. The kitchens at this time of day would be even hotter, with all their stoves running. He ran a hand through his dark brown hair, then wiped it off on his leg. He had a moment of reprieve when he jogged into the castle's cool interior.

The kitchen had two entrances, one in the great dining hall and one in the courtyard, where they accepted deliveries. The courtyard entrance was closest, but it would be completely blocked now. Inside the castle Daryl walked like his mother did on market day, his feet quickly shuffling at a brisk pace with a little extra speed when no one was present. He stopped short when the young Princess stepped into the hallway from the stairs, followed by her training master and three of her peers.

Daryl quickly stepped aside to make room, his arms at his side as he bowed for the Princess.

"Malvoloch? You alright?" Lachie, the Princess' training master, asked.

"Yes sir, just tending to a small issue," Daryl answered. Lachie caught his meaning and raised a hand to his face, rubbing the spot on his forehead just above his nose.

"Malvoloch?" One of the young peers breathed in awe, his jaw hanging open.

"Malvoloch? Are you the dragon rider to Lazuli the Galestorm?" Princess Rinoa asked.

"Yes, Your Highness," Daryl said with another small bow of his head. In the back of his mind he knew Princess Rinoa was here for the season but had forgotten in the moment. Daryl felt mortified now as the Princess beamed at him, his hands tightening at his sides.

"I've heard Lazuli is the fastest dragon that's ever been recorded in history. And in the last contest you both outraced all the others by *leagues*," Princess Rinoa complimented. Daryl could feel a small twitch starting on the outside of his left eyebrow.

"That is what I hear from the archivists, Your Highness," Daryl agreed.

"I would very much like to see the two of you in action one day," she said.

*But hopefully not today*, Daryl thought.

"I am honored to hear that," Daryl said as Lachie politely cleared his throat.

"Your Highness, Malvoloch was on an errand, we probably shouldn't hold him for long."

"Of course," Princess Rinoa said, with a dismissive nod in his direction, before her group continued down the hall. Daryl took a few steps towards the grand dining hall, then chanced looking back to see which direction the group was going. Lachie was at the front of the group, leading the Princess and her peers in the direction of the side courtyard, instead of out the main doors. Daryl counted his blessings and continued on his way.

The grand dining hall had enough tables and benches to sit one hundred people. Between four and six in the afternoon, the kitchen staff as well as the fort staff, served fifty-five dragon riders, seventy-five soldiers, fifteen masters, and whomever else was visiting the fort, such as the Princess and her peers. It was half an hour before the dinner rush would start, and all of the kitchen staff was in the grand dining hall, either standing or sitting, as they waited for him.

The moment the head chef saw Daryl he took a towel from his shoulder and slapped it on the table.

"This cannot happen again!" He shouted, "I must be able to work in my kitchen! The Princess is eating here and I will have the ultimate shame on my shoulders if I can't serve her and the people a good meal."

"I know, I know," Daryl begged, "we are trying hard to work out a solution." He took a deep breath and stepped through the swinging door into the kitchen.

"Work as fast as you fly!" the chef shouted after him.

The kitchen was a large space, with three long rows of tables that served as stations for cutting and prepping food. Multiple stoves lined the northern wall, near the door into the courtyard. Along the western wall were basins for washing. Cutlery, dishes and cups, used to be on the southern wall, but had since been switched to the eastern wall so food could be placed as far from the courtyard door as possible. It was a horrible reminder to Daryl, that such a shift had been made specifically because of his dragon. Lazuli's head and neck blocked the courtyard door and access to all the stoves. He was sniffing heavily as his eyes darted madly around the room.

"Lazuli," Daryl sighed as he walked through the kitchen towards his dragon. "You know you need to talk to me when you get these urges."

Lazuli the Galestorm rumbled, his head was tilted to the side because as much as he had forced his way into the kitchen, he didn't want his antlers to knock everything over, or risk hitting someone. It wasn't his first time doing this, but sadly the only thing he learned after each attempt was how to cause less trouble, and not how to stop.

"It's not fair," Lazuli cried. "I could smell them, and mine don't smell anymore. They've all crumbled."

Daryl put the heels of his hands against his eyes and prayed for patience. Every dragon had a hoard, possessions they normally kept to themselves, but sometimes they were put on display for their dragon friends or riders. These hoards helped keep dragons mentally healthy, it brought them inner peace and happiness. Every dragon's hoard was a little different as the dragons grew and fancied different things. Hayden's brown dragon, Skysong, preferred to have chairs.

There were many times Daryl had seen Skysong's tail happily swish back and forth as she played with her chairs. Stacking and arranging them in different ways, sometimes building them up and then knocking them down with a shove of her head and a giddy roar. Another friend's dragon, an orange dragon by the name of Saffron, liked having four wagons. Saffron would balance a clawed foot in each wagon and then pump their wings as they rolled across the countryside.

Some dragons liked smaller, more delicate items, or at least smaller to them; candles, books, necklaces with large beads, and glass baubles. The problem for Lazuli was his hoard never lasted, because what he really loved to smell, hold, and sometimes cuddle with, was bread. Any kind of bread, and he loved to see the variety. Sourdough was the easiest for him to play with, and croissants often made him cry when they fell apart. He loved the smell of cinnamon rolls and would often put pretzels on his claws like rings.

But whether it was baguettes or soda bread, it would eventually mold, decay and crumble away. Daryl tried to stay vigilant in the upkeep of Lazuli's hoard, working out a deal with some of the bakers in the nearby town to send the fort their old baked goods. However, those shipments were often lacking after holidays, and sometimes there were days when Lazuli would experience the loss of his entire hoard. It would make him spiral into a depressive fit, and, when he thought no one would mind, he'd force his head through the kitchen door to look for more bread.

"Can't I just stay here? I won't be in the way," Lazuli begged.

"My beautiful loaf," Daryl sighed as he rested a hand along Lazuli's jaw, "you block all of the ovens. Besides, the chef won't let any of the workers into the kitchen while you're here. You can't stay. But I will make sure to save my dinner biscuits for you."

Lazuli chuffed, whimpered, but slowly pulled his head back. Daryl guided him so he wouldn't bump into anything further. Once they were outside Daryl firmly shut the door behind him to stop any permeating smells of temptation. There was still a look of desperation in Lazuli's eyes that told Daryl if he didn't escort him from the grounds he was just going to try again.

"Let's go for a flight, okay?" Daryl suggested.

"Fine." Lazuli begrudgingly accepted. Daryl gave him a smile, patted his forearm, then climbed up to settle between his ridge scales near his shoulders. If this was a combat flight Daryl would have to put a saddle and harness straps on Lazuli, or he'd be knocked off the moment Lazuli ramped up his speed. But as this was a leisure flight, he trusted his friend not to knock him off. Lazuli glanced around to make sure he wouldn't knock anyone, then extended his wings and they took to the air.

Daryl was one of the few pilots who had a versatile saddle that allowed him to ride either sitting up or laying down. When Daryl first presented the idea to the Dragon Master, he was escorted to the medical ward to be tested for whiplash and concussion.

"What is the point of laying down in combat?" The Dragon Master had argued with him, "you won't see what's coming at you, and you'll make a bigger target of yourself."

"Lazuli holds back his speed in practice, for me," Daryl protested. "Not only is there a real danger of sitting upright at his speeds, but I wouldn't be able to track what's in front of him any faster than he would. However, because he needs to keep his focus forward, he is vulnerable to the rest of his surroundings. I can be his eyes on what's above and behind him, what's approaching his flank. You know there's precedence for this with a popular winter sport called—"

The Dragon Master cut off his explanation with a quick hand.

"Let's see how it tests in the field," he said.

A prototype saddle was made and Daryl and Lazuli were given two weeks to familiarize themselves with it and the new flying style. If it showed even a little improvement over their previous mock-battle they would be allowed more time to perfect the style. And it did, regardless that Daryl got vertigo afterwards. With more practice he learned to manage the saddle well and Lazuli began to break records. The royal family was even starting to take notice of them, which the Dragon Master forewarned Daryl about.

"I know Lazuli would never hurt any of our allies, but he needs to demonstrate that control. If he's ever caught forcing his way into the kitchen, then it would cast doubt onto his character. They'll wonder what he would do if he ever went feral."

Daryl mused about what extra precautions he could take for ensuring Lazuli's hoard, but he always seemed to hit a dead end. Lazuli made sure their flight was finished when the dinner bell had run, thoughts of the promised biscuits never leaving the back of his mind. Daryl disembarked and straightened his leather jerkin, brushing a hand through his short hair to make sure nothing had gotten stuck in it.

"Wait here," Daryl said to Lazuli, who shifted his weight anxiously from one front leg to the other. Daryl made his way into the fort with the rest of the dragon riders as they were called in by the dinner bell. He could hear their heckled remarks but chose to ignore them. He took his usual spot in the grand dining hall next to Hayden, who had already nabbed two dinner biscuits from the basket for his plate.

"Saved these for you," Hayden offered. Daryl sighed gratefully. "Thank you."

All the dragon riders stood when the Princess entered the hall, then reclaimed their seats when she had taken hers. Food on platters was passed along the table while Daryl's leg began to bounce nervously. Could Lazuli wait for him? If he burst into the kitchen now there would be no way to hide it from the Princess. Before Daryl's plate was even full he started to eat, skipping out on any conversation to consume his food as fast as possible. Hayden only had to pound on his back a few times when he choked for air. As soon as Daryl finished he nodded a goodbye to those around him, gathered his dinner biscuits, and left.

Lazuli was still waiting for him outside, nervously digging at the ground and leaving large trench marks. He stilled as soon as he saw Daryl, laying his stomach flat against the ground as he stretched his neck forward. Daryl held the biscuits up for him to inspect. Lazuli smelled them first, then turned his head to look more closely at them. Then his entire upper lip curled back in an exuberant dragon smile that made Daryl grin from its gleeful appearance

"These are for you buddy," Daryl said. Lazuli extended his left hand and Daryl gingerly set the two dinner biscuits on it. Lazuli brought his hand close to his chest, craning his neck to look down directly at his new hoard. Daryl sighed and sank down to the ground, leaning his back against the fort wall.

"Excuse me, Dragon Rider Malvoloch?" He heard a voice say timidly behind him. Daryl craned his head back to see someone peeking around the fort wall at him. He was pretty sure it was someone who worked in the kitchen, due to her apron, but he didn't know her name or job.

"Yes, how can I help you?" he asked as he stood up. Had Lazuli damaged an oven in the kitchen earlier? What more could happen now?

Hesitantly she stepped out from behind the fort wall, her left hand remained hidden, holding something out of sight behind the wall.

"Beg my pardon for saying so, but, well, everyone in the kitchen knows about Lazuli's…" Her eyes went to the large blue dragon behind him, who paid her no mind as he was completely enraptured by two dinner biscuits. "…Lazuli's need for bread."

"I am very sorry for today, if there were any damages…"

"Oh, no, that's not why I'm here. My friend and I actually had an idea that might help." She tugged her left hand, but nothing moved. With a plastered smile she tugged again harder and pulled another figure out from behind the wall. He was a young man, but not a kitchen hand Daryl recognized, by his garb and age it was possible he was a squire. He kept both his hands behind his back and his eyes on the ground.

Daryl waited but the young man said nothing.

His companion elbowed him sharply.

"Ow," the lad cried. "Stop it, this was your idea."

"Lazuli is only upset when his bread runs out right?" she asked, undeterred by her friend's objections. "Have you ever tried something like a mock-up of bread? Something that would help keep him balanced until more bread arrived?"

"Ah, yes," Daryl said with a soft smile and a nod of his head. "We've tried paintings of bread, scented candles, clay sculptures, but touch is also important to him. It needs to be a similar weight, texture and smell all in one."

"I told you it was stupid," the lad muttered to his friend. Irritated, she pinched her lips together and then snatched what he hid behind his back. He jerked, his face turning crimson as she handed the item over to Daryl. It looked like sourdough with one slash mark across the top. Curious, Daryl took it into his hands, the weight seemed similar. It felt coarse and rigid like the outer layer of sourdough, and when he traced his fingers across the cut ridge, he could feel a softer texture inside. It didn't smell like sourdough, and it didn't feel like he could break off a piece.

"What is this made of?" he asked holding it up to his face for a closer look.

"Fabric and sheep's wool, Sir." The lad answered.

"How do you get the fabric to feel like this?" Daryl wondered.

"I starched it and then sanded it in some locations. I know it doesn't smell like sourdough, but it was just a first attempt."

Daryl was trying to spot the stitches when a shadow fell over his light. He looked up to see Lazuli had crept up behind him, his head craned over and looking down at the faux sourdough. The lad and lady held their breath and stood stock still as Lazuli looked closely at the sourdough. He smelled it, then pulled back his head and tilted it to the side.

"It's not bread." Lazuli stated, having not paid attention to their earlier conversation.

"No." Daryl answered, "it's not."

"...but can I have it?" Lazuli asked.

A lance of hope pierced through Daryl as his eyes snapped onto the lad. The lad could name his price and Daryl would gladly pay it. Lazuli had never shown interest in keeping non-bread items. The lad was staring up at Lazuli, wide eyed but unafraid, while his friend had taken a few steps closer to his side.

"O-of course Galestorm," the lad said before bowing his head.

"What are your names? And where do you work in the fort?" Daryl asked them as a huge claw reached down in front of him, carefully retrieving the faux sourdough. Lazuli pulled it close to his chest in his right hand, next to his dinner biscuits, before waddling away on two legs to examine it further in peace.

"I'm Arc, I work with the cleaning staff, and this is Seng, she works in the kitchens," Arc explained.

"Arc, if I provide you with all the necessary materials, can you show me how to make more of these?" Daryl asked.

Arc smiled, both nervous and proud. "Sure, but I don't have an exact pattern, it's kind of a learning curve," he explained. "And honestly, Seng was the one who helped me with the idea."

"Even though you thought it was stupid," Seng said smiling.

"Great, you can both help, I'll take as many people who can."

~ * ~

Daryl was left with a list of modest materials to grab, and when he explained his plan to the Dragon Master he was granted leave from practice to go into the city. He made sure to get 5 times the quantity of each item needed and loaded his arms up with goods from the bakery. Internally he fought his normal struggle, since becoming Lazuli's rider, to not eat any of the food. He really missed doughnuts.

After delivering Lazuli's hoard, Daryl took his craft items to a table out in the courtyard. His room was too small to host multiple people, and he didn't want to have to use the grand dining hall, where he would have to pack things up between meals.

"I can't believe the Dragon Master was able to change our schedules, so we only have to work on this," Arc commented as he and Seng approached the table.

"Honestly, I'm not. I think Chef is on the verge of bursting a blood vessel if Lazuli gets in his kitchen one more time," Seng said. Arc's eyes widened and he elbowed her for speaking about Lazuli in front of his rider. She winced and smacked the back of his shoulder. Daryl smiled politely to keep himself from acting like his parents and telling them to rein it in and focus.

"What do we do first?" he asked instead.

"We start with dying the material," Arc instructed.

~ * ~

Somehow Daryl made it through impatiently waiting for the dyed fabric to dry, there weren't many tasks to do until then. After dinner they had a few patterns cut out and were joined by Hayden, a couple other dragon riders, and staff members who knew Arc and Seng. They dragged a second table over to help seat everyone.

"Ope," Gerald, a member of the cleaning staff who was older than Daryl said, "I nicked this pattern a little bit, is that going to be okay?"

"Yeah, that's fine," Arc said, nodding in the man's direction before Daryl could bemoan the mistake. "We want them to be similar, but not identical, so it's more like real bread."

"Is that why Lazuli likes bread?" Seng asked Daryl as she leaned over her stitch work, "because they're all a little different?"

"He could answer that much better than I, but how much time do you have? He'll talk your ear off," Daryl said. He was currently working with hot coals in an iron and a metal bowl to shape the fabric.

"Speaking of time, how long are we doing this? How many are you wanting to make?" Hayden asked as he helped sprinkle starch over the fabric.

"This is my life now," Daryl remarked dryly, which got a chuckle out of everyone in their group. Daryl finished his shaping and carefully set aside the hot iron and bowl. While that piece cooled he took a break and a drink, someone had brought out a pitcher of water and tankards. He looked at everyone who had come to help him and Lazuli. He sniffled quickly and rubbed the back of his hand across his nose.

"You all are pretty amazing," he said.

"Of course I am." Hayden grinned as he bounced his eyebrows. Daryl rolled his eyes while Hayden continued, "I was thinking, for the smell. What if we kept some of these in the kitchen? Maybe netted up over the stoves?"

"That or we could try oils? You said you had found some scented candles before, right?" Arc asked. "If there's a candle smell he likes, then it could probably be made into an oil, and you could put a few droplets on the 'pillows' every once in a while."

"That's an idea," Daryl mused and looked at Arc. "How do you get these ideas? I like how you think outside the box."

"He learns it from watching you, and your crazy saddle riding," Seng remarked. Daryl heard from under the table a well landed kick as Arc grew red and Seng swore.

"My grandfather used to make puppets for theater, I learned some tricks from him too," Arc protested.

"Maybe let your Grandfather be the one to inspire you. I've tried using Daryl's saddle once, and—" Hayden cut himself off briefly as the Dragon Master approached their tables, hands held behind his back. Daryl wished his hands had been busy at the moment instead of taking a break for water and quickly set the tankard down. The Dragon Master raised a brow as he surveyed their assembly line of craft making and walked to the end of the table where one of their finished products sat.

"How has Lazuli been with this substitute?" the Dragon Master asked.

"He keeps it, in a separate spot from his bread, but he'll still spend time with it." Daryl answered as he met him at the end of the table.

"Good, let's hope affection for it will grow over time. Princess Rinoa has requested a ride with you in a week's time with her dragon Nyx. I assume you can keep things balanced until then?" the Dragon Master stated with another expertly cocked brow.

"Yes, of course Sir," Daryl promised.

~ * ~

It rained for two days before the appointed ride with Princess Rinoa. The roads from town into the fort became too muddy for the wagons to make their way in and the bakers to deliver their bread. The extra moisture was also doing no favors for Lazuli's cave. Daryl, with the help of Hayden, hoarded the pretzels offered at lunchtime. There were no biscuits at dinner, as the chef for some reason had decided to make cake each night instead. Which added to Daryl's stress levels.

However, Lazuli was ecstatic to receive the pretzels, and didn't appear to reach the melancholy state he sometimes got when his hoard became small.

"The 'pillows', will suffice," Lazuli told him. "But, I require more of them, in the different bread shapes."

"I'll see what I can do," Daryl said, chuckling and shaking his head, his shoulders sagged in relief. Craft nights were starting to become a regular part of his schedule, and he was starting to have a lot of fun with them. Daryl got his saddle onto Lazuli and they set out for their flight, meeting up with Princess Rinoa, Nyx, and their escorts back at the fort.

For the most part the flight went okay, and Lazuli and Daryl were able to show some of their new tricks with the adjusted riding saddle. What kept Daryl from thinking it was a good flight was Nyx being a bit aggressive. The dark scaled dragon often snapped at the other dragons if they got too close, including when Princess Rinoa invited them to come closer, and her own escort, which Daryl assumed would be dragons Nyx was familiar with.

They took a break on the mountainside in a popular viewing spot for dragon riders. Lazuli was in no mood to entertain Nyx any longer and curled up for a nap far from the black dragon. Thankfully the Princess didn't take any offense, as Nyx moved to the opposite side of the ledge from the others.

"Malvoloch, may I have an aside moment with you," Her Highness asked as she motioned to an area away from her guards.

"Of course, Your Highness," Daryl said bowing before following after her.

"You're an innovative rider," she began, "and you work well

with Lazuli the Galestorm. I'm hoping you could assist me with that ingenuity."

"I will strive to do my utmost, what do you need assistance with?" he asked. The Princess sighed and her regal demeanor sloughed off, replaced with the visage of an utterly spent teenager.

"When I'm not at the palace, I'm having trouble maintaining Nyx's hoard," Rinoa said.

"What does she like to hoard?"

Another heavy sigh. "Cake."

Daryl smiled and nodded sympathetically.

"I've got a few ideas."

~ * ~ * ~

**A.B. Martin** hails from the Midwest and writes young adult fantasy. You can find them on X/Twitter @WordsAndSuchAB

# Jacob's Symphony

M. Bloom

Jacob could almost pretend it was quiet.

He could focus his mind on the sound his wheels made, bumping over the stones. The squeak of the wooden axle in its fittings. The rustle of coarse clothing that preceded his every footfall.

These rhythmic sounds helped him block out all else. Jacob knew ignoring the world could make him seem insensitive, uncaring. But he was firmly convinced the alternative, to open himself up to his surroundings, would be to invite madness.

The early months, when the plague first surfaced, the sounds were new, inescapable. Human sounds all—and all unpleasant. Weeping, moaning, praying, pleading. Together they were horrifying. A concert of misery. A symphony of suffering, written and conducted by the devil himself.

For the hundredth time, Jacob suppressed a cruel smile at his own poor joke.

"Jacob! Hold there!"

This was another hazard to letting go of the world. He'd gone straight past the house, oblivious.

Jacob turned his cart and made his way back to the doorframe from which the cleric had bellowed. He had quite the robust voice for a man of his years. Jacob averted his eyes, counted the paving stones, waited for the THUMP that told him his cart had been loaded. Then the cleric's solemn, reassuring hand on his shoulder told him it was time to press on.

The cleric was miraculously unaffected by the sickness, and folks accepted this because he was a man of the cloth. They reasoned it must be God's will.

Neither had Jacob fallen ill. In his case, this earned him naught but a host of scornful and suspicious glances. How dare he live when so many good people had died? How could he transport the dead and not gain sickness as well? The cleric himself knew it was not Jacob's fault, but he'd cautioned that others would not be so charitable. So Jacob kept his eyes to the ground, unchallenging, especially when in the presence of those souls who had just lost a friend or a relative. Those who were looking for someone to blame.

Such might have occurred just now, had a grieving husband or father stood on that porch instead of a compassionate cleric.

Jacob took his full cart through the gates, beyond sight of the town, following the main road, then turning down a familiar side path for half a mile. He looked more than his three and twenty years. The pit he approached had been dug by laborers mere months ago, but it was nearly full now; somewhere within it were those who had once manned the shovels. Jacob knew he was tolerated merely because he could do this simple job as the Collector of the Dead. But soon, when the pit was full to brimming with the bloated remnants of humanity, he would be expected to deal with that new problem as well.

In the gathering twilight, he saw a mound. The pit was now filled to overflowing. Impossible - it had not been so this morning. And no one else would dare approach this place. Superstition was a large part of it. The smell was another.

The mound *shifted*. It was not a pile of bodies, Jacob saw, but one impossibly large body. One that turned slightly at the sound of Jacob's approaching wheels. The great shape cocked its head slightly, regarding Jacob with alien, unblinking eyes. Then the scaled head settled back down as if Jacob wasn't worth the effort it took to stay awake.

Jacob, meanwhile, had decided his blocking out the ravaged world had not forestalled madness after all. Because there were no such things as dragons. There had not been for at least fifty years. And even if there were...a pile of rotting corpses was certainly no one's idea of a hoard worth guarding.

He could not return to town with a full cart, if for no other reason than his legs could not withstand the trek. And he still had enough sense to decide abandoning the cart was unwise—no cart, no job. No job, no excuse for anyone to tolerate his continued presence. So Jacob summarily dropped his five bodies as close as he dared get to the pit. Then he took off as quickly as he could manage his newly lightened load, with numerous glances back to see if the creature moved again.

On no account would Jacob speak of what he'd seen. No one would go near enough the pit to see the proof for themselves. Not even the cleric, who was the closest thing to a friend Jacob had. No, he'd be judged mad—which might yet be true, in Jacob's own opinion—and be run out of town for fear his peculiar mind-sickness might somehow be contagious.

~ * ~

Jacob made extra effort to tune out the world the following day, concentrating on his own personal symphony of wheel thump, axle squeak, burlap rustle, footstep. Forget about that mound, and it won't be there again today. It was that simple.

And Jacob began humming to himself, adding a crude melody to his own personal rhythms. Something to keep the world at bay. Something for his ears alone.

He made it to the gates that evening with only three dead. One, a younger woman, had been hastily dumped in the street. Women were always the worst, because no matter what they looked like, even if their faces were mostly gone, they somehow reminded Jacob of his own loss. But that had been no plague. There was no plague six years ago.

Despite Jacob's resolve, the scaly mound was still there in the evening. It had curled up differently, to more easily watch for any-thing that approached from town. Or so it seemed to Jacob. It also seemed the last bodies he'd dumped nearby had been moved into the pit—at least the two he could still recognize from remnants of their clothing.

The dragon's tongue flicked out, signaling it was awake. There was no other telltale movement.

Again, Jacob dropped the bodies several paces from the pit. He backed away more slowly this time, keeping an eye on the creature. He was rewarded with the sight of a claw reaching out to drag the first of the three bodies toward itself. Perhaps, to a drake's way of thinking, dead meat *could* represent a hoard of sorts.

~ * ~

The next day was a good day. Any day there were no new dead was a good day. Folks would hope and pray such a miracle finally signaled an end to the plague. But Jacob had been through many such cycles and knew better.

He knew better than to hope.

For the first time in months, Jacob walked out through the town gates without a load. "Good days" normally meant he could go straight home after his rounds. He would have no need of this final trek beyond the city gates. This time was different. He felt a curious need to see if that beast was still out there. So he left his cart at the gates and continued his walk unburdened.

The dragon raised its head at Jacob's approach. This was greatest amount of movement Jacob had witnessed so far.

Perhaps it was the uncommon relief—Jacob refused to call it happiness—of having to carry no corpses today. Or perhaps it was the reconciliation this beast was not an imagining of his fevered mind. Or possibly the need to hear his own voice, given no one besides the cleric would engage him in conversation. Whatever the reason, Jacob found himself actually speaking to the thing.

"No one's died today, sorry!"

Jacob knew the beast couldn't understand him. Yet, inexplicably, he found himself worrying his comment had sounded too flippant.

The dragon lowered its head. *"Tomorrow, perhapsss."*

From the dragon, he'd heard a hiss. In his head, Jacob had heard the words.

*"I ssshall be here. On the morrow, then."*

Now Jacob was certain. Certain the dragon was somehow forming words in his head. Either that, or the townsfolk's hateful curses had finally given him a brain fever. Neither option was exactly pleasant.

~ * ~

The next day was worse. Eleven dead, requiring two trips to the pit. Two and a half, for Jacob had been in such a sudden hurry to leave the talking dragon behind he'd left his emptied cart out on the path. He'd had to return for it first thing in the morning. The dragon, though distant, could be seen to glitter in the sunlight if one knew to look. Of course only Jacob knew where to look.

"You! What did you do to him? What unholy thing did you do?"

The burly man stood in the doorway, dead youth in his arms. He didn't want to give up his son. Not to the one who had brushed callously past him nine days ago when retrieving the boy's younger brother. Someone a father's unfocused grief now blamed.

The cleric was not here to rise to Jacob's defense. No doubt he was attending to someone else. There was always need for a cleric's services somewhere…

"You tell me right now! I swear I'll…"

The man began convulsing, likely his own burgeoning sickness adding to his sorrow and the sheer burden of the limp body he held. Jacob forced himself to watch impassively as the boy was finally dropped. The man staggered forward, unable to do more than deliver a halfhearted blow to Jacob's ribs between his own heaving breaths. Finally he staggered back to the supposed safety of his shuttered home.

Jacob fingered his ribs. The grieving man might renew his rage at any moment and charge back out through the front door. If so, his hands were now free to carry a weapon. So Jacob retrieved the limp youth from the man's porch as hastily as possible and loaded him into the cart. Halfway down the empty street, the dull rib ache was supplanted by a greater throbbing. One growing in his mind.

It was bad enough dead young women reminded him of a personal loss, but now young men had begun to remind him of his younger self. How long before every corpse reminded him of something, or someone? How long before he couldn't block out the world anymore?

He was sure he could feel the madness creeping in. Mental tricks, helping to distance himself from the world, were beginning to lose their effect.

Jacob had brought his load to a now-customary distance of five paces from the pit. They hadn't been moved by the time he returned, that evening, with a second cartful. This time, Jacob marched himself right up to the pit proper. If the dragon chose to snap him up, then so be it. That would be a more merciful end than the slow agonies of encroaching mind-sickness.

Still, the barely restrained terror of the monster's proximity coupled itself with the day's fatigue. Jacob's limbs visibly shook as he emptied the cart.

*"Thou shouldst ressst now."*

Jacob forced himself to look up. Save for a subtly twitching tail, he couldn't see that the creature had moved. So, with supreme effort, Jacob ignored it.

Turning to retrieve the load he'd earlier left strewn upon the ground, Jacob neared his physical limit. His legs, spine, and aching ribs wouldn't allow him to bend fully. He could manage to pick up such weight from his elevated cart, or from a front porch, but not when stooping to the ground proper. He collapsed upon the topmost cadaver.

*"Leave them be. I shall collect them."* This time the dragon did raise its head. Then its foreclaws flexed in anticipation, the human carrion in its makeshift nest making unpleasant liquid sounds as it moved and shifted.

Jacob found his limbs ached too much to stand. Ultimately he forced himself. Once on his feet, he used his cart for balance, but pushing into the handles made his ribs hurt anew.

*"Ressst now,"* the dragon repeated. And Jacob collapsed.

~ * ~

He awoke to sparrow song, the morning sun tickling his eyelids. A sun that should not have breached Jacob's carefully shuttered windows. Then the light faded, as if magically obeying this very thought. Jacob opened a crusty eye to investigate this eclipse and found the dragon's head blocking the sun's rays.

Jacob had never made it home.

He tensed—and immediately regretted it, for his spine was unaccustomed to the hardness of the dragon's scales beneath him. Nonetheless, he found the motivation to sit bolt upright.

*"Resssted, now..."* It was either a statement or a question, Jacob couldn't tell which. He scrambled out of the dragon's coils, out of the pit, the instant that scaled head moved aside.

The dragon made no move to stop him. It watched as Jacob gulped for the slightly fresher air beyond the pit.

*"Sssicknesss?"* There was no mistake, this was indeed intended as a question. Jacob answered without thinking.

"You smell...of death," he wheezed between breaths.

The dragon settled its head once more. *"As do you,"* it observed smugly.

Jacob heard himself laugh; an emotional release borne of sheer amazement. He could sense the emotion, the self-satisfaction, in the dragon's comment.

*"Not that any deign come near enough to notice,"* the beast added. *"Nor do they hear thy sssong."*

"Song?" Jacob asked reflexively.

The dragon began humming. The tone would have been impossibly deep for a human, but it was also familiar. It was Jacob's personal symphony.

At once, the dragon stopped. *"Thisss intriguss me,"* the creature confessed. *"We mussst ssspeak more of it…"* And the dragon was silent, gone to sleep in mid-thought without so much as a yawn or a twitch.

~ * ~

Jacob walked off his initial stiffness, plying the streets as was his duty. There were two dead this day. The cleric lingered at the home of the second. It seemed that, after consoling the family, he felt the need to take Jacob aside.

"Neither you nor your cart were at home last night." He managed to keep his tone from gaining an accusing edge. "I was a bit concerned," —a good-natured wink— "seeing as I'm the only one who might be called upon in your absence."

Jacob fumbled for words. "I was uncommon tired," he began truthfully. "I lay down with my cart until morning, just outside the gates." He didn't dare specify how *far* outside the gates, for only a true madman would linger, after dark, in the wilderness.

The cleric took him firmly by the shoulder. "You know better than any the safest refuge from the plague is indoors. You've heard me tell many a poor soul. Away from the sickness of the night air."

Wincing, Jacob gently separated the cleric's hand from his own sore shoulder.

"A singular lapse," he promised. "Unlikely to be repeated. You have my word."

The other seemed satisfied with this, or perhaps it was the new plea of a bereaved family member that drew his attention. Jacob took the opportunity to be on his way.

He found himself humming on the way to the pit. More loudly than usual, but only after he was clear of the gates, with no one around to hear. Blocking out the mournful wailing of the bereaved, whose young daughter now rode in his cart. Blocking out her imagined resemblance to someone else. Blocking out the cleric's earlier, gently suspicious words.

Under other circumstances, Jacob would have been glad of the cleric's attention. Everyone else was either too frightened or too superstitious to engage the Collector of the Dead in conversation.

By comparison, the cleric was quite personable. Well, truth be told, there was one other who would speak with Jacob. And Jacob now hummed not just to forget the world, but to remember something. To recall the song of that Other.

How could it be the same as his own? Jacob pondered, as he walked in the early evening sun, as he made his way to the pit.

"Greetings, dragon." Jacob spoke more boldly than he would have deemed possible—or wise—a scant three days ago.

*"Greetingsss,"* the other responded, a flicking tongue extending the "S" into a mental hiss. The scaled head came up in a manner that reminded Jacob of a puppy anticipating table scraps.

Jacob thought of the cleric, wondering if the man would regard the dragon's use for corpses as a desecration. The dead made into a dragon's hoard? But in this unhallowed mass grave, Jacob could not bring himself to believe one body's fate could be worse than another.

They fed the worms. Or they fed the Wyrm.

*"What tickles thee ssso?"* the dragon asked. Jacob had not even realized he had begun to smile at his own silent pun.

Would this creature take offense at being called a Wyrm? Jacob turned the subject to something more flattering.

"I was merely recalling that song of yours," he replied. Which was true, as far as it went. "You said you wished to speak of it. It is wondrous, especially in the tones you manage."

Perhaps he laid on the praise a bit too thickly. The response was naught but stoic silence.

"Where is it from?" Jacob blurted.

The dragon only craned his neck, inspecting the loaded cart from afar. Very well, thought Jacob, it was quick enough to unload just two. At least the dragon had been courteous enough not to feast in his presence. Thus far.

The creature began to hum as it watched Jacob work. Again, the tones were impossibly deep, but the melody was familiar.

*"Where is thine from?"* it asked finally, nosing the two unloaded bodies into the pit proper.

Jacob didn't rightly know. It had been with him for years.

The dragon settled its head once more. *"Perhapsss...I might help thee to recall."*

With that, the deep *thrumming* began anew. Jacob listened. Unconsciously, he swayed to the tones, as they were nigh hypnotic in their resonance. Finally he joined in. There were long-forgotten subtleties, cascades of intricate notes which his brain had, over the years, slurred into large, crude transitions. It felt better with these intricacies. More *correct*. But the tune's source eluded him.

At the end, Jacob could barely contain a laugh. It was rare enough he could sit and talk with someone. But as the cleric would doubtless say, it was even more joyous to sing out loud. It was something Jacob had not done in many years.

*"Didssst thou recall anything?"* the dragon asked.

Jacob shook his head. But a smile lingered as he did so.

~ * ~

The Collector of the Dead heard rain on his roof that night, and he knew from experience this could only add to the next day's burden. Corpses left out in the slippery mud were much more difficult to grab hold of. Diseased skin was more likely to slough off. Even though Jacob's back was less sore now, and he could bend down properly, this would make his chore more difficult.

Worse still, if the rains were heavy enough, the pit itself could become a cesspool of liquefied remains, finally floating to the surface...

Jacob set out in the early morning, when only a light drizzle persisted. But he did not begin his rounds. He made straight for the city gates and the pit beyond. He did not even bother with his cart. Jacob had been seized by a sudden, inexplicable thought: what if the dragon had fled this change of weather?

It seemed ridiculous, of course. Should Jacob really care that much? Besides, any beast that could comfortably nest upon a pile of infected corpses could not possibly be harmed by a little rain. But dragons were mysterious beasts, and the last one anybody recalled seeing had died off more than fifty years ago. Who knew what would provoke them into action?

The ground mists were too thick to see the pit clearly. Not from the gates, at any rate. Jacob had taken the path countless times in the dispensation of his duty. He could have done it in pitch blackness if need be; the route was such second nature. What was unheard of, what was new, was that he actually *wanted* to go there.

The silhouette of a dark mound rose up where the depression of a pit should have been. The dragon was indeed there, impassive as a statue. Somehow, even through the patter of raindrops, it discerned Jacob's footsteps. Its rain-slicked wings twitched slightly at the man's approach.

It regarded the visitor quizzically. No dragon words needed form in Jacob's mind to read that impassive stare: *Is it not early?*

Then the skies brought forth the only sound that could surpass the depth of a dragon's voice. Thunder. Lightning forked like the drake's tongue. The clouds let loose sheets of rain. Within mere seconds, the path to town became a shallow river.

Wordlessly, the dragon lifted a huge wing away from its body. Jacob had no choice but to accept this leathery shelter.

~ * ~

The dream was strange. Yet while in it, Jacob knew he slept in a dragon's coils, so he reasoned: how could it have been *other* than strange?

A rotund man hummed in the dragon's voice. Jacob sang along. There was a third tone in the symphony, light and gay. It was a woman's or child's voice, then it became a flute, then transformed back again.

When Jacob awoke, that sound had resolved into the musical trickling of streamlets rolling beside the still-damp path. At least the rain had stopped. And the pit, smell as it did, had not quite overflowed.

Jacob stepped out onto solid ground and stretched.

"Return," the dragon said, and slept once more.

By the time he reached the gates, Jacob had an answer ready for anyone who questioned him as to his whereabouts. As expected, it was the cleric who sought him out first. Even before Jacob had reached home.

"The pit is sound," he announced, implying a reason for his absence. "I've seen the rain did not fill it, nor wash its contents across the land."

The cleric nodded in quick agreement. "Else there could be more sickness, yes." Then he wrinkled his nose, though he tried to hide the fact. He quickly departed to resume whatever duties he had that morning.

Jacob knew anything malodorous would be blamed on his visit to the pit. Secretly, though, he knew the dragon's scent he carried on his clothing was something different than mere human death.

~ * ~

"Greetings, dragon."

*"Greetingsss, man."*

It had become something of a daily ritual. Jacob would visit every evening, regardless of whether his cart was full. He preferred an empty cart. The dragon was happier when it was full. Though it was never discussed, there was an understanding that Jacob preferred not to watch the dragon dine.

Several months passed in this way. Sometimes the dragon would sing, and sometimes Jacob would join him. The more Jacob listened, the more he was sure he had once known the entire song. It was not something formed privately in his head, as he'd come to believe, but something taught to him in his youth. Too long ago to remember clearly. But he felt sure it had been part of something pleasant.

Eventually, the plague lessened its hold on the town. Not that many citizens remained: the population had been cut by three-fourths.

The days Jacob had to perform his grim duties grew fewer. Yet he still visited the pit daily, and after several months the cleric could not help but become concerned. Indeed, it was only his own lenient nature that allowed Jacob the benefit of doubt for so long.

Finally, hoping to once again quell the mutterings of the suspicious-minded populace, he consented to follow Jacob on his unpleasant evening duty.

From a respectable distance up the path, in the near-sunset, the cleric saw what any man might see—a charnel-pit piled high with the unfortunate. But then, Jacob appeared to speak to this mound of corpses *and the mound moved to answer him.*

The cleric stumbled back to town in such a blind panic he could not even recall how he made the journey. Townsfolk who rushed to his gasping form, doubled over as it was in the town square, could only make out words like "Jacob" and "Wakened dead."

This could not have come at a worse time. Deaths were fewer, true, which made a day like today—seven dead in all, two of them children—seem all the more horrible in comparison.

Sentiments the cleric thought he'd long since quashed now rose anew among the citizens:

"He makes us sick to insure he has a purpose."

"The way he's never got sick himself, it's unnatural."

"He does things with the bodies."

Even the cleric could not rouse himself to challenge them now.

Since the ravages of plague, the cleric was one of the few remaining elders, old enough to recall Jacob's betrothal more than twenty years earlier. He was not proud of what he had done then, but his actions had helped destroy the last of the winged demons. He would have been glad of his actions, but for the effect it had had on his dearest friend. No, Jacob was never the same after that.

Now Jacob was caught unawares as he wheeled his empty cart home. He hummed; perhaps a bit too loudly. This apparent joy, when returning from such a grim task, made him appear all the more ghoulish to those who lurked in the shadowed edges of the town square.

The first stone caught Jacob between the shoulder blades. He kept his footing by leaning hard into the cart handles, but as he turned to see what had happened, another rock hit him squarely in the temple.

Nor was the cobbled street very gentle with his head when he fell.

His vision was blurred. He saw only forms gathering, kicking him, throwing stones at his face and body from directly above. Incoherent shouting. In a half-conscious reflex, he started humming, as loudly as he could manage, just to block out this world of pain.

It didn't work. His vision, the very sky, began fading into darkness.

Then the darkness began to hum. In tones so deep they must be thunder, the very sky began to hum. This was the end, Jacob knew, with the merciful madness that softens the final agonies of death.

*But the others heard it too.*

In an instant, amidst frightened shouts, the others were gone. The darkness descended upon Jacob. Then the darkness spoke.

*"Greetingsss, friend."*

Jacob felt himself being lifted, and though his vision was blurred, he could see the familiar shapes below: the path, the pit, then the forest beyond.

~ * ~

Humming rang from the walls, echoes making one voice into ten. Jacob opened his eyes and found his vision remarkably clear. But only in one eye. The other was caked with dirt, or blood, or both. Or maybe it was gone completely. Jacob was afraid to check.

*"Thou didst ssing in thy ssleep,"* the dragon noted. *"Thy sssong. Thou wouldssst tell me of it. Now."*

Jacob sat up, knowing it would hurt in a hundred places, but he was past caring.

*"Tell me,"* the dragon's tone was surprisingly soft.

Jacob looked around. He saw a cave, shallow enough to be bathed evenly in cool blue starlight. There were golden glitters here. A more traditional hoard.

Jacob took a breath, knowing this, too, would hurt. "I cannot. I'm...sorry."

The head moved uncomfortably close. *"But thy answer be found, yesss? The answer is known?"*

Despite his resolve, the Collector of the Dead could hold back no longer. Yes, he knew. He'd known since that evening, as if the beating had somehow knocked old memories back into place. They were all there. He sobbed convulsively.

The dragon waited patiently for this to subside, then said, *"This payment is all I asssk. Tell me of thy song, do."*

Jacob understood. The dragon had likely saved his life today. In return, it wanted Jacob's newfound memories.

"Tomorrow..." Jacob half-asked, half-pleaded. He felt if he could sleep through the night, both fatigue and freshly churned sorrow would fade, and these were the only obstacles to sharing his memories with the drake. With his only real friend.

"Tomorrow, I promise."

The dragon curled completely around Jacob's form, signaling agreement. But while the man slept, the dragon—who had proven it could go to sleep in the middle of a thought—never lowered its head, never went to sleep, but waited patiently, unmoving, until morning.

~ * ~

Jacob's aches were not gone in the morning. In fact, they were abetted by stiffness. But grief and sorrow had been supplanted by the beginnings of acceptance, and this granted strength enough for Jacob to keep his promise.

In the morning light, he absently noted the dark gray color of the cave stone. The same stone that formed the town well, made unsafe by the plague. Those were the loose stones used to pummel him. Years ago they would have been gleaned from this very mountain, two days ride from town.

Why did Jacob care to notice? He knew he was searching, in the back of his mind, for a good place to start. He was hesitating now. Stalling. Where to begin?

"Sheryl. Her name was Sheryl. It was she who taught me the song; it was her family's. We were to sing it together. On our wedding day."

When Jacob faltered at this point, the dragon prompted him.

*"A joyousss time for thee, was it not?"*

Apparently dragons did not marry, for the inquiry was genuine.

"Yes, it is a joyous time. But twenty years ago, there was a wyr... that is, there was one like you who hunted the countryside. It even stole children. Or so they said."

The last hasty addition seemed to mollify the dragon. It took no visible offense.

"They wanted to be rid of it, and...and right about then, my Sheryl took deathly ill..."

Jacob's tears came so forcefully now even the impassive drake knew his friend could not resume the tale. So the dragon continued for him.

*"Thine elders decided if one be ssso ill, why not use her flesh to poison this hunter, yesss?"*

Jacob looked up, amazement stemming the tearful tide where nothing else could.

"Yes," he nodded meekly, noting this as the correct memory.

*"Thou hast ssseen me nest upon those fallen by plague,"* the dragon continued in prideful tones. *"Dost thou think any poisons ssswallowed by my prey couldst then harm my kind?"*

"Not poison, but a sickness," Jacob insisted. "Like the plague upon us now, something that cannot be cured."

*"Poisonsss,"* the dragon insisted sternly, its head dipping to within a hand's breadth of the other's face. Jacob could smell the carrion on its breath. *"Most potent poisonsss, mixed by the hand of man. Ssswal-*

*lowed as decreed by thy elders, given unto a sssacrifice, a maiden, to rid the lands of us, shouldst we deign to feast upon that flesh!"*

"No," was all Jacob could say. "This they would not do. Not ever!"

The dragon fairly knocked Jacob down with its angry tongue.

*"Thisss she told me of her own free will! She didst never ssspeak her name, but thisss one thing she told me. And when she sssaw I chose not to harm her, she becalmed, even as you becalmed."*

"They would not purposely harm her. A beloved daughter of our town. My betrothed! And you cannot be the same creature…"

The dragon began humming, powerfully, so the sound reverberated off the stone walls in a deafening torrent.

*"She taught me thisss,"* the dragon intoned. *"It doth sssound like thy sssong, because it is thy sssong. It was my promissse to her. To one day ssseek out her one* love. *To ssseek THEE."*

Jacob rose in anger at the dragon's words, fists clenched, though in truth he had not enough strength remaining to strike down a feather. He thought the dragon a friend, but it now claimed the town had conspired to poison…

Then he found the flaw in the dragon's tale.

"You claim to have known her, and not harmed her? Then where did she go? Did she die? Where is her body? Where is she *right now?"* Jacob's voice had become shrill with anger, and the stone taunted him with his own echoes.

As these faded, the other backed away as if from the sheer force of Jacob's words—no, it backed away to clear the space where it had coiled. There, in the cave's corner, was a single skeleton.

It was neat, passing clean when compared to the filthy chaos of the pit. And it had been protected from the elements such that loose tatters of clothing were still recognizable. Recognizable as the remnants of Sheryl's gown.

In all the time Jacob had carried the dead, he had never been sick, never vomited. Until now.

When he was done, he collapsed in a quivering heap. The dragon came very near. Jacob now lacked the strength even to ball his fist.

*"The poisonsss failed,"* it said in impossibly gentle tones. *"Thy kind may have no cure, but herbs unknown to thee do grow upon this rock. She ssstayed with me a year. I brought her food. She talked with me. She taught me*

*her sssong…"*

The dragon's head came to rest beside Jacob's prone form. *"But thou art the one who taught me her name. The name she wouldst not ssspeak to me. She sssaid it was for thee alone."*

Then the dragon remained still for a very long time. Jacob was filled with hatred. But not for the dragon. Not if even a part of what he'd just heard was true.

"Sheryl…" was all he repeated before he succumbed to exhaustion once more.

~ * ~

Well before dawn, Jacob awoke beside the dragon, his body coiled in the very same position as the first night he'd spent in the pit.

"Greetings, dragon," Jacob spoke with surprising ease.

*"Greetingsss, friend. A question remains lodged within thee, yesss?"*

"Yes," Jacob confessed. "If your story is true…then how did you find me?

The dragon stretched, rose, and faced Jacob directly.

*"The sssimplest of things, truly. When thy mate—when thy Sheryl died, the poisonsss were ssstill within her. I had merely ssstemmed their flow. The poisons mingled with her dead flesh, and created true…sicknesss."*

Jacob thought there was undue hesitation in that last part. "Sickness. You mean plague."

The dragon merely hissed its assent. *"And I didst carry it with me. And it drew thee out, did it not? It drew thee wondrous well, though many towns did I visit until thou wert found."*

Jacob could only think upon this. Sheryl had oft noted how common sickness never seemed to touch Jacob…

"You…*created*…the plague?"

*"Thy poison-sssspinners created it. Condemned themssselves, yesss? I merely caused it to ssspread. And now thou art found, I may end it."*

"The pit should help to end it, casting the diseased so far from town." It was Jacob's reflexive pride in his duty that spoke.

The dragon cocked its head. *"Sicknesss ssspread by the windsss, is sicknesss ssstill. If thou wouldst like, I shall show thee how to end it fully."*

Not waiting for Jacob's reply, the dragon rose, clutching the other in its talons. The dragon rose swiftly. Had this been Jacob's first flight, he would likely have called out in fear. But it was his second. Somehow that made a difference.

Borne aloft by starlight, Jacob could make out the forest below, and the approaching town. They descended outside of town, near the pit. A familiar form toiled there. The only one besides Jacob who would not be caught by the plague.

As far as Jacob was concerned, the fact the cleric dared venture forth in darkness proved he did not believe his own admonitions about wild nighttime dangers. The cleric glanced up and suddenly found he believed in one now.

The dragon swooped within twenty feet of the ground, issuing from its mouth a stream of fire so fierce the oily corpses were set alight instantly. As he ascended to the heavens in the dragon's claws, Jacob knew that cleansing flame would be seen quite clearly against the pre-dawn sky, even from the confines of the town itself.

~ * ~

Jacob awoke strangely content, though his body was wracked with pain from his injuries. Missing eye, broken arm. Things ruined inside that even the dragon's mysterious herbs could not heal. But content, he decided, because he knew his bones would stay here beside his betrothed's. Here in the dragon's true hoard.

*"Greetingsss, friend. Thy sssong be done now, yesss?"*

Jacob smiled. The sound of the drake's voice helped him to weave a new dream, wondrously rich and pleasant. A fat man who hummed in the dragon's voice was the minister; Jacob stood to one side, Sheryl to the other. Then the minister expanded, unfurled into a glittering dragon, and carried them both away.

And Jacob understood.

"Yes. I remember now. Sheryl's song…all of it."

*"Thou wouldst sssing with me, then?"* the dragon asked, and began to hum.

Jacob joined in with uncommon ease. It was just the echo of the cave, he knew, but he could swear he heard a third voice joining them, completing his perfect symphony…

…A woman's voice.

~ * ~ * ~

**Michael Bloom** is a native of Southern California. He has been an amateur reptile rescue volunteer for 40 years, so it is little wonder he also has a strong affinity for dragons.

He has written and performed poetry in Los Angeles and Orange County, CA since 1994, typically with Gothic groups such as League of Vampiric Bards and Casketeria. He has also written Draconic poetry and short stories for the same period of time, but those efforts tend sneak into public view only at Renaissance Faires and science-fiction conventions.

# The Mechanic's Dragon

## Alexandria Wyckoff

Fiora knew nearly every part of the spaceship and its many nooks and crannies that powered the incredible machine. Her father's steady grease-stained hands were the tether between life and death up here, and she much preferred to be alive. Though she wasn't yet old enough to declare an occupation, she still followed her dad around every time he needed to repair something.

There was something thrilling about taking pieces and parts of an engine apart, finding the issue, and having the knowledge to repair and reconstruct the engine the same as it was built centuries ago. The mechanics had created every piece of the original ship, and it allowed Fiora to feel connected to their spirits, even though they had passed many years before she was born.

As she ate her allotted breakfast at the small table in their cabin, a familiar chime echoed into the space. Her father's pager ringing meant one thing—a piece of the ship needed fixing. Giddy, Fiora squealed and hurried down the short hallway to their sleeping area. Her father's fingers were already answering the page, work gear draped across his broad frame.

"Can I come?" Fiora asked, reaching for her own miniature work belt.

"Woah, not so fast miss. Don't you have scheduled lessons today?" he asked.

"Today's a free day Dad. I told you that yesterday, remember?"

"You know how my memory works sweetheart—only when..."

"...it concerns mechanics," Fiora finished with a chuckle. "So, can I go?"

Her father looked down at her with a knowing smirk. "As long as you are ready by the time I finish my breakfast, you can come with me."

Fiora turned into a tornado, throwing on her work clothes and her toolbelt, made from her father's old belt, completing the look with a bandana threaded through her curly brown hair.

"Ready when you are!" She ran into the kitchen area to see her dad drop his plate in the sink.

"Perfect timing. Let's go kiddo."

They left their cabin, stepping out into one of the many inter-connected passenger hallways. Fiora waved to some of her class-mates, but they avoided her gaze once they saw Head Mechanic Clay. Her dad wasn't scary, it was just his work position that made them antsy, and the fact Fiora wanted to follow in her father's foot-steps. Mechanics were the last group added to the ship, even though they built the behemoth. It made no sense to Fiora, who thought mechanics should be like the kings she read about in her books. Prized, honored, respected. Or at the very least not shunned.

Her dad noticed the lack of enthusiasm and stepped out of the bustling hallway.

"What's wrong sweetheart? You lost the bounce in your step."

His caramel eyes melted her anger and she sighed. "My class-mates avoided looking at us again. It makes me mad because you're probably the most important person on this ship!"

Her voice attracted a few stares, and her dad grabbed her hands. "I know it doesn't make sense, and frankly I agree," he whispered. "But not everyone else agrees and that's okay. All that matters is you do what you love. Okay?"

Fiora nodded her head as her lips pulled into a gentle grin. "Thanks, Dad."

"No problem. Now let's get to our job, shall we?"

They rejoined the flow of people, which steadily dwindled to no one as they traveled down level after level. The stairs were covered in a thick layer of dust while the overhead lights occasionally flick-ered like the lightning bugs Fiora had learned about a few days ago. She liked that something so small could be so powerful.

She glanced at the abandoned interior once more before ask-ing, "I've never been this far down in the ship Dad. What do they keep down here?"

He looked around as he reached the final steps, turning back to her with a smirk.

"This is where the main engine and all the life-saving systems are Fiora. The heart of the spaceship."

Fiora's wonder turned into a scowl. "Wait a minute. I thought you told me the engine was in the control center at the ship's bow."

"I did. There is a small engine at the top that monitors the control panel, as there are several scattered across the ship. The difference is what they power. While the small engines power nonessential aspects of the ship, the main engine focuses on powering the ship through space while maintaining our oxygen and atmosphere levels. Pretty cool, huh?"

Fiora sat there for a moment as her jaw dropped. "You mean ...I'll be helping you work on the secret engine?"

He chuckled before turning serious. "Yes, you will, and you'll be seeing something else that is secret too. Promise me you won't tell anyone, okay?"

Fiora's heart skipped a beat. What could be so secret she couldn't tell anyone and it made her dad so serious? Maybe it was a new invention, or possibly intergalactic weaponry, though she didn't think they would meet any invaders in the middle of space. Fiora nodded her head and the smile reappeared on her dad's face as he led her to the engine room door. A palm scanner let them into the area and Fiora gasped. The doorway opened to a cavernous space with the biggest engine she had ever seen right in the center.

A kaleidoscope of lights blinked and flickered on the various panels making up the circular machine, bouncing off the walls like a disco party. Each metal plate was painted white, standing out against the dark blue walls of the ship. Wires crisscrossed the whole thing, all of which led to a large screen that faced them. Her eagerness to be near such a mechanic masterpiece nearly overwhelmed Fiora's senses.

She grinned at her father and tried to run towards the machine, but her dad snagged her shirt.

"Wait, sweetheart. There's someone I want you to meet first."

"Who?"

Her dad just smiled and led her around the side of the engine, each flickering light throwing color onto his face. In the wall to the right, there was an indentation almost as big as the room itself. Fiora's steps faltered as she got closer, but there was nothing in the space except a ratty brown blanket and large troughs for food and water. She glanced at her dad but he seemed as confused as she was.

"He's usually sleeping at this time," he muttered, flipping his wrist out to double-check.

A faint vibration traveled up Fiora's legs and she peered around the engine, trying to figure out where the sound was coming from.

Maybe it was the part of the engine they needed to fix, or the normal creaking from the ship as it hurtled through space. A few steps forward, she noticed a large shadow on the floor, complete with two wings, long claws, and the unmistakable silhouette of a snout.

"A dragon," she whispered.

She crept closer and closer until the shadow became a majestic creature, which was covered in a variety of grey and burgundy scales and had burning emerald eyes. She felt her father come up behind her and place his hands on her shoulders.

"Amazing, isn't it?"

"How…I thought dragons didn't exist after the spaceships were invented and our ancestors left Earth?"

"Most of the dragons were already gone by that point, but there were some left who were able to join us on our journey. We decided it wouldn't be fair to leave them on Earth, especially since we were the ones who pushed the planet to the brink. This is Nox, our ship's resident dragon, and protector of the main engine. All ships have a dragon to protect the main engine from intruders. If you want to be a head mechanic like me someday, you must be able to work alongside Nox."

He gestured upwards and Fiora startled because the dragon had crept to a spot only five feet away from her. Nox regarded her with solemn eyes before bowing his head to her level.

His breath blew against her curls and she giggled.

"Can I touch him?"

"Go slow and wait for him to reach out to you, like this."

Her dad stepped forward with his arm out and Nox copied the movement until they touched. Fiora internally scolded her arm for shaking as she reached out and pressed her palm against Nox's rough scales. She locked eyes with the beast and released a shaky laugh.

"He likes me!"

Nox tilted his head out of her reach and slowly ambled back to his den, curling up on the blanket with a disjointed sigh. Fiora realized the problem right away.

"He doesn't have a hoard!" Her dad looked at her.

"A what?"

"A hoard. You know, the stuff that dragons collect. Like jewels or gold. Can we get him a hoard? I think he'll be happier then."

"Fiora, you know we don't have access to gold or jewels. Besides, it would be dangerous to have a pile of priceless jewels right next to the main engine. Come on; we have to fix a part of the engine over here."

Fiora followed, but she couldn't get the dragon's forlorn face out of her mind.

~ * ~

A couple of weeks passed before her father got another job in the main engine room, and Fiora had a surprise for Nox. Her dad didn't question the extra satchel she held in her hand, nor the persistent sound of metal clinking. They traveled down the unused stairwell again, and her father placed his palm against the scanner.

The second the door was open enough Fiora slipped through, heading straight for Nox's den. His long tail curved into the main room, blocking her view of the dragon's face. She tried not to run as the bag would surely spill all over the floor, and her dad chuckled.

"What's got you so excited Fiora?"

"I brought something for Nox."

"Okay, but be careful. I'll be over on this side of the engine."

Her dad followed the curve of the engine to the other side, out of Fiora's sight. She reached Nox's tail and peered around it. Two green eyes stared back, waiting to see what she would do next. She inched forward, clutching the satchel in front of her body.

"So...I brought you something. I know you probably don't understand a word I'm saying, but I've read about dragons and decided you needed a hoard to guard. I couldn't get jewels or gold, but I did get these."

Fiora turned the bag over and an assortment of nuts, bolts, and metal scraps clanked onto the floor. Compared to Nox the pile was minuscule, and Fiora was thinking her whole idea was stupid when Nox moved his claw towards the pile. He shifted the metal around to his liking before lifting his body and curling around the metal.

Nox nuzzled Fiora's chest, and she threw her arms around him, excited he enjoyed the makeshift jewels she had found for him.

"I'm glad you like your new jewels," she whispered.

Fiora stayed with Nox until her father was ready to leave again, determined to bring Nox more scrap pieces for his hoard.

~ \* ~

Over the years Fiora brought bag after bag and Nox's pile grew to a size worthy of the dragon. He used small amounts of fire to stick the pieces together just enough so they wouldn't fly into the engine. It was almost as if Nox knew he needed to protect both the engine and his hoard, as they were both precious objects to him.

Fiora grew too, finally reaching the age of choosing a profession, and she poured her heart and soul into becoming the best mechanic the ship had ever seen. Some days it was hard to get down to Nox, as she was strapped with schoolwork but at least once a month she made the trip down to the main engine room. Since she was learning to become a mechanic, her hand scan was added to the door so she could visit whether she had a job down there or not.

The day she graduated, the first place she visited was Nox. She adjusted her new official mechanic belt nervously as she headed down the stairs, and wondered why she was fretting about meeting the creature who had been her closest friend for years. She pressed her palm against the door and it glided open.

Nox was standing near the engine, inspecting it with the same gaze her father did after he finished a job. The lights illuminated the burgundy in his scales, and Fiora couldn't get over how majestic he looked in the light. He noticed her movement and turned towards her, waiting for her to speak.

"I graduated today, Nox. I'm a full-fledged mechanic now." Her grin broadened as Nox lumbered over to her and nuzzled her chest, their version of a hug. She held on tight, a few tears dripping onto Nox's scales before they separated.

"Okay, enough crying for me. How's your hoard looking? Big enough for a king?"

She followed Nox over to his section of the engine room, the large pile of nuts and bolts shaped to the curve of Nox's body when he would sleep with his prized possessions. She grinned with pride at the large amount of metal she scrounged over the years, plus the few trinkets that made the hoard extra special. Some of her academic trophies were melded together with pins and medals she had received for passing each grade in her daily lessons, and later her professional tests.

Her hand closed over the newest pin she had received, the

mechanic's emblem stamped into the surface and the sharp edges biting into her palm. She lifted the pin so Nox could see it, his focused gaze absorbing the small details.

"I brought a new addition for you. Only the highest-graded mechanic in the class gets this pin, and since you've shown me so much about this profession and the main engine, it deserves to be part of your hoard. Plus, it's one of the many ways to remember me by."

She swore Nox smirked at her before blowing a low flame on the front of his metal pile. The dark grey metal turned from a deep red to bright orange, and Fiora carefully placed the pin backing onto the melted pieces. Nox gave a satisfied nod and pressed his claw against the pin to make sure it stayed there. They looked at the metal pile for a while, dragon, and human, enjoying each other's presence across a divide of genetics.

After a while Fiora yawned, exhausted from the day's events. Nox noticed and silently curled himself onto his hoard with a small spot left open for her. Fiora picked her way up the metal structure and curled herself into Nox's warm scales, one of the few mechanics who would come this close to a dragon across all of the ships.

The two fell asleep to the soft whirring sounds coming from the main engine.

~ * ~ * ~

**Alexandria Wyckoff** has a BA in Creative Writing from SUNY Oswego. She is the author of *The Pain Cycle* and has had her work published in *Gandy Dancer*, *Planisphere Q*, *The Ana*, and others. When not working or writing, you can find Alexandria curled under a blanket reading a book and sipping mint tea.

Visit her at: lwyckoff2002.wixsite.com/alexandria-wyckoff.

# Evolynn's Skull

## Mabel Ginest

It was nearing sundown on an otherwise normal Tuesday, and an elderly woman was just sitting down to her simple but nourishing supper when a small, fluffy black cat leaped onto the table and sat, curling her tail around her paws. "Galena, I think Yerra's about to go off and do something stupid again."

The elderly woman glanced up and smiled at the cat. "Oh? Well, that's not exactly unusual behavior for Yerra. What's she up to this time?"

"You remember a few weeks ago, when there were all those stories about that boating party of idiots who disappeared after they went to visit Yslen Douen? And Yerra told us she had heard stories Evolynn's Skull was somehow involved?"

"Yes, I remember," Galena said. "She talked about it for some time; she said it was just the sort of collector's item she wanted for her hoard."

The cat flicked her tail with badly concealed irritation. "Well, apparently, she's been doing some digging, and not only has she found out Evolynn's Skull is supposed to be on Yslen Douen, but she even has the exact location. She's leaving tonight to go pick it up."

"What, by herself?" Galena exclaimed. "To an abandoned island with hundreds of ghost stories about it, to pick up one of the arguably most cursed items still left in existence?"

"Exactly." The cat jumped into the woman's lap and glanced up at her. "What are we going to do about it?"

Galena just shook her head. "Honestly, that dragon…well, we can't stop her—you know how single-minded dragons are when it comes to their hoards—and we certainly can't let her go off by herself."

The cat sighed. "We're going to have to go with her, aren't we?"

"I don't see any other option," Galena said cheerfully. "Come on, Analia. I'll just go grab a few things, and we'll head over to Yerra's cave."

The cat glowered at her. "You gave in very quickly," she said suspiciously. "You *want* to go with her; I swear, you're just as bad as that dragon is."

Galena grinned at her cat. "Well of course I want to go! Why wouldn't I? It's been ages since I got to go with Yerra on one of her little quests to pick up something for her hoard."

"Do you think we'll have much trouble getting her to let us come?" Analia asked. "After all, Yerra can be pretty stubborn."

"Nonsense," Galena said. "It's not a matter of her *letting* us come; she doesn't get a choice in the matter. I've been friends with her for over fifty years, and not once has she managed to leave me behind if I really wanted to go along. It's certainly not going to start now."

"Doesn't it bother you that we could be in very great danger on this little trip?" Analia demanded. "I mean, Evolynn's Skull is cursed! It brings disaster wherever it shows up."

"Yes, that's why Yerra wants it," Galena said. "Don't worry, she and I are old pros at this; this won't be the first time we've retrieved something like Evolynn's Skull."

"You're both ridiculous," the cat said groaning. "How you've survived as long as you have without me around to look after you, I don't know. I know I should just stay behind, but if someone of sense doesn't go along, you two idiots are going to end up dead."

"It's always possible," Galena agreed. "But that's what makes it fun!" She slung a small knapsack over her shoulder and draped a shawl over her shoulders. "Come on, Analia; I'll carry you if you'd like."

Still grumbling to herself, Analia jumped into the woman's arms, and together they left the comfortable little cottage they called home. Galena locked the door behind them and started down the well-worn earthen path that led to her friend's cave.

Despite being quite young by dragon standards—she was only 250 years old—Yerra had already amassed a respectable hoard, not by the sheer number of items, but by their rarity and uniqueness. Even as a small dragon, Yerra's taste had always veered towards the dark and macabre, and so it made sense to all who knew her when she started to collect various cursed objects and curios. Always on the lookout for some terrible object capable of great damage, it was no surprise Evolynn's Skull had caught Yerra's attention.

Evolynn's Skull was the name given to the crystalized skull which had been unearthed from an abandoned mountain village several hundred years prior. Nobody knew who the skull belonged to originally, or where it had come from, but it had a long history of catastrophe attached to it; wherever Evolynn's Skull appeared, there often followed a string of calamities in its wake. In short, it was just the sort of thing Yerra loved.

As Galena and Analia approached Yerra's cave, a small dragon with deep, chocolatey brown scales and golden eyes stepped out of the entrance. She smiled and waved. "I thought I smelled you two out here! Whatever are you doing out here so late?"

Galena set down Analia and crossed her arms. "I'm here," she said, "because I have it on very good authority you were planning to run off on me tonight. Something about you finding a new acquisition for your hoard? Evolynn's Skull, perhaps?"

The scales of Yerra's cheeks turned a more auburn shade of brown. "I don't know what you're talking about," she said.

"Mm-hmm," Galena said.

Analia sat on her haunches. "You seemed very excited about it earlier when you were talking to that dwarf I saw here," she said with a purr.

"You were eavesdropping!?" Yerra exclaimed. "You little sneak! I thought I heard something earlier, but I never imagined it was you."

Galena shook her head. "I can't believe you were actually going to go off and try to retrieve Evolynn's Skull without me."

"Well, it might be dangerous," Yerra protested. "You know the reputation Evolynn's Skull has."

"Which is all the more reason why you shouldn't go alone," Galena said. "Come on, Yerra, it'll be fun; it will be just like the old times. Besides, you really don't have a choice in the matter, so you might as well accept it; whether you like it or not, Analia and I are coming with you."

Yerra looked from Galena to the cat and back again. "I'm not going to be able to convince you two to stay here, am I?"

"Have you tried arguing with Galena?" Analia demanded. "You might as well just give up now; you know you're not going to talk her out of it."

Yerra sighed and gave them both a wry smile. "I guess you'll have to come along, then. Come on inside while I finish packing. It won't take long, I'm nearly finished."

Galena gave Analia a triumphant look, and the two of them followed the dragon into her cave. "So how did you hear where Evolynn's Skull is, anyway?" Galena asked.

"I had a couple of dwarf friends passing through, and they told me they had struck a new trading deal with the merfolk," Yerra said. "They're the ones who told me about Evolynn's Skull being in a cave on Yslen Douen. They say no one goes there anymore, especially after that boating party disappeared a few weeks ago, but they have a pretty good idea of where it's at. They even drew me a map. Galena, we're going to get *Evolynn's Skull*; it'll going to be the perfect addition to my hoard!"

Analia shook her head. "Absolutely nuts," she muttered.

"There, all set!" Yerra said, putting the finishing touches on her pack and then stowing it away. "Ready?"

"Ready," Galena echoed cheerfully, scooping up Analia.

Yerra led the way out of her cave. "Yslen Douen isn't too far from here; if we have a good wind behind us, I think we can reach it by mid-morning. That will give us plenty of time to find and retrieve Evolynn's Skull. If all goes well, we'll be back here in less than two days with it."

~ * ~

Yerra flew through the night, and most of the next morning. The sun was just slipping above the horizon when they came to the ocean. A few hours later, Yerra landed gracefully on the rocky shore of a small island: Yslen Douen. Once, many centuries ago, it held a bustling city, the ruins of which still lay scattered around them. One day, however, tragedy struck, and half of the island broke off and sunk into the ocean; no one ever knew why. Since the disaster, there had been many attempts to rebuild Yslen Douen, but none were successful. Over time, the island gained a sinister reputation, and people began to say it was haunted—or cursed. Now, almost no one went to the island; of those who did, none ever returned.

Galena and Analia climbed off Yerra's back, and the three of them examined their surroundings. The island was a desolate one; what little greenery still grew covered the broken remains of stone dwellings, and the air was damp and cold despite the clear skies.

"The cave is just on the other side of where this town used to be," Yerra said. "Near where the island was split in half. It used to be a ceremonial site, I think, but it leads straight into the cave."

"We'll follow you," Galena said. "Analia, do you want to walk, or shall I continue to carry you?"

The cat gave her a dirty look. "I don't like your tone of voice. I shall walk, thank you very much." She jumped out of Galena's arms and stalked off to the side, her tail held stiff in offended dignity.

"This way," Yerra said cheerfully, and led the way through the eerie, deserted cobblestone streets. "You know, there's not so much as a rat out here," she said after a few minutes of silence. "It looks like we're alone here after all. I honestly wasn't sure if we would be."

"That's because we're the only people dumb enough to actually want to come here," Analia said. "I mean, look at this place! It's not exactly a tourist destination."

Galena looked around at the deserted ruins. "Well, no," she said thoughtfully. "But that hasn't stopped people from coming; the usual ghoulish thrill-seekers, usually. I wouldn't think we'd see any though; the boating party incident is still too fresh, I'd think."

"Well, I wasn't referring to sightseers anyway," Yerra said. "My dwarven friends said there were stories about something living out here."

"Something...human?" Galena asked.

"Maybe. Nobody's certain. Some people say it's some crazy old hermit woman, others say it may be a siren, or a ghost. Most of the stories are pretty vague; I wouldn't be surprised if the locals on shore just made them up to help discourage anyone from coming out here."

The dragon led them down a rocky path carved into the side of the island. The wind was colder here, and the ocean spray more pronounced. After a few minutes the path curved inward, away from the salty spray of the ocean, to a wide plateau surrounded by tall rocky outcroppings. There was a black, yawning cavern in one side of the rock, and Yerra stopped in the middle of the plateau, facing it. "This is it," she said. "At least, I think it is. If my friends were right, Evolynn's Skull should be right in there."

"I hope you brought a torch," Analia said, staring with distaste at the cavern's opening. "It looks awfully dark in there, even for me, and I happen to have excellent night vision."

"I brought a lantern," Galena said. "Yerra, would you light it for me?"

"Of course," Yerra said, and obligingly blew a puff of flame into the lantern. "Let me go first, though. Evolynn's Skull should be just a straight shot in and out, but there's always the chance something unpleasant could be living in there. If that's the case, I'd much rather be the first one to meet it."

The three of them, with Yerra in the lead, proceeded into the cave. They were almost immediately swallowed up by blackness Galena's small lantern could do little to dispel. After what felt like ages, but was probably only a minute or two, the tunnel widened and opened into a large space. The flickering lantern only illuminated a small circle around them, but all three had the impression the cavern was a sizeable one. Analia shifted uneasily; she clearly disliked being unable to see around her, and she pressed closer to Galena's leg.

Up ahead, there was a narrow stone pedestal, about Galena's height, with a patch of what looked like moonlight shining down on it, seemingly generated out of nowhere. On top of the pedestal, glittering in the strange light, was a human skull, encrusted with delicate crystals.

"There it is!" Yerra breathed. "Evolynn's Skull!"

"Where's that light coming from?" Analia demanded in a low voice. Before Galena could reply, she continued, "You know what, never mind; I don't really want to know. I have a bad feeling about this place. I think we should go."

"I'll just grab this," Yerra said absently, slowly approaching the pedestal with a starry expression. "And then we can go."

"Galena..." Analia protested. "This isn't a good idea!"

Galena reached down and stroked Analia. "It's alright; we're almost done." She watched Yerra cautiously approach and prepare to lift Evolynn's Skull off the pedestal, readying the small, elaborate chest she had brought along to transport it.

"*Galena*," the cat hissed. "*There's something in here.*" Analia stood stiffly, her back arched and her tail fluffed out to twice its usual size.

Galena gave a quick look around the cavern. "Where is it? I don't see anything."

"It's right over there," Analia said, staring off to the right. "It's all misty, like a cloud of gray smoke, but there's definitely something in here."

A cloud of swirling gray mist snaked out of the darkness into their midst, and began shaping itself into a tall, indistinct figure. Galena and Analia backed away from the woman and the evident malfeasance and ill-will emanating from it.

"Uh-oh," Galena said. "Yerra, you'd better hurry; we have company, and it doesn't look happy."

Yerra turned around in time to see the wraith reaching for her, and the glittering skull now securely packed away in the wooden chest. She squeaked and dove to the side, narrowly avoiding a collision with the creature. The ghostly apparition screamed raspily and tumbled after Yerra, not even stopping for breath. It swiped at Yerra with a clawed hand and missed, but deeply scored the stone floor.

"We should go," Analia squeaked. "Right now!"

Yerra narrowly dodged another attack from the wraith and shot a look at Galena. "Get moving! I'll be right behind you!"

Galena scooped Analia up in her arms and then turned back to the fight. "Yerra, duck!"

Yerra scrambled out of reach of the wraith as it slashed at her again. The wraith screamed in frustration, but before it could make another attack on the dragon, Galena threw her lantern at it. It screamed again and disappeared in a sudden burst of flame, which died down as the lantern hit the floor.

"Let's go," Yerra said. The threesome tumbled out of the cavern and took off running down the tunnel, back to the entrance of the cave, as quickly as they could. They burst out of the cave and went sprawling across the rocky ground. Up above them, the sun shone brightly, and the crash of the ocean could once again be heard. Slowly, carefully, the trio got to their feet and took stock of the situation.

"Is everyone alright?" Galena asked. "Analia? Yerra?"

Analia coughed. "I'll probably live," she said. "I *told* you we should have left earlier!"

Galena glanced over at Yerra, who was frantically turning in a circle, examining the ground. "Yerra, what's wrong?"

"Evolynn's Skull, where is it? I must have dropped it somewhere around here—"

Analia had been staring intently into the tunnel, and she suddenly turned and scrambled up Galena's leg. "We have to go!" she said. "That thing is back, and it's coming straight for us."

"But Evolynn's Skull!" Yerra protested. "It was right here…"

"I think Analia's right on this one," Galena said, scrambling up on Yerra's back. "I think that thing must be protecting Evolynn's Skull; you were the only one it went after in there, and it was because you were the one with Evolynn's Skull. I think we're going to have to call it a loss and get out of here. We can't fight it off with just the three of us; I think it'll leave us alone if we don't have Evolynn's Skull."

Yerra hesitated a moment longer, but as the wraith creature came barreling towards them out of the tunnel, she quickly turned and took off into flight. The wraith stayed below, looking up at them as they flew away from Yslen Douen as quickly as they could.

~ * ~

Yerra, Galena, and Analia made the lengthy trip back home in silence. Even after they landed outside Yerra's cave, well into the night, no one said anything. They all just sat, staring thoughtfully into the darkness. Finally, rousing herself, Yerra said, "It's pretty late; why don't you two just spend the night here? You can go back to your cottage in the morning."

"That would be lovely," Galena said. "Analia, are you alright with that?"

"There's no way we are walking back home at this time of night," Analia said firmly. "After what happened on that island? We are definitely staying here."

One by one, they went inside Yerra's warm, comfortable home; Analia immediately went over to the ever-present fire and began grooming herself in front of it. Galena made herself a mug of tea while Yerra took out the leg of a deer to snack on, and the friends joined the cat by the fire.

Yerra sighed. "I can't believe I actually *held* Evolynn's Skull. It was so beautiful! I wish we hadn't had to leave so quickly. It would have been such an acquisition for my hoard."

Analia snorted. "Yes, it would have come with its own personal haunting. How delightful. That thing guarding it would have torn this place apart; I think it's just as well you couldn't bring it home. It gave me the heebie-jeebies."

"Don't be so disappointed, Yerra," Galena said. "At least you got to see Evolynn's Skull, which is more than most people can say.

Besides, I think Analia's right; it just wouldn't have been good addition to your hoard."

"I suppose you're right," Yerra said regretfully. "It's definitely out of the question now. It's such a shame, though. It was so pretty."

"There, there," Galena patted her friend's shoulder. "There's always next time. You know how it is; cursed objects always seem to be popping up. You'll find another addition for your hoard before you know it."

"Hopefully one that doesn't have a screaming ghost attached to it," Analia muttered.

Yerra brightened slightly. "Now that you mention it, I *did* hear about a cursed spinning wheel a couple of kingdoms over, that's supposed to be responsible for—"

"You had to get her started, didn't you?" Analia grumbled to Galena, as Yerra happily prattled on about the cursed spinning wheel. "I suppose we'll have to come along with her to pick that little item up too. Honestly, Galena, you enable her!"

"Well, she's a dragon," Galena said. "It's only natural she wants to add to her hoard. And anyway, if we go along with her, at least we can make sure she doesn't get herself killed. You'd never be able to live with yourself if something happened to her while she was off on a trip."

"Speak for yourself," Analia grumbled. "Oh, I suppose you're right. It won't be too bad, I suppose; it has to be better than going after that blasted skull was!"

"—in the tower, but it really could be anywhere. I have some contacts in that area I can ask for more information, but it should be no problem to get to it!" Yerra finished excitedly. "What do you say? Should we go after it? It's not every day you hear about a cursed spinning wheel like that."

Galena and Analia looked at each other. The cat just gave a resigned sigh and curled up. Galena grinned and looked over at her friend. "Why not? It sounds like fun!"

"Perfect! We can leave in a week; it will take me at least that long to talk to people and get everything ready," Yerra said. "I don't want to go in blind again like we did with Yslen Douen; that was my fault, I got so excited about Evolynn's Skull I didn't want to wait. Now, let's see…if I go and talk to Sylvester about getting that cabinet, I can mention I have an interest in that castle, and maybe he can connect me with that old man he mentioned before..." The dragon turned away, muttering plans to herself, while Galena stretched her legs out in front of the fire, and slowly drifted off to sleep.

~ * ~ * ~

**Mabel Ginest** has had a love affair with writing for as long as she can remember; even as a small child she enjoyed crafting quirky and unique stories, something that has remained constant in her life. When she isn't plotting out another story, Mabel spends her time enjoying the company of her family and friends, and pursuing her bachelor's degree in criminal justice at her local community college. She currently lives in a tiny house with her (extraordinarily spoiled) cat Polly, two potted plants of astonishing hardiness, an embarrassingly large collection of mugs, and far more books than she has bookshelves.

# Bookworms & Bookwyrms

LA Knight

Dragons are Fair Folk. People forget this sometimes.

When I'm born, I'm chunky, and sweet, and my mother's thorns don't leave so much as a scratch on my soft skin as I slide into the arms of the goat-eyed midwife. The only unusual thing about me in the months that follow is the little creature on the other side of the mirror only giggles along with me instead of trying to reach through the glass and bite.

By the time I'm four, I've picked up the biting habit of some neurodivergent mortals and faerie babies. I learn to read and begin devouring books like crows feasting on the dead. My mother occasionally trades strands of her curly, black hair to the crow-witches, nesting materials in exchange for children's books from bookstores staffed by the winged and frog-eyed. My father reads me the ones about dragons—they're one of his special interests—voicing each character and pulling gruesome faces to make me flap my hands and shriek with hyena-laughter.

When I'm five, the teacher insists I'm not the right kind of child somehow: too hungry-ready to bite; too many twitches in hands and feet; too many grown-up words spilling like diamonds and toads from my tongue.

At the pediatrician's office, the doctor diagnoses me as either autistic or a changeling.

My mother, a changeling herself, is wholly unsurprised but very pleased. Her garden-skin breaks out in amber roses like iridescent tattoos. She hisses at the doctor, baring her needle teeth when he suggests burning me with an iron poker so the Fair Folk will take me back. His face pales like curdled milk. She grins, silver against golden-brown skin, and takes me to the bookstore for ten new human books, and afterwards for pancakes as a reward for passing the autism tests.

"The doctor said I failed," I point out.

"The doctor is human and ignorant, and something is going to eat him one day." Mom shrugs. Other restaurant patrons slap at her with their scandalized looks. She focuses on pouring strawberry syrup over her French toast in the perfect ruby sugar pattern.

Dad is pleased when Mom tells him I passed.

"That explains a lot!" He opens his arms and I walk into them; he smells like vanilla and sunscreen. His beard tickles my cheek.

Neither of my parents make assumptions about touch-boundaries. Mom has too many rose thorns writhing under her skin, ready to pierce.

My father is autistic. My mother is a changeling. They agree it means the same thing, and don't care which I am.

~ * ~

After my diagnosis, my parents teach me to walk the tightrope of autistic and changeling. First rule: if it's mortal and it hurts me, avoid it.

First day of first grade, I scorch my hands on the steel push-bar of the girls' bathroom door. Dad spreads aloe sap across the red rawness and later Mom slinks cat-tense out the door into the desert, seeking sand-sidhe. She returns from the faerie market missing all ten of her rose-thorn claws, carrying a pair of black fingerless gloves in one bloody hand and a stack of books under one arm.

"They'll grow back," shrugging over the empty nailbeds and handing me the gloves. Suede-soft leather. A sheen like the rainbow on a crow's wing. "These," grinning silver needles, "will grow with you, and cannot be lost or stolen. A fair trade, rosebud. Our kind can't be cheated."

The books are for me, too—Zetta Elliott, Robin McKinley, Laurence Yep, known for their dragon tales. An apology for scaring me with her meat-raw fingers. They're the last I can fit on my second bookcase. Going to need another one soon. Mom delights over my growing library and asks to borrow a couple books from my hoard in exchange for helping me reorganize it.

Second rule: never break a bargain to iron-laced or immortal.

The first bargain I make is with my mother when I'm eight— I'll never agree to a pact without asking three questions and giving the answers three moonsets' pondering. Because it's bound in motherlove, and my mother is a thing of ragefire and quicksilver briars, the Folk will respect the oath.

Third rule: keep your true name secret.

The only time my mother has ever spoken it was in the moment of my birth, when the labor-heat and fresh blood and water-scent kept us both safe from everything to fear. It sits where a heart, that may not be flesh, beats the syllables (one way to discover if a heart is a changeling one is to cut open the suspected changeling with a steel scalpel).

There are smaller rules. Never stand in a crossroads; wear your socks inside-out; you may hum but never whistle in a wood. Be generous with the crows, give way before the cats, offer friendship to the hounds. Don't tease the mirror-things that mimic our reflections, or treat your treasures carelessly, or kick down a saguaro (that's illegal, anyway). Ignore lights like candles in the wilds; mind your manners even when alone; decorate your jacket with safety-pins but never touch them.

Dad does that one for Mom and me because pins are made of steel and burn our fingers.

"Well, that settles it," Dad's father says one afternoon when he thinks I can't hear. Grandpa Glenn is helping Dad build another bookcase for my room (*helping* means criticizing everything my dad does, like making the bookcase out of hawthorn because other woods make Mom sneeze herself unconscious). "Can't touch steel? Changeling."

"Or a metal allergy," Dad says. "Or a sensory issue, or just a trace of fae blood. Anyway, who cares?"

"You don't care your child isn't yours? Isn't even human?"

My parents don't speak to my grandfather for three years after that. Dad makes a point to explain the reason to me, to remind me it doesn't matter, I am exactly what my parents want because I am myself and they love me.

On the hard days, when the human children call me *hobgoblin* and throw salt at me, I come home and look at my safety-pinned jacket, the seven hawthorn bookcases so tightly packed with my literary treasures, the black gloves that have grown seven sizes since kindergarten—proof my father speaks the truth.

My parents love me for eighteen years, even when the world doesn't.

The world doesn't, which is why at the end of those eighteen years, when I tell my mom I want to go to college, she bites her lip hard enough to draw mulberry-dark blood like garnets at the tips of silver pins, before nodding and promising to help.

~ * ~

My mother prowls while my dad helps me unpack in my dorm. The hallway is cramped, and thorns press sharp against her skin, trying to rip through. She rubs long, scarred fingers up and down her arms to ease the prickling.

Dad handles it better, but the noise drills into him. I recognize the wince behind his gray-streaked beard. It matches mine.

College is new for me, but also for them. They never went, and they struggle with newness. It doesn't matter. Even though Mom's garden-skin has lost its roses, and there's only empty thorny branches twisting black against the brown, she's *here*. They're both *here*.

When everything's set—my room crammed with specially-made tiny bookcases to hold the most important volumes in my collection, and the bed mounded with homemade quilts embroidered with book illustrations, a new little microwave on my desk— my mom scratches a symbol on my windowsill and another in the doorframe with a claw. Protection. Our house has that mark in the same spots.

We hug. My mother presses her face in my hair to feel it on her cheeks. I do the same. An old tradition. Dad kisses my forehead; the scratch of his beard soothes. We vow love and letters.

"We'll send you books on the solar days," Dad promises. "Something to look forward to. Just send us your lists. Come visit for the solstice."

"Avoid the crossroads," Mom whispers against my hair. "Guard your name. Mind your manners. Be kind to your new mirror-creature. Take care of your treasures." Then, so quiet it's barely a sigh on the wind, "There is a dragon underneath the library. A book-wyrm. She is safest to bargain with."

They only leave me when they're forced to it. I watch them go from the window, my father driving so carefully, my mother slumped against the passenger-side window. I've never seen her look so tired.

~ * ~

There is too much new and hurting in this place. My brain and blood rebel, despising it.

Everything is gonging bells and whooping students and biting-edged desks shriek-sliding on icy linoleum that hurts my knees when I walk or stand for more than ten minutes. The air conditioning is winter-cold, dry in a way different than my desert.

No wonder my mother never went to college. She barely survived regular school. Her parents didn't understand being a changeling.

I shiver through each period, each day, desperate for the New England sun to give even a little of the desert heat I'm used to. Cold freezes my bones; I struggle to grip my pen to take notes, even with my gloves. My feet ache bundled in three pairs of socks. I never get warm, even in the dorm showers in the middle of the night, trying to blast the cold away in a spray of water; it's never hot enough to melt the frost in my blood.

I live on cup ramen and hot cider nuked in my teensy microwave; they barely thaw me. At night, I leave a tiny cinnamon bun from the Student Union and a cup of cinnamon-sprinkled cider for the new creature in the mirror above the desk I don't use for homework; instead of my desk, I study under a mountain of the illustrated book-quilts Dad's mom made for my birthdays.

In the mornings, my offerings are gone. I know they're acceptable because nothing tries to strangle me while I shiver-sleep through the night.

Changelings don't bargain lightly. I'm not even sure I *am* a changeling, magic gloves and iron-aversion notwithstanding, but I am my mother's child.

Ice crawls through my veins and I can't stand it anymore.

There is a dragon underneath the library. I need her help.

~ * ~

The push-bars on the library doors aren't made of steel. Because of the dragon? Does the school even *know* there's a dragon here?

A man in his fifties guards the front desk. Bald on top, flowing auburn waves down to his skinny shoulders matching a rust-red goatee. A Viking in a white button-down shirt, plain gray tie, drab khaki slacks. He peers at me through wire-rimmed glasses. Frowns. He reminds me of my mom's dad, which makes no sense. Grandpa Brett is dark-skinned, curly gray hair buzzed short, neatly trimmed beard, stocky, quick to smile. Good at doing silly voices. Pretty sure if this man did a silly voice, his head would explode.

"You're here to speak to the Great Lady."

I blink—once, twice.

"Did...did my mom talk to you?"

"I don't know who your mom is. You have the look, though. Come on."

When I was eight, my mom drank a gallon of chamomile tea spiked with sea mist, hawthorn elixir, and seven shots of spell-courage. She booked a flight with help from Grandpa Brett and Grandma Jaqui and took me on a two-day trip to the New York Public Library. Even with her thorns roiling and churning under her clammy, golden-brown skin. Even twitching like the wild thing she was every time a taxi honked or a human shouted on the street.

She introduced me to rat lords and pigeon queens as she bore me along on her shoulders; she didn't trust merely clasping my small, gloved hand. Eventually she brought me before the proud stone library lions. Showed me their secret golden eyes with a trick of her Sight. Introduced me to the literary goddesses History, Romance, Religion, Poetry, Drama, and Philosophy encased in stone above the entryway. When I bowed to them the way my mom told me, they smiled and complimented my manners.

Then Mom led me inside to revel in the impossible treasure trove of books upon books upon books.

*This* place is bigger than my collection back home or even my mother's living room assembly of bookcases, but it's no New York Public Library. Most of the space is taken up by computers. There's maybe two rooms' worth of actual tomes. Do they at least have a bigger e-book collection?

The librarian—nametag says 'Roy' with quotation marks; I'm guessing not his real name—leads me past everything, to a back-room and a plain wooden door. When I blink, there's an ouroboros etched into the golden knob. Another blink, it's gone.

"Down there."

"Just like that?" To see a dragon?

'Roy' shrugs. "Either you're on the up-and-up or you're not. If not, she'll eat you. Either way, not my problem."

Fair enough.

Major upside to being a bookworm with a changeling for a mom? I know the rules for fairytales and quests and surviving under the hill. Pro-tip: never touch a doorknob. They bite.

*Mind your manners*, Mom said.

"Please may I enter?"

The door to the dragon's lair swings open.

~ * ~

The air is heavy with ink smell and parchment perfume. There are echoes, each step and each breath. An entire cave beneath the library, lined with bookcases carved of ancient fire-maple, sigils glowing in a rainbow of colors etched in the petrified wood. Twisted sculptures of gold filigree and crystal tears cast light across books that gleam on their shelves. Gilt text? Glitter-painted spines? I'm not close enough to see. Dare not risk getting closer.

This place is no New York Public Library; it's a different kind of hoard. The hoard of a bookwyrm.

And there she is.

In the middle of a circle of flat-topped boulders, a mound of crystal the size of a pair of charter buses heaves. A glittering cable, as big around as a redwood, lifts from the jeweled pile of dragon flesh—at the end of the long neck, a massive head, almost leonine. When she breathes, embers glow in her throat. A forest of spikes like lances of glass grace her spine.

The air shimmers hot with a familiar scent—baking sand. Desert smell, desert heat. Homesickness stings my eyes; I knuckle away unwelcome salt. Even if she says no, for the first time since leaving the desert, I'm not shivering. It's a small blessing.

She looks at me.

Have you ever gazed into an eye bigger than you are?

I can see myself reflected in the inky midnight blue of all three eyes. Triple illusions of an exhausted freshman who might be fae-blooded, or might be autistic, or might be both. Whose aching weariness writhes like shadows and thorns through my three mirror-selves. I study the image while the dragon studies me.

Curly dark hair, brown eyes, golden-brown skin. Black coat a little too small, white shirt. Black slacks, my only pair; I only ever wear black bottoms, but I almost never wear dress pants. They're tailored so they don't cover my feet. Hate that. Even in black socks and boots, my feet feel naked, and that makes *me* feel naked. My familiar black gloves look brand new, even after thirteen years.

"You dress like a mortal, but you move like a fae thing."

The dragon's whisper is as loud as drums. She blasts heat-shimmer at me with a slow breath. Inhales, and the brief wind pulls.

"You smell like something caught between both."

I practiced this. I've had to explain this all my life. I can talk to a stranger about this without stuttering. I *practiced*.

"My mom's a changeling." Nailed it.

"I see." A blink hides the triple-mirage of me for a moment. "What do you want?"

"I," each word rolled around in my mouth, weighed on my tongue, "wish to bargain."

"The semester has barely started; you need extra study time already?"

"What?"

People come to a dragon for *that*? That's brilliant, I never would've thought of it. But…

"No. I'm…" Will she laugh at me? Or will she understand? "I'm…cold. I can't g-get warm." No, don't stutter. Go slower so I don't stutter. "I'm cold," slowly, carefully, "and nothing works. This place…it's so cold. It's barely end of summer, but I'm so *cold*."

The dragon stares at me. A huge, slow blink. Another. The glints of light across her crystalline scales flicker between cobalt and carmine.

"You believe I can help you?"

"Dragons are Fair Folk." My mom taught me this. "Fair Folk can do a lot of things. And," swallowing, reminding myself to speak slowly so I don't trip over my tongue, "dragons are lords of air and fire sometimes." Sometimes they're creatures of other stuff, but water can be hot and ground-ovens are a thing, so it can still work.

"And what will you give for a dragon's warmth?"

*Never make an open-ended promise*, my mother warned me at the beginning of first grade. *Never say "anything."*

I'm the child of a changeling. I know the instructions for surviving fairytales. I've practiced what to say and what not to say my entire life.

"What would you ask for a dragon's warmth, Great Lady?"

Titles. Manners. Always be polite when asking one of the Folk a question.

The glints shift color, chartreuse and magenta, before turning to blue again. There's something like molten silver and steam in her voice when she says, "Organize my library, and I will give you warmth for a year to stave off the cold of this place."

Organize her...oh. Oh, *yes*.

But the bargain I made with my mother fills my throat and spills onto my tongue. Three questions. Three moonsets' to ponder the answers.

"The library upstairs, or the one down here? Or both?"

She cocks her head to one side, fresh interest in her eyes. "This one; I have the librarians for the one upstairs. But my hoard has received at least seven-thousand new titles in the last year, and I have been too busy to catalog them. It's disorganized. I detest that."

"Ugh, I feel that," I say without thinking. Reorganizing our bookshelves is An Event at our house, a party. We play music and order pizza. If we didn't, the living room library and my room would be a *mess*.

The dragon blinks at me but says nothing.

"Is there a time limit on when I must finish or when I must do the work? I wouldn't wish to disturb you or cause you trouble, Great Lady."

"You may work when you wish, but you will not be compensated until you are finished."

"And do I have your promise of safety while I'm here, and from your bargain? No being incinerated by dragon-warmth, no time passing in weird ways while I'm down here, no rules about eating or drinking or sleeping that mean I'll be trapped?"

*She is the safest to bargain with*, Mom said.

Doesn't mean she's *safe*. No dragon is wholly safe, not even a bookwyrm.

"While you are here, no harm or ill shall befall you. My word upon it. No time-tricks or fae-traps, nothing untoward. A straightforward exchange—you organize my hoard-library for me, and I will give you warmth, and nothing more be done to you."

"May I have three days to think on it, Great Lady?" At her narrowed eyes and vermillion-tinged scales, I add quickly, "I swore a bargain with my mother as a child, that before I enter a pact with anyone, I ask three questions and think over the answers until the moon has set three times."

The blood-orange tint to the crystal scales fades.

"Your mother is a wise creature. She has raised a cautious child who will perhaps grow to be just as wise one day. You may have your three days."

"Thank you, Great Lady."

"You may go."

I bow, and do not turn my back on her as I make my way carefully up the stairs, praying I don't trip and break something.

My lungs don't draw a full breath until I'm back in my dorm, huddled under my quilts. I don't even bother taking off my boots. In moments I fall into shivering sleep.

~ * ~

In the morning, there's a note in front of the mirror. The letters sparkle on a post-it note so old the adhesive is gone.

*You can trust the Great Lady of the Library. Bookwyrms only care for their books. Thanks for the cinnamon buns. Good luck on the math test today.*

I stare at the note, then look in the mirror.

My reflection winks at me with eyes that are not mine. I grin, and my reflection grins. The teeth in the mirror are jagged shards of glass.

"Thank you," I say.

*Mind your manners.* I always do.

~ * ~

Turns out *good luck* from a mirror-creature is just as potent as *good luck* from jacaranda dryads or the Twelve Months or a witch in a chicken-legged hut. It's the first test I've taken all semester where clicking pens and screeching desks don't drill bleeding holes in my ears. The half-muffling only lasts the duration of the test, but a small gift is still a gift.

That night, I buy a large cinnamon bun with extra frosting and a go-cup of hot chocolate with whipped cream and chocolate sauce from the Student Union. I split the cinnamon bun but give the mirror the bigger half. Leave the go-cup on my desk. Before I go to bed, I cup my hands in a heart symbol at the glass. My reflection gives a shard-grin and winks.

The dragon's offer sits in the back of my mind. I let my thoughts on it percolate. It's how Dad taught me to ponder things.

At the end of three days, I go back to the library.

~ * ~

"How would you like these organized, Great Lady?"

Every librarian has their system. My dad arranges his books by title, my mom by the Dewey Decimal System. Mine are by author's last name. I don't want to kerbobble the dragon's shelves.

"You may call me Lady Taramarth. Author surname will suffice; most of these are fiction. Anthologies are by editor's surname."

There are twenty-six white sheets on the floor of the enormous cave. There are at least thirty-thousand books in this library; the number tingles through my hands. I'll have to pull them all off the shelves and organize them into piles on the sheets. This is going to be...wonderful.

I pop two Tylenol, wash it down with rowan berry tea. Strap on wrist-braces, black canvas and Velcro. Set my phone down on a boulder. Blue silk thread ties a charm to the rainbow pop-socket, a chunk of lapis lazuli carved by mother-claws into the shape of a jay; a trinket-spell to make my phone work in fae-touched places.

"May I have music?"

Ink-dark eyes study me. She nods, graceful, massive. I bow to her. Press play on the music: thudding drums like heartbeats, a pair of violin bows raked across silver strings, trilling flutes. Lady Taramarth's head jerks back. Her scales flash cobalt and carmine.

Shake out my hands. Pop my neck. Stretch: bend my back, touch my toes, roll my shoulders to the music. Snake my head back and forth, up and down in rhythm. Hands up. Sway to the melody pulsing under skin.

Okay. Let's have a party.

*"O, I forbid you, maidens all*
*That wear gold in your hair*
*To come or go by Carterhaugh,*
*For young Tam Lin is there!"*

The dragon watches me shuffle-spin to the first bookcase. Watches me snag a book, spine cold under my fingers. Glittering in the glow of chandelier prisms. A book bound in ice...no. Diamonds. Bound in *diamonds* supple as leather, shining with glacial starlight fire. And the other books, each as big as my torso, ensorcelled to be lighter than clouds (how else could I lift them?). Words and stories and dreams bound in jewels that give under my touch like suede. Titles etched in letters like abyss, like void.

I blink at the title. Turn to the dragon.

"The Hitchhiker's Guide to the Galaxy?"

Crystalline scales glint, flecks of magenta and chartreuse. "You object?"

"No, just surprised."

Where did she get *this* version? I want to get one for my dad, he loves this series. Maybe in garnet, for his birthstone?

Where did she *get* these?

When I open a jewel-bound tome, pages of silver-golden faerie metal shine with etched letters, marked by a white silk bookmark the width of my palm. Of course metal pages—dragons are massive and sharp with spine and claw, paper would never work.

I lose myself in repetition: grab a book, feel the huge cover of peridot or alexandrite or onyx or sapphire or moonstone or aquamarine or jasper give under my touch, read the spine for title and author, carry it to the respective sheet. It's immediately obvious the books are out of order. I find Moorcock and Hideyuki and Valente mixed with Adams and Addison Allen and Atwater-Rhodes, Gaiman and Dokey and Jemisin with Barker and Bishop and Brennan, Datlow and Mafi and Pierce with Capote and Chokshi and Coville.

This will take weeks. *Months,* since I have class…but the underground library is desert-hot and lovely, and I don't care. I'm jazz-sliding and ballet-twirling, singing along as I stack books on the sheets, far enough from the edges to avoid any dust.

> *"Hear the clear flute calling low,*
> *The King of Elfland singing slow*
> *From the wildwood that tangled grows*
> *Beyond the shield of fire's glow…"*

Time slips away. There's only music, motion, the sweet scent of ink, the delicious heat of the library melting the frost under my skin. I shrug out of my sweater after half an hour; it's wonderful to be in just short sleeves again. Lady Taramarth just…watches, her scales dancing with vibrant pink and yellow-green and lavender flecks. An occasional twitch of tail or slow blink of a great eye is the only way to tell she's not a crystal-carved statue.

Five bookcases taller than me are empty by the time she calls for me to stop. I pause my music.

"Did I mess up?"

"The hour grows late, little betwixtling," she says gently. "Dorm curfew comes soon. You've worked hard. I did not expect such progress so soon. Come here."

Up close, she looms. She towers. There is more of the terrifying in her than ever could exist in the stone lions and library goddesses of New York City. She is more ancient than anything I've ever seen. She is a living work of art, carved of bejeweled ice and indigo ink, and I really hope she's not about to eat me.

No. I have her promise.

Dragons are Fair Folk, after all. We do not break our word.

Lady Taramarth slowly lowers that massive head and breathes in my face. Lightning strike, bonfire smoke, molten metal—the mixed scents sting my nose. Heat spills honey-thick down my spine. Twines like ferrets around my bones, stretching along my skin. An ember flickers to life in my chest inside the cage of my ribs. A sigh shudders out of me.

"I will not send you back to the cold you loathe so much after such service. Return tomorrow, and the warmth will burn on."

It's more than I ever expected; I bow to her.

"Thank you."

~ * ~

My days are history and literature singing of long-ago stories, math and physics that whisper alchemy. My evenings are studying, music, dancing, books, the heat of dragon-embers in an echoing cavern full of treasure-tales.

Lady Taramarth teaches me the names of stones I've never heard of—morganite, pink as roses; prehnite like cat's eyes; sunset spine, vibrant with dusk's dying sun. I teach her about my music, old bands and new, YouTube artists and famous rockstars. She knows a few old ballads even my mom didn't teach me.

She learns to read my twitches and tells, and I learn to read her colors. Dragons are a little like chameleons—they subtly change color depending on their emotional state, like facial expressions on some humans. I wonder if she finds me as fascinating as I do her.

One day, there's a cushy black chair waiting next to one of the huge book piles. A plate of pale cookies glittering with crystalline sprinkles sits on a matching ottoman.

"Oh!" I drop my bag to the floor by the first bookcase.

"You work hard, little bookworm," Lady Taramarth says. "You deserve a soft place to sit, and something sweet. These cookies are my favorites; I had some brought for you. They are safe for your kind."

I wonder if she means humans or changelings. Doesn't matter, really. I've always just assumed I'm both, to be on the safe side.

"Thank you, Lady Taramarth."

"Just...just Taramarth." Her peridot-tinted face mirrors my own surprise, then she flicks her tail. Twin plumes of silver steam waft from her nostrils. "I grow weary of being called 'lady' when relaxing in my own lair."

"Of...of course, La—Taramarth."

I start to bow, and her scales shimmer with vermillion. Annoyance. I'm learning her colors. Jerking out of the bow, ignoring the bite of strained muscle in the small of my back, I shove a cookie in my mouth—snickerdoodle, yes!—turn on the music, and get back to work. When fire pulses through my feet and knees, I sink into the chair. Soft as clouds. Warm as a sunbeam. Perfect place to curl up and read, or just talk about books.

Every day after that, during my breaks, Taramarth tells me about different favorite books I haven't read yet. I write down every single one.

~ * ~

Across days and weeks, I work from B.B. Alston to Octavia Butler, David Chariandy to Samuel Delaney, Michael Ende to Cornelia Funke, William Golding to Barbara Hendee, onward ever and on. Black diamonds and blue, chocolate diamonds and canary. Ruby, sapphire, topaz, emerald. Bookmarks of gold wire lace and moonbeam silk, silver lattice and satin the color of nebulae.

Repetition soothes and stimulates: dip a cloth into a bucket of water, sun-warm; wipe down each empty shelf, damp rag swiping up dust-bunnies; dry the shelf with the towel draped across my shoulders; move on to the next. Rest when my knees ache and my feet throb.

I don't want to stop. There's a quiet in my mind as I empty and clean the shelves. Even when Taramarth asks questions about my life before college, my classes, what I hope to major in, the tranquil quiet within me remains.

Sometimes, we both sing along to my music. She learns fast. Her voice is a ringing bronze bell turning the air to dawnglow.

*"A hawk came to me, trembling afraid;*
*It broke the pieces of my heart.*
*I knew it's strength and loved its soul,*
*And vowed never then to part…"*

~ * ~

The day of the Homecoming game, electricity crackles in the October air. Threatens to bite. Familiar paths are marked off with poison-yellow tape. Detestable signs throw me off course as I stumble around campus. Nothing is where it should be. Nothing is where I can find it. The compass inside me spins, spins, spins.

Run back to my dorm. Corridors crowded with people as I shove through pillars of flesh, more people than there should be. So many, too many. Why are they here? The game. The teachers warned us about drinking on campus, the redirection signs are *every-where*, I can't *be* here. Stumble into my room and slam the door, flapping hands, rock-pacing to my desk, what should I—

Tiny tap-tap. Like on a window. Chest heaving, I look at my desk from under my hair. Lungs squeeze hard, harder. Skin screaming. My fingers dig into flesh, shoulders hunch around my ears.

My reflection does none of this. The mirror-creature watches with eyes that are not mine, eyes full of worry. Long fingers tipped in silver claws touch the other side of the mirror. One fingertip scrapes silently over the glass. Traces quick letters that shimmer like craft store glitter.

*You're overstimmed. Go to the library. To the bookwyrm.*

It's so far. It's never felt so far but what if the path is taped off like everywhere else? They didn't *tell me* the paths would be blocked. Nobody said there'd be different walking routes today. Nobody warned me classes would be moved; why did they move them? What if the library is different? What if I'm not allowed?

*Go to the library. They won't change the way. It will help.*

Okay…okay. I nod. Make a heart symbol with shaking hands full of buzzing blood like hornets. Manners. And I love my mirror-friend.

A reflected pair of hands make a heart. I grab my bag and stumble out of my room on wobbly knees.

~ * ~

I stagger on the last stone step. Taramarth looks up, gaze like three vast pools of darkness, scale-sparkles oscillating between lime and crimson. Somewhere between the dorm and the library, I started crying. Now breath wheezes shrill in my throat. My face is sticky. My fingers itch to rip away the gritty feel of drying tears.

"What is it?" Taramarth demands. "What's wrong?"

"I'm sorry, everything's all d-different, I can't...I just..." Breath saws in my throat, burning. Pain pulses through hands, jaw, forehead. Panic tries to pulp my heart. Words tangle, bramble-briars in my throat. The only reason I've made it through the changes that come with starting college is because of my time in the dragon's library. This is one too far. A change lodged in my throat like bones. "I, I can't, I'm s-sorry, I—"

Taramarth breathes on me. Wash of delicious, sand-scented heat crashing over me in a wave. Tarry film of panic and saltwater disappears from my skin. The grip on my chest loosens. Cavern library warmth, gentle book-scent, familiar soft light from the chandeliers: they soothe me.

"Tell me five things you can see," Taramarth's drum-beat whisper thuds through the lingering fear-haze.

"I...what?"

"Five things you can see, little bookworm. Tell me."

"I..." Images smash together in my head and fragment. I grasp at shards, desperate to hang onto a handful. "Chandelier, arm... armchair..."

"Good. Three more."

"Um...um, c-cookie plate, book piles...um..."

Salt packs my throat. Squeeze my eyes shut to block out panic. Press shaking hands to my lids. Fifth thing. Can't think of a fifth thing. The more I try, the more ravenous static chews through my skull, I *can't*—

*"Look at me."*

I open my eyes.

Crystalline wonder fills my vision. The lime and crimson have faded from the facets of her jewel-scales, replaced by soft rose, misty blue. Such wonderful colors, always. Sometimes I think I could watch her scales forever, the way I love to watch dust motes in the sun or water spilling over a miniature falls or dancing flames in the fireplace.

"You," I whisper. "I see you."

"Very good," her voice more gentle than I've ever heard. "The goings-on upstairs have upset you. The game?" I nod. "They change the geography of the campus to accommodate the revelry. I'm unsurprised they didn't think to warn anyone. So, you seek refuge here."

"May I stay with you? I can work on your books some more."

"You seek refuge…with me?"

"I feel safe with you." Honesty, though I don't mean to confess it. I'm not ashamed. "May I?"

Rose light deep within her scales shines softly.

"Of course. We can listen to your music and talk while you work."

It helps: the music, the talk of inane things, the lunch she has brought down by a library page; the warmth of the cavern and the warmth radiating from her; the soothing repetition of the work—cleaning the gemstone binding and metal pages of each book with a solution of hawthorn oil, jeweler's soap, and preservation spell, then placing each book in its proper place on the shelf. All of it.

I want to stay forever.

~ * ~

"You may call me Tara," the Great Lady of the Library says one November day as I'm reshelving *Goth Girl and the Ghost of a Mouse* by Chris Riddell. A children's pastiche, not the sort of thing I'd expect an ancient dragon to keep, but it's one I read back in elementary school. My copy was black hardcover, silver spine, purple end-pages, silky purple bookmark; hers is bound in amethyst chased in silver, but the satin bookmark is just a bigger version of mine.

The words process slow as syrup. The sweetness hits all at once. Heat flushes my face. If I had garden-skin like my mother, I'd bloom pinks and violets and yellows.

"I…can?"

Taramarth—no, *Tara*—inclines that gleaming, elegantly sculpted head. "You have come to me faithfully every day for three moon cycles. We are friends, are we not? For I believe you would come here even if I offered you no dragon's warmth to fight the chill you so detest."

Denial is pointless for so many reasons. The northern cold of this New England university town drove me here, but if I'd known about the library hoard of precious stone tomes, if I'd known about the wonder that is Tara...I'd have come anyway. Who wouldn't come to a place like this? Who could possibly resist someone like her?

"Yes," I say. The light as softly pink as blush roses shimmers in the depths of her scales, brighter at my words. "I would."

She settles down against the stone floor, brilliant as diamonds.

"Will you read to me, little bookworm? Your task can wait awhile."

The best smiling is so wide and warm, it hurts. If I had my mother's needles, my grin would shine like silver in the sun.

"Sure. What are you in the mood for?"

~ * ~

"You're nearly finished," Tara says a week before the winter break.

I'm slouched in the chair with one of the huge books—*One Good Knight* by Mercedes Lackey, bound in ruddy andesine polished to a glassy finish—and the words hover at the edge of my awareness until they dart in one by one and sink teeth into me.

My head snaps up. Pain twinges in my neck. "What?"

Tara doesn't look at me. Her beautiful ink-blue eyes are fixed on the sole empty bookcase. Almost all the sheets laid out on the cave floor are empty, too. Just the rare Z volumes left. I hadn't... realized.

"Your task is almost finished."

Finished. Yes. Her hoard is nearly organized. Every precious book-jewel in its place, save for the last. A day's worth of work, *maybe*. Probably not even.

"Oh. Um...okay."

Words clog my throat. Can't taste the shape of them, only the salt. Finished. Already? It's only been...it hasn't even been four months. I don't...I don't want to leave yet. It's warm here, and

peaceful. The light is soft, not stinging-bright. There are no screeching intercoms or shrilling desks. There are books. There's a dragon
who loves *books*.

There's *Tara*. I can't leave *Tara*.

"Great Lady," the words fly into my mouth, cold as diamonds
and sharp. I carefully set the rust-silk ribbon into the book. Close
it. Slide out of the chair and put the book on the seat where it won't
fall. "Great Lady."

For the first time in weeks, I can't read the colors of her scales.
Can she read my expression?

"Yes?"

"I, um…I'd like to bargain with you."

The slowest of slow blinks. "I see. What do you want?"

Quick flash of panic, vinegar-sharp in my mouth. Fingers twist
and twitch; I clasp them still. Try to think. What can I ask for?

Never lie to the Folk. That doesn't mean always tell the entire
truth, but this time…this time, I do.

"I want to stay here with you. I mean," scrambling to forge my
wish around the bittersweet rules of adulthood, "I have to do
school, obviously. And I want to see my parents on the breaks and
stuff. But I want to keep coming here. Taking care of your books.
Hanging out with you. I want to keep doing this with you."

"But the task is nearly finished."

Is that regret in her voice?

I *can't* leave Tara. Not just because I love this place, not just
because I love spending time here, but because…

"Well…well, maybe I can do a new task." I think to all the
libraries I've seen, public and private. "Why don't we do a different
organizing system?"

Her eyes gleam, midnight sapphire. "What system?"

I think of all the rainbow shelfies I've seen on social media.

"What about by color?" When she hesitates, I add, "We can
always put it back later. We can arrange the library by color, then
take some pictures, and then put everything back the way it was. Or
maybe a different system, and then put it back the way it was."

I'll do whatever she wants. Whatever it takes to stay.

"I see. And what will you give me for this privilege?"

Is…is she going along with this? Buzzing in my blood, in my
hands. I keep them still and down by my sides.

"What would you ask for this privilege?" Familiar script. It soothes the vinegar-sting in my mouth and the hornet-hum under my skin.

Tara studies me for a split-second eternity. I taste woodsmoke and my own heartbeat, the stardust of faerie promises and the bittersweetness of ink.

"I ask for the truth. Why do you wish this privilege? Tell me that, and I will grant your request."

Three questions, three moonsets.

"The entire truth, or only part of it?"

"The entirety."

"Do you have to approve my reasons, or is giving them enough?"

"Giving them is enough." Her voice thrums with tension like harp strings.

"And the terms of safety from our first bargain apply?"

"Always."

*Always*. It says more than a single word should be able to.

I roll the words around in my mouth, taste the risk of them. I can't break my word to my mother. "Can I have three nights to consider the bargain?"

"You may. Will you finish this task?"

Nerves fizz through my fingers, wobble through my knees, but I nod and start shelving the Zs.

~ * ~

At the end of three days, 'Roy' helps me move my desk and its mirror and my teensy microwave and all my small bookcases into the underground library. Tara watches us. Inclines her head to 'Roy' when he bows to her and leaves.

"You accept my bargain?" Tara asks when we're alone.

Risk tastes of salt and ink, cinnamon and hot chocolate, pancakes and rose petals on my tongue. I sink into the armchair the dragon brought here for me all those moons ago. Set my elbows on my knees.

"You asked why I want this privilege."

Words hold power. Bargains can be shackles, or their keys. Confessions can be curses or enchantments. I am the child of a changeling. I hold magic in the briar-tangle of my heart.

Tara watches me and says nothing.

"I love being in your library," I say slowly. "I love taking care of your books. I love talking about books with you, and eating cookies, and singing, and talking about school with you. I love all of that. And," fighting every instinct screaming to swallow the spell of my own truth sitting heavy on my tongue, "and I love you, Tara. I want to stay with you."

Her scales shine with rose light. Her eyes are midnight ink flecked with stardust.

"Good, because I want you to stay. Because I love you."

"Oh," inanely. Relief makes me drunk. "Cool."

"We'll have to get you a bed, though."

"Yeah," dazed, joy spilling like heat and light and honey over my bones and into my heart. "I brought quilts big enough for a queen-size."

"We'll see to that later. I believe you said something about arranging my books by color, little bookworm?"

It's going to take *months*.

I can't wait.

~ * ~ * ~

**LA Knight** is a disabled autistic queer Black person. He uses any pronouns except it/its. Xe is active on Twitter at @LA_Knight89 and on Patreon. Their work has been published in *Foliate Oak Magazine*, *The Young Adult Reader*, *Tomorrow's Cthulhu*, *Combat Magazine*, *New Legends of Fantasy: Caster\*Castle\*Creature*, *Fiyah Literary Magazine*, and *We're Here: The Best Queer Speculative Fiction of 2021*. They are going to be published this year in the anthology *Fairy Rites* and the anthology *Maleficence: An Anthology of Queer Disabled Villainy*. Fae lives with jør genderfaun spouse, two life-partners, and eir cats in the Sonoran Desert. She has over five-thousand books in xyr own literary hoard (including a pristine copy of the now out-of-print *The Flight of Dragons* by Peter Dickinson and the entirety of *The Memoirs of Lady Trent*).

# More Books from
# WolfSinger Publications

### The Hounds of Ardagh – Laura J Underwood

Ginny Ni Cooley never desired more than the simple life she had, living in Tamhasg Wood and using her magic to occasionally assist the folk of Conorscroft while putting up with the machinations of the ghost of her former mentor Manus MacGreeley. But her peace is shattered one night with the arrival of a lad who is fleeing a pack of red-gold hounds led by a hound-shaped demon known as Nidubh.

So much for peace and solitude. By rescuing Fafne MacArdagh, Ginny becomes wrapped in the fabric of an intrigue involving a family feud, a traitorous son, and a blood mage named Edain who is determined to keep her soul. It is she who cast a spell on Fafne's family and household and transformed the MacArdaghs into hounds.

Ginny gives Fafne her word to take him to Caer Keltora so they can report the matter to the Council of Mageborn. But Edain is determined to keep her secret and her soul intact and moves to thwart Ginny at every turn.

For Ginny Ni Cooley who has faced many bogies, dealing with a demon, a bloodmage and the Dark Lord of Annwn will be no easy task. But she will do what she must to undo Edain's spells. If not, Manus' soul will become part of Arawn's Cauldron of Doom. Ginny will become a demon's feast, and poor Fafne will join the Hounds of Ardagh.

### Wee Folk and Wise: A Fairies Anthology
#### – edited by Deby Fredericks

All over the world, fairy tales are told.
There are big fairies and little fairies.
Ugly fairies and pretty fairies.
Wise fairies and silly fairies.
Sweet fairies and scary fairies.

Seventeen authors share their own fantastic fairy tales in this magical collection. What kind of fairy will you meet here?

## Infinity – Ted Pennella

In the distant future, when peace between humanity and the artificial intelligences their ancestors created has been settled, Conrad Conner tries to live a quiet and unassuming life in orbit about Jupiter on the city-station Socrates' Odyssey. When Conner's attempt to create a prototypical communication artificial for use by the Sol-Humana Confederation's Stellar Fleet gets derailed by the attempted murder of the very artificial he's created, his life spirals into a mad flight back to Earth to try and save at least his sister's children, if not his sister herself. Past failures and heartaches resurface as seemingly unconnected dots become a plot by the First Admiral to steal not just power over the Confederation, but a secret Conner holds within himself.

A secret not even Conner knows about.

## Flatlanders - Mike Sherer

Young theoretical physicist Mickey Haiku has fallen into Eden's trap. She is a much smarter scientist who is intent on saving her own dimension by destroying his. Unbeknownst to either, beings from several yet higher dimensions have their own strategies. This sends the mixed-up pawns off on a wild odyssey through a dozen weird, twisted dimensions. As if this hyper-dimensional odyssey isn't challenging enough for Mickey, he has the additional difficulty of embarking on this whacko tour as a (pregnant!) female. Which means Eden is stuck in Mickey's body. The two are soon forced to cooperate since each holds the other's body hostage.

The strangest relationship this side of the 11th dimension develops between the two.

## Fires of Rapiveshta: Book Three: A Familiar's Tale
### – Verna Mckinnon

With Obsydia's chaos growing and more kingdoms falling under her control, Runa, Mellypip and their friends scramble to find a way to stop her from discarding her mortal form and claiming their world in the name of her Eternal Father Ahridum and plunging it into a never-ending age of darkness and evil.

The dragons of Rapiveshta are awakened from their long slumber by Obsydia's attempt to steal the egg that holds the unborn dragon who will become the next leader of the dragon clans. The egg is given to Runa's grandfather to protect it. When it hatches, Mellypip finds himself bonded to the baby dragon as her guardian.

As Obsydia reaches the climax of the ritual that will burn away her mortality, Runa, Opaline and Panthara find themselves captured to be used as sacrifices. Will the Gate of Souls claim Runa and Mellypip as the Winged Fey have foreseen? Or will the Fires of Rapiveshta and those chosen to be the Scions of Light be able to save them and their world.

## Borne in the Blood — edited by Carol Hightshoe

Delve into the mysterious and powerful world of blood in "Borne in the Blood"

This collection of enthralling stories explores the multifaceted essence of blood—as a symbol of life, a medium of magic, and a bond of kinship. From the chilling tale of a minstrel haunted by a spectral king to the whimsical account of a vampire ice cream vendor, each story weaves a unique narrative around the theme of blood. Encounter a woman whose body bizarrely intertwines with metallic elements, and follow a girl's journey as she confronts her isolation due to her heritage. Feel chills as those who were wronged reach across the years to have their final revenge on the blood descendants of those who oppressed them.

Shifters, Vampires, Witches, and other ordinary and extraordinary folk—all bound together by that which they carry in their blood.

These tales will transport you through a spectrum of emotions, from the depths of fear to the heights of fantasy, as you unravel the mysteries and power that lie within the blood.

Proceeds from sales of Borne in the Blood will be donated to the Multiple Myeloma Research Foundation – themmrf.org/

## Winter Emergence — Dana Bell

Kat has lived in the mountain her entire life. Going outside is allowed only to a select few, many of which never return, including her brother Ned. She doesn't want to believe he might be dead and tries every night to contact him via the coms. Silence is the only response.

Desperate to find an answer to his disappearance, Kat steals a snow cat and searches for her brother, putting the safety of everyone in jeopardy. She's joined by a cat who, for some reason, wants to come with her, and leaves once they reach the city, leaving her alone to face unknown challenges and threats for which she's not prepared.

In the city Word Warrior faces a new threat. A Striped One stalks the cats, wolves and snow ghosts killing any unfortunate enough to be caught as if they are rightful prey! He must find a way to stop the predator or all he has worked to accomplish might fail, forcing them to revert to the old laws of challenge and mate.

A new female appears bringing news of two legs, an enemy they all feared, who lived in a strange world where she had been forced to stay until she managed to escape. In fact, one was in the city and close by.

Faced with multiple threats, including worse snowstorms, Word Warrior faces the responsibility to protect their community from all dangers, knowing if he fails - they could all die.

## Space Brides, LLC – edited by Dana Bell

Tired of those lonely dark nights? No one in your settlement suitable? We are here to help! We will help you find the bride or husband to keep you company, raise your children, and be your partner building a dream together. Contact us directly and give us your specifications. Success guaranteed.

In this collection of 15 testimonials read about the challenges and triumphs of some of our clients as they found love on the frontier of space.

From aliens to vampires, we brought these couples together and together they found acceptance and love—each in their own way.

A man with three kids finds an unexpected match in the brother of the woman he had contracted to marry when she runs away.

A woman running away from an abusive marriage finds acceptance and respect with a colony group that marries everyone to everyone in order to ensure they know they belong to a family.

A woman constantly rejected because of her skin color and origins finds acceptance and love with a wounded soldier.

Even though we encourage absolute honesty in your profile and correspondence with your potential spouse—many people don't. However, like some of the testimonials you'll read here; they still manage to expand their horizons—together.

Contact or walk into any of our offices 24/7. We are here to help you find that special someone and start a new future!

Other conditions apply.
Please ask for more information before contract is drawn up and signed.

## The Dragon's Hoard – edited by Carol Hightshoe

Dragons are well known for their hoards—but not all hoards are created equal.

A young dragon starts his hoard with some very precious gifts.

One dragon shares her complaints about taxes with a friend as they wait for a lunch delivery.

Another dragon defends her most precious treasures against a group of greedy goblins.

And yet another may hold the solution to saving the Earth after a devastating apocalypse in his collection of bottled treasures.

In addition to the normal gold, silver and jewels here you will find dragons who collect many different treasures. 25 storytellers invite you to enter *The Dragon's Hoard* and share the treasures within.

## The Dark See: Book Three: The Moleskin Cap
– M.R. Williamson

As Helen Durkin's journey to find out about herself continues, she finally realizes that she needs the help of someone with more knowledge than dwarves, elves, or even dragons. But, just how do you approach the old Wizard Andsell Phagan?

As she tries to solve that problem, yet another dangerous situation presents itself. This mysterious person is not friend of the Phagan family. Helen quickly finds herself on a collision course with a halfling who most refer to as Scar—one who dabbles in the dark side of magic.

With this added pressure, the effort to approach and perhaps train under Andsell Phagan intensifies. As time progresses, an old friend comes to her aid. Now, the race is on, and the old Dragon Pragamore takes the lead in Helen's plight.

Will Helen finally find out why the Faes are calling her Bright Helen?

What of Pragamore? Will his years keep him from helping?

And, who is Scar really after—Helen, the old wizard, or Pragamore?

## *And more – check out our books at www.wolfsingerpubs.com*

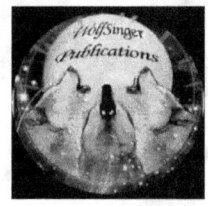